PRAISE FOR THE NOVELS OF JANE PORTER

"Jane Porter has written her way into this reader's heart."
—Susan Wiggs, *New York Times* bestselling author
of *Snowfall in the City*

"Porter writes with genuine warmth and quiet grace about the everyday problems all women face."
—*Chicago Tribune*

"She understands the passion of grown-up love. . . . Smart, satisfying."
—Robyn Carr, #1 *New York Times* bestselling author
of *Return to Virgin River*

"[Porter's] musings on balancing work, life, and love ring true."
—*Entertainment Weekly*

"Once more Porter is able to write about painful life situations with dignity, grace, and authenticity. What might be heavy and depressing in other writers' hands is gentle and cathartic in Porter's."
—*Library Journal*

"Two stories of heartbreak and loss wrap into one, demonstrating the depth of emotion humans are capable of and how extensive the healing process can sometimes be."
—RT Book Reviews

"An extremely well written, emotional, and resonating story of grief and with an ending that isn't traditionally happy and neat. . . . For fans of Porter's Brennan Sisters trilogy, you'll be delighted with a number of guest appearances."
—Chicklitplus.com

"An introspective, some
en's fiction by the exce
From tragic loss of lov
and from the end of a lo
romance, *It's You* will
sionate side."

—Harlequin Junkie

BERKLEY TITLES BY JANE PORTER

FLIRTING WITH FIRE
FLIRTING WITH THE BEAST
FLIRTING WITH FIFTY
IT'S YOU
THE GOOD WIFE
THE GOOD DAUGHTER
THE GOOD WOMAN

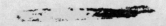

FLIRTING
with
FIRE

JANE PORTER

BERKLEY ROMANCE
New York

BERKLEY ROMANCE
Published by Berkley
An imprint of Penguin Random House LLC
penguinrandomhouse.com

Copyright © 2023 by Jane Porter
Penguin Random House supports copyright. Copyright fuels creativity, encourages
diverse voices, promotes free speech, and creates a vibrant culture. Thank you for buying
an authorized edition of this book and for complying with copyright laws by not
reproducing, scanning, or distributing any part of it in any form without permission.
You are supporting writers and allowing Penguin Random House to continue to
publish books for every reader.

BERKLEY and the BERKLEY and B colophon are registered trademarks
of Penguin Random House LLC.

ISBN: 9780593438428

First Edition: July 2023

Printed in the United States of America
1 3 5 7 9 10 8 6 4 2

Book design by George Towne

*For my mom and dad, who loved the arts
and supported my passion for the theater*

Chapter 1

MARGOT HUGHES, WHILE GOOD WITH COMPUTERS, WAS by no means an expert and when her desktop froze mid-task—forcing a reboot—the spreadsheet she'd been updating all day was gone.

She was finally able to locate it, but when she did, none of the changes were there. All her work that day, disappeared. Vanished.

Margot pushed back from her desk and stood, angry. Jen, the office receptionist, looked up, alarmed.

But instead of melting down in the office in front of everyone, Margot grabbed her sweater and went for a brisk walk down Main Street, threading her way through shoppers and tourists, walking as if she were back in New York with its huge blocks and hectic pace, rather than the sleepy coastal village of Cambria, California, population 5,555.

This is such a small thing, she reminded herself. *The loss of a day's work isn't big.* Frustrating, but not earth-shattering. Not like death, or divorce, not that she'd ever officially been married, but she'd had a long-term relationship, eleven years, and he'd proposed year two. He'd given her a ring. She'd never doubted him, never imagined there wouldn't be a wedding, and she'd made plans, had everything picked out in readiness: the dress, the venue, the flowers and music. It hadn't been easy to wait, but she had. In the end, she'd waited too patiently.

Sam had ended it abruptly, and at forty-one Margot was single. It had been a devastating breakup. She'd supported Sam for years so he could focus on his work. She'd trusted him. Believed in them. Fortunately, that was eight years ago. Unfortunately, there hadn't been anyone to replace him. At first it was because she was still working in New York, but even after returning to her hometown of Paso Robles, she discovered that dating remained hard, and finding someone special . . . well, that had proven impossible.

Now she just focused on work, and living an ordinary life among good, kind, ordinary people. It hadn't been a painless transition from actress to office manager, but after twenty-five years working on Broadway, Margot was tough. A computer glitch wasn't going to knock her off her game.

Exhaling, she dashed across the street and then slowed her pace as she passed the manicured entrance for Cambria's playhouse plaza, the 1938 stucco theater, a gem of a place, only recently reopened after two years of renovation.

It was her boss Sally's pet project. Sally had bought the entire block three years ago, spent a year getting permits and plans drawn and then a year renovating the buildings and courtyard, bringing them up to code, before finally opening in January for the theater's first season. Either Sally's expectations were too high, or local interest too low, because casting the production had been challenging, and attendance for the winter and spring plays had been dismal. Margot had gone with Sally to see both winter and spring productions and had cringed. The acting was awful. She wasn't the only one uncomfortable—half the audience left at intermission—but Margot had remained with Sally until the bitter end.

After the spring show, Sally offered to pay Margot to step in and take charge of the show.

Margot declined. When she left New York two and a half years ago, she'd left her acting career as well. She was done with theater. Done with acting, done with actors, done with writers, all of it.

She just wanted a normal life now, one with regular office hours, and regular office headaches. Like lost spreadsheets.

Smiling ruefully, Margot entered the Cambria Coast Development office. Several of the women had already left. Jen, the pretty young receptionist, was about to leave, and she mentioned to Margot that she'd already put a call in to Malcom, their IT guy, and hopefully he'd phone in the morning.

Margot thanked her, praising her initiative, before looking to the back, checking Sally's office. Sally Collins, the owner of Cambria Coast Development, was still there, on the phone. Sally was always on the phone or out in meetings, showing properties and making deals, generally big deals, as she owned significant real estate. For a woman who'd been born with virtually nothing, she'd accomplished a lot in her life and was now, at sixty-seven, very comfortable financially.

Margot had become Sally's right hand and rarely left work before Sally did. It wasn't that Sally expected Margot to work late, but Margot didn't feel right leaving Sally alone, all too aware that Sally didn't know when to quit and would continue making calls and following up on leads when she should be home, or at least off with friends, doing something relaxing.

Not that Sally knew how to relax.

Like tonight. Sally had a chamber of commerce meeting to attend. And then there was a dinner with some Los

Angeles investors who'd come to town to explore opportunities in Paso Robles, and Sally owned significant property there as well. Ranch land, wineries, commercial real estate.

Eventually, Sally hung up the phone, and Margot left her desk to stand in the doorway of Sally's office. "The chamber mixer is starting soon," Margot said, folding her arms across her chest, and giving Sally a meaningful look. "You don't want to miss it. You insisted I get you there on time."

Sally glanced at her watch, shook her head. "I'm already late."

"Not too late if we leave now."

"There's not enough hours in the day," Sally said, rising from her desk to slip on her unstructured blazer. She glanced into the framed mirror on the sidewall, fluffed her silvery-blond hair, which today was more blond than gray. "Are you still going to the cocktail party with me?"

"Of course. I agreed to be your date."

"But not the dinner after?"

"Not tonight. After the mixer, I just want to go home, relax, and get my eight hours of sleep. Don't know how you do it on five or six."

"Sleep is overrated. I'll have plenty of time to rest when I'm dead."

"So morbid, Sally."

"But true." Sally took her oversized purse from the chair near her office door and turned off the light. "Taking my car?"

"Sure." Margot would just walk back for her own car later. The Fog Horn was only a couple of blocks away, and Cambria was safe.

"Jen mentioned your computer. Do we need to get you a new one?" Sally asked. "Maybe a laptop you can take home at night?"

The last thing Margot wanted was to spend her evenings working at home. "Let's just see what Malcom can do. It might simply be a software update, something easy to fix."

"We could also have someone take over data entry jobs, freeing you up to join me for more of the sales meetings."

Margot shook her head. "I'm not a salesperson. I don't have your teeth, either. You're comfortable with these high-powered investors. I'd be lost."

They'd stepped outside, and the sky was clear, the sun still high since summer was coming. Sally used her key to turn the dead bolt. "I can teach you."

"I know, and I'm grateful." Margot smiled at her boss, one of the most generous, smart, successful women Margot had ever met, and that was saying a lot. Sally could have been a Broadway producer in New York. Sally knew everyone, was incredibly skilled at getting people to do what she wanted, and never took no for an answer.

"It's all about listening," Sally said. "You have to make people feel heard."

"And then convince them that what you want is what they want," Margot teased.

Sally shrugged as she unlocked her white Cadillac, an older model she'd bought used, fifteen years ago. "I never can resist a challenge."

"Which is why you're the boss, and I'm your assistant." Margot opened the passenger door and sat down. After buckling the seat belt, she popped the mirror open on the sun visor, applied fresh lipstick, brushed her long blond bangs into a tidier side sweep, wishing yet again she hadn't been persuaded to add bangs to her style, before closing the mirror. At the time, adding bangs seemed wiser and less invasive than trying Botox, but she'd gone ahead a couple of months ago and done that, too, after noticing how tired her face looked all the time. The Botox had definitely "brightened" her eyes, and she'd do that again. The bangs? Never.

Sally started the car. "Someday you could be the boss."

Margot reached over, lightly placed her hand on Sally's before removing it. "Thank you, but no. You need someone a lot smarter than me. Maybe that's my next task. Finding you the person who could head up Cambria Coast Development for when you're ready to retire."

"Which won't be for twenty years at least."

Margot grinned. "Fair enough."

AN HOUR AND A HALF LATER, MARGOT MANEUVERED through the crowded private room at the Fog Horn restaurant, trying to reach the exit without getting drawn into another conversation. She'd promised Sally she'd stay for an hour, and had stayed an hour and a half. Surely it was safe to slip out now, especially as Sally was engrossed in conversation with the mayor of Cambria. Sally loved people, was an extrovert to the core, and did not need a wingman.

"Ditching me already?" Sally asked, catching Margot near the door.

"You were talking to Bill," Margot said. "I didn't want to interrupt you."

"We were talking about you. He has a crush on you."

"Sally, stop. He must be what? In his sixties?"

"At least."

"I haven't even hit fifty yet. Don't rush me."

"You'll be fifty in a year, and he owns two big car dealerships. He has money, and he'd be able to take care of you—" Sally broke off, seeing Margot's shudder. "But wouldn't it be nice for a change? Having someone take care of you?"

"I don't need anyone to take care of me."

"Well, Sam certainly didn't."

"You never even met him. Leave him alone. You promised." Margot smiled at Sally. "Now pretend you didn't see me slip out, as I'm dying to get home, kick off my shoes, ditch my bra, and watch the new episodes of—"

"You won't meet a man crashed on your couch," Sally objected.

Sally, with five ex-husbands, was still a big believer in love. Margot, with no husbands, not so much.

"I'm not hunting for a man. If a good one falls into my lap, I'll deal with him then." Margot shouldered her purse. "Drive home safely—"

"Wait, Margot. Please. I need advice."

Margot eyed her boss suspiciously, because Sally never needed advice. Sally had a golden gut. She made decisions swiftly, effectively. "What's happened?" Margot asked.

"Cherry, the director, quit. Just as we arrived here tonight."

"She called you?"

Sally shook her head. "She quit through a text."

"Not very professional," Margot said.

"Cherry wasn't happy with the leads, and she told them that. In front of the entire cast. So they quit—"

"Tonight at rehearsal?"

Sally nodded. "And then after they quit, Cherry quit. So as of the last hour, we have no director, no Paul, no Corie, and the show opens June ninth, less than a month from now. What do I do?"

"You refund the tickets, skip the summer season, and concentrate on your September show," Margot answered.

"I can't do that. The show must go on."

"Sally, *Barefoot in the Park* has been nothing but a headache since you announced the summer season. Let it go. Hold the auditions for *Next to Normal* and use this summer so that opening night late August will be wonderful."

"Margot, people are expecting a summer season."

"This is Cambria, not Ashland. After COVID, no one's surprised by anything."

"Which is why we're not scrapping the summer season. You had a twenty-five-year Broadway career. If anyone can save this show, it's you."

Margot had loved theater ever since she was a little girl.

She'd performed in every community theater production in Paso Robles she could while growing up. She'd been a dedicated theater geek at Paso Robles High School. And as soon as she'd graduated from PRHS, she'd flown to New York, found a tiny studio room—in a dark basement, no less—and began juggling jobs while auditioning. She'd been on the East Coast eighteen months when she was cast in her first off-Broadway play. She'd never looked back, working hard, so hard that she'd been able to later support her talented playwright boyfriend, thrilled to have someone to share her love of theater with.

But when he disappeared on her, she'd thought— hoped—he would realize he'd made a mistake. He was having a midlife crisis. Sam was in his midforties, the age for it. She kept working, giving him time, giving him space, but Sam never missed her, and he never returned. At forty-three, Margot had waited long enough and was forced to accept she was single, without financial security, and paying rent for an apartment she was never at.

It took her another year and a half to realize she was burnt out, sick of acting, sick of traveling, sick of hotels, sick of being one of the older cast members, and most of all, sick of pretending to always be someone else. Sam had broken her heart, but performing had sucked her dry.

Margot's eyes burned and she swallowed hard, pressing the memories back. "Sally, no. I can't. I love you, but I *can't*. You know I can't."

Sally wagged a finger at her. "That's all in your head, you know. The past shouldn't own you. You're stronger than that."

Blinking, Margot looked away. "You're merciless at times," she said huskily.

"I'm realistic. Everyone has a price. You have yours. I know you're saving for a house. Help me on this, and I'll help you with your down payment. No strings attached—"

"There is a string. A huge string!"

"Just this one production. I won't ask again."

"This isn't advice, this is bribery." Margot struggled to smile but couldn't. "I can't act anymore. I'm burnt out."

"What about direct?"

"Sally."

"Just this one time."

Margot held her breath and looked from Sally's hopeful expression to the chamber members mingling behind them. She glanced back at Sally, the most fearless person she knew, as well as the hardest-working person she'd ever known. "You're killing me."

"You might discover you enjoy it."

"Ha!" Margot reached up and wiped the moisture from her eyes. "Let me think about it tonight."

"You'll love directing. You're a natural."

"I haven't agreed yet."

"Just remember I need to tell the cast and crew something tomorrow, especially since we'll need to hold new auditions for the lead roles of Corie and Paul."

"How can I forget? You won't let me."

Margot slipped out the exit and inhaled deeply. The night had cooled, and a breeze rustled through the trees, tugging at her hair.

She walked the two blocks back to the office parking lot to retrieve her car. She felt raw and emotional, and disappointed that Sally couldn't—wouldn't—take no for an answer.

Sally simply didn't understand. She was always the strong one in her relationships, the dominant one. An alpha female, Sally wasn't afraid to walk away from a bad relationship or a bad marriage. She loved love but wouldn't be disrespected.

Margot wasn't that strong. She didn't love love. She'd loved Sam. She'd loved his mind and his wit, as well as his immense talent. An Idaho native, raised on a ranch not far from Harrison, he'd been tall and lanky, with a cowboy's laconic charm. His dad had been a bestselling author of crime fiction, and his mom had been a singer with more talent than ambition and had been happy to give up her career to be a stay-at-home mom.

She'd met him the night of her thirtieth birthday. He was at the same restaurant as she, and he sent a bottle of champagne to her table. She invited him to join her and her friends for dessert, and she'd been smitten. Charmed. He was brilliant, and funny, and they liked the same authors, and even after her friends left, she and Sam stayed talking until finally the bar closed. He'd walked her home, all those many blocks, and she'd invited him up to her tiny apartment. He never left. Well, they got bigger places, nicer places, but they were together for the next eleven years, and she'd loved him every single day of those eleven years.

It was one of her friends who'd let her know Sam had eventually married Lorna, the producer he'd moved in with when he left her. Thankfully they hadn't married right away, but still, he had married Lorna.

It brought back all the pain. The sense of inadequacy . . . not just as a partner, but as a wife, a woman. What had happened to all the promises and plans? They were supposed to have children. They'd wanted to start a family. She'd wanted it more than he did, but he kept pushing things back, saying next year for sure. Next year they'd try.

Now she was too old to have babies—at least, make babies of her own—and it hurt. She felt robbed. Cheated. If only he'd been honest with her, she might have been able to do something, plan something like freezing her eggs, or saving money for IVF. But he hadn't, and so she hadn't, and now there were only regrets. In her car, Margot rolled all the windows down and drove home to her rental cottage, letting the force of the air rushing in and out clear her head.

Two years ago, Sam had been nominated for his first Tony Award. He hadn't won, but his play was still a huge hit, and Lorna was financing his next play, scheduled to open in London next year. She was glad for Sam. She'd believed in him from the beginning. But that didn't ease the ache inside of her. If they'd married, she wouldn't be forty-nine and single. She would have had babies, and her dad—such a good dad—would have been a grandfather.

The drive from the office to her rental house took eight minutes. Sally had turned the former vacation rental—a snug one-bedroom 1930s cottage just steps away from famous Moonstone Beach—into a long-term rental for Margot.

Margot loved the tiny, gray-shingled cottage with the living room bay window and its extensive window seat. The old stone fireplace was made with the smooth rocks typical of Moonstone Beach, and the exterior window trim had been painted a whimsical lilac, which charmed Margot to no end, especially now that she'd tackled the once neglected yard and turned it into a garden filled with plants that called to the butterflies and hummingbirds. After a lifetime in New York City without any green space, Margot couldn't get enough of her own little garden with its patch of grass, bright red picnic table, and pair of pale blue Adirondack chairs not far from the front door, where she had a peekaboo view of the ocean.

She smiled at her cottage as she parked in the gravel driveway. The front porch light was on, casting a glow on the gray shingles, making the little house look like something from "Hansel and Gretel."

Inside, she locked the door and set the alarm—something her dad, a retired sheriff, had insisted on—not that there was much crime in sleepy Cambria, but she wasn't about to argue with an eighty-eight-year-old man. Dad lived a half an hour away in her hometown of Paso Robles, and she wanted him to sleep well at night instead of worrying about her.

After changing into comfy pajamas, Margot heated up the leftover chicken tikka masala from two nights before, sat down on her couch with a wedge of warm naan and the masala, and turned on the recorded show. She watched one episode, and then another, and then a third, unable to resist the cliff-hanger at the end of each episode. Margot had nearly finished the third when her phone rang. She glanced at the antique clock on the stone mantel. A little after eleven. Her first thought was her dad. But as she reached for her phone on the end table, she saw it wasn't Dad, but rather Sally.

Margot answered quickly. "Sally, everything okay?"

"I've called an ambulance, and it should be here soon. I haven't felt well for the past couple of hours. Not sure, but I might be having a heart attack."

"I'm on my way—"

"No, the ambulance is already coming and there's nothing for you to do in the ER. I just thought you should know. Tell everyone at work that I'm fine, that I'm going to be fine, and honestly, it might only be heartburn, but I'll feel better knowing."

"Absolutely. Where will they take you?"

"I imagine it'll be Memorial in Paso Robles."

"Will you take your cell phone with you to the hospital?"

"Of course."

"Please call me when you need a ride home. I'll be there as quick as I can."

"I hear the siren. The ambulance is here. I'll call you when I know more."

"Sally, I love you."

Sally's voice deepened. "Nothing's going to happen to me. I love you, too."

Margot hung up the phone and stared blankly at the TV. Her eyes burned. Her throat squeezed closed. She dragged a hand through her hair, trying not to panic. Sally was tough. Sally was a legend. She'd be fine. She *had* to be fine.

Chapter 2

MAX RUSSO HADN'T EVEN WOKEN UP PROPERLY WHEN his agent, Howard Levering, called, wanting to get Max's thoughts on upcoming projects. Max glanced at his watch. Eight thirty. Five thirty for Howard, who was based in L.A. but already amped up and ready for the day.

Yawning, Max put Howard on speaker while he poured a cup of coffee, and then carried the phone and coffee into the living room, where he dropped onto the low butterscotch-leather couch. "Howard, I haven't been to hot yoga yet. Slow down."

"I'm just saying you have a name now," Howard said. "You're a hot commodity right now. You can't let these opportunities pass. This is what you've been working for your entire career. The best roles, significant money. Respect. This is not the time to—"

"Howard," Max interrupted, "I only got home last night. I'll look at the scripts this weekend. But I won't do it today, or probably tomorrow. Give me a chance to do some laundry, go through my mail, water my plants—"

"You have plants?"

"Yes."

"Who waters them when you're not home?"

"I have a plant-sitter."

"A plant-sitter?"

"Like a dog-sitter but for plants. She comes by several times a week and waters and mists them."

"I didn't even know that was a real thing."

"The point is, I'll read through everything you've sent, and then we will talk."

"Good, because the Finlay brothers want you to read for them. It's a big feature film. They've already cast Chris—"

"Which Chris?"

"Does it matter?"

Max laughed, and sipped his coffee. Howard was still Howard. He'd never change. "Do I have that screenplay here?"

"You do. It's a crime thriller set in New Orleans. Read that first, and then have a look at the screenplay by Lee Sheridan. He's waiting to hear from you. I can't keep making excuses."

"He knows I was in Italy. He's aware I've been working nonstop this year."

"Because people want you *now*."

Max bit back his smart-ass response. Howard was a good person, and he'd done a lot for Max's career, sticking by him when he'd been typecast as a soap actor and no one else wanted to take a chance on him. "Thanks to you," he said. "You've always been there for me, and I'm grateful."

"You're one of the good ones, Max. You deserve the success, but you know this industry. Now that we have some momentum, we need to keep it going—" He broke off, changed the subject. "How did the commercial go? Okay?"

"It was fine. A couple days' shoot."

"I told you it was easy money. Those foreign commercials can put significant cash in your pocket. The big stars won't do commercials in the US, but they all do them in Japan and Italy. Because no one knows. Now that you've had your first, there will be more."

But Max couldn't even think about another job, not when he was jet-lagged and beat. He needed to catch up with friends and become a person again. He'd been working so much he didn't even know who he was anymore. "Let's touch base on Monday, okay? I'll have read everything by then. We'll compare notes."

"Remember the crime thriller story, and Lee Sheridan's screenplay. Both are big."

"Okay."

"What time Monday?"

"Any—" Max broke off to glance at the text vibrating on his phone. Call me. It was Johnny texting. Johnny being his father. Max hadn't heard from him in months. "I'm usually up by eight."

"Then let's say eight."

"Maybe eight thirty," Max answered.

"Remember, you can't get comfortable," Howard replied. "Now is the time to be proactive."

"I understand."

Max's phone vibrated again. It's about Sally was the text.

"Would you want to do another commercial?" Howard added.

"Later. Eventually."

She's in the hospital came the next text.

Max couldn't focus anymore. "Howard, we'll talk Monday. Enjoy the rest of your week." He hung up and immediately phoned Johnny. "What's this about Sally?" Max asked when his dad answered.

"She was hospitalized last night. Had a heart attack. Melinda called just a few minutes ago with the news, and I figured you'd want to know right away."

Melinda Rojas had been Johnny's last girlfriend, a sweet,

hardworking nurse at Memorial Hospital in Paso Robles. Her late husband had been a truck driver and died in an accident, leaving her to raise their five kids. Johnny liked Melinda, and appreciated her cooking, but didn't do kids—he hadn't even taken care of his own son—and broke up with her for Allison, a self-taught horticulturist who grew strawberries and marijuana in Watsonville.

Max rose from the couch and walked to the big window with the view of the Hudson River and city skyline. "I didn't realize Melinda knew you'd been involved with Sally."

"She saw the photo of you and Sally at your Yale graduation, and I filled in the missing pieces. Melinda called me because she felt funny calling you, now that you're a big star and all."

"Whatever," Max said, tensing. Mentions of his career usually led to requests for money. He'd cut off his dad a year ago because Johnny threatened him, demanding some "parental support" or there would be problems. Max wasn't afraid of Johnny. He just wasn't going to put up with his bullshit.

"You must make plenty of money, though, if you can afford a seven-million-dollar condo in New York."

Max had never told his dad about the purchase, and he'd certainly never tell him what it cost.

As if reading his mind, Johnny added, "Allison follows you, and then looked it up online. Real estate is public record."

Max focused on the river, but his thoughts were on airplanes and flight schedules. It wasn't even nine yet, early enough that he could still catch a flight to the West Coast, and then a connecting flight into either Monterey or San Luis Obispo.

"Sally's at Memorial?" Max asked.

"Yes."

Max hadn't stayed in touch with her, not properly, not the way he'd intended. Life had just gotten so busy and he'd juggled work and relationships, but not well. But he owed Sally, and he should have been there. She was the one who'd financed his college years. She'd made it possible for him to attend Yale, covering everything the small scholarship hadn't.

"You're going to call her?" Johnny asked.

"Yeah." Max wasn't about to tell Johnny he was going to go visit Sally. His dad would hit him up for money, ask for another loan, play the guilt card . . . the very same things that made Sally walk away from him. *Them.* "Thanks, appreciate the heads-up."

MARGOT SLEPT BADLY, CHECKING HER PHONE ALL NIGHT for an update. Finally at seven fifteen she got a text from Sally.

Was a heart attack but I'm fine. They're keeping me here a few days. Nothing to worry about.

I want to come see you, Margot texted.

Room 313, Sally replied.

Margot drove the thirty minutes to Memorial Hospital, picked up her visitor's name tag, and headed to the third floor. Sally's room was at the end of the hall. The light was off and the curtain was drawn against the bright morning light. Margot stepped into the room, thinking she hadn't been in a hospital room in years, not since Dad's prostate surgery, which became yet one more reason Margot knew it was time to move home.

Approaching the bed, Margot swallowed hard. Sally looked so pale and still. Margot quietly pulled a chair close to the bed and waited.

It was a few minutes before Sally opened her eyes. She smiled weakly at Margot.

"Hello."

"Hello yourself," Margot said, leaning forward to put her hand on Sally's forearm. "How are you feeling?"

"Fine."

She didn't look fine. She looked ashy. Pale. Her voice sounded hoarse. Margot forced a smile. "That's good. I've been so worried."

"Why? Nothing's going to happen to me."

Margot's eyes burned, and she had to hold her breath a moment to make sure her voice was steady. "Sally, something did happen to you. You had a fairly major heart attack. The doctors want to observe you for a few days. You need to rest and cut back—"

"You sound like my doctor now."

"Because we're all concerned!" Margot was still fighting tears. "I'm not happy with you right now. You've been working too hard. You stay up too late and get up too early. You drink, you smoke—"

"You smoke."

"I gave it up in January. You were supposed to quit, too."

"I've tried."

"Case in point," Margot said tautly, wiping away a tear before it could fall. "I'm not going to let this continue. You are taking an extended vacation, and you're going to rest. You're not going to the office. You're not going to worry about your little theater."

Sally had closed her eyes but she opened them again. "You'll direct?"

"Yes." Margot held up her finger for emphasis. "Just this one play, just this one time." Her voice cracked. "Because I don't want you to worry. I don't want you to do anything but take it easy, and come back to all of us. We need you. I need you."

"I'll be back at work by the end of the week—"

"No."

"But I will leave the play to you." Sally wheezed a

breath, before adding, "And Max. You and Max will be a good team."

"Max?"

"Russo. He's an actor. On *Stardust Ranch*—"

"I know who he is."

"Well, he's flying in today. I told him you'd pick him up at the San Luis Obispo airport."

For a long moment, Margot just stared at Sally. Sally wasn't making any sense, and Margot didn't even know where to begin. "Max Russo is coming to see *you*?"

"Yes."

"Why?"

"We're old friends."

Except Max Russo wasn't that old. He was either Margot's age or a few years younger. Hard to ever know one's real age in Hollywood. "And I'm picking him up?"

Sally gave her a look. "I would, but the hospital won't let me."

"Still so sarcastic," Margot retorted, adjusting Sally's pillow.

"I had a heart attack, I didn't die." Sally waved at the tray table, which had been pushed aside. "Hand me my phone. His flight details are on it. I think Max is flying United, landing just after five. He knows you're coming for him."

Margot was still trying to piece it all together. "How do you know him?"

"He was raised in Morro Bay."

"I know that. And . . . ?"

"I used to live in Morro Bay. Briefly."

Margot studied Sally's face. She was terribly pale, but there was the old hint of mischief in her eyes. "Tell me, truthfully, is he coming to see you, or is he coming for the play?"

Sally hesitated just a moment too long. "Both?"

Margot frowned. "He doesn't know about *Barefoot in the Park*."

"Not yet."

"But you want him involved."

"I want a lot of things, but I don't always get my way."

"You get your way more often than not."

Sally allowed herself a small smile. "Just bring him here, and I'll handle the rest."

MAX WAS FINALLY USED TO BEING RECOGNIZED. YEARS back, women who watched the soap *Forever Young* would stop him and ask for a photo or an autograph, but then he'd left the show and become obscure. Now he was on a big show again, an even bigger TV show, with season 4 of *Stardust Ranch* drawing on average 1.7 million viewers an episode, making him a recognizable face once more. In August they'd begin filming season 5, and then it'd be another four intensive months. This summer Max was determined to have a break so come August, he'd be ready to film. Right now he just wanted sleep. And peace.

During the flight to Los Angeles, a woman stopped by his seat. She'd already passed him three times, each time smiling at him, friendly, nonthreatening.

She finally spoke after her fourth trip to the restroom. "Hi."

He tipped his head. Smiled. Not wanting to encourage her, but conscious that he couldn't really be rude.

"Are you Max Russo?" She gave him a hopeful look, a smile that was a little nervous, very self-conscious. "I bet my friend you are. Were." She flushed, stammered. "I loved you in *Forever Young*, and I've followed your career ever since. I'm not asking for an autograph, I just wanted you to know that I think you're wonderful. I used to have your posters all over my wall." She made a little face even as she flashed her hand with the wedding ring. "I'm married now, it would be weird to have your posters up. My husband's a good sport, but you know." She laughed. "I'm rambling. Sorry. I talk too much when I'm nervous—"

"It's okay. It's nice to meet you." He put out his hand. "Your name is?"

"Jasmine." She blushed. "And you really are Max?"

"I really am."

"Wow." She let go of his hand quickly. She kept staring at him as if she couldn't quite believe any of this was happening. "Have a good flight, Mr. Russo."

Mr. Russo. That sounded so old. But she was trying to be respectful, and she was sweet. She'd also been a fan for a long time. "You, too. And it was nice to meet you, Jasmine."

Jasmine disappeared back behind the slight curtain into the economy section of the plane. Max only recently began flying first class. He'd been making good money ever since *Stardust Ranch* became a hit, but he hadn't wanted to spend the money. But lately, he wanted more privacy and more legroom, which he wouldn't get in economy.

There was no first class on the commuter plane that took him from L.A. to San Luis Obispo, though. Fortunately, it was a short flight, just an hour, and they landed before sunset, fifteen minutes early.

Sally had told him one of her employees, a Margot Hughes, would be picking him up and that Margot would drive him to the hospital before getting him settled.

He'd answered that he'd already booked a car and a hotel, but Sally insisted he use her car and not spend the money. At least she hadn't fought him about the hotel room, as the last thing he wanted to do was crash at Sally's place while she was at Memorial. Hopefully he wouldn't need her car, either, and could just use his ride-sharing app.

The plane didn't pull all the way up to the terminal, but

parked on the tarmac. He was one of the first down the stairs, and he tugged his baseball hat lower, the brim bumping his sunglasses. This used to be his home airport. This used to be home. It seemed like another lifetime.

THE AIRPORT IN SAN LUIS OBISPO WAS A FIFTY-MINUTE drive from Margot's home off Moonstone Beach, and she'd left early to make sure she was there before Max's flight arrived, but she'd hit traffic on the 101. She'd given herself a thirty-minute cushion, but with his flight landing early, she'd only just reached arrivals when she heard the announcer say the incoming flight from Los Angeles was on the ground and everyone would soon be deplaning.

Margot took a quick breath and tightened her ponytail. There was no reason to be nervous, but she felt unsettled. It had been tough at the office today, the staff emotional, everyone upset about Sally's condition, and Margot had worked hard to reassure the team that Sally would be okay, even as she secretly worried about a future where Sally couldn't do as much. What would happen to Sally's empire? Had Sally made any plans for the future?

Margot had initially planned to leave for the airport straight from work but at the last minute dashed home to change into something a little more chic, swapping the white work blouse for a purple paisley tunic with a hint of gold embroidery at the neck and hem. She'd put on some makeup, too, not a full face, but lip liner, mascara, eyeliner, and a hint of bronzer. She wasn't trying to impress Max Russo as much as feel confident. In control.

Sally's heart attack had shaken her deeply, making Margot think of her mom, who hadn't survived her heart attack. But then, no one even knew her mom had heart issues. She'd still been relatively young, and healthy. But her mom hadn't been strong, almost fragile ever since Margot's sister, Charlotte, died at seventeen. But Sally was tough. A fighter.

Sally wouldn't give up. Margot didn't need to be afraid. But she was afraid, and sad. The intensity of her feelings surprised her. She couldn't lose anyone else.

And she wouldn't lose Sally. Margot was determined to take care of her, stepping in at the office and anywhere else she was needed.

Sally was depending on her. The office team was depending on her. Everyone was counting on her to keep things together, and she would. She could.

Margot might not be as fierce as Sally, but she wasn't a lightweight. She'd been through her share of hard times. She could handle this.

And she could handle Max Russo.

Five years ago, Max Russo had been just another good-looking, hardworking actor who'd played numerous secondary roles on popular TV shows. He'd started out in theater, got a role on a soap, and when his character on *Forever Young* was killed off, he disappeared for a while before appearing as a guest on other TV shows, making appearances in numerous TV pilots. And then three—four?—years ago, he was cast in the new Western, *Stardust Ranch*, and the show became a huge smash, with Max the breakout star. In a matter of months, he'd gone from likable, recognizable actor to heartthrob. This year he'd graced the cover of a number of magazines, including a four-page spread in *People*'s beautiful people issue. The public couldn't get enough of Max—Jen, the receptionist, couldn't stop talking about him—and somehow, he knew Sally, and was flying in from New York just to see her.

Margot had tried to get more details from Sally, but Sally had closed up then, becoming unusually secretive.

Margot knew Max had been born in San Luis Obispo County, with Templeton claiming him, while others in Morro Bay said he'd been raised there. Regardless, he was a native, and he'd left—much like she did, right after high school—but unlike her, he'd never moved back.

The terminal's sliding glass doors suddenly opened, and there he was.

Max wasn't hard to recognize even with the baseball cap, polarized aviator-style sunglasses, and dark bristled jaw. He was taller than average, and lean, with big shoulders, long legs. He was wearing jeans, cowboy boots, and a brown leather jacket over a tight-fitting T-shirt and looked every bit the film star. If Jen were here, she'd die.

Margot heard someone next to her murmur, wondering aloud if that was the guy from *Stardust Ranch*. She stepped forward, meeting him partway. "Max," she said.

He nodded. "You're Margot?" he asked, shifting his leather backpack to the other shoulder.

"I am. Flight okay?"

"No problems." His dark eyebrows flattened, his bristled jaw tightening. "How is she?"

It went without saying that he was asking about Sally. Margot swallowed around the lump suddenly filling her throat. "She's looking forward to seeing you. I'm to take you straight there."

"Is she really going to be okay?"

The lump in her throat grew. "I hope so." She nodded at his backpack. "Is that all you have, or is there a checked bag?"

"Just this," he said. "Only here for a few days."

"So, you're really not here for Sally's play?" she asked, trying to confirm what Sally told her.

Max looked at her, gaze hidden by his polarized glasses. "What play?"

"*Barefoot in the Park*. It launches the Cambria Playhouse's summer season." They were walking out of the terminal now, across the street to short-term parking. The sun had dropped lower in the sky, creating a fine line of gold across the horizon.

"Just yesterday she told me the director had quit," Margot continued, "as well as the leads. She asked me to step in and direct. This morning I agreed." She glanced at Max as they reached her car. "I should have agreed last night. I shouldn't have left her stewing all night. Maybe if I hadn't, none of this would have happened."

He lowered his backpack and then removed his sunglasses. His dark brown gaze met hers and held. "You think you're the reason she had a heart attack?"

His eyes were beautiful. His face . . . beautiful. She sucked in a breath, suddenly a little light-headed. "She was fine at the cocktail party."

"I can't imagine you were actually the trigger. Sally is driven. She has always worked hard, and unless something has changed, she doesn't exercise, doesn't eat right, and starts her day with a good vodka tonic."

"She's switched to vodka and orange juice."

Max laughed, creases fanned at the corners of his eyes, and his teeth flashed, blindingly white. Her pulse jumped and her mouth dried. Wow. "If you know her favorite drink, you two must have some history," Margot said, unlocking the car and popping the trunk.

"That's an understatement," Max answered, dropping his backpack into the trunk before closing it.

Margot shot him a quick look, curious. There were a dozen things she wanted to ask, but right now, she needed to get him to the hospital. Sally was waiting, and if Max could buoy Sally's spirits and help her recover, then Margot would roll out the red carpet for him.

Chapter 3

SALLY WAS DOZING WHEN MAX ENTERED HER ROOM ON the hospital's third floor. It was almost six and the deep gold sunlight spilled across the bed, but her face was shadowed.

He stood in the doorway for a minute, glad Margot chose to wait in the lobby, because seeing Sally like this, so still, so much older, filled him with guilt.

He shouldn't have waited so long to see her. He should have been better at staying in touch and returning her calls. He liked the brevity of texting. Sally loved a good long conversation, something he didn't always have time for, something he didn't have the energy for.

He felt selfish now, seeing her, realizing that in the four years since they'd last met, she'd aged. He couldn't even remember where they'd had dinner—it had been in San Francisco, he knew that much—and once again she'd made the effort to come to him, just as she'd gone to see him at the Cape Playhouse, where he was starring in *The Glass Menagerie*. She'd surprised him, showing up unannounced, hoping they'd have dinner after the play, but he'd already made plans and he couldn't change them. She'd left that evening disappointed. She'd tried to hide it, but he knew, because he knew her, and so the next time he was heading to California, he called and suggested they get together, and she said she'd be in San Francisco, so they met for dinner and then walked around the Marina. It was a nice night.

But was that four years ago, or five?

Pathetic that he couldn't remember exactly when. He'd been so busy these past few years that everything blurred together.

His boots thudded on the floor as he crossed to Sally's side. She stirred and slowly opened her eyes. It took her a moment to focus, and then she tried to sit up. "You came."

He drew the armchair closer to the bed and sat down. "There was no need to have a heart attack. You could have just asked me to visit."

The corner of her wide mouth lifted. "You wouldn't have come."

"You don't know that." He saw her fumbling with the bed controls. "What do you want? Let me help."

"I want my head higher. Can't see you properly."

He leaned over the bed, pushed the up button and then stopped midway. "Not sure you're supposed to be all the way upright." Max glanced to the door. "Should I check with the nurse?"

"Don't bother them. They're so bossy as it is."

Max couldn't hide his smile. "That's their job."

"I'm the guest here. They're billing me. They should listen to me more."

He laughed quietly, amused as always. Sally was fierce and wonderful, perhaps fiercely wonderful. "You're a patient here. They're trying to help you."

"I'd rather be at the Ritz."

"Have you ever even stayed at the Ritz?" he countered, aware that frugal Sally didn't do luxe vacations or fancy cars. She'd become wealthy by being conservative, and investing her money, not spending it. Whenever she'd come to see him, she flew economy because first class was a waste of money. She wouldn't approve of his flying first class here, not even to see her.

"That's not the point," Sally said faintly, before sighing and closing her eyes. "Can't even banter," she said after a moment, "not without tiring out."

"Then don't banter. Rest. I'm not going anywhere for a few days."

She opened her eyes and looked at him, her brows pulling together, creating a deep crease between them and another strong line in her forehead. "Did Margot mention the play?"

Max sat back in the chair. "She said you'd asked her to direct and this morning she agreed."

"I've invested a fortune in the playhouse. It's the old theater complex, I'm sure you remember it, on Main Street."

"It was closed for a long time."

Sally nodded. "I refurbished it but maintained the original character. What's the point of having a historic theater and making it look new?"

"Like the Cape Playhouse," he said.

"Only ours doesn't date to the nineteen twenties, nor was it a nineteenth-century meetinghouse." She wheezed a moment, before adding, "But yes, Cambria has its history, and I want to protect it for the next generation."

"Maybe you shouldn't talk right now," he said, reaching out to take her hand. "Maybe you should just rest."

"I am. I'm lying in bed. So frustrating, especially when there is so much to do."

"What needs to be done?"

"The office—"

"It seems as if Margot has that in hand."

"And then there's the play. We need leads. I lost them both last night. As well as the director."

"I thought Margot told you this morning she'd direct."

"Yes, but she'll also make a good Corie. That just leaves Paul."

Max wasn't going to touch that one. "Margot didn't mention acting in the play, just directing."

"She said she'd help. She promised."

"She promised to direct, I believe."

"She said she'd do whatever she could so I wouldn't worry. And I'm worried about the leads. Worried that the playhouse is doomed—"

"It's not doomed."

"Years of COVID and now this!" She fussed with her bed, raising the head higher. "Where is Margot? Did she just drop you off? I thought she was going to take you to the cottage. That was the plan anyway."

"She's here. She's just in the lobby waiting. She was trying to be thoughtful and give us time to catch up."

Sally gestured impatiently. "Well, go get her. We need to figure out our leads now. Rehearsal starts at seven."

MAX TOOK THE ELEVATOR DOWN TO THE LOBBY, DEEP IN thought. He'd only just met Margot, but he sensed she wasn't going to like Sally's plans . . . for either of them.

As he crossed the lobby, someone stopped and stared at him, and then a couple discussed him as he passed by. Max ignored the attention, focused on Margot, who was sitting in a row of chairs across from the small florist and gift shop, reading on her phone.

She glanced up as he approached, wispy blond strands framing her face. "How is she?"

"Ornery," he said. "Doesn't like being in bed."

Margot smiled and stood. "What's next? The cottage? Or food first?"

"Actually, Sally wants you to come see her." He paused. "I'm to return with you. She wants to speak to both of us together."

She pursed her lips, lifted a delicate winged brow. "Hmm."

"You sound suspicious."

"I am."

"What do you think she wants to discuss?" he asked, curious as to how well Margot knew Sally.

"I suspect it's about the play, and probably rehearsal which should begin in, oh"—she pulled out her phone, checked the time—"an hour." She looked up at him, a faint smile on her lips. "Am I wrong? I'd love to be wrong."

"You are not wrong."

She clapped a hand to her forehead. "The woman could have died last night and all she can think about is that play."

"You're going to have to bring me up to speed."

"I will," Margot promised. "As soon as we leave here." She shouldered her purse, walked with him to the elevator. "How did she look?"

"A little gray. Her voice isn't very strong. She sounds pretty wheezy."

"I asked the nurse about that this morning. Apparently, that should pass soon. It's worse after she gets up and moves around the room."

"She has gotten up, then?"

"Briefly." Inside the elevator, she leaned against the wall. "They want to do a balloon angioplasty, and she hasn't agreed. She said they could give her medicine that would do the same thing—"

"How is that possible?" he asked, punching the button for the third floor.

"It's not. Sally would just prefer medicine, but they need to do both, in conjunction, and it's a fairly routine procedure. It's important she have it done, if she wants her life back."

This was all news to him. Sally hadn't mentioned anything about the heart attack itself, or treatment. "Have you talked to her about it?" he asked.

"Sally only wants to discuss the play."

"That's pretty much our conversation, too." He felt it only fair that Margot be prepared. "Apparently you're going to act *and* direct."

Margot laughed out loud. "*No.*" The elevator doors opened and she stepped out, glancing at him as he followed her. "That's not happening. That wasn't part of the agreement."

"And the agreement was?"

"I'd step in for Cherry, the director, and we'd audition for new leads."

"Do you think she's confused?" he asked as they walked down the hallway.

"No. She's just . . . managing . . . us. As she does."

"Manipulating, you mean."

Margot didn't immediately answer. "I want Sally to make a full recovery. Her business needs her to make a full recovery. I'll do everything in my power to see she gets well."

"Including playing Corie?"

They'd been passing patient rooms with open doors, and she stopped between rooms, faced him. "Have you agreed to play Paul?"

"Would it make a difference?" he asked.

"No," she answered. "I'm just trying to figure out what Sally is planning."

"I think she'd like us to star together. I think that's her goal."

Margot studied his expression. "That would mean you'd be here for weeks, not days. Could you do it?"

Max thought about Howard and the screenplays in his backpack. He thought about the past year where he'd worked steadily, job after job, day after day, and he was tired. Close to burnt out. "I don't know. I was hoping to take a break for a couple weeks. Read, eat, sleep, get some writing done."

Her expression changed, becoming more guarded. "You write?"

"A little."

She glanced away, gave her head the smallest of shakes. "I don't want to act," she said quietly before looking at him, her gaze meeting his, "but if we can use this as leverage to get Sally to agree to the PCI—"

"PCI?"

"Percutaneous coronary intervention," she said in a rush. "I think that's what it's called. But it's the procedure Sally refused, and it's the one that will make the biggest difference to her quality of life . . . as well as extending her life."

"Then let's team up. Make her play ball."

They started walking again, and neither said anything until they'd reached Sally's door. Max didn't want to go in until he knew Margot's position. "Are you with me?"

"Obviously I want Sally healthy, and I want her to be around a long, long time."

"So we'll do what she wants, if she does what we want."

"She won't like it," Margot warned.

"Not right away, but she loves to make deals. We're just negotiating with her, and as you said, she's passionate about the play. If we come together, and we're in agreement, she won't be able to fight us, not when she is so close to having what she wants . . . a successful summer season."

"With the world's most boring play," Margot muttered.

Max laughed. "It's not my favorite, either."

She sighed, clearly unhappy at the prospect. "But we could pull it off. If we had to."

"Sounds like we have to."

"Let's go in and talk to her. See if we can make her happy."

IT WASN'T EASY MAKING SALLY HAPPY, NOT WITH THEIR insisting she agree to the procedure in exchange for their taking on the leads in *Barefoot in the Park*.

"I don't think two against one is fair," she complained.

"We're not prepared to lose you," Margot answered. "And as you're not prepared to give up on the summer season, I think it's a win-win."

"Now who's being merciless?" Sally glanced from Margot to Max. "And you agreed to this?"

"You wanted me to spend time with you." Max smiled cheerfully. "Well, here I am."

"With conditions," Sally retorted.

"You don't mind a few conditions, not when it means you get everything else you want."

Sally stared at him hard, and then her expression softened. "I don't like being put under. What if I don't wake up?"

Max moved closer to the bed, sitting on the edge so that he could take her hand. "You'll wake up, and I'll be here."

"You'll be glad you had the procedure, Sally. No one is ready to take over your empire," Margot said.

Sally sighed. "Fine. Then let's get this procedure scheduled so I can get out of here and get home. You two should be at rehearsal. Isn't it starting soon?"

Margot shook her head. "I canceled tonight's rehearsal. It didn't make sense to have a rehearsal when everything was up in the air, but we'll meet tomorrow, at seven."

"So, what are you going to do tonight?" Sally asked.

"Find some food," Max answered, "and get some sleep. It's been a long travel day, but don't worry, tomorrow I'll begin reviewing the play."

"Sally, should I take Max to your house for the night? Your car is there. He'd probably like to have wheels."

"As long as it's not her Cadillac," Max answered. "That's a gas-guzzler if I ever saw one."

"But it's free," Sally said.

"Gas isn't." Max leaned over the bed and kissed her forehead.

"In that case, cancel your hotel room and take the Leopold Cottage." Sally looked at Margot. "It should be available for the rest of May, and see what we can do to make it work for him for this summer. No point making Max move if we don't have to."

Sally glanced at Max. "It's a Cambria gem, designed by Warren Leopold in the sixties, built from old-growth redwood. It's a special place, right on the ocean, next to Fiscalini Ranch Preserve."

"Sounds wonderful," he said, "but I don't need a big place."

"It's not," Margot answered. "It's just a one-bedroom cottage, but it's stunning, with epic views and a private staircase down to the water."

The nurse entered, and then a doctor. The nurse gave Margot and Max a pointed look.

"That's our cue to leave," Max said. "But I'll be here tomorrow, Sally." He winked at her. "Looks like you've got me for the summer."

"It took long enough," she grumbled.

Margot stepped away from the bed. "I'll be back tomorrow in the morning, before work."

Sally frowned. "What is tomorrow?"

"Thursday."

"I've a conference call with the Bay Area group."

"I'll cancel it," Margot promised.

"No, take the call," Sally said, trying to sit up. "Don't let them know I'm in the hospital. Just fill in and try to be me."

Margot's mouth opened, closed. There was no point arguing with her boss, not now. Margot managed a weak smile. "That's a tall order, Sally, but I'll do my best."

The strain in Sally's expression eased. "Consider it practice for the future."

Margot joined Max in the hall, slightly nauseous and trying her best not to panic. "What have we gotten ourselves into?"

"I wasn't expecting any of this."

"One would almost think Sally had the heart attack on purpose."

Max's lips quirked. "You never know with her."

"Wow. What a day. I'm exhausted, and I haven't just flown in from New York. Let's go get you settled. But first, I need to swing by the office to pick up the cottage key."

Forty-five minutes later, they had the key and were approaching the Leopold Cottage on Sherwood Drive. Sally had acquired a number of architect Warren Leopold's homes in Cambria, along with one in Big Sur. Leopold had done most of his Cambria design work in the 1960s, his designs incorporating his love of nature and craftsmanship, and even if his work was a little too quirky for some, he did know how to frame a view.

Margot parked in the driveway, and from the back, the house was almost windowless and nondescript. The roofline was sharply defined, and walls rose to dramatic angles. Max glanced at Margot as they walked up the path leading to the front door. "It looks like something a hippie might have built in Santa Cruz in the seventies."

She could tell he wasn't impressed. She hadn't been the first time she'd visited the house, either. "The house is designed to take advantage of being right on the ocean. You'll see."

She unlocked the door and stepped aside, letting Max enter first.

He passed her, his backpack lowered, and she gave him a moment to explore on his own. There wasn't a lot to explore; it was a one-bedroom cottage, with a platform couch in the living room that could be used as an additional bed. Otherwise it was a snug wood and stone cottage with views of the ocean from nearly every angle. The small but full-sized kitchen had recently been updated with new appliances and a limestone counter.

Margot entered the cottage a moment later and found

Max standing in the living room at one of the enormous plate glass windows, hands in his jean pockets, gaze on the horizon.

She joined him at the window. "Will this do?" she asked, lips curving.

He said nothing for a moment before turning to her. "It's spectacular."

He was, too. Theater people were talented, but not necessarily jaw-droppingly beautiful. Max was the whole package—that face, the lean, muscular body, and his style . . . casual but sexy, confident, a man comfortable in his own skin.

He caught her staring, and his gaze met hers and held. She felt a crackle of awareness, an energy she couldn't explain. Suddenly shy, she looked back at the water, where blue waves crashed on the rocks below. "A seal," she said huskily, pointing to something playing just past the rocks. "Or possibly an otter. I know the guests that stay here comment regularly on all the marine life."

"I like this place."

"Good." Margot left him to step into the kitchen. She checked the gas stove, and then the refrigerator. The appliances were new and immaculate, and the cleaning service always did a fantastic job.

"Did I hear Sally right? Will I need to move end of this month?" he asked, entering the redwood kitchen.

The kitchen suddenly felt small. Max was tall, and with his big shoulders and long legs, he easily filled the space, charging it with a very masculine, almost tangible energy. Margot's pulse did a little jump as she stepped around him, moving closer to the dining nook with its built-in bench along the windowless wall. "I don't think you'll need to move," she said, remembering Sally's words about "see what we can do to make it work," meaning, have Heather, who managed all the residential vacation rentals, adjust the upcoming reservations. "The team will manage the bookings."

"She's not going to cancel anyone's reservations, is she?" he asked, sounding uncomfortable.

"We have plenty of time to sort it out." Margot smiled, evading his question before glancing at her watch. "Are you sure you don't want me to take you for groceries, or to dinner? You have to be starving."

"I'll order something in for dinner." He suddenly yawned and tried unsuccessfully to hide it. "I might not even do dinner. It's been a long day."

"Call me if you change your mind. I'm just five minutes away off Moonstone Beach."

"Is that walking distance or driving?" he asked, following her to the door.

"Driving." She opened the door, stepped outside. She could hear the crash of waves below. Dusk was quickly giving way to darkness. "There's some coffee pods for the Nespresso machine in the pantry, along with creamers, sweeteners, and teas. Next to the pantry, you'll find a water dispenser. There should be an extra water in the garage. Cambria relies on two streams for its water supply, and toward summer we get very low on water. Thus, we all like short showers and these big forty-gallon containers of water instead of what you'd buy at the grocery store." She handed over the house key, promising to send him the wireless password and all other details once home. "I should have done that at the office, but I forgot. I'll look it up at home and text you the info."

"Wait until the morning," he answered. "I've got my phone, and lots to read. I'm good for the night."

Chapter 4

MAX WATCHED MARGOT DRIVE AWAY.

She intrigued him. He didn't think he had a type, but he had married two blondes—not that he was looking for a third wife. He wasn't marriage material, but he liked women, and he was drawn to Margot, with her wide green eyes and shoulder-length blond hair, which she'd run a hand through when uncertain.

But she wasn't just pretty, she was smart. Sharp. He could see why Sally had made Margot her right hand. Margot might look like a small-town girl, but she knew how to get things done, and Sally would like that. Whereas he liked the curve of Margot's high cheekbones, the fullness of her mouth, and the look in her eyes when she didn't think he was paying attention. She'd spent a fair amount of time looking at him, trying to figure him out. It was almost as if she'd been thrown in a cage with a wild, unpredictable animal. Maybe he was.

Half smiling, Max closed the door, took another walk through the cottage before unpacking his leather backpack, putting everything he'd brought into the built-in drawers in the bedroom and then heading to the shower.

The bathroom featured more glass with a big window overlooking the ocean, providing views from the sunken bathtub to the green-tiled shower. Since Margot left, the outdoor spotlights had come on, illuminating the dramatic coastline with its dark rocks and foamy waves. Another light hit a large, gnarled Monterey pine, turning the weathered tree into a living sculpture.

Max, who hadn't thought he'd ever be back on the Central Coast for any length of time, was impressed. The house was so unique. He wasn't surprised that it rarely came open. It had a small footprint but lived large with the floor-to-ceiling redwood walls, huge windows, angles and verandas, all designed to capture ocean views. Sally knew him well. This was his kind of place. It would be good to be close to Sally for the next few months. She'd spent so much of her life looking out for him, and he was glad he could finally do something for her.

He turned on the hot water, giving it a minute to warm up, thinking he'd sleep well tonight. There would be no flying tomorrow. He'd wake up, make coffee, find some breakfast, and begin reading through a *Barefoot in the Park* script he'd download tomorrow. Then later tomorrow, after he was properly fortified, he'd email Howard and let him know there'd been a change of plans and he'd be performing this summer on the West Coast at the Cambria Playhouse. For free.

Max stepped beneath the shower spray and grimaced, anticipating Howard's reaction. Poor Howard. He was not going to be happy.

THE MARINE LAYER COVERED THE STREETS OF CAMBRIA in a cool gray mist. After an early visit to the hospital, Margot was at the office, wanting to be one of the first to arrive. She hoped to get organized, go through Sally's calendar, making notes of things that would have to be handled promptly. She was still at Sally's desk when Jen arrived, and then Heather, Kelly, and finally Ali.

Jen offered to do a quick coffee run, and when she returned with the lattes and the one Americano for Ali, Margot gathered everyone for a meeting, filling them in on Sally's condition as well as Sally's determination that things continue as if she were there. Nothing should change.

"When does she get to go home?" Heather asked.

"She needs a fairly routine procedure to open blocked arteries, and then she should be released the next day."

"I'd think after a heart attack any procedure would be dangerous," Kelly said, troubled.

"Actually, they'd wanted to do it sooner," Margot said, "but Sally refused."

"So Sally," Jen said with a sigh. "She can be very stubborn. My grandma is like that. Once she has her mind made up, she won't budge."

Margot checked her smile, thinking Sally would not appreciate being compared to Jen's grandmother. "She doesn't like being put under," Margot explained. "I think she'd hoped medicine would break up the clots, but it's not enough. Fortunately, she's in good spirits." She hesitated, wondering how to work in the play and Max's visit. Not visit, but arrival. Just thinking of him, and her stomach did a sudden freefall. She'd found it hard to fall asleep last night, overstimulated from the day and just being near Max. He was not like any man she'd ever met before.

"I have just one more bit of news," Margot added, avoiding looking at Jen since Jen would lose her mind once Max's name was mentioned. "As we all know, Sally is very committed to the playhouse, and she's—" Margot broke off, held her breath a moment, before finishing the thought. "She's asked me to take over *Barefoot in the Park*. So I have."

"That's exciting," Kelly said. "She's wanted to get you involved ever since I started working here."

"Fortunately, I don't have to manage the play on my own."

Margot swallowed, adding, "Max Russo will be costarring in the play with me."

For a moment there was just silence and then Jen leaned forward. "Max? My Max?"

Margot's lips curved. She knew Jen would be excited. "He's here—"

"In Cambria?" she squeaked.

Margot nodded. "I checked him in to one of the rental properties on Sherwood Drive last night. Which reminds me, I need to get him the Wi-Fi password, and basic property info. I didn't know where that was."

"I can take it to him," Jen volunteered.

"We can just text him the password and then email him the rest." Margot saw Jen's disappointment. "But maybe if we can find an extra script, you could run one over? He's going to need one."

"I'll get on that," Jen said, grinning.

"What *is* he like?" Kelly asked, curious.

"Nice. Easy to talk to." Margot hesitated, swallowed. "And good-looking."

"Wow," Jen breathed. "This just might be the best summer of my life."

Everyone laughed. Margot shook her head. "You do have a boyfriend, Jen."

"I know," Jen said, "but a girl can dream." Her expression turned speculative. "I don't suppose you need any help with the play?"

Margot pursed her lips. "I probably will. The first rehearsal is tonight. I'll know more after that."

MAX WAS UNPACKING GROCERIES WHEN MARGOT called. "Hey, Margot," he said, recognizing her number. "Thanks for the script."

"That was all Jen. I'm glad she got it to you. Everything good?"

"Yes." Max folded the paper shopping bag and tucked it in the cupboard under the sink. "I've got a car now, a long-term rental. It was dropped off a couple hours ago. I've already hit the grocery store, bought some clothes, and even found a cheap printer at the Walmart in Paso Robles."

"You've had a productive morning. Did you happen to see Sally? I went by early this morning, and she was a little grumpy. Hadn't slept well last night."

"She was in a better mood when I saw her."

"Good. Is the procedure still scheduled for Monday?"

"Yes. And if all goes well, she'll be cleared to go home Tuesday, and then she's going to need someone to stay with her for a few days."

"I can do that."

"So can I." Max leaned against the counter. "But it seems she doesn't want either of us. She's hiring a home health nurse."

"That doesn't make any sense. Why have a stranger come in?"

"Sally doesn't like to be fussed over, and then there's the play. She wants us to focus on that—"

"Ridiculous!"

"But it seems to be what's motivating her right now, and if that gives her incentive to get through her physical therapy program when she gets home, that's fine with me."

MARGOT ARRIVED FORTY MINUTES BEFORE REHEARSAL to open the theater. She sat now in the middle of the audience, feet up on the back of the chair in front of her. The lights were on. The stage was empty. The red curtains were open, revealing the scuffed and scarred wood stage. Rows of red velvet seats were in front of her. More seats behind her.

The theater was small, just one hundred seats total, although there was room to add a row of folding chairs to create a new front row. Not that extra seats were needed.

There hadn't been a sold-out show since the playhouse re-opened. Nor had there been a sold-out show before the theater closed all those years ago.

Margot knew Sally had hoped the summer season would change that, which is why Sally clung so stubbornly to her dream. But dreams could be problematic.

Margot sighed and stretched, and then glanced at her watch. People would begin arriving soon for rehearsal. She wondered how they'd react to Max. Margot, who rarely got starstruck, was more than a little in awe of him. He was so . . . everything.

She flipped open her notebook, studied her proposed schedule. Introductions. Updates on cast and crew changes. And then read through. There'd be no blocking tonight. Margot just wanted to gauge how comfortable everyone was with their part. She'd spent her lunch studying the script, refreshing her memory, as she'd played Corie several times before. It had been years, though, and Margot once had a great memory, but memorizing took longer now. She had to work harder to remember lines. Fortunately, she'd learned tricks over the years to help new lines stick.

A door opened in the lobby and then closed. Footsteps sounded, heavy, masculine steps, and then disappeared, as if muffled by carpet. She looked over her shoulder. Max had entered the auditorium.

Her stomach knotted, and her heart jumped.

He looked impossibly cool in his jeans and black T-shirt. The neck of the shirt was slightly stretched, showing a little collarbone, while his arms were tan and muscular. His thick, carved biceps were on full display. The jeans hugged his lean waist and sinewy thighs. His dark wavy hair was tousled. His jaw had a proper five-o'clock shadow. In short, he was walking testosterone, and apparently whatever estrogen she had left wanted what he had. "Hi," she said, heat and a prickling awareness heightening the flurry of butterflies in her middle. "You're early."

"Just by ten minutes." His gaze swept the intimate theater and returned to her. "How long have you been here?"

"Awhile." She saw the lift of his dark eyebrow and tried to smash her breathlessness. Breathless was not good. Her surge of hormones was dangerous. Just because she hadn't felt . . . anything . . . in ages didn't mean she needed to lust after Max, who was, after all, an actor, and actors weren't her favorite human beings. "I wanted to be calm and collected when everyone arrived."

"Is it working?"

Well, it was until he arrived. "Sort of," she hedged.

"What makes you nervous?" he asked, walking toward her with the same slow, deliberate walk she could picture him doing in cowboy boots on the set of *Stardust Ranch*.

Her pulse jumped. She lifted a hand, gestured broadly. "I gave all this up."

"Why?" Max took a seat in her row, leaving an empty chair between them.

Up close there were more muscles—in his triceps, in his forearm, in the taut line of his quadriceps. She swallowed hard. "Too complicated to explain now."

"But you'll explain it later." He said it as a statement, not a question.

She shifted, closed her notebook, hooked the pen on the notebook cover, avoiding eye contact. Even though Max sat back in his seat, looking comfortable and relaxed, something else was happening. It was that seductive energy of his. He exuded physicality, sensuality, *sex*.

The sex part was wreaking havoc on her brain. She honestly didn't know how to handle the awareness. Or him. It had been years since she'd dated. Years since she'd made love. "It's not a very interesting story."

"Tell me anyway—"

Thankfully, voices sounded in the lobby, saving her from an answer. Several people had arrived all at once, two men and a woman. Margot jumped to her feet, grateful for the interruption. "Here we go," she said.

"It's going to be fun," he said, rising.

She shot him a swift, sardonic glance, even as she heard the woman say, "Is that Max Russo?"

"Does that happen all the time?" she asked Max, knowing he had to have heard it, too.

"More than it used to."

It suddenly crossed her mind that once the public knew Max was starring in the play, the playhouse would be selling a lot more tickets. In fact, they might even sell out for the summer season. Sally would be thrilled.

And savvy Sally had probably already thought of this.

MARGOT NEEDED A DRINK AFTER THE READ THROUGH.

That rehearsal—if it could even be called a rehearsal—was crazy. The whole night had been crazy. It was terrible, awful, worse than awful. So awful that she could only laugh as the other three cast members left, leaving her alone with Max.

Thankfully, Max was laughing, too.

"Oh good Lord, what are we going to do?" she asked, reaching up to dry her eyes. "We're in trouble."

"They're rusty," he said, the corner of his mouth tugging. "They need a lot more rehearsal time."

"Be honest. Can this play be saved?" She gave him a serious look. "Tell me the truth."

"Yes."

"Were you here tonight?"

"I was, and it was rough, but it's also the worst it will ever be. It'll just improve from here on out." He met her gaze, held it. "You'll make it better. A week from now it won't even be remotely the same."

"I wish I could be so confident."

"They're just trying too hard. They're overacting. With some direction they'll pull back, find their characters, settle into the role." His lips twitched. "At least Saul is projecting. That's a plus. The others are all but inaudible."

Saul was bellowing, not projecting, but hopefully Max was right and they just needed to rehearse. A lot.

"Feel like a drink?" Max asked.

Her gaze swept his features, avoiding his eyes, which she was already noticing could be gold sometimes and a darker brown other times. Part of her needed to escape and collapse—tonight had been a lot—but she felt drawn to Max and was reluctant to say goodbye to him yet.

"Yes."

"Any suggestions?"

"The restaurant on the next block has a little bar. Let's see if we can squeeze in there."

The bar was virtually empty on a Thursday night, and they took a small booth in the corner. The server appeared almost immediately. "What can I get you?" she asked.

"Whiskey, neat," he said. "Margot?"

Margot pushed back her bangs, barely able to think, as she looked at the server. "A glass of red, something from Paso?"

"I really like the Petite Sirah from Tobin James Cellars," the server said. "Just opened the bottle tonight."

"Sounds great," Margot said. "I'll have that."

The server walked away, and Margot settled back against the booth with a sigh. "I think this is the first time all day I've felt like I can breathe."

"It's been a lot," Max said. "I'm impressed with how well you're coping. Taking on the play and Sally's business? Wow."

"There's not a lot of changes at work. Sally has a good team in place. When I first came on eighteen months ago, there had been a lot of turnover, but since then, there's been no staff changes and I'm grateful to be working with people who know what they're doing and care about Sally."

"So Sally has good people around her?"

"Really good people. Conscientious, hardworking, loyal."

"I'm glad to hear that."

Their drinks were delivered. Max lifted his whiskey. "To Sally Collins, someone we both admire."

Margot clinked the rim of her goblet to his glass. "To Sally, someone we both love."

They sipped their drinks and Max hid his yawn. "Sorry. Still adjusting to the time change."

"It's late for you. You're on East Coast time."

"Not sure what time zone I'm used to. I was in Italy for almost a week and had only just returned home when I got the message about Sally's heart attack."

"On vacation?" she asked.

"Work. I'd gone over to shoot a commercial."

"For?"

"A fragrance." He tipped his glass, gave the golden liquor a swirl. "I'm a brand ambassador for an Italian fashion house, and it's their first fragrance, so there were a lot of people on set standing around making sure everything was done right."

"Were you shooting in Rome?"

"In Positano. I started out in designer threads, and by the end I was—" He broke off, shook his head, amused. "Naked in bed."

"Alone?"

"No. I had a gorgeous young Italian model for a costar. I think she was wondering what she was doing with an old guy like me."

"I seriously doubt that. You're not old, and you've got that face and body."

"I'm hoping that's a compliment?"

Margot laughed and he smiled back at her.

"Anyway," he added. "I was aware I was old enough to be her father, and I love women, but prefer them closer to my age."

"Really? Why?"

He shrugged. "I think mature women are more confi-dent, more interesting, which usually means less drama."

"I noticed an emphasis on the word *usually*. Have you just escaped a drama-filled relationship?"

"My divorce was finalized late April."

"So recently. I'm sorry."

"No, it's a good thing. We were together four years and then the divorce took another eighteen months. I'm ready to move forward. It's time."

Margot waited for him to say something else. He didn't. But she was curious. She hadn't gone to Wikipedia to dive into his personal life, but maybe she should.

"And you?" he asked. "Single, married, divorced?"

"Single. Never married."

"What?"

She smiled, grateful it didn't sting anymore. There was a time it had hurt, but years had passed and she'd accepted that she'd probably never marry. "I didn't expect to be sin-gle at my age. I wish there had been children, but I suppose things happen for a reason."

"It's not too late. You're beautiful. And young."

Margot's cheeks burned. "Older than you, by four years I think." She lifted her goblet. "Sally told me your age. I haven't been stalking you online . . . although I'm consider-ing it."

"Should you, just know a lot of stories online are fake. I've never done interviews where I talk about my relation-ships, that's always been off-limits, so whatever has been written, it's conjecture, or downright fiction."

"You're smart to keep your personal life private. More people should. It's one of the reasons I don't have a Face-book page. I don't do Instagram or TikTok. Even when I was acting, I avoided social media. I'm happier out of the limelight."

"It's not going to last, you know. Once it's announced

that we're being added to the cast, things could get a little chaotic."

She'd thought of that, but had pushed the thought aside, too content in her little bubble in Cambria. She had no real problems here. She didn't lose sleep over her job. She was making good money, saving for the future. "You don't need to worry about me. I won't be talking to the press about you. None of Sally's staff will, either. They're very loyal to her. Everyone else? That remains to be seen."

"I give it three days," he said, looking down into his whiskey.

"Three days?" she echoed.

"Before our secret is out."

"Then I guess I need to figure out how the theater's front office works. I don't even know who handles ticket sales or manages the website."

"I noticed it hasn't been updated in some time."

Margot reached for her wallet but Max beat her, pulling out cash and putting two twenties and a five on the table.

"That's way more than the drinks cost," she said, gathering her things.

"I know, but better to be generous and stay on the good side of the community."

Chapter 5

FRIDAY MORNING MARGOT WOKE EARLY, STOMACH IN knots, head already pounding. She'd had terrible dreams about the play, dreams about performing to an empty theater, dreams about being booed offstage.

They were just dreams, but still, her mood was low, and Margot had to give herself a pep talk as she made coffee, and then downed painkillers, before leaving for the office.

But she wasn't the only one early for work. Jen arrived just a few minutes after Margot did.

Margot was glad it was Jen who'd arrived. "Do you have time to talk this morning? We could also go to lunch."

"I'm not in trouble, am I?" Jen asked.

"No. Not at all. I need your help."

"We can talk now. Let me just get my laptop." A minute later Jen rolled a chair closer to Margot's desk and sat down, laptop open. "What do you need?"

Margot hesitated, trying to formulate the words, not even sure what she was needing, as she felt like she needed everything. "You said you'd be willing to help out with the play, and I wondered if that offer was still on the table—"

"Yes."

"You don't even know what I'm going to ask," Margot said.

"Does it matter? Sally's in the hospital. You're in charge of a play you didn't want to be part of. Max Russo is in town for the play. Considering all the problems the play was having, I'm anxious just thinking about it."

"You summed that up very nicely."

"I'm direct. Why waste time?"

"I agree. I learned last night that there isn't really any crew. There are a couple of people who have volunteered, but the two people who have built sets in the past are out, having quit under the former director. Apparently, nothing had been taken care of." Margot hesitated, thinking of the daunting tasks ahead. "Now that Max is involved, we need a publicity team—real publicity—and costumes, set design, crew . . . everything."

"How are you sleeping at night?" Jen asked, deadpan.

Margot laughed. "Not well." But it wasn't just the production making her toss and turn. Max had infiltrated her sleep and she was dreaming about him, and the dreams were every bit as hot and provocative as he was.

"No wonder. That's a lot. You need an assistant."

"I do. An assistant director." Margot hesitated. "Want the job?"

"What does an assistant director do?"

"Everything."

Jen tucked a strand of long brown hair behind her ear. "Sure. I'll do it. Who needs sleep?"

"You might want to think about that one," Margot warned her.

"I told you I'd help. I'm in."

"In community theater, it's not usually a paid position, but you'll be paid—"

"I don't care about the money," Jen protested.

"You will when all your free time through the end of July is sucked into this production." But just having Jen on her team made Margot breathe easier. "So, we will figure out compensation. It's important to me that I don't take advantage of you—"

"Like Sally takes advantage of you?" Jen said. She glanced around at the still-empty office but dropped her voice anyway. "I'm not trying to be rude. I just know that Sally squeezes you a lot, and I think it's because she trusts you, but one person can only handle so much. I can't even imagine my mom coping with everything you do."

"Your mom?" Margot said faintly.

"She was one year behind you at Paso Robles High. She said you didn't have any classes together, but she remembered you from school, and how you were always the lead in the school plays and musicals."

"Your mom must have been young when she had you."

Jen shook her head. "Not that young. Twenty-five, I think."

Margot suddenly felt old. It was strange thinking she could have a son or daughter Jen's age, if she'd stayed in Paso and gotten married, instead of going to New York.

Margot forced herself to focus. "So, as my assistant director I don't expect you to take on everything, but rather, help me find the people who can help out at the theater, hopefully people with some experience as crew, but if not, I can train. The goal is warm bodies who will commit."

"What exactly does the crew do? What kind of people am I looking for?"

"People who can build and paint sets. Manage props. Sew costumes—or find things that could serve as costumes. Hair and makeup—in this case, the cast will be responsible for their own. But we'll definitely need sound and lighting technicians, as well as someone to design programs and posters. Assist the director—"

"You," Jen said, smiling.

Margot nodded. "And then during performances, work the box office, take tickets, pass out programs, and behind the curtains, move those sets, get props in the right place, help with costume changes. Never mind clean and organize."

"Was none of this in place?" Jen asked, clarifying.

"The director had alienated a lot of people from the last production and hadn't told Sally what was happening. It wasn't until she quit that all the problems came to light."

"But if it's been done before, we can do it again," Jen said, unfazed. "I don't have experience in theater, but I've done a lot of events. That's what I did during college. I worked for an event planner, handled everything from weddings to fund-raisers." Jen had been typing notes, and she looked up at Margot. "My degree is in marketing, which required some internships with companies. They'd always just throw you in the deep end, handing off their social media and publicity. I'm not going to let you down. I love challenges."

"Then why are you working as a receptionist?" Margot asked. "You are underutilized here."

"I took what I could get when I graduated from Santa Clara. I had lots of opportunities in Silicon Valley, but my little brother had some health stuff going on, not sure if you knew that, and I wanted to come home to be closer to him."

"I didn't know."

"He's a really sweet brother, and before you feel weird, he's doing well. He's finishing high school and he's hoping to get into college." Jen glanced down at her laptop. "I'm thinking we will need at least ten to twelve people, four or five for crew, preferably people with some theater experience," she said briskly. "And then we'll want a publicity team, but I can do a lot of that." She rose. "If there's nothing else, I'll get going. Sounds like we have a lot to do."

"You're good to go? No other questions?"

"Oh, I'm sure I'll have questions, but I have a general idea of what is needed and I think the first thing to do is get word out on social media that the playhouse is looking for volunteers." Jen hesitated. "So now that the cat is out of the bag about Max being here, should I share on social media?"

Margot remembered her conversation with Max last night at the bar, and how he'd warned her that things would change. "Could we wait until Monday? Give us the weekend to concentrate on the play, and then take everything live Monday?"

"Good plan." Jen closed her laptop. "Do you need me at rehearsal tonight?"

"No. Not until Monday, but then it'll be every night for quite a while."

"I'll use the weekend to read through the script, see about getting familiar with it. I don't know a lot about theater, but I'm going to learn."

FRIDAY NIGHT REHEARSAL DIDN'T GO MUCH BETTER than the night before. Margot remained in her folding chair onstage even after everyone had left. She'd thought Max was gone, too, but suddenly he was there, crossing the stage to pull out a chair and face her.

"What's wrong?" he asked quietly.

"This doesn't seem right." She frowned and rubbed her temple where she'd had a throbbing ache all night. "It's boring."

"It's not boring. It's just . . . familiar. We've both done the play, and we've seen the play performed—"

"Way too many times." She hadn't planned to ever act again, but now that she was, she wanted it to be good. No, better than good. She wanted the audience to love it. She wanted them on their feet at the end, giving the entire cast a standing ovation. "Why Sally picked this play is beyond me. I like Neil Simon, but this is dated. He wrote it in the early sixties, it premiered in 1963, and the world isn't even remotely the same. Audiences won't get it. Technology has taken us too far. Our tastes are more sophisticated than silly humor."

"But it's what Sally wanted." Max stretched and leaned back in his folding chair. "And it will be fine. You heard the cast. They were all excited tonight to be part of the show. They think it's going to be a hit."

"Of course it's going to be a hit. You're in it. America's new favorite smoldering cowboy."

He leaned back, a dark eyebrow lifting. "Do I smolder?"

She made a face at him, trying to hide how he had this uncanny ability to make her feel like an awkward prepubescent girl who hadn't figured how to be cool around the popular guys. "And brood and make the ladies fantasize."

"I sound pretty amazing."

She tossed her script at him. "Just a little bit vain?"

Max caught it easily with one hand. "Margot, it only took me twenty-some years to become an overnight sensation. Let me savor my hard-earned success."

"Fine, savor away. In the meantime, let's put that Yale brain to work, shall we?" Margot jumped to her feet, paced the length of the stage before returning to face him. "We've got to do more than join the cast. We need more to make this special. You know, Broadway tried a revival a number of years ago, and it closed early."

"So how would you change the play? How would you reinvent it if you could?"

"Besides not doing it?" She paced the other way. "That's a good question. I actually haven't thought that much about it. But I probably . . ." She hesitated, voice fading as she considered all the possibilities. But then an idea came. "I'd flip it."

"Flip it?"

She nodded. "I'd flip the two main roles so that it was different, so that it could possibly say something about our world now, about our society now. I would be the ambitious partner, and you could be the happy, free-spirited husband. You could take care of the apartment and getting them settled into their new place." Margot walked toward him, enthusiasm building. "We could play with the idea of relationships, and gender, and who is responsible for what. I think it'd be interesting, and it would be something different for both of us. It'd give us a different character to play. The audience wouldn't expect it, but then, they also might hate it."

"There are risks in everything."

Margot grabbed her chair, pulled it toward him. "When is the last time you played a laid-back character? Have you ever been a beta male?"

He thought for a moment. "No, come to think of it, never."

She chewed her lip. "I didn't think so. But would the audience like you as a beta male?"

Max pulled his rolled-up script from his back pocket, flipped through some pages, stopping at one scene, and then another. "However, even if we switch the roles, the new Paul wouldn't be a beta. Corie is a full-on alpha female. She's in charge of this relationship. Poor Paul is along for the ride, which means, if I became the Corie character in character, I'd be running you ragged. I'd be bossy and stubborn, and would the audience like that?"

He had a good point. Margot sat down, looked through scenes in her script. Read the dialogue carefully. "The dialogue is funny. Neil Simon's incredibly clever. And this is comedy. We'd have to be funny." She looked up at Max. "I'm not very funny."

"You're an actress. You're funny."

"We can try it out," she said. "Run through some scenes now, see what we think."

"So I'm reading Corie's lines," he said. "You're Paul."

Margot glanced at her script, now filled with scribbled notes and highlighted lines. "Want to switch scripts? I've marked up all of Corie's lines."

"Good idea." He handed her his. "Let's give it a go."

For the next hour they read through one scene after another. At first it was stiff and cold, but by the time they got into the second scene, and then the third, Margot was having fun. Max was making her laugh. He was really good at this, and had impeccable comedic timing.

They finally took a break. Max stood and stretched. Margot looked at him, impressed. "You're good," she said. "Really good."

"You sound surprised," he teased, uncapping his insulated water bottle.

"No, just pleased. I think this could work. We just need to go through the script and adjust a few pieces." She glanced at her watch. It was almost eleven. "Too late tonight, though."

"Let's meet tomorrow," he said. "Come over to my place. It's Saturday. You won't be working, will you?"

"No. Thankfully." She closed the script. "I'm starting to feel better. I think I have hope."

"Good." Max held out a hand to her, pulling her to her feet. "I'll wait while you lock up."

The moment she put her hand into his, her palm against his, she felt a hot spark of sensation that made her pause and look up at him, startled. Was it her imagination, or had he felt it? She drew her hand swiftly away, and yet Max was looking at her, a question in his eyes, and no, she didn't think it was her imagination, because she still felt the tingling in her palm and that hot streak of sensation up her arm, only to curl in her middle.

She shot him another quick look, and went to work turning off lights, but the entire time she thought of him and the way he made her come alive. It wasn't just her skin, either, it was her heart and her mind, and she just felt so much again, and after the past eight years, it was exhilarating. It was also addictive.

Max walked her to her car, always a gentleman, always focused on making sure she was safe, but as Margot drove away, it crossed her mind that she was tired of being safe, playing it safe. She craved adrenaline, energy, Max's energy.

She felt like she wanted danger. But that couldn't be. It didn't make sense. For the past eight years she'd been the epitome of cautious. Safe. Sensible.

But she didn't feel sensible right now. No, her pulse was racing and her body felt hot, and sensitive. She'd liked that shock she felt when her palm met his, liked the jolt and heat, the coil of desire in her belly. Best of all? She'd be rehearsing with Max again tomorrow.

BACK AT HIS PLACE, MAX LAY IN BED STARING OUT THE window at the ocean. The spotlights had gone off, but the moon was full, and he could see the reflection on the water, dark waves and foam.

He liked this cottage, but he'd like it better if Margot were here, giving him that oh-so-very-Margot look, which was curiosity mixed with caution mixed with something else she didn't want to recognize. But he recognized it and felt it every time they were together. The sparks, the heat, the awareness. It didn't happen often that he was this physically drawn to anyone, but when he'd reached out to Margot tonight to draw her to her feet, he'd felt a jolt. A sharp little current of desire. He'd looked to her eyes and then her mouth, and she was just as aware of it. There was serious chemistry between them, and whereas he had a history of acting on attraction, he suspected she did the opposite.

She was probably smart to be cautious. He should take a page from her book and proceed carefully, but he liked fire, and was drawn to challenges. Danger intrigued him. The unknown was appealing, but he couldn't be an asshole and he couldn't risk hurting her, not when she was so important to Sally. Sally would kill him. And then there was the fact that Margot was different, and brainy, and interesting, and he didn't want to hurt her. She deserved better than that.

Max rolled over and smashed a pillow. It was strange

being so close to his childhood home. He could almost remember the boy he'd been. He could almost feel the power Johnny once had over him. Johnny had been big, incredibly strong, and terrifying at times. He liked scaring Max, liked backing him into a corner and making Max tremble. Once Max had been so scared he'd peed himself, and his dad had laughed and laughed. It had been a great joke to Johnny. For years after, his dad had referred to him as Peepee Pants, and it was only when Sally came along that the name-calling stopped.

Max didn't know what would have happened to him without Sally. She changed everything. She'd become his rock, caring for him, providing for him, opening doors where he'd seen only obstacles. Before Sally, his life had been mostly poverty and abuse, but she'd given him confidence and love, believing in him until he learned to believe in himself.

But that didn't make taking on this role in *Barefoot in the Park* easier. He really did need time off. He needed a break, and quiet so he could have time to himself. It had been a hard year, and constantly working, coupled with a bitter divorce, had taken a toll. Annaliese, his second wife, was undeniably beautiful, and complicated. Like him, she'd had a difficult childhood, and he'd thought he could help her, be her rock the way Sally had been his. It hadn't worked out that way. His love didn't make Liese feel secure; instead their passionate relationship only created fear and anxiety within her. She didn't want him to take jobs that required his traveling, and yet he was already in *Stardust Ranch*. He had to go to Wyoming, and he wanted the movie roles starting to come his way. He loved his wife, but he also loved his career. He promised her he wouldn't do her wrong. He vowed to always return to her. Max loved and admired women, but he wasn't a cheater. That was Johnny, not him.

Tossing back the covers, Max left his bed and went to get water in the kitchen. Moonlight streamed through the huge windows and spilled across the floor, a ghostly white light illuminating the redwood walls and floor.

He leaned against a counter and sighed, aware that even performing in a tiny theater in a small town was not going to let him hide or be quiet. But Margot and Sally needed him, and Max had the most unfortunate hero complex. When he was needed, he couldn't walk away.

The scripts stacked on the narrow dining room table caught his attention, reminding him that he hadn't said anything to Howard yet about *Barefoot in the Park*.

Max returned to the bedroom, sat down on the edge of the bed, and grabbed his phone off the nightstand to quickly text his agent. Let's talk tomorrow. I need to update you on some developments.

Howard thankfully didn't call early, but he did phone while Max was making scrambled eggs, and Max put Howard on speaker so he could talk while he cooked. "Good morning, Howard," Max said. "How are you today?"

"I'm fine. Just curious as to these developments, as I had thought we weren't going to talk until Monday."

"Yes, well, a lot has changed since then." Max leaned across the counter, put the sourdough bread down in the toaster. "I'm in California."

"I thought you just wanted to do laundry and water your plants for a while."

"That was the plan, but a friend wasn't well and I jumped on a plane to see her."

"Everything okay now?"

"She's still in the hospital but doing better."

"Glad to hear that."

Max turned the heat down beneath the small skillet. "It looks like I'm going to be here until late July. Haven't done it yet, but I'll book my return to New York for the twenty-fourth."

"Her health is that serious?"

"It's complicated."

"Where are you?" Howard asked.

"Cambria."

"By Hearst Castle?"

"Yes." Max gently flipped his eggs. "So, I'm not travel-ing for the next few months. I'm here, I have a place, and I can audition if it's remote."

"What about Lee Sheridan? He's expecting you in L.A. to read for him."

"I don't know what to tell you."

"How about you tell me you'll be heading to L.A. to meet with Lee."

"I'd like to, but I don't know when that could happen. I'm in rehearsals—"

"For what?"

Max checked the bottom of the eggs. "A community theater production."

"You've got to be kidding." Howard added a few more colorful words. Max just waited.

"You're serious?" Howard added after a moment. "Com-munity theater?"

"Yes."

"Why?"

"My friend, the one in the hospital, owns a theater and needs help. So, I'm helping her."

"Are you in love with her?"

"No, Howard. No. Sally's like a mom to me."

"Oh, Sally," Howard said, having met her years ago when Sally had come to see Max in a summer theater pro-duction. "What play?"

"Barefoot in the Park."

Howard groaned. "No one can be Robert Redford but Robert Redford. Why does anyone try?"

Max smiled. "I'm not going to try to be Redford. We're switching the roles. I won't be Paul. I'm playing Corie."

"What?"

Max reached into the cabinet for a plate and began

dishing up the eggs. "That's all I can say now. You'll just have to come see the play. We open Friday, June ninth. I'll save you a ticket."

"How much are they paying you?"

"It's an amateur production, Howard. We're all volunteers."

"Absolutely not."

Max had known Howard would say that. "I'm already committed," he answered, buttering his toast, and then carrying his plate to the narrow dining room table.

"What about the screenplays? Have you read any of them?"

"No."

"Max, we're talking about your future. These next steps are critical."

"I get that, but sometimes we have to take care of the people who have been there for us—"

"I've been there for you, back when no one else would touch you."

"Now, Howard, that's an exaggeration, but I'm glad you're thinking big picture." Max glanced out the huge window with the fog pressing against the glass, swallowing the ocean and sky. He'd forgotten Cambria could get so gray. Where he'd been raised in Templeton, summer was warm and sunny. "Let's still talk next week. Let's shoot for Wednesday."

Call ended, Max finished his breakfast, aware that Margot would arrive in a little over an hour. He had some thoughts on her suggested changes, and he'd made some notes of his own.

He retrieved his laptop and returned to the table to check email and then review his notes. Most of the emails went straight to trash but there was one that gave him pause.

Annaliese.

He stared at the subject for a long moment. Can we talk? He didn't even want to open it because there was nothing to say. It had all been said before the lawyers got involved. Everything Annaliese had wanted, he gave her. He had nothing more to give.

Max deleted the email without reading it.

Maybe it was a good thing he was here in Cambria, far from New York. Maybe this was the summer he needed. And while his new condo was luxurious, a summer in New York was not. Summers in the city were hot, muggy, miserable. He'd had enough of miserable. He'd had enough of marriage and wives. Ex-wives.

Max closed the laptop, pushing it away. He didn't want to think of Annaliese. Or New York. Or Howard.

Once he had a handle on his role in the play, he'd have some free time. He needed to protect that time. This would be the summer he'd finish his novel. This house was perfect for writing. The dining room table was rather small for a dining room table, but ideal as a desk. With his back to the solid wall, he had that view, and the lighting was good, and with the kitchen close, he'd be able to refill his cup of coffee without losing his train of thought.

But for now, no writing, not until he and Margot had the play sorted, because that was his priority. Max did nothing halfway. Once he was in, he was all in.

MARGOT ARRIVED AT MAX'S COTTAGE AS THE MARINE layer began to lift, revealing a beautiful morning sky.

She paused on the front walkway, hearing his voice coming from someplace near. It sounded like he was on the phone, and she hesitated as he laughed, a deep, sexy rumble that made the hair on her nape lift and her skin prickle. His voice was sinful, just enough rasp, just enough warmth. She shivered, remembering last night when he'd taken her hand and it had been electric.

Margot crossed to the side and peeked around, past the little Zen garden to a pair of chairs in the sun. He was sitting in one of the chairs, feet propped on the other. He was bare-foot, but wearing a gray hoodie. She watched him a moment, filled with emotions she couldn't define, and a desire she hadn't felt in ages, and then he spotted her and waved, gesturing for her to join him.

Margot used the stepping stones in the Zen garden to reach him. "That was Sally," he said as he hung up. "She's a little grumpy."

"You sounded as if you were making her laugh, though."

"I was doing my best. She hates the hospital's coffee, and she's upset they'll only let her have one small cup every morning."

Margot smiled. "She loves her coffee. She'll be happy to get home."

"It's just a few more days. I'm scheduled to drive her home Tuesday." He gestured for her to follow him up the stairs to the deck. "Do you want anything to drink? Coffee? Tea?"

"Tea would be great. Anything without caffeine. I'm already a little too amped up." She followed him upstairs, his perfect butt beautifully defined in the soft, worn Levi's.

Inside, Margot glanced around the narrow dining area. On the table was a computer and a stack of screenplays. "Looks like you have a lot of reading to do. Or have you gone through it all?"

"Need to." He put the kettle on a burner and leaned against the counter. "My agent isn't happy that I've procrastinated."

"What did your agent think about you being in the play?"

He shrugged. "I have nothing booked until *Stardust* begins filming again, and that's not until the end of August."

"But those are all opportunities?" she asked, nodding at the screenplays.

"Yes."

"Wow." She'd never reached the point where people

pursued her and sent projects to her. She'd always had to fight for the next job. "Is there anything your agent is excited about?"

"A couple of things, but we're at a crossroads. What he wants for me isn't necessarily what I want for myself."

"What does he want for you?"

"Big money."

She smiled faintly. "He's an agent."

"Exactly," Max agreed, moving the kettle off the burner as it started to whistle. He looked in the pantry for the boxes of tea he'd bought, and carried them to the counter. "But personally, I'd rather pursue some of the smaller-budget films if it means I could try different things. I want to keep growing, not just take my shirt off for shower scenes."

Margot's lips twitched. "Do you have a lot of those?"

"Have you never seen *Stardust Ranch*?" he asked, pouring the hot water over the tea bags, filling the mugs.

"Only part of one episode."

"That's okay. I actually feel better knowing you haven't seen my butt yet."

Margot's face grew warm, and her chest felt hot, her insides filled with the strangest fluttery sensation. "Guess it's time I caught up on the show," she said lightly, accepting the mug from him.

"That's not necessary. I can just show you a butt cheek sometime this summer and save you hours of time."

She laughed, even as the butterflies fluttered wildly in her middle. She'd never fallen for the hot, hunky actor before, and the virile alpha had never appealed until now. But Max Russo with his faded Levi's and muscular chest and gorgeous face appealed, big-time.

Chapter 6

OUTSIDE ON THE DECK, MAX MOVED CHAIRS AND TA-
bles, clearing the furniture so they had plenty of space to
work. "Should we take it from the top?" he asked once the
area was open.

"Yes," Margot said.

"That wasn't a very confident yes," he said.

She wasn't going to tell him it was because she'd lost
focus, and instead of thinking about the play had spent a
night thinking about him. But it was time to get serious.
Opening night wasn't that far away. "Do you think these
changes will work? Or should we go back and do the play
the way it's written? After all, no one's expecting anything
but the original Neil Simon comedy."

"Let's not panic yet. Let's run with the changes and see
what we think."

For the next hour, they read aloud, working straight
through the entire play, sometimes sitting and reading, other
times walking, pacing, even circling the other as they got
into character. Margot as Paul became the rather intense

single-minded lawyer, while Max fully embraced his Corie, the happy, optimistic husband who was in charge of getting them settled into their first apartment.

As they read, Margot realized one of the biggest changes was that Max now had to carry the play, and she was the foil to his humor. Fortunately, Max was funny, and Margot giggled more than once at Max's portrayal of Paul. It was Max's suggestion to switch the phone installation into Wi-Fi installation, which made far more sense today, and also heightened the urgency of getting the service installed. But together they agreed they'd leave everything else as written until they announced the changes to the cast on Monday.

"I like it better," Margot said, finally sitting down. She'd spent the past hour on her feet, moving as she ran lines, but then she'd always done that because it helped her memorize. "What do you think?"

"It's different," Max said.

"Different good, or bad?"

"Hard to say at this point, but once we really know the lines, it'll become all about timing, and that's where the humor is. Line. Reaction."

"You're funny already. The audience is going to love you."

"As long as they laugh with us, not at us."

She looked at him more closely. "You're not really worried about that, are you?"

"No. I have a pretty tough skin, and I think flipping the script was a clever idea. I wish I'd thought of it myself."

"You're the award-winning actor. I've never been nominated for a Tony or an Emmy or an Oscar."

"I've only been nominated for an Emmy."

"And won," she said, before frowning. "You did win, didn't you? I could have sworn Jen said you had."

"Jen from the office? The one that brought me the script?"

Margot nodded. "She's quite a fan."

"She's very sweet."

Margot hesitated. "I was pretty nervous about taking this on with you."

"Why?" he asked.

"I was just . . . intimidated. I haven't acted in years. I was afraid I might have forgotten how."

"Acting is like riding a bike—"

"I don't think so." But she smiled as she said it. "Nice try."

He laughed, and the sound, another low rumble, did crazy things to her heart.

"If you hadn't confessed," he said, "I wouldn't have ever known. You're talented, and a natural director. I was impressed with how you handled everything at the playhouse. You might think about directing again in the future."

"No. I'm happy to do this for Sally, and it's cool to work with you, but this reminds me of who I used to be, and what I used to want. I had so many big dreams. I was determined to become someone. Now twenty-five years later, I'm back where I started. An ordinary woman from an ordinary town. Still single. But now instead of big dreams I'm wondering how to possibly save enough so I can retire one day."

"You've returned with twenty-five years' experience, wisdom, and skills you didn't have when you moved to New York. That girl who went to New York couldn't step in and run Sally's business, nor could she save a play."

"Oh, she could have saved the play."

Max gave her a smile that was all heat and appreciation. "I would have liked to meet that young woman. She sounds fearless."

"She was." Margot hesitated. "And determined. Nothing was going to keep me from New York."

"That ambitious?" he asked.

"I loved acting. It was my passion, my everything."

He said nothing for a moment. "I left the area because I was angry. I left and vowed to never return."

"Now here we are." Margot drew a breath, slightly envious that he'd found so much success, and not just great parts, but good money, big money. Theater didn't make you rich, at least none of the roles she'd played. If she'd earned more money, she would have more options today. Not that she would have ever pursued becoming a single mom, but she might have felt more confident about being a parent, or starting a family. "How do you feel being back?" she asked.

"I'm glad to be here for Sally." He hesitated. "I'm not sure it's something I could have done while married, so the timing is good."

"Why would it not have worked while you were married?"

"Annaliese would have been jealous of Sally. She didn't like me being close to anyone but her."

"But Sally is like part of your family."

"I know, but it would have created a lot of friction and ultimately it would have made everyone miserable, Sally included."

"I can't even imagine. After a few years, Sam and I spent more time apart than we did together. I was traveling almost constantly at that point, in one touring Broadway show after another."

"There were no jobs in New York?"

"Not enough steady work. Touring was steady work, and it paid the bills."

"What about Sam? He wasn't working?"

"He was writing, and I supported him so he could pursue his passion."

Max's eyes narrowed. "He was okay with that?"

She shrugged. "Sam was far more talented than I was, and he never asked me to do it. It's what I chose to do. What I wanted to do. I believed in him and thought that once he made it, we'd be able to do what we wanted, which was marry and have kids."

"Did he make it?"

"He did. After we'd split up." Her chest felt as if it were

being squeezed into a tiny ball. She forced a smile because it would keep her from tearing up. She wasn't usually so emotional, but there was something about Max that kept her honest, real, and made her feel.

"That hurts."

Margot wasn't going to cry. She'd loved Sam, but given the chance to do it all again, she'd make different choices. "It does."

"He was an actor?" Max persisted.

"No. A playwright. Sam was up for a Tony this year."

"You don't mean Sam McCully?"

She blinked hard, and nodded. "We were together eleven years."

Max whistled softly.

Margot blinked again. "I told you he was talented."

"I've heard some stories about him," Max said.

She looked away, not wanting to discuss "stories." Margot had never caught Sam in the act, but yes, there had been rumors toward the end. She'd refused to believe them. She hadn't even addressed them with Sam because she found it too insulting, to him, to them. People liked to cause trouble, and there was no way Margot could listen to the gossip and then get on the tour bus and drive away. She'd chosen to have faith in him, choosing to focus on the future. How could she just walk away after pouring all of herself—and eleven years of her life—into their relationship?

She rose, gathered her empty mug and the script. "We did good work today," she said briskly. "Thanks for making time to rehearse."

Max took the mug from her. "I've got this," he said. "Don't worry about anything."

"Let me at least help move the furniture back."

"No, leave it. I like it like this. I could work out here, do some yoga."

"You do yoga?"

"Helps when you spend a lot of time filming in a saddle."

"Or shooting those nude scenes." She was glad she could make a joke. She'd felt a little too raw a few moments ago.

"That's right. I owe you a butt cheek," he teased, heading into the house.

Margot smiled as she followed him to the kitchen. "You really don't. I'm fine. But thank you."

He put the mugs in the sink and faced her. His jaw was firm, his gaze narrowed. "I'm sorry. I shouldn't have mentioned the gossip. That was tasteless on my part."

Max's apology caught her off guard. She bit into her lower lip to keep it from quivering. "It's okay."

"It's not. I know what it's like having the tabloids constantly speculate on your relationship. It's hard enough making something work, much less while being under the microscope."

"Most of my time with Sam was good. It was only near the end—" She broke off, steeled herself. "We had eleven years together, and as I said, most of them were good years."

"That makes breakups even harder."

"Fortunately, I found a great job with Sally, and she's even been trying to introduce me to people. I think she's attempted to set me up with every single man in a sixty-mile radius." Margot rolled her eyes. "We have different taste in men."

His laugh was so warm it burrowed inside of her. "Any good dates?"

"I haven't actually gone out with anyone Sally's tried to set me up with," she confessed. "But the newest candidate owns two car dealerships. He's in his sixties but she claims he'd 'take care of me.'" Margot shuddered a little bit. "I don't want a sugar daddy. I have a father—whom I'm meeting for dinner tonight—and the last thing I need is someone to support me. I can do that just fine, thank you."

"Your dad lives close?"

"In Paso Robles. That's where I was born and raised."

"I'm from Templeton."

"I know. They're very proud of you. And now I really should head home. I'm going to see Sally before dinner with Dad."

They both walked to the front door. "Where are you and your dad going tonight?" Max asked. "Have you decided?"

"I don't know. It's his turn to pick the restaurant." She hesitated. "What are your plans for the night?"

"Doing nothing, and enjoying it."

"You're sure?"

"Absolutely," he said, smiling, creases fanning at his eyes, teeth white.

She sucked in a breath, momentarily dazzled by that smile of his. She didn't get her head turned by a pretty face very often, but Max Russo knocked her sideways. On TV he was handsome, but in person, his energy was electric, and she didn't know how not to respond to him, or that gorgeous smile of his. And it was gorgeous, setting off the strong, bristled jaw, the straight nose, wide brow, and thick dark brown hair that didn't want to be tamed.

"Okay, then," she said, taking a step back, her voice a little too high, a little too breathless. "Enjoy your evening, and thanks for working with me today. I feel better about the play already."

"It's going to be good. We just need to put the time in."

She nodded and walked quickly to her car on legs not altogether steady.

She didn't fall for her costars. She didn't like actors. She didn't want to date anyone in the business. She didn't even *want* to date. But Max. Wow. He was . . . something else.

AT HOME MARGOT SHOWERED AND DRESSED, THEN quickly ran the flat iron over her shoulder-length hair. With a final glance in the mirror, making sure there were no mascara dots beneath her eyes, she grabbed her car keys and headed out.

Paso Robles was inland from Cambria, considerably hotter, and usually with a dazzling blue sky. Today was the exception, and Margot relaxed as she drove. She'd become a city girl, but there was something comforting in rolling hills dotted with massive coastal oaks.

During the last thirty years, Paso Robles's open pastures and cattle ranches had been replaced with vineyards, but the land was still beautiful, the golden hills lined with tidy rows of grapes. Fortunately, the oak trees Margot had always loved remained. She was sentimental about oak trees, as they'd had an immense one in their backyard when she was growing up. Her dad had built a tree house in it for her and Charlotte, and her mom had sewn yellow daisy curtains for the windows, and painted the front door red and the shutters purple—Charlotte's favorite color. Her dad had made window boxes for those windows, and every spring they planted new geraniums. It was an adorable girl tree house, and even as teenagers she and Charlotte would go there, escaping their parents, as well as each other. Charlotte liked to hide out with her boyfriend. Margot liked to memorize her lines there, and sing, practicing her songs for the school musicals. After Charlotte died, it's where Margot would go to cry, not wanting her parents to know how deeply she grieved. Her hectic schedule helped her stay busy, but her drama teacher, Mrs. Ortiz, helped, too, teaching her to use her pain for her art, to tap into those emotions to power her performance.

In some ways, Charlotte's tragic, senseless death cemented Margot's future. Margot needed outlets for her emotions, and the theater, whether acting, dancing, or singing, gave her a place where she could channel everything. Margot's dad, Joe, had work as his outlet. But Margot's mom was a full-time stay-at-home parent and losing Charlotte, her firstborn, when Charlotte was only seventeen and just learning to spread her wings was more than Mom could bear.

Margot reached the hospital, parked, and headed to the lobby to check in and get her name tag.

Sally was awake and watching TV when Margot reached her room. Sally immediately muted the TV and used her bed control to raise her head up higher. "I was afraid you weren't going to come after all," Sally said, but her tone was cheerful, and she looked better than the last time Margot had seen her.

Margot pulled the chair close and sat down. "Wouldn't dream of not coming to see you."

"How is everything at the office?"

"Good. The team is working together to make sure everything runs smoothly in your absence. Heather has been able to shift the reservations so that Max will be able to stay at the Leopold Cottage until end of June. She's still working on July."

"How did the meeting go with the Johnson Group from San Francisco?"

"They seemed interested in the property in the Willow Creek area. They like the possibilities and the acreage."

"It's not going to be on the market much longer. It's rare to have one hundred and fifty acres perfect for viticulture be available. The price is good. I should call Jim."

"You should probably wait until Tuesday, after your procedure."

"I'm not calling him now. It's Saturday night after all."

Sally sounded so indignant that Margot smiled. "Just checking. I know how hard it is for you to relax."

"Tell me about the play. You've had, what, two rehearsals now?"

Margot nodded. "Thursday night was dreadful. I can see why Cherry quit. It hurt to even read through with Max and the cast."

"But it was better yesterday?" Sally asked hopefully.

"Marginally. We're going to need every minute, of every day, to get everyone ready for opening night." Margot hesitated, making an effort to keep her tone light. "You never told me there is no crew."

"There's no crew?"

"There is Robyn and Graham, but Graham hasn't been well this year, and can't build anything, or lift anything, and Robyn can help paint and manage props, but as of now, there is no set, or props, or costumes." Margot drew a breath, trying to stay calm, not wanting Sally to feel any of her stress. "There are just so many needs, and I didn't mention any of this to Max as I don't want him to feel obligated to problem solve—"

"He can, though. He's good at problem-solving. He went to Yale, you know. Max is very smart. He's not just a pretty face."

"I know," Margot answered, "but since he's just arrived and doesn't know people here, it doesn't make sense to put him in charge of recruiting volunteers to work backstage. So I've asked Jen to help. I'm hiring her to be my assistant director."

"You don't need to pay her. She's probably thrilled just to be around Max."

Margot counted to five. "Jen is a huge Max Russo fan, but I'm not going to drag her into this without some compensation."

Sally frowned. "Do you think we need to pay everyone— the crew, I mean?"

"No. I think once we get the word out that Max is starring in *Barefoot in the Park*, we'll get volunteers. But I want someone reliable as my right hand, and I know Jen. She won't abandon us if things get rough."

"I don't want Max to be embarrassed by our production. He's going out on a limb for us. For me."

"I know." Margot took Sally's hand and gave it a light squeeze. "The last thing any actor wants is to be in a weak production. We're going to make this work. It's just going to take a lot of effort."

"Be honest. Are you upset you've had to take this on?" Sally's gaze met hers and held. "I know I forced you—"

"Stop. We're good. I'm good. I should have stepped in before. I've been kicking myself for not helping out sooner. It's just that theater isn't comfortable for me anymore, and I was thinking of myself, not of you. I'm sorry."

"You shouldn't be apologizing to me. It's my playhouse, it's my dream, not yours. I think I'm a frustrated thespian. I always thought I'd be a good actress, given the opportunity."

Margot grinned. "Get better and we can make sure there will be a part for you in a future production."

"Does that mean you will help out in the future?"

Margot gave Sally a severe look. "Don't start. Let's just focus on *Barefoot in the Park*. I'm trying not to freak out as it is."

"But Max is good, isn't he? He'll make a great Paul."

Max was better than good. Max was gorgeous and gifted, sexy and real. He was the perfect costar, as well as the subject of some very hot dreams. But she wouldn't share any of that, nor would she mention yet that Max would actually be playing Corie, but answering to the name of Paul, because Sally might not get it, and would panic, and the last thing any of them needed was stress on Sally.

"Max is great," Margot said simply. "Very talented. Did he study theater at Yale?"

"No, not initially. He went for economics and then somehow got involved with a campus production, I don't know all the details, but he enjoyed it so much he changed majors to theater. He nearly dropped out of school for a film role, but I convinced him to finish his degree, and he did. Reluctantly. I'm glad he did, and I think he is, too."

Margot didn't go to college, which had disappointed her parents as her dad graduated from Fresno State, and her mom from Cal Poly, San Luis Obispo, but they respected her choice, knowing how much she wanted a career on Broadway.

"So, he never did acting around here," Margot said, shifting her attention back to Max. "I wondered. His wasn't a name I was familiar with growing up."

"He didn't come from a family that would have supported acting. But then, his dad didn't support anything Max did."

"I hate hearing this."

"It's what made Max who he is today. He's tough. He works really hard. And he's grateful for those in his corner."

Margot suddenly caught sight of the clock on the wall, hanging above Sally's whiteboard with all her information. "Oh my gosh, I'm late. I'm supposed to meet Dad for dinner. He's made a reservation for six thirty and I still need to pick him up first."

"Then go. Don't be late." Sally reached for her hand, clasped it firmly. "Thank you, Margot, for everything. A true friend, and a lifesaver."

The sincerity in Sally's voice moved Margot. She swallowed around the lump filling her throat. "You've been a good friend to me as well. You've given me a life here, and purpose—" She broke off, blinked, clearing her eyes. "I love you. You know that."

"I do."

Margot was climbing into her car when her phone rang, and it was her dad calling to say he wasn't feeling one hundred percent and had a fever. He didn't think it was a good idea to go to dinner, and wondered if they could do a rain check for the following weekend.

Margot agreed, but offered to pick up some dinner for him or run some errands since she was already in Paso Robles. Her dad declined. He'd just put one of those Marie Callender's potpies in the oven and watch some TV. There was nothing he needed and it was probably only a little cold, but why take chances?

Driving back to Cambria, Margot thought of Max, wondering what he was doing tonight, and if he was truly alone. Did he have any friends still in the area? Would he try to see his dad?

Part of her was tempted to stop by his house and check on him, and then another part of her—probably her dignity—urged her to have some self-respect. They'd met only a few days ago. He probably was enjoying his downtime and space.

Margot was impressed he'd gone to Yale, which had one of the most competitive theater programs in the country. She knew because she'd looked at it while still in high school, when her guidance counselor wanted her to consider college. Margot had always thought she'd go, but then when Charlotte died, Margot was desperate to leave school and *live*. She wanted to be onstage. Life was short. If you had a dream, you had to go for it, no excuses.

Which is why giving up the theater had been so painful for her. It had been her dream. It had been virtually everything, but because of it, she'd never had the chance to do other things. Like be a mom. She thought she'd be a good mom, too, and maybe she'd meet a man who had kids from a previous marriage, or maybe she'd meet a man who wanted children, but she didn't want to do it on her own. She'd been raised by a wonderful mom and dad, and maybe she was too old-fashioned, but she wanted a family with a significant other, sharing the joy and responsibility with someone who loved her, and who'd love their children. She couldn't get discouraged, though, not when she still had a long life ahead of her.

MAX WAS READING WHEN HOWARD CALLED AT NINE thirty. He wished he could say that Howard would be calling on a Saturday night only because it was something important, but that wasn't true. Howard called whenever he felt like it. Whenever he had something on his mind, urgent or not.

But Max, tired of his own company, answered the phone, curious as to what Howard had to say, considering they'd already spoken that morning. "How is your evening, Howard?"

"Could be better. Your ex can't reach you, so she's blowing up my phone."

Max didn't have to ask which ex. "I got an email from her. From a new account."

"You blocked her?"

"I did."

"Apparently she's been trying to get a hold of you for the past few weeks."

Max said nothing, not having anything to add.

"She wanted to know where you were. It sounds as if she talked to someone in your building, and they said you hadn't been around for quite some time." Howard paused. "When was the last time you were in touch?"

"April."

"Your divorce was finalized in April."

"Yes."

"Is she getting her spousal support?"

"Of course." Max was certain this wasn't about money. Annaliese didn't need more money. She needed attention. She needed an anchor. But he couldn't be that person anymore. He wouldn't be. "You actually talked to her?"

"She wouldn't stop calling. Marlene thought maybe there was an emergency."

Marlene was Howard's wife, and a really nice woman. A really smart person. But also, a woman who liked to protect her time with her husband. For her to encourage Howard to pick up the phone meant Annaliese had been absolutely terrorizing them. "Maybe you should block her, too," Max suggested.

"Has that ever worked with her? No. It makes her more unpredictable. Maybe you should talk to her."

Max rose from the couch, walking to the door to step out on the deck. The spotlights illuminated the waves, turquoise waves and white foam. "I can't be her therapist. I won't. We're divorced and there is nothing we need to say to each other."

"I agree, but you're about to star in a play, just five hours north of her place in Malibu. If you don't want her on your doorstep, or talking to the press, try to nip this in the bud."

Hanging up, Max remained outside. The air was cool, a little misty. He leaned on the railing, watching the waves, soothed by the sound of the water rolling, crashing. He hated conflict and negativity, and talking to Howard about Annaliese made him uneasy. The marriage had been a mistake from the start. They should have had a longer engagement, and he should have listened to that voice inside of him saying that this woman, and this relationship, could be a problem, but he'd ignored common sense. He wanted to be the good guy. He wanted to prove he wasn't a quitter and didn't give up on people. His first wife, Cynthia, hadn't given him a chance to fix things, and so Max had doubled down on his marriage to Annaliese, doing whatever was needed to make things work. He couldn't make it work, but he tried. For four years he tried. The divorce itself took over a year to finalize. The divorce had been hell, too. But finally in April he was free, and he wasn't going to get pulled back into Annaliese's world. Not for anything.

Chapter 7

THE PLAY.

Margot woke up nauseous Sunday morning, filled with dread. This wasn't going to work, flipping Paul's and Corie's roles. If she played Paul as written—she'd be unlikable, a bitch. If Max was as dramatic as Corie was written, he'd be over-the-top. The audience could be uncomfortable. They might not get the humor, and the laughs—would they be for the wrong thing?

She'd fallen asleep worrying about some of her decisions, seeing certain scenes, hearing the lines, and it had made her nervous. All night she dreamed about the play, and now she was heartsick, aware that Friday and Saturday had been spent learning new lines, creating new characters, and it was a mistake. She'd wasted Max's time. Neil Simon's play wasn't meant to be reinvented. The roles weren't exactly stereotypes, but they were rather a humorous poke at classic gender roles—the warm, emotional, optimistic young wife. The tense, hardworking, driven husband.

People laughed because it was funny to see the two

together, and sometimes pitted against each other. But if she were to be the tense, hardworking, driven woman . . . it wouldn't be as appealing, not in the current social and political climate. Personally, she loved this flip, but not everyone was open to change and it was all too easy for things to blow up on social media.

Would anyone enjoy watching Max fling himself about the apartment, making plans without considering his new wife's needs?

No.

Margot suspected they'd prefer Max better as the hard-driving lawyer, tense, exhausted, and struggling to understand his new bride.

Margot was too queasy to even contemplate a cup of coffee. She exhaled, grabbed the script from next to the bed, and began reading it from the beginning, trying to read it as it was written, trying to see how to play Corie as Neil Simon had wanted her played.

The first thing that struck her—besides the loopiness of the story—was all the touching. There was so much touching and kissing. A kiss here. A kiss there. A kiss on the neck. Sitting on laps. Bouncing on laps.

Which meant she and Max would be touching, and kissing. A lot.

The second thing was that this lovely couple, so in love in the beginning, fall out, but then find their way back to each other, and really, wasn't that the true point of the play? Love was everything. Did it matter who was who in terms of casting just as long as Paul and Corie still loved each other at the end?

MAX WOKE UP IN ONE OF THOSE MOODS THAT WOULD only be improved by pummeling something. Fortunately, he'd found a small gym in Cambria that would let him join through the end of July, and he headed there early, on a treadmill running by six. After forty-five minutes, he moved on to free weights, and then finally a long session with one of the punching bags in the corner.

He liked that no one talked to him or bothered him. He had earbuds in, not just to discourage conversation, but he worked out to specific albums—Nirvana, Linkin Park, AC/DC, Rage Against the Machine, Metallica, Led Zeppelin. He always got more out of lifting listening to heavy strings, lots of synth, and loud drumming.

Leaving the gym at 8:40 a.m., he stopped at a little café for breakfast, sitting at the far end of the counter. With his script in front of him, he ate while poring over lines, appreciating the waitress who kept his coffee hot.

He was on his way out of the café when he realized someone had snapped his photo. Max ignored it. At least he wasn't in New York, where photographers trailed him every time he went somewhere for dinner. Crossing the street was easy, as it was virtually empty. Shops and galleries wouldn't open until eleven. A light silver mist swirled around the buildings, keeping temperatures cool.

Max drove to his place on Sherwood Drive. As he entered the cottage, the view drew him. He hadn't realized until he was here how much he'd missed being close to nature. He'd grown up outside. He'd run pretty wild as a kid.

Templeton was a small town, just four thousand people. Max's family lived on the outskirts of town, with the foothills his backyard. Their house had three bedrooms and it had seen better days, but at least they had acreage. True, it was weedy, undeveloped land, but it was open, and his to roam. When not building forts and using his toy cowboy pistols to shoot at imaginary bad guys, he'd ride his bike into town, where his dad was a mechanic at Templeton's only filling station. Johnny tried to work on the side as well, which is why the metal garage next to their house was always full of cars and trucks, things his dad was going to fix, but didn't necessarily get around to. Too often his dad used his free time to take off on his Harley, go ride and drink, meeting women that weren't appropriate to take home, especially as he was married.

Max didn't remember a lot about his mom. He had snapshot-like memories, specific moments that stood out, but there was no moving film, no camera roll except for the day she died. That still played in his head, over and over.

She'd been beautiful, he remembered that. She'd been young, too, just twenty-one when she'd married Johnny. She'd gotten pregnant almost right away, and even after Max was born, Johnny was rarely home.

His dad and mom were always fighting and breaking up, and then they'd get together again, but mostly Max remembered yelling. Johnny yelling, his mom yelling back, Johnny smacking her, and then his mom crying. Johnny would take off then and not come home for a while. Max liked it when his dad was gone. He wished his dad would never come home.

His mom struggled. She needed pills to sleep, pills to wake up, pills so she wouldn't eat. Pills to relax. Pills to make her function so she could go to work because they needed money. And then when the pills weren't enough, his mom found harder stuff, guaranteed to do what the pills no longer could.

This is where the moving pictures rolled fast. His mom died the day before his seventh birthday. Max was the one who'd found her, still in bed. Stiff, cold. Blue. A syringe tangled in the sheets. He threw away the syringe. He tried to call his dad at the gas station, but he wasn't there yet. Max didn't know his grandparents' number—he never saw them. He checked on his mom again. Definitely not breathing, definitely not living.

His dad hadn't come home that night. It was happening more and more. Sometimes neither of his parents were there, but Max would just watch TV, and sleep in front of the TV with his cowboy pistols next to him.

But with his dad still gone, and his mom blue, he had to do something. Reluctantly he called 911, saying that his mom wasn't breathing and he needed help.

The ambulance came. The police came. After the ambulance took his mom, the police took him back to the little police station. He'd thought they'd go get his dad. Instead, they called some lady who drove him to a place for problem kids. He was there for three days while they worked out whatever they needed to work out.

When he was finally reunited with his dad, Max waited for him to apologize for not coming sooner, say something about his mom, something about Max's birthday, anything, but his dad said nothing, just drove them home.

Sometime later in the year, Max overheard Johnny tell a lady who was over at the house sitting on the couch that Lucy had moved to Morro Bay and just abandoned them. Abandoned her little boy. Johnny said Lucy didn't want Max because Max looked exactly like his dad.

The lady on the couch had cried, and she'd tried to hug Max, but Max just stared at his dad, confused by the lie. Why would his dad make up something like that? How was being divorced better than death? He didn't know, and the lie just made him despise Johnny more.

Johnny liked to be rough, and scare Max, but he never acted that way when ladies came over, and after his mom died, women were always over, hanging around, moving in, moving out. Sometimes there would be two women disappearing with his dad into the bedroom. Sometimes Johnny even forgot Max was there. Other times he'd point to Max, saying, "That's my boy, Max." Inevitably the lady would say how handsome he was, just a little miniature of his father. Lucky Max.

Max was in sixth grade when his dad met Sally. Sally wasn't like his other women. She was older, and successful. She could pay for things, make things easier. For two and a half years, Johnny cleaned up his act, cut back on drinking, stopped womanizing, and tried to be a good partner to Sally. Sally bought him a new motorcycle, and even a new car. They went looking at houses together. They talked about marriage. Max was happy. He liked Sally, and not just because she was far better than any of the other women his dad brought home, but because she was smart and funny, and when she was around, Johnny was a better man. Johnny became almost like a real dad.

But leopards don't change spots, and Johnny eventually cheated on Sally, and that was the end. Sally didn't mind paying most of the bills. She didn't mind a lot of things, but she wasn't going to be disrespected.

Max struggled after Sally moved away, moved on with her life. He was angry with the world, but mostly with his dad. He understood why Sally left, but he felt abandoned. His once good grades dropped. He couldn't focus in school. He began doing stupid things, acting out, anything but to be home and feeling what he felt. Sally, miraculously, had kept tabs on him, and even more incredibly, she took him under her wing. He finished his freshman year of high school at her house, and he'd been happy, really happy with her. She challenged him, made him go to summer school to take a class over since the low grade wasn't good enough, and he wouldn't get into a great college if he didn't apply himself.

Sally had a new man at that point, but her boyfriend, Walt, liked Max, and Max liked him. They were almost a family, but then over the summer, Johnny showed up. He was drunk and belligerent, and he got into it with Sally, and then when her boyfriend interceded, Johnny threw a punch, knocking Walt down.

Max lost his mind. He launched himself at his dad, fists flying. Sober, Johnny was strong. Drunk, he was unhinged. Max ended up bruised and bleeding, but he'd at least held his own. But when it was over, Max moved home to the house with the peeling paint, not because Sally said he had to go, but because he had to go back to protect Sally and Walt.

After returning home, Max and his dad didn't speak for months. They never really talked again.

Fortunately, Max had learned what he needed to learn. Take responsibility for yourself.

Don't wait for others to make things better. The world owes you nothing. If you want something, you have to fight for it.

Those lessons had helped him succeed.

Based on his past, having survived a miserable childhood, Max knew he'd never have kids, not because he didn't like them, but he knew it was impossible to have everything, or to do all things well. If he was going to be a dad, he'd have to scale back work, be home, be involved, be a good parent. Good parents were selfless. Good parents put their children's needs first. Max wasn't sure he could do that, either. Better not to have children than to risk messing them up. It had been years since he'd made that decision, but he still felt that way.

Turning from the window, Max stretched an arm, easing the soreness in his biceps. It had been a good workout, and he was feeling it now. In the bathroom he stripped off his workout clothes, showered, and after dressing, made a fresh pot of coffee. He was still learning lines when his phone rang an hour later. It was Margot, and she sounded out of breath.

"Good morning," he said. "Everything okay?"

"Yes, just out for a walk, but I've had an epiphany. Max, we can't switch the roles. People won't get it. They won't like it. They won't like you being Corie, or me being Paul. Our culture is filled with stereotypes, and most people are comfortable with those, comfortable with the man being dominant and successful, and the woman supportive—"

"Wait, slow down. You're talking too fast."

"I think I've made a mistake." Margot gulped a breath.

"I can't do this to you. People don't want to see you as Corie. They want you as Paul. Intense, single-minded, impatient with a wife who has picked out the wrong apartment, and refuses to accept she's made a mistake. Audiences will think that's funny because she's stubborn and impractical, you know, typical of a woman—"

"But why do we have to play it that way? Why can't a man be stubborn and impractical?"

She didn't say anything for a moment, and then she drew another breath, a shaky breath. Was she crying?

"Margot?" he asked, concerned.

"Our world is complicated. What I'm good with isn't necessarily what others are comfortable with. It seems like now people are much quicker to judge and criticize, and I would hate for people to judge or criticize you for a decision I made." She took a deep breath before continuing. "I've wasted your time. It was stupid to think I could reinvent Neil Simon, especially toward the end, where they're struggling together. The shift is going to rub some people the wrong way."

"Which scenes specifically?"

"The fight scene after it snowed. Where the telephone—Wi-Fi—guy returns and Paul and Corie aren't speaking."

Max said nothing for a moment, picturing it in his head, thinking about the lines, and the tension between the couple. "I think you're panicking."

"I know I'm panicking, but I think I'm right—"

"I'm not sure you are, not this time."

"Max, this is a little play that will get a lot of attention. I don't want you to get flak. I don't want anyone to shred you, or your performance. Sally made me promise you wouldn't be embarrassed. I can't let either of you down."

"Listen, it's Sunday. We've worked on this play for only three days. Nothing is set. We're free to do whatever we want, but anxiety isn't going to make anything better. I've got a tough skin. No one needs to protect me. Not you, and not Sally."

"She's so proud of you, Max. Last night she was telling me how you went to Yale, and how smart you are. Your success is really important to her."

"Margot?" he said when she paused to take a breath.

"Yes?"

"What if we meet at the theater? Got onstage, ran some scenes together? If it's not going to work, then we can switch back to the original roles. I already know those lines. I'm sure you remember Corie's lines, too."

"I hate doing this to you."

"You're not doing anything to me. We're actors. Entertainers. We're trying to figure out what would be the most entertaining for the audience. What time do you want to meet?"

"How about an hour?"

"See you there."

MARGOT HAD TO FORCE HERSELF TO FINISH HER WALK, to at least hit a mile. She walked faster, pushing herself, trying to get her heart rate up and her emotions down.

She was grateful Max had been calm and matter-of-fact. He didn't seem worried either way, which reassured her. She had a feeling he tended to be the cool head in a room. She wasn't. Although Margot had always wanted to be the logical one, the one that didn't get upset, that was Charlotte, not Margot. Margot had always been more emotional, and her drama teacher, Mrs. Ortiz, said it's what made Margot such a good actress. That she was sensitive and responsive and could slide into a character's skin. But Margot didn't like being sensitive. It didn't make real life easier.

Returning home, she cleaned up, made a late breakfast, and filled her water bottle before driving downtown. Max was in the parking lot when she arrived. He had hot tea for them both, and a box of pastries from the French Corner Bakery, one of Margot's favorite places in town.

"You brought treats," she said, smiling.

"Croissants, chocolate éclairs, and an apricot cream cheese Danish."

"All my favorites. Did Sally tell you?"

"No," he said. "I like them, too."

Her gaze swept his tall, lean frame, lingering briefly on the width of his chest and the outline of pecs beneath the thin knit fabric of his long-sleeve shirt. "You don't look like you indulge much."

"That's because I go to the gym and pound things. It helps."

"Impressive."

They crossed the small empty brick plaza, the courtyard surrounded by big trees and strings of lights running over-head. Margot knew Sally hoped to serve wine in the court-yard during intermission, taking advantage of the summer weather, but there could be no wine until there was a play.

Passing the box office, they approached a pair of dark-tinted glass doors, and Margot unlocked one and flicked on the lights. The crystal chandelier in the little lobby shone brightly, casting colorful prisms on the whitewashed walls.

She locked the door behind them and headed for the auditorium. The doors were open, and it was just a short walk down the carpeted aisle to the stage.

Just facing the stage filled her with fresh butterflies.

She must have made a sound, because suddenly Max's hand was on her back. "Breathe," he said.

She glanced at him, her eyes meeting his. His gaze was warm, and it made her insides do strange things. "Why am I losing my mind? This is a tiny community theater pro-duction."

"But at the same time, it's not," he said. "It's our career, so of course we internalize it all differently."

"People will expect it—us—to be good."

"Or great."

"So no pressure."

He laughed at her sarcastic tone. "Oh, there's pressure. That's why you're stressing, but we'll put the work in and it'll be great." Max brought a folding chair onto the stage, and with his tea and script, he looked ready to go. "Should we start with the scenes you're most worried about?"

Margot forced herself to stand still. "Which is virtually all."

"You need to eat a pastry."

"Do I?"

"And breathe."

"Anything else I should do?" she muttered, because he wasn't helping. He was the one she was worried about. She'd given up her career but his was thriving, and the last thing Max Russo needed was to be humiliated onstage night after night. Although, she supposed the play could just close early. End the agony sooner than later.

Sally wouldn't be happy, though. And Margot had promised Sally she'd have a successful summer season.

"Don't lose your sense of humor," he said. "This is comedy. We're going to be over-the-top, and I mean really over-the-top. Your Corie isn't merely ambitious, she's prim, buttoned-up, uptight. She has no sense of humor, but you, Margot, do. You're going to have to lean into Corie's nerdiness. I can see your Corie now in your sensible heels, with sensible glasses, barely able to leave your brief. You've only been married six days when the play begins, and I'm quite certain you were a virgin when you married—"

"And you were, too?" she interrupted sweetly, dropping onto the ground and reaching for the box of pastries.

"Perhaps. Because I'm probably a little nerdy, too, and since I don't have a job at the moment, I'm doing my best to create a home for you as I'm dependent on you, and very grateful you're the breadwinner."

She lifted the apricot cream cheese Danish from the box and took a bite. The Danish was flaky and sweet, the cream cheese just creamy enough, and she closed her eyes, chewing with pleasure. If only life could be this uncomplicated—happiness found in a perfect pastry.

She opened her eyes and saw Max watching her, a smile playing at his lovely mouth. "It looks good," he said.

"It's delicious." She took another bite and brushed flakes from her lips before pushing the pastries toward him. "Have one," she said, still chewing, knowing you weren't supposed to talk and eat at the same time, but she felt out of her element with Max. He was interesting and handsome, articulate, and so easy to talk to. He was the total package, the one she didn't think existed in real life.

Max took the chocolate croissant and ate it. For a minute there was no conversation at all, and Margot had to admit that she felt buoyed by the treat. Her spirits weren't quite so low. "So . . ." she said, brushing off her hands and then blotting her mouth, wanting to be sure there were no leftover crumbs, "comedy."

"Yes."

"I haven't done comedy in years."

"Neither have I."

"And this is a comedy, regardless of what role we play."

"Exactly. Comedy requires energy," he said. "And every live performance needs energy, but comedy even more so. I had one director—and this was years and years ago—who made the entire cast run around the auditorium as a warm-up before rehearsal. Down the stairs, into the lobby, back through the auditorium to the stage. Five times. It was a big theater, and by the end, everyone was breathless, blood was pumping, but it energized the cast, and then, we'd dive straight into rehearsal."

She arched a brow. "Are you suggesting we run around the theater?"

He stood. "Why not?"

Margot tipped her head back, looked up at him. "I was joking."

"I think we should do it. Comedy is all about commitment. Let's commit."

She jumped up, removed her long sweater, and tightened her ponytail. "It's not a race," she clarified.

"It's not," he agreed. "We don't want to fall down and break anything. We just want to warm up and have fun."

"I'm not going to break anything," she said, dashing down the stairs, wanting to be the first one to the lobby. But Max was right behind her, on her heels, as she pushed through the door to the second aisle and was running for the stage. He passed her before they reached the steps. "Hey," she cried, "I didn't think it was a race."

"It's not," he answered, crossing the stage. "You are just really slow."

"Ha! So rude," she retorted, needing to slow down as she went back down the stairs. "How many times are we doing this?"

"Until we've chased the jitters away," he called back to her.

"That will take a lot of running," she said.

"We have all day."

But they didn't run all day. They just made five circles around the theater and returned to the stage laughing. At least, she was laughing. The run had been fun and silly, and it was just what she needed to help her loosen up, because there was no faking it with comedy.

"No shame, no embarrassment," Max said, facing her onstage.

"We're going to create quirky, lovable characters," she said, jumping up and down a little bit, wanting to stay loose.

"We're committed." He reached out to her for a fist bump.

Grinning, she fist-bumped him back. "One hundred percent."

They returned to rehearsing and were making significant progress with their blocking and lines, but as the afternoon passed and the day grew later, Margot was struck all over again that *Barefoot in the Park* wasn't just a comedy, but a romance, filled with laughter and affection.

Margot had been doing her best not to dwell on all the touches and kisses. They'd figure out what and where, and the rest would be easy. But this afternoon it wasn't easy. Everything felt different. The earlier silliness had disappeared, and she felt increasingly aware of Max—not Max the actor, but Max the man. She was glad that with the character switch, Max's character would be the more assertive, affectionate one. Margot didn't think she could throw herself at Max and kiss him, or jump on his lap and bounce like a little girl. Maybe at twenty you bounced on laps, but at nearly fifty? No.

Yesterday they'd blocked scenes, reading lines and stage directions, but now they were acting the script out, and suddenly, they were close, really close, as the scene called for a kiss—more than just one kiss, actually—and Max was just inches away, and Margot couldn't think, her body a little too sensitive, her nerves dancing a little too much. "We could do this part tomorrow," she said, voice somewhat strangled. "No need to continue. We've made good progress tonight."

But Max didn't move away, and she didn't know where to look. She probably should move. He was close, ridiculously close, and the look in his dark eyes made her heart race. He was gorgeous, and he had so much energy and charisma. Maybe he kissed a lot of costars, but she didn't. She couldn't even remember the last time she'd kissed anyone onstage. Of course she'd kissed on some of her dates, but that was private, and not something other people watched. Those men were also rather ordinary, and not jaw-droppingly beautiful like Max Russo.

She couldn't even imagine kissing Max—

Max took control and made it happen, his head dipping, his mouth covering hers. It should have been a brief kiss, just the briefest of touches, but the moment his lips brushed hers, she stiffened, feeling as if she'd just been zapped again, her lips quivering beneath the pressure of his.

He lifted his head, looked down at her, brow creasing.

Had he felt it, too?

Confused, Margot stepped back. She still tingled from head to toe. "What was that?" she said.

His eyes were even darker, and they glowed with an emotion she couldn't name. "Growing up where I did in Templeton, we called it a kiss. Not sure what you-all called it in Paso."

The edge of her mouth tugged. She smiled at him, even as her limbs felt weird and her pulse thudded too hard. "Do you do that to everyone?"

"I think that was you," Max answered.

"Hmm." She moved farther away, trying to figure out what had just happened. "Maybe we should call it a night."

"I was going to suggest the same thing. I'm hungry. I need to eat. Want to join me?"

"As long as you keep those hot lips to yourself."

He laughed and began gathering his things, but Margot was secretly worried. She'd been kissed plenty of times in her life, but no one, and she meant no one, had ever kissed her like that. Max Russo was going to be one dangerous costar.

Chapter 8

MAX DROVE THEM TO THE LITTLE ITALIAN RESTAURANT at the end of Main Street. The restaurant was empty and staff were straightening tables and sweeping, preparing to close. But Max was starving and he wanted food, a lot of food.

Leaving Margot on the doorstep, he entered the little restaurant and asked to speak to the manager. The manager appeared, looking irritated, but Max gave him a smile, and the manager's frown faded, turning to surprise.

Max introduced himself, explained they just wanted a quiet place to eat, assured him that they wouldn't be there overly long, an hour at most, and promised he'd make it financially worthwhile—if the restaurant could accommodate them.

The manager's attitude changed. "Of course. Give us a minute to ready your table."

Max returned to the door where Margot waited. "They're keeping the kitchen open for us," he said.

"How did you pull that off?"

"I said we'd eat and leave and wouldn't overstay our welcome."

"I'm sure there was more," she said.

He shrugged. "I did promise a very good tip, for all the staff."

The manager appeared and escorted them to a big leather burgundy booth in the very back. Their table was covered with a classic red-and-white-checkered cloth. A candle burned in an old Chianti bottle, dripping colorful wax down the sides. Bread arrived, and olive oil, along with a little carafe of balsamic vinegar.

The waiter handed Max a wine list, which he promptly handed to Margot. "I don't know wines like you. Want to order us something?"

She smiled at him, her green eyes warm. "No whiskey tonight?" she asked.

"Wine and pasta—how could you go wrong?"

Her smile widened. "I don't think you can." She turned to the waiter then, and consulted with him on their wine choices. Once again Margot picked a local wine, something from the Paso Robles area.

After the waiter went to get their wine bottle, Max asked her if she ordered wine from the Paso area because she was back, or if she'd always been a fan of it.

"I didn't drink much when touring. It was a good way to manage my weight, and also keep within my budget. If I craved a glass of something, I'd splurge a little, but I always ordered something safe—a Napa Chardonnay, or an Australian Shiraz. It wasn't until I moved back that I wanted to learn more about wine. Dad and I did a wine tasting one weekend, and then last year I attended a class about Paso Robles wine, and it's become a hobby, learning about the local wineries and what they bottle."

Max listened to her, liking that she was down-to-earth, hardworking, and humble, much like the community she'd been raised in. "Did you have a happy childhood?"

"It was wonderful—up until my sister died. That was such a shock, and it changed everything."

"But until then, your parents had a good marriage?"

"They did. They were very devoted to each other, and really loving parents. I've heard that after a tragedy some couples turn on each other, but they didn't. They loved Charlotte and grieved together. I've always felt lucky to have had the family I did."

"How did your sister's death change things—unless it makes you uncomfortable talking about it. I don't want that."

"No, I'm fine. And it was so long ago. Sometimes it doesn't even feel like my life . . . or that I'd had a sister, but I know I did, and I loved her." Margot hesitated. "It was my mom who changed the most after Charlotte died. My mother became far more protective, almost obsessive about where I was, and who I was with. Dad just got really quiet. He disappeared inside himself, and you could feel his sadness. Their grief was oppressive, and I was just a teenager. I wanted out, I wanted to be free, and by the time I was a senior in high school, all I wanted was to move away. And I did."

"That couldn't have been easy, though, knowing that you'd become their everything and you wanted to pursue your thing."

"It was awful." Her voice thickened and her eyes deepened to a darker green. "To choose Broadway over my parents?"

"I doubt they saw it that way."

"But I'm sure my decision hurt them, and I've always felt guilty about that. It wasn't what my mom wanted. But I was afraid that if I stayed, even another month after graduation, I wouldn't have the courage to go later. So I kissed them, hugged them, and left."

The waiter returned with the wine bottle and two glasses. Max nodded at the waiter, not interested in inspecting the label or watching him open and pour. Instead he focused on Margot. "On the other hand, I can't imagine your parents wanting you to give up your dreams just so you could remain close."

"Dad got it. But Mom struggled. She was never the same after I moved away."

"Or maybe it was losing your sister? You weren't dead, Margot. You were just in New York. Five hours on an airplane."

"That's true, and we did see each other. But I was thrilled to be in New York. I've always known what I wanted to do. I fell in love with acting after seeing my first musical in elementary school, and that was it. I wanted to take acting classes and dance classes and voice lessons. I did summer theater and children's theater, and auditioned for everything I could. My mom drove me to every audition. Mom and Dad came to every show I was ever in. I was lucky. I *am* lucky." Her gaze met his. "Why did you want to be an actor? What was the appeal?"

"I didn't even think about acting until I was in college. I was at Yale studying economics and one day the casting director for an upcoming Yale production approached me on campus, mentioned I would make a good greaser. They were putting on *The Outsiders* and were short a couple gang members. They asked me to read, even though I was mostly supposed to stand around and look cool. Maybe run a comb through my slicked-back hair."

Margot's gaze never wavered from his face. "And?"

It crossed his mind that when Margot listened, she was truly focused, and it wasn't an act. She wasn't trying to score points or bed a star. She was being herself, and it was wonderful. Refreshing. "They asked me to come back and read again, and then again, and I ended up playing the part of Dallas, or Dally."

"Matt Dillon plays him in the movie. He was *mean*."

"Cold," Max agreed, remembering. "But it was a good

fit for me. Dally had a serious chip on his shoulder. He was intense. I found it really easy to get into character. It was freeing becoming someone else. I didn't realize that there's a freedom in acting. Most people don't ever get that chance to escape themselves and reinvent themselves, but when you act, you do. And you get paid for it."

The wine had been poured and the waiter took their order and left.

Max studied Margot across the table, aware that she had a sweetness and kindness to her, but she also had a surprising amount of strength. She wasn't a pushover and she wasn't concerned about her image, or her reputation. From the beginning she'd been worried about what the public would think of him. "Why theater and not TV or film?"

"I'm not pretty enough—"

"That's not true—"

"It is," she interrupted. "My face isn't symmetrical. My nose is a little too crooked, and I never wanted to get it fixed." She touched the bridge, rubbing a small bump. "I ran into an open door in fourth grade, and broke it. I've always liked the bump. I like not being perfect, but for film, you either make a great character actress, or you make a gorgeous leading lady, and I, unfortunately, fell somewhere in the middle. A little too attractive to play those interesting character roles, but not beautiful or interesting enough to carry a film."

"Did an agent say that to you?"

"Casting directors did. I used to do a lot of auditions when I was growing up. Mom drove me to L.A. a number of times to meet with agents, or go to an open casting call. I got fairly far with a couple roles, getting several callbacks, but in the end I was never hired. I wasn't quite right. They'd tell me while I was talented, I might want to focus on theater. It seems I had a Broadway face, and since I could sing and dance, that would probably be the best direction for me." Her expression turned rueful. "However, being told at fifteen I had a Broadway face was definitely discouraging."

"Not discouraging enough you gave up."

"Oh no. Margot Hughes is tenacious. She doesn't like to give up."

"Well, I respect her tenacity and I'm glad she didn't quit. I also think the casting directors meant you had presence, and you do." He meant it, too. She was different from Hollywood actresses. She had no attitude and focused on the product. Margot was also witty, creative, and vivacious, and he loved the little bump in the bridge of her nose and the slightly crooked left front tooth. It was easy to fix things—surgery, veneers, spray tans, and personal trainers. It was far harder to keep it real. "So why did our tenacious Margot give up acting?"

She smiled at him, but it was a bittersweet smile. "As much as I loved performing, over time it became an issue of diminishing returns. I'd given so much of myself to the theater world but had nothing at the end of the day for me, Margot. I didn't like living in a hotel room. And when not on tour, I didn't like returning to an empty apartment."

"And Sam?"

"He'd been gone for almost two years at that point. I'd been trying to continue without him, and my heart just wasn't in it anymore. I was lonely, and my dad was a widower now, and I realized it was time I grew up and got a real job—"

"Performing is a real job."

She shrugged. "It was all I had at that point, and in hindsight, I'd sacrificed too much. I wanted other things. I was ready for other things. Like coming home, being near my dad, having a family."

"You've been home several years now," he said.

"I moved back when I was forty-seven. I'm forty-nine now." She played with her butter knife. "For the first couple of years I lived with Dad, and did some temp work. I also dated, thinking if I just focused on being me, and putting myself out there, I'd find the right guy, fall in love, and have my happy-ever-after."

"What happened?"

Her shoulders lifted and fell. "It just didn't happen. I dated a lot. I had a boyfriend for a little bit, and I thought with time he could be a possibility, but it turns out he was already married and enjoying playing the field. That hurt." She looked up at him. "I learned something, though. You can date all you want, and meet every available individual, but it doesn't mean you'll click. It doesn't mean there'll be a spark, or anything remotely like love. Affection, sure. Companionship, yes. Someone that helps you kill time? Those people are out there. But what I wanted, true love, forever love, that proved to be ridiculously elusive."

"But you thought you had found it with Sam?"

Her expression changed, eyes darkening with pain. "That's true. I thought I'd found it with him, maybe that's why it was so hard for me to let him go. I wanted us to work. I would have done anything to make us work."

He felt a pang. She was sweet and trusting and very much a romantic. "It takes two, doesn't it?"

She nodded, a shimmer of tears in her eyes.

"Maybe, then, it's a good thing acting was your passion," he said. "It gave you a lot of pleasure."

"That's true."

"Not that it means anything, but I'm glad I get to be on-stage with you now, and see you shine in your world."

Margot exhaled. "It's not my world anymore."

"And Sally's real estate empire is? Come on. I don't believe that for a second."

He saw her open her mouth, but then she closed it, lips pressing tightly together. Margot looked away, brow furrowing, and he had a feeling he knew what she would have said.

The job pays the bills.

I work normal hours now.

I have more free time for myself.

"What were you going to say?" he prompted.

"It's a good job," she said, lifting her wineglass. "Sally is an awesome boss. But is it my dream job? No. Am I content at the moment? Yes."

"Do you ever miss New York?"

"Of course. It was home for twenty-five years."

"When is the last time you were there?"

Her clear green gaze met his. "When I moved away."

"You haven't wanted to return?"

She shook her head. "When I returned to California, I discovered I didn't want to see plays or musicals. I didn't want to hear an orchestra tune up. I didn't want to feel that hum in the auditorium just before the curtain rose. I was like an addict. I had to make a break with my addiction, cold turkey."

"I'm beginning to understand why you didn't want to take this play on."

"I think it's good I was pushed back into it. I have missed it. But is it my future? No. Being a professional actor is in the past." She chewed on her bottom lip, teeth sinking into the softness. "But it still feels weird to say that. Maybe it'd be different if I could see into the future and know who I'll be in a year, or five years, but life doesn't work that way, does it?"

He tried not to focus on her mouth. She had a very lush, kissable mouth. A mouth he'd like to taste properly, a mouth he wanted to explore.

She suddenly looked up at him, her gaze piercing. "Have you ever felt that kind of addiction to anything? Is there anything that's taken over your life?"

Annaliese suddenly came to mind, and Max shifted uncomfortably. He didn't want to think of her, not when he was enjoying Margot's company, and he was enjoying

Margot's company. "Our industry is filled with beautiful, creative people. It's easy to get lost in a role, or caught up in something when on location. Having made mistakes in the past, I try to keep it honest and real now."

"So what's in your future?"

He thought for a moment. "To keep acting. Maybe direct someday. And finish my book. I've been working on it for the past year and I'd like to make it a priority."

"Do you enjoy writing?"

"It's different from acting. It's private, personal, and only mine." He could tell she was studying him, but he couldn't read her expression. "What are you thinking?"

"That I am quite shallow because I like looking at you."

It was the last thing he expected from her, and he choked on the wine he'd just swallowed. Max set down his glass. *"What?"*

"Women must fall at your feet," Margot said. "Is that weird for you, or is it normal?"

"Women are available. But so are bagels and ice cream, and just because it's there, doesn't mean you want it all the time. Or even any of the time. I can't tell you the last time I had a bagel."

Margot laughed. "You can't compare bread and women."

"I'm just saying if it's a stranger, then it's just a body, which also makes it just sex, which I don't find satisfying."

"Come on. Men like sex."

"And women like sex. But as I've gotten older, sex without emotions feels gratuitous. I might as well go to the gym and get a workout in."

"I would think a workout and an orgasm feel quite different."

He loved how she said *orgasm*, so bold and sassy. "What about you? Let's talk about your orgasms—"

Margot snorted. "Can't. There isn't one. Haven't wanted to get naked with anyone in ages."

"But all that dating you did, where you put yourself out there and gave so many nice, boring guys a chance."

Margot gave his arm a push. "I didn't sleep with all of them. I didn't sleep with most of them. The last man I slept with was the one who was married, and while the sex wasn't bad, I was never into him."

"You said he had possibilities."

"I hoped I could work with him to break some of his more annoying habits."

"Give me an example of one of his annoying habits."

"This," she said, before clearing her throat loudly and repeatedly. "Adam did that a lot, at night, in the morning, during movies. Not a deal breaker—not like already being married—but it got on my nerves."

"Anything else?"

"He had to be right, and he had this need to correct me and make sure I was aware that I'd said something wrong. It wasn't even about big things. Did it matter that I'd bought mandarin oranges and called them tangerines? If I said I'd arrived at ten thirty, and I'd arrived at ten thirty-five, Adam would interrupt me, it didn't matter where we were or who we were talking to, and say, 'No, Margot, you're wrong. It was ten thirty.' What was that? Who does that?"

Max looked perplexed. "Are you sure his wife wasn't trying to get rid of him? Maybe she'd hoped you'd take him off her hands."

"Not a chance. The moment I learned the truth, Adam was out of there."

"How did you learn the truth?"

Margot flushed and glanced away. "She spotted us, in a restaurant, having lunch. It was horrible. It wasn't even the scene, but the shock. Her walking over and just calling Adam out. I didn't even know what was happening. I thought she was a lunatic, and then Adam got up and left with her." Margot leaned toward Max, dropped her voice. "I've never told anyone that before. Not my friend Andi, not Sally, and certainly not my dad, so let's keep that between us."

"That's a deal," he said.

"Thank you, and to ensure your silence, I'm paying for dinner tonight." She reached over and covered the bill hidden in the black leather folder.

"No. It's mine tonight. It's also going to be expensive."

Her chin lifted. "I have a job. I can afford the dinner and the additional tips—whatever they are."

"I know you can afford to pay, but tonight is my night. You can pay the next two times if you'd like." He covered her hand with his. Her skin was soft, and warm. "Deal?"

"No deal."

Max slid his fingers between hers. She sucked in a breath. Her eyes darkened. "Now you're not playing fair," she protested.

"You're the one fighting me."

"I was trying to do something nice."

"Speaking of nice," he said. "How long has it been since you got naked with someone? Just wondering if you're due for an orgasm—"

He broke off as Margot jerked her hand out from beneath his.

Max smiled at her and then checked the bill. "Looks like I won. But you can pay next time. I promise."

Margot gave him a look of outrage, and then ruined it by laughing. "You didn't even care about the answer. You just wanted to win."

"I did." He tried to sound remorseful but failed. "I hope you'll forgive me."

"I'm not sure if I can." But she couldn't stop smiling.

Max slipped a handful of one-hundred-dollar bills into the leather, and then he and Margot were heading out.

On Main Street, Margot glanced at his car and then toward the theater. "I can walk back," she said. "It's just a couple of blocks."

"No. I'm driving you."

"This is a very safe town," she said.

His gaze skimmed her face, with the high cheekbones, the vivid eyes, the full mouth that had felt so good against his. Her lips were kissing lips, warm, soft, sweet. He was looking forward to the play. Looking forward to a summer with her. "I know you're fine. You're always fine. But I'm going to take you to your car, make sure it starts, and wait for you to pull out of the parking lot so I don't have to worry about you getting home." He saw her expression and sighed. "Just do it for Sally if you can't do it for me."

Margot grinned, amused. "Okay."

He had her back to her car in just a minute, and as he told her, he stayed and waited while she slid behind the steering wheel. Margot glanced at him, smiled, and waved, before pulling out. He shifted into drive, and pulled onto Main Street behind her.

She wasn't with him, but she was. He could still feel her warmth and her brightness, her smile, and could hear that laugh. She liked to laugh. She liked to be happy. He couldn't remember when a woman had last made him feel this way, and if the restaurant hadn't needed to close, he could have sat across from her for another hour, or more. He wasn't ready for the night to end, but he also couldn't invite her back to his place. It was one thing in the morning when they were rehearsing, but not after dinner and wine, after an hour of staring at her mouth, and thinking how much he wanted to kiss her again. A proper kiss. A kiss where she forgot all the Adams of the world, and boring, uninspiring men.

But Margot wasn't a prize to be won, or a woman to be taken. If he hurt Margot, it would hurt Sally, and he couldn't do that.

He wouldn't do that.

God knows, he had a legacy of disappointing women. Whether he liked it or not, he was Johnny Russo's son.

Chapter 9

JEN WAS ALREADY AT HER DESK IN THE OFFICE WHEN Margot arrived the next morning.

Margot was concerned by her grim expression as she passed Jen's desk on the way to her own. "What's wrong?" Margot asked, sliding her sweater off and hanging it on the back of her chair.

Jen left her desk and walked to Margot, her phone in her hand. "It was on TMZ last night, and then *Daily Mail* shared it, on their TV news show and online."

"What?" Margot asked, although she had a sneaking suspicion she already knew the answer.

Jen scrolled on her phone, pulling up the screenshots she had taken. She handed the phone to Margot so Margot could see the headlines and accompanying stories. Each of the screen grabs featured photos of Max leaving the gym, others were of him exiting a coffee shop with coffee, and another was of him getting in a car. He looked like he'd just worked out—his T-shirt was damp, his dark hair disheveled. Lucky for him, he looked sexy disheveled.

"They don't know what he's doing here," Margot said, handing the phone back. "Just that he is here."

Jen gave her a pointed look. She took her phone back, went to a website. "And these were from this morning," she said, turning the phone around so Margot could see the photos of her and Max at dinner last night.

"We were in the back of the restaurant," Margot said. "How did they get this?"

"Probably a telephoto lens through the front window," Jen said. "They followed you back to your car, too." And yes, there were more pictures of her and Max in the parking lot, his car next to hers.

This was all new territory for her. Margot was familiar with performing, but fame? Never. Of course, there were always the hopeful autograph seekers standing outside a theater at night, hoping to meet cast members after a show, but paparazzi and tabloids? Not for her. And Max was whom the photographers wanted, not her.

Thank goodness there had been no kissing at her car. She'd certainly wanted to kiss him last night. It had been on her mind throughout dinner.

He'd been on her mind all night.

Her sleep had been hot and bothered, with dreams that left her feeling incredibly dissatisfied.

"I think we have to announce the new cast today," Jen said, putting her phone away, and thankfully saying nothing about the dinner photos. "Max generates a lot of press. Max here, in our play, is going to get serious attention. It could get crazy."

"Yes," Margot said even as her insides knotted. She was not ready for crazy. There was too much to do. "We need to update the playhouse's website. Add Max's bio and photo—"

"And yours. You're a name here, too."

"I'll track those down," Margot said. "It would be good to get the website updated today. Do we have access to it?"

"Kelly built the website, and Heather keeps it updated,"

Jen said. "I'm sure between all of us we can have it done this morning." She hesitated. "We need those links for purchasing tickets to work. Let's face it. Max's fans will go nuts. Imagine seeing Max Russo live, here. It's a such tiny theater. People will feel as if they're able to reach out and touch him."

"As long as they don't actually reach out and touch him," Margot said dryly. "That's more *Jesus Christ Superstar.*"

"Have you been in that one?"

"I did play Mary in a traveling show. It was my last tour."

"You've done it all," Jen said.

"It was my life for a long time." A thought came to Margot. "If people want to call to buy tickets, how does that work? I know seniors don't always feel comfortable making purchases online."

"According to Heather, most people buy their tickets online. If someone does call the box office, the phone number goes to voice mail, and then Heather returns the calls when she can." Jen glanced at Sally's empty office in the back and sighed. "The truth is, most of the calls Heather has had to return have been people asking for a refund. They were subscribers for the season, and after the first two plays, they wanted their money back. But Sally refused to give refunds, which is why the theater has some bad reviews on Yelp."

"Oh dear. I had no idea. Lots of bad reviews?"

Jen shrugged. "Enough."

"Anything else I should know?"

"Sally wanted to do a wine tasting during the intermissions, and once had some wineries lined up to do the tastings, but with attendance so low, they backed out."

"There's not really enough time to do a tasting at intermission," Margot said. "But we could certainly sell glasses of wine. Or offer complimentary glasses—"

The front door opened then, and Ali entered with Heather. They were talking, and giggling. Definitely in high spirits, which wasn't how they usually arrived for work. "Max

Russo is parking outside," Ali said, excited to share the news. "I'm not sure if he's coming in here, or going somewhere else, but he's outside, and there are photographers out there, too."

"He's taller than I expected," Heather said. "He's not a short actor."

Margot drew a quick breath, feeling as if things were spinning out of control. "He's probably just getting coffee somewhere." She looked at Heather. "I had no idea Sally had put you in charge of the playhouse's website and ticket sales."

Heather walked to her desk and tucked her purse in the bottom drawer. "It's not a big deal. The website takes no time, and there have been no ticket sales."

"Do you think you'd have time to update the site today? With photographers stalking Max, we probably should announce the cast changes."

"Give me everything I need, and I'll do it this morning."

"I'll pull it together," Jen said. "Just give me an hour—"

She broke off, and all four turned to look as the front door opened. Max walked in.

He was not sweaty or disheveled this morning. But he did look sexy. And Margot's traitorous heart gave a little beat of joy.

"Good morning," Jen said brightly to Max. "We were just talking about you."

Margot had to admire the girl's pluck.

Max just smiled. "Is that so?"

"We're going to update the website today with the new cast," Jen added. "We'll need your bio and whatever head shot you'd like us to use."

"I can send both to you right now," he answered. "Just give me a sec." He pulled out his phone, tapped a few things, and then asked what email he should use.

"Mine," Heather said promptly, giving him her work email address.

"I'm going to need it, too," Jen said, looking at Heather. "For publicity."

"I'll forward it to you," Heather answered, sitting down at her desk and turning her computer on.

Jen and Ali returned to their desks, leaving Margot and Max standing.

For a moment Margot didn't know what to say. Max had a way of knocking her off-balance. "I hear that the tabloids know you're in Cambria."

"They're everywhere," he said. "It was inevitable." His gaze scanned the office. "I didn't realize the office was this big."

"It's bigger than it looks from the outside. Sally doesn't like cubicles, so we've been able to spread our desks apart, have space." She again glanced at Sally's dark office. "She's going to be in procedure any minute."

He nodded. "I'm heading that way in a little bit. Wondered if you'd want to go with me. That way we can see her after she's moved to recovery."

"I'd need about an hour," Margot said. "I've got some things to handle here, but I could be ready by nine thirty."

"That works for me. I'll be back in an hour to get you."

MAX HAD WANTED BREAKFAST; THAT WAS PART OF HIS reason for driving downtown this morning. The other part was checking on Margot, seeing if she was upset about the photos being splashed about. He didn't care. He paid them no attention, but it wasn't always easy for others, especially women. There were a lot of haters online. The trolls were just that, trolls, and often cruel. He knew Margot avoided social media. Hopefully she'd continue to ignore the noise. It wasn't good for anyone. It certainly hadn't been good for Cynthia.

At the café across the street, he seated himself at the

counter, at the far end. The waitress appeared almost immediately with a pot of coffee. "Coffee?" she asked.

He turned his cup over and pushed it toward her. "What do you recommend here?"

"Any of the specials," she answered. "I'm partial to the pork chop and scrambled eggs. Comes with country-fried potatoes and toast, but you can sub the potatoes for fruit."

"Sounds good. But no potatoes," he said, "and just one slice of toast. Sourdough."

The waitress gone, Max sat with the coffee, his thoughts on Cynthia, and Gigi, who'd been only three when Max and Cynthia started dating.

They'd been happy together until that stupid mistake in Australia. Max didn't even know about the photos until Howard told him. Howard found out because the magazine called him asking for a comment.

Max flew home to talk to Cynthia. But she was packing when he arrived, not her things, but his. She was throwing him out. She wanted him gone.

He stood there, watching her empty his drawers into a suitcase, crying as she flung shirts and boxers in. "Why?" she demanded, scooping up things from the closet. "Why? I gave you everything."

He couldn't answer. He had no answer. Because she was right.

He should have fought for her, just the way he'd fought to win her heart initially, but he'd been young and embarrassed, and he hadn't realized until much later that maybe the marriage could have been saved, that her anger and hurt might have passed, if they'd taken steps to working through the pain together.

Instead he'd taken a page from his dad's book and moved on.

For the next six years he played the field, which was better for his career and lifestyle.

And then he met Annaliese, and it was an incredibly physical relationship. Annaliese couldn't get enough of him, and he got lost in her body. In the beginning, they spent hours in bed, hours where it was just the two of them. She was a model and trying to break into acting, but finding it difficult. Wanting to make her happy, he introduced her to people, helped open doors for her. But she found the rejection—such a big part of his industry—hard, painful, and the rejections frustrated her. She felt dismissed when she wanted respect.

There were things Max could help her with, but he wasn't a producer or a casting director. He couldn't give her a job, but he could encourage her, and support her. And love her, because he realized he did. They had a mad, passionate kind of love, a love that could feel all-consuming. She mentioned marriage after they'd been together for a year. He wasn't ready for that. She stormed out after a terrible scene. He felt sick, hating to see her cry, hating her pain.

He got a call from Howard telling him that Annaliese was in the hospital. She'd overdosed. It had been a close one, but she should be okay.

He went to the hospital and sat on the side of the bed, holding her hand. She was pale and bruised, a broken woman.

He'd done this to her. He'd failed her, just as he'd failed Cynthia. Max kissed her and told her to plan the wedding of her dreams. Annaliese did, and they married. The first year went well, but every time he needed to travel, especially when he'd be on location, she'd become explosive. She'd accuse him of being unfaithful—he wasn't. She'd insist on being there on set to make sure he didn't cheat on her. He told her she was welcome anytime. But once on set, she'd do things, say things, start things.

It'd get so bad he'd have to ask her to go. She'd leave, creating drama, and then she'd call him incessantly, apologizing. He told her to focus on her acting career, if that was what she wanted. Take classes, get a drama coach, put in the time.

She was cast in a few shows, small roles, but she was acting. She was going to auditions, and continuing with her acting coach, but it bothered her that the only time photographers took her picture was when she was with Max. Without him, she felt like a nobody, and she resented him for that.

His career kept getting bigger and hers was at a standstill. Her insecurity grew, making her jealous every time he was mentioned in a magazine or on an entertainment program. She didn't celebrate with him when he was nominated for Emmys or any other awards. The night he won for lead actor in a drama series, she got drunk, and then got into an ugly fight with him at the after party. Max tried to get her out of the party without a scene, but the next morning footage of him trying to drag her out of the ballroom while she swore and screamed was carried on every channel.

He still didn't want a divorce. He still thought they could salvage their relationship. They needed counseling, and when she wouldn't go to counseling, he went on his own, and then got back to work. Fortunately, he had a lot of work, filming in Wyoming, and then press in Los Angeles for his new film's premiere. Press in L.A. was easy. They were living at that time in Malibu, but then he had to go overseas for the premiere in London and would be gone for a couple of weeks, and Annaliese told him not to go. She said she wouldn't be there when he returned if he did. He told her to do what she needed to do, but he had obligations to fulfill.

While in London, Annaliese made tabloid headlines, photographed at a club making out with a young up-and-coming actor, and then five days later, captured leaving a hotel with a musician, shoes in her hands, makeup smeared, hair messy, expression blissful.

She was pleased with herself. She was getting the attention she wanted.

Instead of returning to Los Angeles, he flew from London to New York, where he initiated the divorce, as it was where they'd married, and he still had a home there, a place he lived when he was filming in the city. He'd hired a good attorney, and because of the prenup, she'd receive a generous alimony, but not enough for her to never worry about money again. She'd need to eventually work, or marry again, or whatever she needed to do to make ends meet.

That was when she came after him, and when he answered that this was the agreement and she'd signed it, she tried to sell her story to any media outlet that would pay for it. There were weeks so uncomfortable Max wouldn't pick up a paper or turn on the news, but finally the drama had played out, and finally she'd accepted the terms of the divorce.

Max was in Georgia filming a few weeks before the divorce was finalized. Annaliese came to see him. She was quiet and articulate, saying she owed him the biggest apology, and he was right, she'd needed help and she'd been in therapy for the past six months. She hoped he'd forgive her because she loved him, dearly, desperately.

They went to dinner and it was bittersweet. She cried at dinner, saying she needed him, and she'd do anything to get him back. He held her as she wept. He hated seeing her pain. He assured her they'd remain friends, but he wasn't going to get back together with her.

Annaliese left the next day, but suddenly there were photos of them everywhere, pictures of them at dinner, pictures of him holding her, pictures of him kissing the back of her hand, pictures of her leaving his hotel room with him standing in the door, watching her go. She had sold the story to a UK tabloid, and had a feature in another magazine, and every story was about Max's love for her, and how they'd soon be together again.

It was humiliating being featured in Annaliese's clickbait. But he couldn't blame her entirely. He'd spent time with her, listened to her, had dinner with her. Giving Annaliese access to him allowed her to twist facts and create a story that tabloids could splash on their pages.

Now she was reaching out to him again, and it wasn't okay. But he wasn't sure what the next best step was. All he knew for certain was that Annaliese needed to stay out of Cambria and steer clear of Sally, Margot, and the playhouse.

IN THE CAR, MARGOT GLANCED AT MAX AS HE DROVE. HE didn't seem troubled but rather thoughtful. Something was on his mind. She was already getting to know him, and when he was thinking something through, he'd retreat and be quiet. She was comfortable with the silence, and used the time to run lines in her head.

She didn't run lines too long, though, distracted by thoughts and memories. She didn't want to compare Max and Sam, but she found herself doing it anyway. They were both brilliant men, creative and ambitious men, but Sam's energy was always inward. He was a profound introvert, needing a lot of silence due to all the words and stories he carried in his head. Max seemed to need time alone, but he also needed people. He liked people, and made sure he took care of others, whether it was leaving a generous tip, opening a door for a stranger, allowing others to merge. He was considerate. Protective. In many ways Max reminded her of her dad—

Dad.

Margot stiffened. "Oh no," she whispered, realizing she hadn't even checked on her father after their canceled dinner Saturday night. He hadn't been well and she'd forgotten him.

Max glanced at her. "What's wrong?"

"I need to call my dad. We never got to have our dinner Saturday, and I haven't even checked in with him. What's wrong with me?"

"You've had a lot to juggle," Max said, glancing at her. "It's been an intense forty-eight hours. But what happened to Dad date night?"

"He thought he was coming down with something and didn't want to expose me, so after I left the hospital, I drove home. I was going to call him yesterday and I forgot."

"Call him now."

"You don't mind?" she asked, reaching into her bag for her phone.

"Of course not."

They were on the outskirts of Paso Robles, with the last of the golden pastures and green vineyards giving way to new housing developments. She'd grown up in one of the older neighborhoods, not far from downtown. "Max, could we stop by the house for a minute? We're not that far. Let me just run in and make sure he's okay? It won't take long, and Sally is still in procedure—"

"Definitely. Just tell me the exit."

"It will be the Seventeenth Street exit. I'll give directions from there."

It didn't take long to get to the neighborhood she'd been raised in. It was quiet in this part of town. All the new growth had shifted the desirable neighborhoods away from the city center, but she liked where she'd been raised. The houses had been built in the 1940s and '50s, the lots generous, the houses shaded with mature trees. Her home, gray with white shutters, had a long white picket fence next to the sidewalk with thick pink shrub roses lining the fence, the roses in full bloom thanks to the late-spring heat and her father's devoted care.

"That's my dad's car," she said, gesturing to the driveway. "So he is home."

Max pulled up behind her dad's car and parked. "I'll wait here."

"It's ninety-eight degrees out, you can't wait in the car."

"I'll stand in the shade, then. Go in. Don't worry about me."

Margot nodded, and hurried up the walk to the front door. She had her keys with her and let herself in. "Dad?" she called, entering the house. She could hear the air conditioner but it was warm inside. Her dad, like other retirees, had a fixed income and didn't like big energy bills. "Dad, it's me."

"In here," he called from his bedroom.

"You okay?" she asked, entering his bedroom, dark with the curtains drawn.

"Just a sore throat and congestion. It's a head cold."

"Must be bad if you're still in bed."

"It's just cooler in here."

She approached the bed, taking in the bottle of NyQuil and box of tissues. "Are you still running a fever?"

"I don't think so."

She placed a hand on his forehead. He was warm, not hot. His skin wasn't clammy. "Are you eating?"

"Had some chicken noodle soup last night. Nothing this morning, but I'm not hungry."

"I could make you some eggs—"

"Margot, I don't want any eggs, but thank you, sweetheart. I'm okay. It's just a cold, nothing serious. I promise you."

"I should have checked on you sooner."

"We talked Saturday. It's what? Monday? Stop fussing and know if I needed something, I would call you."

"I just worry."

"Well, don't. I've lived by myself for ten years. Just because you stayed with me when you first moved back from New York doesn't mean I'm not happy alone. I have friends. My buddies stop by. I go to their house. We golf. We have beers. We watch the big games. Stop feeling guilty for having your own life. Kids are supposed to grow up and be independent."

"You know I love you."

"I do. And I love you. We'll go have dinner—or lunch,

breakfast, whatever you want—as soon as I'm feeling better. Okay?"

"Okay." She moved forward to kiss him, and he put up a hand to stop her.

"Don't," he said firmly. "You've got your Sally in the hospital. The last thing you want to do is pass on my germs."

Outside the house, Margot found Max standing in the shade beneath one of the tall evergreens lining the driveway. It had once been a living Christmas tree in a fifteen-gallon container, one of Charlotte's trees, they called them, because when Charlotte was ten, she insisted they buy only live trees, as she couldn't bear to have a "dead Christmas tree" in the middle of the house. *Why are we celebrating Jesus's birth with dead things?*

Her parents had honored Charlotte's need for living trees for years, and the property boundaries were dotted with them, creating shade and privacy between their little gray house and the neighbors.

A lump filled her throat. There was something poignant seeing Max beneath one of Charlotte's trees, and it struck Margot that this was yet another reason why her dad stayed here. The family house. The memories. And Charlotte's living trees.

Ah, Charlotte.

Margot's eyes burned and she suddenly, fiercely missed her big sister, and of course her mom. You didn't get to be Margot's age without losing people, but that didn't make it easier.

She felt Max's scrutiny, and she forced a smile. "I should have had you come in. It's hot out here."

"New York is hotter, with twice the humidity," he answered, meeting her at the car. He was still studying. "Is he okay?"

She nodded. "He's so strong. He's been through so much—losing my sister, losing my mom, losing his partner on duty—and yet he's always cheerful, always positive. Such a good man." And then she was wiping away tears. "I don't know why I'm crying."

"Because this is home," Max said, standing outside the car, looking at her over the roof. "And even when we love home, it's still complicated, isn't it?"

"So true." She was grateful he understood. "It is complicated. Makes me feel like a kid, and emotional. Happy and sad. Grateful but also guilty."

"Why guilty?"

"Because Charlotte was the one who died. Why was it her? Why wasn't it me?" Margot blinked hard, fighting the tears. "She was such a good person. Beautiful. Sweet. She had a heart so full of love. She loved all living things— trees, animals, bugs." Margot laughed and then reached up to wipe away tears. "I'm sorry I'm crying."

Max came around the car and wrapped his arms around her. "It's okay to cry. It means you feel."

She nodded, her face pressed to his chest, and he was solid, his body big, hard, real. His arms were warm, strong. His warmth and strength just made her struggle more. "I never cry like this."

"Maybe it was time."

She nodded again, and then after a deep, rough breath, she stepped back, undone. Embarrassed. "Wow," she whispered, turning away to dry her face. "I don't know what's happened to me."

"It's been a hard few days," he said. "There's been a lot going on."

She managed a faint smile, grateful he understood. "Don't tell anyone I'm such a crybaby."

"Lips are sealed." Max opened her car door for her. "Let's go check on our Sally."

Chapter 10

SALLY'S PROCEDURE WENT WELL, AND AFTER A NIGHT at the hospital for observation, she was now home. Max had picked her up Tuesday morning and helped her settle back into her house. He stayed until her nurse arrived, and then he left, but then Sally and the nurse had words, and Sally, in one of her rare tempers, sent the nurse packing.

Margot was at the office when Sally phoned and asked Margot if she'd mind staying with her for a few nights, as it was a requirement from her doctor. Margot agreed, and left work to pack an overnight bag before returning to town to pick up miso soup and salmon teriyaki from Sally's favorite Japanese restaurant. But once Margot arrived, Sally wasn't ready to eat, and so Margot left everything in the kitchen to join Sally in the family room.

Seeing Sally enthroned in her favorite leather recliner with a computer on her lap and reading glasses on the bridge of her nose was reassuring. Sally's color was good and her voice was strong. She looked like the Sally of old. "I have heard nothing from the office other than a few feel-better-soon messages. What's going on? Why am I out of the loop?"

"You probably have forgotten," Margot answered dryly, sitting down on the couch and crossing her legs, "you had a heart attack a week ago today. You had some issues and needed a procedure, which was done yesterday. You just got home a few hours ago."

"Yes, but there are no emails to read through. There's nothing for me to do."

"We were thinking you might like to have a Zoom with the team tomorrow. What would you prefer? Eleven? One?"

"Eleven or one? What is everyone doing all day? Sleeping in?"

Margot checked her smile. Sally really was feeling herself. "No, we still open the office at eight. We just thought you might want to take it slow."

Sally looked at her as if she were crazy. "Why?"

"My goodness, what was I thinking? Sally, what time would you like the Zoom to be? It is your company, and your team."

"Yes, it is. And I don't intend to fritter away my morning doing nothing. Set up the Zoom, send out the link for eight thirty."

"Done." Margot grabbed her phone, shot Jen a text, asking her to set up the Zoom meeting for the morning, and to be sure to send Sally a link as well. Finished, Margot looked at Sally. "Feel better now?"

"Don't patronize me. I'm the boss."

Margot hid her exasperation. "You're still the boss, no one is trying to replace you."

"I know that. I *am* the boss. And I need to hear from everyone. I've had almost no emails, no calls, no texts. It's as if I dropped off the face of the earth."

"To aid in your recovery, I told everyone to leave you alone, and if there were big things, to come to me and I would bring them to you. I wasn't going to have people bothering you when you just had a heart attack. 'Should we get the new toilet paper now or later? There's a sale on toner, three cartons or five?' You don't need to be bothered with such trivial things. Your staff should be able to make those decisions without having your input, especially when you're in a hospital."

Sally smiled reluctantly. "So what did you tell them about toilet paper and toner?" she asked, drawing her reading glasses off and placing them on the arm of her recliner.

"I said buy what was needed, another sale would come again." Margot glanced at the table next to Sally, noting the water bottle and pills. "Do you have all your prescriptions? Is there anything else you need?"

"Max took care of all that earlier."

"I'm glad. And aside from frustration over office silence, how are you feeling? You look good."

"I feel great. I feel better than I have in a long time. I had no idea how hard my heart was working. It just wasn't getting enough blood flow. Who knew?"

"Good." Margot hesitated. "Just out of curiosity, has Max talked to you about the play?"

"Only that he said things were going really well. He said you are a lot of fun to work with, and incredibly talented."

"I'm okay. I wouldn't call me incredible."

"So why did you star in all those shows? Why did you work in the business for twenty-five years?"

"I wasn't a star, Sally. I was a supporting actor."

"You were the star on almost every touring Broadway production."

"Because the real stars don't travel the country on the tour buses, Sally. People like me crisscross the country on buses. I'm just one of hundreds of solid hardworking actors who can sing and dance and love performing so much, we're willing to live on the road for years and years and years—" Margot broke off, remembering, and then smiled slowly. "I did love it, though. I'd forgotten how much I enjoyed being in a theater, onstage with a great actor."

"Is Max great?"

"He's a very good actor, and he has star power. He's also pretty gorgeous." Margot shifted uneasily. "Although I don't know why I'm telling you that."

"He was always a good-looking kid. In high school he reminded me of a young James Dean. He had a look, but he was angry, and he didn't want to be pretty. He got in so many fights in junior high, angered at being perceived as this pretty face. I finally sat him down and said, 'This isn't going to work. You can't fight everyone who wants to pin a label on you. You can't fight everyone who has something to say. The best way to handle negativity is to do something in life. Focus on your goals, and getting ahead. Trying to silence the detractors will just keep you stuck. You don't get anywhere in life doing that.'"

"How is it you have so much wisdom?"

"It's street smarts, not book smarts," Sally answered. "I never had a lot of schooling. Didn't have the opportunity. Or money. But I wasn't going to let that stop me."

"I wish I had your fire. Your focus."

"You do. It's what sent you to New York in the first place. You were what? Just eighteen?"

"Yes."

"Your fire isn't gone. It's there. You've just built walls around it, banking it—"

She was interrupted by a knock on the door, and the front door opened.

"Sally," Max called. "Is this a bad time?"

"No," she replied. "Come in, Max. It's just me and Margot. Join us. We're talking about you."

Margot shot Sally a reproving glance but Sally ignored her.

Max appeared in the spacious family room with the wall

of windows and view of the sea. It was going to be another stunning sunset, the sky gold, the waves metallic, everything gilded.

"I hope you won't stop talking about me," he said, crossing to Sally, kissing her cheek, before sitting down at the other end of the couch. "I'm sure it's all so nice. Please continue."

Margot tossed a pillow at Max. "You're ridiculous," she said, and yet she was smiling, and her heart was beating faster. From the moment she heard his voice at the door, she felt filled with tingly energy. "I don't know how you can wear hats with such a big head. What makes you think we were saying *nice* things?"

"What could you possibly say that wasn't nice?" he teased.

"Oh, we could talk about all kinds of things, we can discuss your. . . ." She frowned, glanced at Sally. "Sally, what could we discuss?"

"Well, to be honest," Sally said, "we were discussing how good-looking you are."

Margot covered her face with a hand. "Oh, Sally. Why?"

"It's true," Sally answered. "There's no reason we can't appreciate Max's good looks. It's what's made him popular."

"I would hope it's my talent. I don't want to just be a pretty face," Max protested.

"We were discussing that, too," Sally said. "I was telling Margot that you did not like being called a pretty boy, that you'd fight anyone who said something about your face."

Max shook his head. "I don't even know why you're talking about this." He glanced at Margot. "What does this have to do with anything?"

But his tone was playful and Margot smiled wryly. "I'm not sure. I think we were talking about the play and that I was having fun working with you, that you were easy to work with—"

"And very easy on the eyes," Sally interjected.

"For Pete's sake, you're both impossible," Margot

muttered. "I need to go. I want to grab some tea before rehearsal. You two can do your thing." She glanced at Max. "Can you try to get Sally to eat before you leave? I brought her food. They're in the kitchen ready to be served. And you, Sally, I'll see after rehearsal."

Margot disappeared out the front door, pulse still beating a little too fast, her body warm, full of energy and emotion. In her car, she backed out of the driveway and headed south for town. She was feeling again, not quite everything, but more than she'd felt in years. She was also hoping again, and she wasn't comfortable with hope, not at all. Hope was like an expressway to disappointment.

She had to be careful and remain on guard. She couldn't let her emotions get out of hand. Hope and love, those were not on the table. Fortunately, she wasn't in love with Max. She wasn't even close to being in love, but she was attracted to him, possibly a little infatuated, but that was a far cry from forever and commitments.

Driving downtown, she wondered how she'd even become infatuated. She hadn't come into this looking for anything. Truth be told, she'd tried hard to avoid feelings and entanglements.

It seemed as though she'd just have to try harder.

Margot abruptly made a U-turn in the street and headed back the way she came, going to her house, though. She was going to show up tonight in character. She'd be reserved Corie. She'd wear a suit and a prim blouse and keep Max at arm's length.

She would not let his warmth melt her.

It was time to resist.

THEY'D DECIDED FOR MOST COMEDIC RELIEF TO DO every scene as written, every line as written. Neil Simon was funny, deadpan funny, and *Barefoot in the Park* was about two newlyweds wildly in love with each other, pairing a passionate physical partner with the more practical, reserved one. Because they'd switched roles, she'd be practical and reserved, which, honestly, was something of a relief for Margot. She preferred playing the straight man to his funny man.

Max would be the over-the-top, dramatic one, full of energy and wild ideas. He'd be passionate, physical, the one kissing her. Touching her.

He'd be the one unbuttoning the top button of her blouse in act 2, scene 1 and kissing her neck. They were just about to rehearse act 2 now. Margot swallowed hard, trying not to anticipate his lips on her neck, because her neck was very, very sensitive.

She scanned the scene, making sure she knew the lines, and when she was comfortable, put the script down on the folding chair behind her. "Ready whenever you are."

He took a last drink of water, nodded. "Ready."

They took the scene from the top, where the stage is empty and Paul comes rushing through the front door, carrying a pastry box and some bottles of wine. He's dressed sharp, for the evening's festivities. He's barely out of breath, as he's getting used to the five flights of stairs. After moving around the room, turning on lights, arranging things for Corie's arrival, he goes to the front door and shouts down the stairs to where Corie seems to be struggling, and he has a one-sided conversation with her where he fills her in on everything that's happened that day, including the wrong lamps being sent, her parents planning to visit them the next weekend, her sister's boyfriend having acne—and everyone hating him.

He calls down some sweet nothings then, warning her to get ready to be kissed for five minutes, and then the neighbor passes him and slams a door.

Paul is embarrassed and goes to the kitchen for an ice bucket, Corie enters the apartment, breathless, exhausted, and drops onto the couch.

Paul steps from the kitchen, and seeing Corie on the couch, crosses over, scoops her up, and deposits her on his lap.

They'd never actually done this. They'd blocked it, but not performed it. They were rehearsing properly tonight, but when Max lifted her up, set her down on top of his lap, she tumbled forward, sprawling onto his chest.

Heavens, he was big, and muscular, and warm, his body generating some serious heat beneath her. Margot struggled to sit up, but it meant rocking back on his lap, and as she fought to get her balance, Max arched an eyebrow.

She wasn't sure if she was mortified or amused, because she wasn't oblivious to the sparky energy zapping between them. She still wasn't comfortable on his lap, but didn't dare wiggle anymore, not needing any extra stimulation. She had a job to do, lines to say, a conservative lawyer to play.

"You're supposed to wince in pain, from my overenthusiastic manhandling," Max said. "Should we try that again?"

"No. Let's just push on," Margot said. "But I do think it's going to be awkward with you trying to pick me up twice just a few lines apart."

"Then just stay put, and we'll continue the lines with you here, which makes sense as I'll be unbuttoning your blouse soon—"

"But there is that line where you ask if I won," she interrupted, not wanting to think about him unbuttoning her blouse yet. "It has a lot of physicality in that section."

"It will be fine. We'll make it work. Let's just go for it," he said.

So they did, continuing with the scene, blocking and rehearsing, trying to act as if everything was normal and Margot wasn't sitting on Max's lap, facing him.

"Maybe that's how we handle the jumping up and plopping down again. Maybe instead of me jumping all the way up, I start to get up, and you pull me back down so now I'm sideways on your lap."

"Good idea," he agreed.

They had some lines—which she more or less remembered—and then he was unbuttoning her blouse to kiss her neck. Margot's mind went blank.

She was trying not to feel, and trying not to feel was making her brain freeze. Her neck was so sensitive, and just the brush of his fingers against the silk of her blouse made her shudder a little. His gaze met hers, and held. Margot couldn't breathe.

Act.

Act, she told herself. But her brain wasn't working, hijacked by the warmth of Max's skin. He slowly undid the top button on her blouse, and a tremor coursed through her. She prayed he couldn't feel it. He unbuttoned the next button, and she sucked in air, her heart pounding, nerve endings screaming.

Again his gaze met hers and then his head dipped, dropping, his lips brushing her exposed neck.

She tried to feel nothing. She tried not to care. But her eyes closed as his mouth moved across her neck, the kiss so warm, her body so hot. Shiver after shiver coursed through her, her insides squirming with pleasure. She let out a soft sigh.

His head lifted. She gulped air, dazed, thoughts scattered. "Whose line?" she whispered.

"Mine," he said, smiling into her eyes, making her quiver. She felt scalding hot. Her lips trembled. She shouldn't feel this much sensation. They were rehearsing—blocking the scene still—there should be no feelings involved. No pounding heart. No desire.

And yet with his gaze locked with hers, all she could think was *Kiss me.*

Now.

Max said his lines.

Her mind was still gone. Margot stared blankly at him. "Whose line?"

"Yours," he said huskily.

She had no idea what her line should be. She couldn't even remember the rest of the scene. For that matter, she couldn't even feel anything but heat and desire. "Could we take five?"

He nodded and lifted her off his lap as if she weighed nothing. "Good idea. I'm sure everyone would enjoy a break."

Margot walked away from the couch and, after scooping up her water bottle, headed outside.

She paced the brick courtyard, completely unglued. She'd lost her mind in there. She'd completely blanked out, overwhelmed by Max and his lips against her neck. But it had started before that. It had started when he put her on his lap, and she'd felt him beneath her thighs, against her butt, and it was bewildering. She couldn't remember ever feeling that much, never mind while in character, acting.

Where was her control? Her discipline?

What had happened to her memory? It wasn't okay to snap. There was no forgetting one's lines. She had to pull it together. They had to finish the scene, and she had to stop behaving like a ninny. Like a virgin.

This wasn't real. Max wasn't seducing her. They weren't lovers. They were acting in a tiny community theater production, and she had to stay in character. She had to focus. Even if Max's lips were on her neck and his hands at the buttons on her chest.

"What's making you uncomfortable?" Max asked.

She turned to find him standing in the shadows. She hadn't heard him join her outside, and had no idea how long he'd been there. "You," she said bluntly, softening her words with a smile. "You're a lot."

"Good or bad?" he asked.

His voice was so deep with that slightly raspy tone that always made her think of bed, and sex. "Both." She faced him, arms crossed. "I'd find this easier if you were not so appealing."

"You'd rather kiss unappealing men?"

She laughed because there was nothing else she could do. He was handsome and funny, and she was feeling all kinds of emotions, emotions she didn't expect to ever feel again. "We've done different kinds of acting in our careers. I sing and sometimes dance. You kiss and sometimes get naked. We're experts in different things."

"I'm not usually completely naked. There's a nude-colored thing I wear to cover the real thing."

"Alright, I did know that. I was trying to be funny."

"You are funny," he said, walking toward her. "But you're also nervous and you don't need to be. Would it help if we just practiced out here first? Away from everyone? It might be easier than having that first super hot kiss onstage, with the cast watching."

Her heart did a jagged tattoo. "Hot kisses can be awkward," she agreed, pulse beating even faster. She wanted to kiss him. She'd been wanting to kiss him properly for days. And yet, she should want the kiss to be bad. She should want it to be the kind of kiss one endured because it *had* to be done—

"It's not going to be bad," he said, stopping in front of her, and smiling down into her eyes. "Stop wishing it would be."

"How do you know I'm thinking that?"

"You're far too revealing right now. It's written all over your face. Maybe you should try acting? You're quite good at it, when you focus."

She lightly punched his chest. It wasn't even a punch. It was a press of her fist to his pectoral muscle, a muscle that was very hard, and warm. She left it there, as if holding him back. Or keeping herself away. "You should just get it over with, then."

His laugh was such a deep rumble that she could feel it all the way through her hand, her arm, her body. Desire knotted in her belly. Her legs went weak. She would love being in bed with him, would love his warmth against her, from head to toe.

"Why don't you kiss me," he retorted, "since you have this desperate need for control?"

Her lips parted to protest, and then one arm wrapped around her, his hand settling low on her back.

Heat surged through her. Her skin flamed. She was a mass of nerve endings, both exquisite pain and pleasure. Margot didn't think she'd ever felt so sensitive before.

His hand slipped lower on her back, toward the curve of her cheek, and she breathed out and then in. "I don't think I can kiss you," she said. "You're too tall."

"Let me help."

He tipped her chin up, and his head lowered, his mouth covering hers, and this was not a professional kiss. It wasn't light. It wasn't a peck. It was hot and demanding, and his tongue traced the seam of her lips before she opened her mouth to him, and that was another lesson in pleasure. He teased the inside of her upper lip and then drew her tongue into his mouth, and she felt him everywhere—sensation everywhere, and she welcomed the friction of his tongue on hers, she welcomed the pressure of his chest, his hips, his thighs, and if they were naked, she'd want him inside of her, too.

Deep. Hard and slow. And every which way he wanted to move because she suspected Max would be an expert at that as well.

She didn't know how long the kiss went on, but she was a puddle of need when he finally lifted his head, and she looked up into his eyes but couldn't see. Her brain was completely foggy. Her body craved more.

"Better?" he asked, his hand on her jaw, his thumb just beneath her ear, over her wildly beating pulse.

She loved the way his hand felt against her neck. It was all she could do to keep from shuddering with pleasure. "Sure."

"Do you think we can go back inside and finish rehearsal? Have we worked out the nerves?"

Margot forced a smile. "Absolutely."

She had a feeling he didn't believe her, but thankfully he didn't call her on it, and he stepped back and let her pass so she could return inside.

However, Margot wasn't sure she should be thankful her costar turned her on.

BACK AT SALLY'S THAT EVENING, MARGOT DISCOVERED Sally had already gone to her room for the night, but she wasn't sleeping. Instead, she was in bed watching a TV show. Margot knocked lightly and stuck her head around the door. "How are you doing?"

Sally paused the TV. "Good. Happy to be back in my own bed. No nurses to poke me during the night. No annoying doctors on their early rounds."

"This is why we need to keep you out of the hospital."

"I won't be going back there anytime soon."

Margot smiled, leaned against the doorframe. "Do you need anything?"

"No. But you were out late. Rehearsals all this time?"

"Yes. Sometimes Max and I grab a drink after to talk things through, but tonight we had some hiccups, so we kept going until we ironed them out."

"I can't wait to go to a rehearsal. Hoping to drop in later this week."

"About that," Margot said, stepping closer to the bed, "we think you should wait, until opening night."

"Why?"

"We want you to love it, and right now, there are kinks, which will get worked out, but Max and I agree that if you wait until opening night, it'll be a better experience."

Sally pushed herself into a more upright position. "Is it that bad?"

Margot laughed. "Not the way you're thinking, but we're feeling the pressure. There's no set yet. We don't have props. We don't have a real stage manager who can do the heavy lifting on this, so it's Max, me, and Jen right now, and Jen is awesome, but she's not a theater person, so her learning curve is pretty steep."

"Can she handle this?"

"Yes. But when this is over, she deserves a nice long vacation."

MARGOT HADN'T BEEN EXAGGERATING WHEN SHE TOLD Sally that Jen was amazing. The next morning at the office, Jen filled her in on her progress. With her social media acumen, she already had volunteers for the stagehands, because once she mentioned that Max Russo would be starring in *Barefoot in the Park*, there was no shortage of interested bodies. But since most had zero experience, Jen told Margot she planned on reaching out today to the theater arts department chair at Cal Poly, San Luis Obispo.

Margot wouldn't have thought of that, but it was a great idea. "How did you think of that?"

"I didn't graduate from college all that long ago. Students are always looking for opportunities and experience."

"Maybe I should have gone to college."

"Not everyone has to go to college. My best friend dropped out at the end of her freshman year. She wasn't ready."

"Did she ever go back?"

"Yes. It took her a couple years, but honestly, college isn't for everyone. We all have different paths."

"How come you are so mature?"

"I don't know if I'm mature, but having a brother with disabilities has taught me to focus on what we can do, not what we can't."

"I'd love to meet your brother someday."

"I'm going to get tickets for my family to come see the play. Hoping to give them a backstage tour after."

"Definitely."

Heather gave a shout from her desk. "Zoom with Sally in two minutes, everyone."

"I almost forgot," Jen said.

"I'm in the same boat," Margot said. "I also need more coffee."

MAX WAS HOME DOING SOME WRITING—THE FIRST TIME since he'd arrived in Cambria, but also, the first time in a long time—and he was finding it difficult settling into the story. He'd been to the gym this morning, he'd had breakfast, he'd reviewed his lines, and he had nothing pressing, so he thought he'd be productive and write. Only the words weren't coming, and his attention was scattered, distracted by a bird hopping on the railing outside, and then by texts coming through on his phone, almost all from Howard but then one from Lee Sheridan.

Max picked up his phone, opened the message. Lee wanted him in L.A. to read. Was there any way Max could be there Friday?

Max checked his messages from Howard. They were all about the same audition. Howard reminded Max that the screenplay was sitting there, waiting for Max's attention.

Lee Sheridan didn't just produce and direct, he also wrote his own screenplays. He was something of a maverick, but Max liked him. He phoned Howard.

"Finally," Howard said, disgruntled. "I've been trying to reach you for hours."

"I was at the gym."

"And then?"

"Showering, eating breakfast, reading scripts."

"Sheridan's?"

"Just about to."

"It's good, Max. You've got to get down here. Make it work. You're still in rehearsals. You could miss Friday."

Max could miss Friday, but he wouldn't want to miss more. Maybe he could leave after rehearsal Thursday. It'd take four hours if he went then, as traffic would be light. Unless there was road construction. "I can do it. I'll make it work."

"There's a six a.m. out of San Luis Obispo Friday that gets into LAX at seven. There are still seats available, if you didn't feel like driving."

Normally in Los Angeles, Max liked having his own wheels, but all the rideshare apps had made getting around L.A. much easier. "I'll let you know what I decide."

"So I can confirm with Sheridan?"

"I can confirm," Max said.

"Want to have dinner while you're here? Haven't seen you in a while."

"I'll probably be heading back by then. But if we can get lunch or coffee, it'd be great to catch up."

Hanging up, Max answered Lee's text, letting him know he was coming into town, and just needed to know where and when.

Lee responded with a thumbs-up.

Max put the phone down, stretched, and glanced at his computer. The screen was dark, having gone into sleep mode. He closed the laptop. He wasn't going to be writing today. And then after sitting there a few minutes, feeling increasingly restless, he decided he'd go for a drive. Maybe he'd head to Templeton, drive down Main Street, see the park, have lunch there. He wondered if his old house was still there or if some enterprising person had torn it down and built something new. He hoped there was something new. He'd hated that place. Nothing good had ever happened there.

Templeton looked just as he remembered, the small downtown sandwiched between Main Street and Old

County Road. At one end of Main Street were all the schools, including the middle school and high school. At the other was the post office. In between, enormous oak trees lined the street, from Templeton Park with its pretty gazebo, through the historical district with the landmark Templeton Feed & Grain structure, rising 105 feet high, towering over other businesses. Tom Jermin Sr. opened the feed store in 1946, and the store grew to encompass a city block dominated by its iconic grain elevator.

The grain elevator had fascinated him as a boy. He used to ride his bike from his house down Main Street, circling the park, and then on to Templeton Feed & Grain. Max pulled over across from the grain elevator and just looked.

He was glad it was the same. Downtown Templeton had been a safe place. Home had not. He'd liked being down here, getting books from the school library, and then reading hidden away in the gazebo. There was a lady in one of the offices near the school who knew his dad, and when she saw him, she'd always come out and give him an orange Fanta. He never told her that he didn't really like orange. He'd always drink it and thank her, and then hand the bottle back.

One day she walked out with a grape Fanta. "I just found out you like grape best," she said. She smiled at him but she didn't seem happy.

He drank the soda and watched her face. No, she definitely wasn't happy. He suddenly thought of his mom, and he didn't like that. "How did you find out I like grape?" he asked, when he'd almost finished the soda.

"Your dad told me." She tried to smile but instead had a look that made him think of basset hounds. They always looked sad, too. "I won't be able to bring you drinks anymore," she added when he handed her the empty bottle. "Your dad said no. I'm sorry."

He felt sorry for her. He didn't understand why she was so sad. "It's okay. I was probably costing you a lot of money anyway."

"Not that much," she answered. She glanced down the street, uneasy. "I better get back to work."

"Thank you." He hesitated. "What was your name?"

"Lucy. Like your mama's."

For a long time after, Max avoided that one block, riding his bike behind her office building instead of in front. She'd always been so nice to him, but thinking about her made him feel bad, and there was enough yelling and breaking things at home that he didn't need more bad feelings.

Sitting in his car now, Max wondered whatever happened to that nice Lucy lady. He hadn't thought about her in years. Twenty years or more. He wished he hadn't thought of her now, not because she'd ever done anything wrong, but because she'd tried to be nice to him, and Johnny hadn't liked it.

That was what angered Max.

Why had his dad cared that people were good to him? Johnny certainly didn't love him. He hadn't wanted anything to do with him until Max was famous. And rich. That's when his dad reappeared, asking for a handout, demanding his share because he'd raised Max, and surely Max realized he owed Johnny something for all the sacrifices he'd made over the years.

But Max's dad was nothing like real dads, good dads, and Max owed him nothing.

Starting the car, Max was ready to return to Cambria. He'd had enough of a drive down memory lane.

Chapter 11

MIDAFTERNOON, JEN APPROACHED MARGOT'S DESK. "Success," she said, waving a handful of papers. "Applicants from the university, all with theater production and design experience, all very eager to be part of the summer season. You will have your crew very soon."

"You are brilliant," Margot said. "Thank you!"

"I'm also getting questions from prospective actors, wondering if the Cambria Playhouse needs understudies, and I didn't know how to answer."

Margot nodded. "Absolutely, yes, we do. That's been one of my fears. If someone gets sick or hurt—we're in trouble."

"Do you want to audition them?"

"We should." Margot opened her phone, studied her schedule. Today was Wednesday. Two weeks from today, they'd be deep in dress rehearsals. Time was of the essence. "Tonight? Before rehearsals?"

"And when should we have the applicants for the crew meet?"

Margot glanced down at her phone calendar again. "Tomorrow, if they can make it?"

"I don't see why they couldn't. Let's try."

Margot exhaled, relieved. They were finally getting some momentum. "Could you be there tonight, too? In fact, I want you at everything. I need your young brain to keep me on track."

"I already promised you my brain is yours." Jen smiled, clearly not worried. "I'm here until the bitter end. There's no way I'm leaving you to deal with this on your own. We're a team, and Sally's always talking about teamwork."

"That's right. Teamwork makes the dream work."

Rehearsal that night was better than any rehearsal so far, but then, halfway through the second act, Edgar, who was playing Victor, stepped backward and fell off the stage. It was a very dramatic fall, and for a second he didn't move and Margot feared the worst. Thankfully Edgar just had the air knocked out of him, and after Sharon—who was playing Mother—a retired nurse, looked him over, Max and Saul helped him to his feet and onto the stage.

The actors who'd auditioned to be understudies were in the theater at the time, watching. Margot glanced at them, thinking this is why they had understudies. Rehearsal continued after a ten-minute break, but they couldn't get the energy back. No one's heart was in it with Edgar limping around the stage. He kept insisting he was fine, only a little stiff, but Margot wasn't convinced, and she called the rehearsal early and suggested Edgar see his doctor in the morning.

Max walked her out. "It's going to be okay," he said, reading her discouragement.

"What if he's really hurt?" Margot asked, leaning against her car.

"Sally has good insurance. He'll get seen by a doctor, and patched up. And if he can't continue? We have those understudies."

"Who don't know anything."

"Not yet, but they all have acting experience, whether in community theater or at college, and they could fill in. We still have two weeks."

She rubbed her face, tired. "Why doesn't this stress you out?"

"Because it's just a play. Not life or death."

Life and death. Margot knew the difference, too, flashing to the night Charlotte had died. According to the official reports, Charlotte had swerved, overcorrected, and ended up in another lane, where she was struck by an SUV, dying instantly. The sheriff on the scene, one of Dad's colleagues, had recognized Charlotte and come straight to the house to break the news. "You're right," she said. "But I struggle to detach. Are you able to do it because this is an amateur production, or are you like this with all your jobs?"

"Most of them. I love what I do, but let's face it, acting is fairly frivolous. I'm not saving the world. I'm not a brain surgeon. I'm not finding a cure for cancer. I act. I entertain. I provide people an escape. And I have no desire to lose my mind, not doing what I do. It would be pointless."

"How can you be so chill?"

"Because this is easy, compared to what I knew growing up."

"I thought you had Sally."

"I didn't meet her until I was eleven. Those first eleven years were rough. My dad was rough. My mom—" He broke off, shook his head. "This is never easy to talk about. Do you want to come over for a drink?"

"Yes," she said. "I do. I'd like that. Let me just give Sally a call, make sure she's comfortable, and if so, I'll meet you there?"

When Margot phoned Sally, Sally said she didn't need anything, she was happy watching her show, and told Margot to enjoy herself.

Max had a glass of red wine waiting for Margot when

she arrived. It was a cool night with a strong breeze, and they opted to sit in the little living room with the gas fireplace on.

Neither of them spoke right away, and Margot sipped her wine, good with the silence. Max was easy to be with. She liked his company, even if they were just sitting side by side, doing nothing. But after a few minutes, she glanced at Max and realized he wasn't completely okay. He looked as if he had a lot on his mind.

She didn't know what to do, wasn't sure what to say. They weren't exactly friends. They didn't pour out their hearts to each other. But she did care for him, and she was concerned. "Want to talk about anything?" she finally asked.

He stretched out his legs, crossed one boot over the other. "I visited my old stomping grounds today. Colossal mistake."

"Why?"

"As you've figured out, I didn't have a happy home and two loving parents. My mom passed when I was seven and then it was just Johnny and me for a long time."

"Johnny?"

"My father."

"He asked you to call him by his name?"

"No, but I wasn't going to call him Dad. He was a shitty dad. He was—" Max broke off again abruptly and rose, disappearing into the kitchen. He returned with the wine bottle and a refreshed whiskey. "He didn't know the first thing about raising kids," he said, topping off her wine. "Johnny did one thing right, though, and that was meet Sally. If it weren't for her, I'm not sure I'd still be here. She saved my ass. Straightened me out. Which is why I'm here now, doing the play, keeping an eye on her. She's the closest thing I've ever had to a mom, and I'd pretty much do anything for her."

"Did you see your dad when you went to Templeton today?"

"He doesn't live there anymore. He's up in Watsonville now with his girlfriend. She's a farmer, and he smokes the weed she grows."

"She grows cannabis?"

"And strawberries." His upper lip curled. "I'm sure she's a nice enough lady. All my dad's girlfriends are nice. They fall for his looks, and think he's charming. By the time they figure out he's not, he's moved into their house or double-wide and maxed out their credit cards."

"He doesn't work?"

"Hasn't in twenty years or more. His girlfriends support him. He's been this way his entire life. Growing up, he barely kept a job. We had so many unpaid bills, just piling up. So much debt. Dad would buy things, and lose things. A car, a couch, a refrigerator, motorcycles. All bought and then re-possessed because Dad didn't continue the payments."

"Your refrigerator?"

"Nice, huh?"

"How awful for you."

"Made for good stories. I'm full of them. I've got a good one about a motorcycle. Want to hear?"

She nodded, fascinated.

"Dad got word that they were coming to repossess one of his bikes, a newer Harley, and he was so pissed off that he destroyed the bike. Drove his truck into it and over it. If the dealership wanted it back, well, they could have it back."

"Flattened," she said, shocked.

"And that's Johnny in a nutshell."

"I'm sorry."

"Me, too. Because my one goal as a man was to be nothing like him. But I guess the DNA is strong, and I don't know if it's nature or nurture, but I'm no better with rela-tionships than he is. I always thought I'd be different, but I've been married twice, both marriages failed, and I'm not going to do that again."

"More mistakes?" she asked.

"Yep."

"Why did the marriages end?"

"Different reasons for each, but my takeaway was the same—enjoy women, love women, but don't make promises. I'm terrible at commitments." He frowned into his whiskey. "How did we even get on this subject?"

"I'm not sure, but I'm glad. I've been trying to figure you out. You seemed awfully perfect there for a while."

"Ha! Had you fooled."

"Take it easy, handsome. You're still pretty perfect."

"I'm not. Trust me. My first wife was an angel, and I blew it. She was a makeup artist working on *Forever Young*, the TV soap I was in. We'd known each other for a couple of years before we ever dated. I'd known her when she was still married, and then after her divorce, I gave it six months and asked her out. The divorce made Cynthia a single mom, and I convinced her to give me a chance. We were supposed to start slow, but within a year we were talking marriage and buying a place together."

"Did you?" Margot asked.

"Yes. And everything was good, really good, until I screwed up."

"You had an affair?"

"Not a physical one, no, but I grew close to an actress I was working with in Australia. We spent a lot of time together. I was never in love with her, we never got physically intimate, but we talked a lot, and shared things with each other that I probably wouldn't have if I was home with Cynthia. One day we'd gone to a café and we were talking. She was upset. I took her hand, and we were photographed like that. The pictures were sold to tabloids, and Cynthia was devastated. She felt humiliated and betrayed, and that was that. Trust had been broken, and Cynthia wanted nothing more to do with me." Max gave Margot a crooked smile. "I learned another huge life lesson. The people you love most should be treated the best, and when you find the one, fight like hell for that relationship."

"She wouldn't give you a second chance?"

Max dragged a hand through his hair, pushing it off his forehead. "I understand why she didn't. Her former husband, a stunt actor, couldn't keep his dick in his pants. She hoped I'd be different, and instead, I was as unfaithful as he was."

"I thought you said you didn't sleep with the actress."

"I didn't. But we were close. If I was just banging some young actress, that would be bad, but to actually have feelings for her? In Cynthia's mind that was unforgivable."

Margot didn't say anything for a long moment, imagining how hurt Cynthia must have been, and then picturing Max on set, immersed in a role. "It's tough, because I can see both sides," she said, looking up at him. "In our world, you're away from your family a lot. The people you work with often become a second family, especially when you're on set, or traveling with a show. There were so many affairs and hookups when I was on tour. It wasn't for me, but it's hard not to be lonely."

"As long as you don't defend me. I was wrong, and it's a mistake I will never make again."

"So you might marry again," she said.

"No. And no kids, either. I have no desire to screw up another generation."

"You're very hard on yourself."

His gaze met hers, held. "I'm determined to hold myself accountable."

Their eyes remained locked. She couldn't look away. Margot was hooked, impossibly drawn to him, everything in her responding to him whenever they were together. Her body was humming right now, and although she'd struggled to stay detached, and she'd been determined to keep her distance, it wasn't working. Max had this uncanny ability to pull her in and make her feel. Care. Need. She hadn't realized how numb she'd been until she felt these intense quivers and sparks as sensation and emotion returned, waking her up, bringing her to life.

But she didn't trust desire. She didn't trust lust. Not even infatuation. Max was not sticking around. He wasn't going to be her person, not for the long haul, and that's what she really did want. If she were being completely honest with herself, she hoped one day to find her person. Someone to share life with. Someone to grow old with. And yet Max had just said he didn't make promises. He didn't do commitments.

She forced herself to focus on what he'd said, not what she wanted. "Was your divorce really painful?"

"We'd been separated for almost a year before the divorce was finalized."

Margot tried to imagine being married to someone like Max, and she couldn't picture it. Couldn't even visualize what a normal day would be like. "It still had to have hurt."

"To be honest, it was a relief."

"That bad?"

"We had a stormy relationship. It was exhausting."

"I'm sorry." She was, too. Because despite his warnings, despite his tough words, she liked him. Wanted him.

He was from her world—not the acting world—but the area she'd been raised in. Their towns were just ten miles apart. He'd driven the same backroads she had. He'd played beneath the same hot summer sun. She wondered if he'd run through sprinklers, and sucked on Popsicles. Those were the things they did in Paso in the summer. You played. You tried to stay cool. You enjoyed being a kid.

She worried that Max didn't have that childhood. His mom died when he was seven. His dad wasn't loving. Margot suspected he'd been terribly lonely as a boy. Thank God for Sally. "I'm glad you're here now," she said, meaning it. "Sally needed you. And considering the state of the play, I did, too."

"You are one of the most sincere people I have ever met," he said, the corner of his mouth lifting in an incredibly sexy, bone-melting smile.

"You like sincere people?"

"I like you." His gaze locked with hers. "But I think you know that."

She swallowed hard, feeling the heat in his eyes and the invitation in his smile. "I should go," she murmured, setting her nearly empty wineglass down.

"Or not," he said.

Shivers raced through her, and her pulse drummed, a beat she felt all the way through her. She was so tempted by him, so hungry for touch and pleasure. Skin. She had a feeling he'd be amazing in bed. She had a feeling she could get lost in him.

But what about after?

She wasn't good with breakups and pain. She dreaded being cast off. Discarded.

Margot rose. "I can't." *But I want to.*

"I'm driving Sally to her doctor's in the morning," she added for good measure. Mentioning Sally was always a reality check. Neither of them wanted to hurt her, or disappoint her. Margot picked up her purse, checked that she had her phone and keys. "Don't get up. I'll see myself out. Good night."

It was just five minutes to Sally's, and after parking, she slipped quietly into the dark house, and locked the door behind her.

Margot peeped into Sally's room—Sally was sound asleep, the TV on low, but that's how she liked it—and headed to the guest room, where she changed into pajamas and climbed into bed, trying not to think or feel.

It was hard, though.

She could still see that smile of Max's, and the way it heated his eyes. He'd looked her up and down, desire humming between them.

She'd wanted to stay.

She'd wanted the fire, wanted to burn. But at the last second sanity prevailed.

Maybe when the play was over . . . maybe in the last week she could take a risk. Let go of her ridiculous need for control. But not yet.

That didn't make sleep come, though. She couldn't relax. Couldn't stop replaying Max's words in her head. He told her stories that shocked her, but more than the shock was the pain. To lose his mom so young, and then to have such a destructive, callous father. Her heart hurt for him, for the boy he'd been. But she also found herself admiring him even more. Considering his examples, he was a caring man, a loyal man. A man she liked very much.

A man she could love, given the chance.

It was almost three when she fell asleep, and Margot slept fitfully. When she woke it was after eight. Margot left bed in a panic. She'd overslept. In the kitchen she found Sally at the table drinking coffee and talking on the phone.

It sounded like a business call, so Margot quietly poured herself a cup and was about to slip away when Sally ended her call and turned to look at Margot. "Are you coming down sick?" Sally asked, concerned.

"No. Just a headache. Didn't need that second glass of red wine," Margot said, which was true, but her headache wasn't as much about the wine as how she felt.

"I can get someone else to drive me—"

"No. Absolutely not. I'm fine. Just need coffee and maybe a couple Tylenol." She forced a smile. "Are you hungry? I could scramble some eggs."

Sally shuddered. "I don't like breakfast. You know that." She waved Margot off. "Go deal with your headache, but we should leave in a half hour if that works for you."

"Definitely."

The coffee helped her head, and a good shower did the rest. Margot was ready with ten minutes to spare. The drive to the medical center near the hospital was easy, and the appointments went well. Sally's doctors cleared her to return to work for a few hours each day, and instructed her to start physical therapy twice a week. Sally was thrilled she'd been cleared to drive, provided she didn't jump back into her busy schedule.

Margot listened, thoughts drifting to Max. This morning she remembered what he'd said about his childhood, and his dad. It made her heart ache a little. She'd had an almost idyllic childhood. His had been anything but.

Margot made a mental note to call her dad later. She hadn't checked in with him for a few days. Time was passing so quickly. It seemed as if she wasn't getting anything important done.

Margot had just dropped Sally back at her house after the doctor visit when her phone rang. It was Jen.

"What are you doing right now?" Jen asked. "Can you break away for a little bit? Meet for lunch?"

"Now?"

"It is one, which is considered lunchtime," Jen answered dryly.

Margot couldn't believe that her day was already half-gone.

"It's not a social lunch," Jen added quickly. "I've met a really interesting theater major from Cal Poly. She's into design. Costumes, sets, all the visuals. I think you should talk to her. She came to the meeting with me today prepared. She has some really good ideas for *Barefoot in the Park*. I'd mentioned to her that you want to update the story a little bit, but not all the way, and she'd love to show you her ideas."

"Where are you?"

"Linn's. We've got a table by the window."

Linn's was just a few blocks away, south of the theater, and a brief walk. Passing the outside of the restaurant, Margot spotted Jen and the student inside. Entering the restaurant, Margot slipped past the hostess and walked to the table.

Jen moved over, giving Margot the outside chair. "Margot, I'd like you to meet Capri. Capri is entering her final year at Cal Poly, and has wonderful ideas for the play. At least, I think they're wonderful. Capri, this is Margot Hughes, the director, as well as one of the stars of *Barefoot in the Park*."

Capri rose partway and held out her hand. "It's very nice to meet you. I've followed your career."

Margot shook Capri's hand. "Mine?"

"Hometown girl makes good. You and Max are two of the biggest names to have come out of this area—well, you two and Josh Brolin."

"I forgot Josh was from San Luis area. Which town?" Margot asked, settling into her seat.

"Templeton. Same as Max." Capri smiled. "I know because I'm from Templeton, too. Well, I was born there. My parents moved to Santa Maria when I was in junior high, so I still think of Templeton as my hometown." Capri adjusted her oversized black glasses, which weren't quite cat eyes, but definitely statement glasses. Her hair was short and spiky, shaved on one side, with the other dyed a rich burgundy. She had a piercing in her nose, more piercings in her ears, and despite her colorful appearance, her expression was serious and all business.

"I brought some ideas with me," Capri said, shifting topics. "I spent some time last night researching the play, and how it reflects its time period, and I think the sixties are important for a lot of reasons, from the rise of cold war politics, to the civil rights movement, assassinations, student protests, and the Vietnam War. Much like today, it was a tumultuous time, and historians claim it was perhaps the most divisive in American history—although I think many would say today is equally divisive. The point is, America gave birth to this generation gap, and Neil Simon was very aware of all these cultural and political shifts. His play reflects the sixties beautifully. Corie is a free spirit. She's outspoken and passionate, young and idealistic. Paul isn't as idealistic. He's quite practical, and he's struggling to keep up with his bride, not wanting to be the 'heavy,' but he is the provider, and his profession is quite conservative."

She took a breath, looked at Margot, waiting for comment.

Margot smiled. "You know your stuff," she said approvingly.

"As I said, I've brought some ideas for you. I'm very visual and think it's easier to show you my vision than try to explain it." Capri pulled out a tablet and typed something in. She'd sketched the apartment set, showing the front door, the window, the stairs, the closet, and the bedroom door. The sketch was basic, just the essential outline, and then she changed screens and the set was in color. Decorated. The walls were avocado, the couch was gold. The lamp next to the couch was teal. Throw pillows were orange. They were most definitely the colors of the sixties, but not the soft tones that might have been seen in the late fifties. These were psychedelic, the hues loud, and cheerfully clashing.

"This is a rather classic nineteen sixties interior," Capri said, using the stylus to zoom in on some details. "This is how the apartment looks at the end of the play. We know the apartment is empty in the beginning, they've only just moved in that day. During the play, Corie continues to add to it, and she's young and hip, as well as eclectic, so we'd embrace that, because she embraces her own aesthetic. Paul isn't as comfortable in this environment. It's not particularly restful for him," she added. "After all she's often teasing Paul about being a stuffed shirt, which we know he doesn't like."

Margot was impressed with Capri's research. "This is *really* good."

RTER

s." Margot nodded, pleased. Relieved. "Looks
plan."

een typing away on her keyboard, making
are we going to move forward?" she asked,

riends at Cal Poly who can build the set," Capri
get in a pinch, I can always enlist my dad. He's
tion, and he knows everyone. I'm going to focus
es."

re an angel," Margot said.

aughed. "Not at all. But I do love the theater world."
too." Margot smiled at her warmly. "I'm looking
to working with you."

'll see me at the playhouse later tonight," Capri an-
. "Too excited to stay away."

Capri took the praise in stride and swiped the screen, pulling up a very good illustration of Max in different dark burnt-orange pants, flared at the bottom, and fitted at a slightly higher waist. With the burnt-orange pants, he wore a bright orange-gold shirt with a wide white collar. In another illustration he was dressed in fitted blue paisley pants with a dark blue button-down shirt, again with that wide collar. Over the blue shirt was a brown vest. In another sketch he was wearing a rust corduroy jacket, paired with matching rust pants. "Jen mentioned you were considering changing the roles, flipping Max and Corie in your production, which is why I'm showing you Max as the cool one."

"He's definitely mod here." Margot smiled, imagining Max wearing these fitted shirts and trousers that would hug his chest, thighs, and butt. Every woman in the audience would swoon. Margot felt a little swoony just thinking about him in such tight shirts and pants.

"Obviously, if Max is going to play the role as written, we'd put him in classic nineteen sixties suits, and you'd have the fun wardrobe. But for the sake of consistency, here is how I'd dress you if you are the lawyer." Capri tapped her screen, and this time it was Margot in the sketches, wearing dark suits that looked like a flight attendant uniform. The straight, narrow skirts hit below the knee, and the double-breasted jacket was cropped at the waist. The blouse underneath was white, and boring. There were a couple of variations of the suit, but in each the colors were neutrals—charcoal, navy, and black. But Margot appreciated the details Capri included—gloves, leather handbags, neat hairstyle, discreet pearl earrings.

"You make me wish I was the fun one," Margot said. "I love your vision."

"Thank you."

"Did you design all of these yourself?"

"Yes, and I do have an alternative idea," Capri said. "If you're open to it?"

"Definitely," Margot said.

"I've moved the time period up, taking the play from the sixties and moving it into the nineties."

"Why the nineties?" Margot asked, intrigued.

"Well, it's the advent of the world as we know it today. Technology was making huge strides, and communication was forever changed. We had our first cell phones, we saw the introduction of email and the internet. Eventually people could text on their phones. We were no longer tied to a desk, or locked into one method of communication. In terms of design, it's a fascinating period, as it was the decade that became a reaction to the excesses of the eighties. Interior design became much more minimalistic. Fashion saw a lot more monochromatic design. The silhouettes were lean, streamlined. There was a strong Asian influence in interiors, as well as that black-and-white and neutral color palette." Capri held up a finger. "But music was having an influence, too. Think grunge. Bless Kurt Cobain. Rock, indie, British pop, ska."

Margot felt like she was sitting across the table from a pro. How was Capri still a college student? "You're blowing me away. How do you know all this?"

"I'm a designer. I pay attention to culture and history and society."

"And art," Jen said. "Because you are an artist."

Capri flashed Jen a smile and then continued with her presentation. "In this version, Margot, your suits would have those big padded shoulders, and loose, boxy shape. Wide-legged trousers. Low heels. You'd wear those neutrals again, cream silk blouse."

"And Max?" Margot asked.

Capri swiped twice on the screen, pulling up a compilation of photos featuring not Max, but a young Brad Pitt. "All these pictures were taken in the nineties. Like other young hipsters, Brad wore lots of black and jeans. During

the day, it might b
sweater, paired with
ence right there. At n
black shirts, or black l
nineties wardrobe it wo
accessible." She looked

"Yes." She realized th
get their attention, but Ma
food right now. She held
needed one more minute. "Th
soon as the waiter slipped aw
way, the sixties or the nineties.
be able to meet with Max later, s

"I have a job this afternoon, bu
later tonight, maybe when rehearsa

That was a lot of driving back an
was expensive. Time was valuable fo
thought a moment. Did Max need to
care?

Jen must have been reading her mind.
tor. You're taking such an original approac
with your gut. Max will be happy with whate

"You want me to go with the nineties," M

"Has it been done that way?" Jen asked. "N
matters, but imagine the music you could d
young to ever be into the Seattle music scene, b
most hear Nirvana's 'Smells Like Teen Spirit'
that theater as the curtain rises and Paul is getting t
ment ready to show Corie. Talk about setting the sc

Margot bit into her lip, thinking Nirvana blaring
be a cool and edgy way to kick off the play. Margot
liked the simple minimalistic set and the monochrom
wardrobe of the nineties. It would work well. "Okay."

"Okay?" Jen repeated, glancing at Capri and then bac
to Margot.

"Nineties it
like we have
Jen had b
notes. "How
glancing up
"I have f
said. "If we
in constru
on costum
"You
Capri
"Me,
forward
"Yo
swered

Chapter 12

MARGOT WENT TO SALLY'S AFTER WORK TO GATHER HER things from the guest room since Sally didn't need "baby-sitters" anymore. When she arrived, she was happy to see Max's car in front of the house, but once she went inside, Max and Sally were nowhere to be found. Puzzled, Margot packed and carried her overnight bag out to her car and was just about to leave when she saw Sally and Max walking up the driveway.

"Hi." Margot shielded her eyes as they approached. "You went for a walk?"

"He insisted I get exercise." Sally sounded indignant, but she had good color in her cheeks. "I would have rather had a cocktail."

Margot smiled. "I'm sure you can have those again soon."

"*If* she exercises," Max said. "Sally was saying she doesn't need the physical therapy, so I took her on a walk to show her that yes, she does. Her strength has diminished and she's winded from a little walk."

"I know what I need to do," Sally said tartly. "And I'm

grateful for all your help, but you two may go. I'm ready to have my house—and life—back, and I'm sure you have rehearsal soon."

"We do," Max said. "I'll be heading to the theater once I see that you drink some water and cool down." He glanced at Margot. "Remind me later that I need to talk to you."

Margot nodded, waved goodbye, but as she drove to the theater, wondered what he needed to speak to her about. Hopefully everything was good. When she'd left his house last night, things between them had been good. A little hot, a little bothered, but positive.

She wasn't going to worry, though. She trusted Max. He didn't play games. Whatever he had to tell her would be fine.

And it was, she realized two hours later, when Max pulled her aside at the theater, walking her to the lobby so they could talk without others close, his hand on her back, so warm against her skin.

She glanced at his profile, trying to read his expression. He looked like Max—rugged and handsome.

In the lobby his hand fell away and he gave her an encouraging smile. "Don't look worried. Nothing's wrong. I simply wanted you to know that I'm not going to be here for rehearsal tomorrow. I've got an audition in L.A. but I promise I'll be back before Monday's rehearsal. Will you be okay with that?"

"Of course. I'm excited for you. What audition, or can you not say?"

"Remember the Lee Sheridan screenplay you saw at my house?"

She nodded.

"I'm going to read for it," he said.

"Very cool." Margot leaned in, hugged him. "You'll be fabulous."

He wrapped an arm around her, keeping her close. "Want to go with me?"

She lifted her head, looked up into his eyes. "To L.A.?"

He nodded. "I'm leaving after rehearsal tonight. Come with me. I've booked a room at Shutters in Santa Monica. We can make a weekend out of it."

"The play—"

"Will be here when you get back. And so will Sally, the office team, all your work. When is the last time you went anywhere, besides beautiful, scenic Paso?"

"So ruthless," she laughed, patting his chest.

"Is that a yes?"

"I have nothing packed. I'm not prepared."

"So go home and pack. I'll pick you up when you're ready to go."

She knew why she should say no, and yet a big part of her wanted to say yes. She'd never stayed at Shutters but had seen photos. It was right on the beach, close to Venice, great restaurants nearby. But Shutters wasn't the main draw. Max was the draw. Being alone with Max in a luxurious hotel? A hotel with room service? They could stay in bed—

Margot's head jerked up and she looked at Max, really looked at him, and the fantasy faded.

The moment she slept with Max, everything would change. Was she ready for that? Was he?

And beyond Max, what about her commitments? She'd promised her dad she'd be there for dinner Saturday night. She was going to pick something up and they were going to stay in, maybe play cards or Scrabble. Her dad and mom used to play a lot of Scrabble.

Her dad was looking forward to her company. She couldn't cancel, not only because he'd been sick this past week, but because it didn't feel right putting him off, putting him last. She'd done that when she was younger, only she wasn't a girl anymore. Her family was important to her, as important as her dreams, as important as her needs.

"Max, I can't," she whispered. "I promised my dad we'd have dinner Saturday. He'd understand if I asked for a rain check, but I don't think I can."

"It's okay," Max answered, bringing her even closer. "You love your dad. I respect that."

She tipped her head back to better see Max's face. She couldn't tell what he was thinking. She was still getting to know him, and he wasn't always easy to read. "Maybe when you come back . . . maybe we can have dinner?"

His eyes searched hers, and then his head dropped and he kissed her. No tentative kiss here. It was demanding, almost consuming, and she didn't know how long they stood in the lobby, lost in each other. They might have remained there all night if it weren't for Jen's knock on the door. Margot and Max broke apart. Margot blushed, laughed. Max was smiling, completely at ease.

"Ahem," Jen said loudly, clearing her throat. "Everyone's waiting for you guys. But no hurry," she said dryly. "When you're ready."

They returned to the stage, but Margot's head was spinning. Oh, those kisses. Heaven help her. What on earth was she doing?

Max Russo was gorgeous, and he made her feel things she hadn't felt in forever, but this wasn't safe, or smart. Why did she think she could play with fire?

MARGOT USED FRIDAY TO WORK WITH THE CREW. THE set was starting to come together. There were hanging racks with costumes. Tables were filling with props. They were making progress, and according to Heather, tickets were selling quickly, so quickly that all of the opening weekend was sold out, and most of the tickets for the next two weekends. If sales continued like this, the season could very well sell out—even before the show opened.

Saturday morning Margot slept in and then after a walk and some stretching, she showered and tackled chores at home. Laundry. Bills. Responding to emails she'd let slide.

Saturday evening, Margot picked up dinner from her

dad's favorite Italian restaurant downtown. She'd called and asked him what he wanted, and he'd said lasagna, chicken Parmesan, garlic bread, maybe one of those big, chopped salads. Margot had laughed. "That's a lot of food, Dad."

"I'm saving some for tomorrow. It'll be my lunch and dinner."

"I guess after not eating this week, you have an appetite."

"That's right."

"Tiramisu, too, Dad?"

"I've got some ice cream here. That should do."

Margot arrived at the house just before six, and let herself in, giving a shout so her dad knew she was there.

"In the den," he called back. "Watching the end of the game."

Her dad was a huge San Francisco Giants fan. She grew up watching him watch games. He loved the 49ers, too, and the Golden State Warriors. Dad had played both baseball and football for Fresno State, but when he blew out his knee his sophomore year, he shifted his interests, got a degree in criminology, and moved back to Paso, where he got a job with the county, working for the sheriff's department. He spent his entire career with the sheriff's department, was getting close to retirement when her mom died. He stayed on another couple of years because he needed that family since there was no one else at home.

Margot joined her dad in the den, glanced at the game. It was only the fifth inning. "You should have told me there was a game on tonight. We could have rescheduled."

"I'm taping it. I can always rewind and watch it later."

"Even after you know the final score?"

"I like to see the big plays. If there are no big plays, I might not watch it."

"So what should I do? Dish up dinner . . . wait?" she asked.

"How about we wait until the bottom of this inning? Sit with me a minute. It's nice to have my favorite girl here."

Smiling, she sat down on the arm of his chair. He took her hand and held it. Together they watched the first batter strike out, and then the next. The program cut to commercial break, and her dad looked at her. "You look pretty tonight," he said. "Are you doing something different with your hair?"

Margot reached up, smoothing her hair. "I just left it down. I think you usually see me with it in a ponytail."

"It looks pretty like that." He kept looking at her. "Is any of that your natural color, or do you have to do things to keep it lighter? Your mom did things to her hair. She'd get it done every couple months or so."

"It's all color now, Dad."

He looked a little embarrassed. "I didn't know. It's very nice. Natural."

The game was back and the pitcher got rid of the third batter as quickly as he dispensed with the last two. Inning over, Margot rose to go dish up dinner. The doorbell rang. Her dad started to get up and she waved him down. "I've got it."

"Check the peephole first. Don't open to any strangers."

It was Max on the doorstep. He was holding a pie box and a bottle of wine. She couldn't believe it. Her hand shook as she unlocked the door and swung it open. "Max!"

"Margot."

"What are you doing here?"

"Heard we're having Italian tonight." He held up the bottle of red wine. "It's a Paso red."

She wasn't sure what to think and shook her head. "Your audition? How did it go?"

"Well, really well, and so I came back, hoping I could see you. Spend time with you. As well as get to know your dad."

"I'm not sure this is a good time," she said. "He's watch-ing his game—"

"I know. He invited me to join you. I'm a Giants fan, too. Hope that's okay."

She darted him a sidelong glance, her insides all butterflies and hope. Soft, tender hope. She opened the door a
little wider. "When did you talk to him?"

"This afternoon, after I returned from L.A."

She blinked and exhaled, and then thanked him for the
pie—banana cream, a family favorite—and put it in the
fridge. She handed Max a wine opener. "Do you mind?"

"Not at all."

"Margot, who is here?" her dad called from the den.

She shook her head at Max, and then walked into the
den, and leaned over to kiss the top of her dad's head. "As
if you don't know."

Her dad reached up to catch her hand and give it a little
squeeze. "Did he bring the right pie?"

"He did." Margot knelt next to his chair. "How did this
happen?"

Her dad shrugged. "We had a little man chat."

"I didn't know men chatted."

He smiled, pleased with himself, and his happiness
made her heart ache in the best sort of way. It was lovely to
see him in such good spirits.

"Max came over earlier today. He was on his way back
from L.A., and he stopped by to introduce himself. He wanted
me to know he was a big fan of yours, and he said if I ever
needed anything, to let him know, and gave me his number."

"When did you invite him to dinner?"

"An hour or so after he arrived."

"He was here an hour?"

"Well, two, but some of that second hour was watching
the Giants. Tonight's a doubleheader."

Her eyes stung as she got to her feet. "Oh, Dad, what
would I do without you?"

"I don't think we have to cross that bridge now. But I
would like my lasagna and garlic bread, if you don't mind."

They had dinner together in the den, and then when the
Giants game ended, they played Scrabble. Her dad usually

won, but Max was getting the high scores tonight. Clearly his fancy education had paid off.

But then it was nearly nine and time to go. Margot said good night to her dad, kissing his cheek. Her dad and Max shook hands, and then her dad surprised her by pulling Max in for a hug.

Outside the house by their cars, Margot looked at Max. She didn't want to say good night, not yet, but she was wading into dangerous waters. "This isn't supposed to happen," she said, leaning against her car. "I can't get involved with you."

The corner of his mouth lifted. "Was that in the Cambria Playhouse volunteer contract?"

She smiled, a little of her tension easing. "You know what I mean. We have a responsibility to the play, and Sally. If something were to go wrong . . ." She shrugged. "It could get so messy."

"What would go wrong?"

"Oh, come on. Everything could go wrong."

"Or, everything could go right. I like you. And I think you like me."

She flushed and bit her bottom lip because yes, she liked him, way more than she should. "I do like you. But I'm not into gratuitous sex, either. I'm not someone that can easily separate love and affection. If we get physical. . . ." Her voice faded, and she looked at him and then away. "We don't want to doom the play before opening night."

"Let's not have sex, then."

She lifted her head, her gaze locking with his. "Seriously?"

"Let's take it off the table. Agree it's not going to happen. That way you can feel safe spending time with me, and not have to worry about fending off my advances."

Margot laughed. "I also know about reverse psychology."

He smiled, his expression warm. "I do mean it. I want to spend time with you. I want to kiss you and touch you, but we can have limits. Keep things tame. Keep you feeling in control, because I think that's what you're afraid of."

Her cheeks grew hotter, and her tummy did a flip. She'd never wanted anyone as much as she wanted him then. "You're dangerous."

"Not that dangerous. Ask Sally."

She shook her head and then took a step toward him, and another, until she was in his arms. "What's happening?" she whispered.

His hand stroked the length of her back, ending on her hip. "You tell me."

Margot searched his eyes, the desire thudding in her veins, drumming low in her belly. She wanted him, craved him, craved his mouth and his body and his skin.

"What if I come over?" she said.

"We could do that," he said, cupping her backside, setting everything within alight. "See how we feel."

Margot's mouth dried and her heart was pounding and, unable to speak, she simply nodded.

He opened the door of her car, waited for her to be seated and buckle up. "Want to follow me?" he asked.

She nodded again and, once he was behind the wheel, shifted into drive and followed him back to his oceanfront cottage.

Max waited for her to park, and then as she left her car, he took her hand and walked her to his door. The first kiss came as he unlocked the door. "What do you feel like doing?" he asked, securing the dead bolt. "We can watch the news, play some cards—"

"You're hilarious."

He smiled, and her stomach did a dramatic free fall. She leaned forward and kissed him. "What do you want?" she asked him.

"You already know the answer to that one."

"But that's off the table," she teased.

"That's right. We'll just chat," he said, pressing a kiss to the corner of her mouth. "Talk about our signs, and our favorite colors, and whether we liked mac and cheese as kids."

"I didn't," she said, hooking her fingers over the waistband of his jeans. "I thought it was gross."

"I did. I liked it even more when Sally would add tuna to it."

"Ew."

He smiled and kissed a spot on her jaw, and then below her jaw. She shivered, her pulse doing the wildest, most erratic dance ever.

"Thirsty?" he asked, trailing kisses along her jawbone to her ear.

"No."

"Is there anything you want?" he persisted, holding her close.

She sighed at the feel of his hard body against hers. He felt so good, all that muscle and warmth. She swallowed hard. "Just you," she said, dizzy, aroused, wanting everything that she hadn't experienced in so long.

He stroked her cheek, slipping his hand under her hair to cup her nape. "I can help you with that."

"Thank goodness."

His head dipped, his mouth covering hers, his lips parting hers. He sucked the air from her mouth, drawing her breath into him, and she shuddered, melting into him. Max held her easily, his body solid, strong. He shaped her to him, her hips to his, thigh to thigh. She felt him everywhere, pleasure and sensation.

Max started with her neck, kissing beneath her ear, and along her jaw, one slow, deliberate kiss after another, before tilting her chin up, giving him more access to her skin. He kissed his way down her neck, until halfway down, he bit at a tendon and she gasped. Desire flooded her. Her insides were hot. Those kisses, and that bite, had her humming, her nerves all exquisitely alert, and waiting.

He made her wait, too, pausing between kisses to let her breathe, and feel. He unbuttoned her top, pushing it aside so that his tongue could lick her collarbone, even as his palm captured her breast, fingers closing around her nipple.

It was hard to focus, feeling as much as she was, her body tingling, her breath hitching as he made her arch and press closer to him.

His mouth moved to her nipple, tugging on it through the lace of her bra, the heat and pressure of his mouth making her hotter, wetter. Margot's heart raced. Her body was boneless. She didn't want him to stop, she wanted every touch, every sigh of pleasure. It had been forever since she'd felt like this. Since she'd felt good. Alive. Beautiful.

Max swung her into his arms, carried her into the bedroom, and placed her on the bed. His hands smoothed her shoulders, caressed her arms, and then while kissing her, he unhooked her bra, pushing the delicate straps off her shoulders. Somehow she was flat on her back, and he was giving her breasts attention again, teasing, sucking both nipples until she was panting, squirming. He worked his way down her rib cage, exploring her ribs, her skin, peeling off her remaining clothes as he went, finding her hip bone, blowing a breath across the skin. She shuddered as he kissed the inside of her thigh.

He was so good, and he took so much time, and Margot didn't know what to do other than feel. By the time his mouth found her there, his tongue on her most tender, sensitive skin, she wasn't just boneless, she was mindless. The man had exceptional technique. She was a puppet in his hands, and Max wasn't in a hurry to bring her to climax, apparently enjoying her whimpers, her sighs, her hand on his shoulder and then tangling in his hair. She could feel the orgasm building, knew it was coming, and it was extraordinary, the tension, the anticipation. Margot had never been more ready for anything, every nerve ending tensing, every nerve screaming, and then the first wave almost hit, it was almost there, almost but not quite, and she exhaled hard, frantic, and then his hands, his mouth all came together, exerting the right pressure, in the right way, and she lost it, shattering. It was all fireworks, all brilliant little specks of light exploding in her mind, her body lit with the most incredible sensation.

And emotion.

Joy. Relief. Release.

She'd never felt anything like it. Ripple after ripple of pleasure, she was out at sea, lost in space, completely out of her body. Detached from the world, and worries. Suspended in feeling, and oh, how she felt, feeling everything and nothing.

Wrecked, Margot couldn't move or speak.

Max moved behind her, his arm around her chest, holding her against him.

Tears pricked the back of her eyes as she struggled to return to herself. No one had ever taken so much time to touch her, pleasure her. No one had ever made her feel so safe and yet alive.

She put her hand on his arm, holding him. But still there were no words, the shudders continuing, the sensation overpowering.

Thankfully, Max seemed content to simply hold her.

She knew she ought to ask what he wanted or needed. Was he impatient for her to reciprocate? But then, feeling him against her, feeling his calm, his warmth, she realized he wasn't asking for anything. He was okay, he was good. And so she closed her eyes, savoring how wonderful it felt to feel safe, and whole, and beautiful.

To feel so good with him, in his arms, in his bed.

When Margot woke later in the night, all the lights in the house were out, but Max was still there with her, holding her. It felt good, and right.

She turned a little, pressing her face to his chest. He smelled delicious, and he was so warm, and solid. She'd never been with anyone built like Max. He was strong, his chest wide, his arms thick with muscle. She put a hand to his biceps, gently touching it.

Her touch woke him. He stirred. "Hey," he said huskily. "You okay?"

"So good. Sorry I fell asleep on you."

"You were tired."

"Still, it seems rude, especially as I didn't even say thank you."

He laughed, a deep, sexy rumble she could feel vibrating through his chest, into her. "Are we supposed to say thank you each time? Is that a Paso Robles tradition?"

Margot pressed her lips to his skin, choking back her laugh. She felt light. Happy. "What? They didn't teach this to you in Templeton? Crazy. Only ten miles away and yet clearly rubes."

He laughed and shifted his weight, rolling her onto her back. Max nudged her legs apart, settling between her thighs. Margot could feel his hardness against her. The tip of his erection pressing against her body. It felt good there. But then he felt good on her, against her. He felt like . . . home. He felt like the place she'd grown up, he felt like the people she'd loved, he felt like who she was and what she believed.

She stared up into his face, that beautifully masculine face, with those straight dark eyebrows, the angular cheekbones, the mouth. Oh, that mouth. She reached up and lightly ran her fingertip over his lips, relishing the firmness of his mouth and then the hard bristle on his jaw. He was the most beautiful man she'd ever been with, the most beautiful man she thought she'd ever know. Equally impressive, he was so generous in bed. So generous with her.

She slipped her hand around his nape, stroked it, her nails lightly grazing his scalp, his skin. "You're kind of a big deal, Max Russo."

"Oh, babe, I'm not that big. Don't get too excited."

She laughed, her eyes stinging, the happiness unexpected. But then, he was unexpected. "What a surprise you are. You've completely rocked my world."

"And we're just getting started."

She drew his head down so that she could kiss him, and this time she took charge, wanting his mouth, his tongue, his taste. He kissed her back, and it was fire, and she shifted restlessly, wanting him.

He lifted the kiss, traced her cheek. "Sweetheart, I don't have any condoms here," he said, resting his weight on his forearms.

Disappointment rushed through her, the disappointment so strong she couldn't speak for a second. She wanted him in her. She could feel the tip of him against her, smooth where she was slick, thick, warm. Margot couldn't even imagine the pleasure of him inside of her. "I can't get pregnant anymore, too old," she said. "I haven't been with anyone in ages, and I'm always very careful about everything."

He kissed her temple, and then her jaw, and then her lips. "I have been with someone, but I always use protection. And I get tested."

"Then kiss me. Be with me, in me. I want you."

He took her lips, his tongue stroking the inside of her mouth, even as his body slowly filled her, warming her, making her feel. The thrust of his hips had her sighing, and meeting him, welcoming him. The friction was incredible. The sensation mind-blowing. It was as if he'd been made for her, as if she waited all these years to be perfectly, truly loved, because that's what it felt like. She could feel him everywhere, on the inside and on the outside, and combined it was better than an orgasm.

She felt whole, full, complete.

Being with him was comforting and healing in a way she hadn't expected, and she didn't think the pleasure could be any greater, but then he reached between them, and he touched her, making sure she came when he did.

Margot could have cried. But she didn't.

The thought flashed through her—she could love this guy. She could love him forever. It was a crazy thought, completely unrealistic and impractical, and yet in that moment, she knew he'd changed her life.

She would never be the same. When Sam left her, it had cracked something inside of her. For years she'd struggled to move forward, struggled to find herself, and it had taken until now to heal.

How? How had it happened? It was a miracle.

She kissed Max and snuggled close, the afterglow a blaze. She felt as if she'd gone to a revival, one of those summer traveling churches, and found her faith. Found God. Found hope. Found life.

She was okay. She was better than okay.

She had a whole life to live, and it was going to be incredible.

MAX LAY ON HIS BACK, HOLDING MARGOT. HE'D DOZED off when she had earlier, but he hadn't slept long, waking after a half hour, glad to discover her still in his arms.

He didn't want to overthink. He just wanted to be. It felt good to simply be. No past, no future, only right now. And now was peaceful. Right now, he was utterly content.

It didn't happen often. He rarely felt this way. Which was why he didn't want to sleep. He wanted to be present and grateful. He was grateful, too. Margot was lovely. A surprise. A gift.

She stirred in his arms, eyes fluttering open. "Should I get out of here?" she asked sleepily.

"No," he answered, pulling her closer. He stroked her back. She had the most lovely back—beautiful shoulders, that long spine, the curve of hips. "It's two thirty. Do you feel like driving at two thirty in the morning?"

"I wasn't sure how you felt about me being here in the morning."

Max shouldn't laugh, but it was funny. "Did your last guy like to kick you out in the middle of the night?"

She giggled, her soft lips pressed to his shoulder. "No, but some men don't like it, I guess. I don't want to be a bother."

"A bother? I have the most passionate, gorgeous woman in California in my bed, and you think that's a bother? A distraction maybe, but who needs sleep when I have you?"

"Such a sweet talker."

"Totally being selfish. If you left, how would we make love in the morning?"

"Will we do it in the morning?"

"Unless you're ready now?"

"Now?"

"Normally I'd need a couple of hours to recover," he said, "but there's something about you that drives me crazy, because I could go again. Right now. I'd love to be in you again."

She lifted her head to look at him, her gaze locking with his.

God, she was gorgeous. So sexy.

"Really?" she murmured, and then as if to confirm, she put her hand on him, her palm and fingers wrapping around his shaft, sliding upward, her touch firm, making him even harder. "Oh, you have a lovely one."

Not just sexy, but sweet. Margot was sweet and open, the quintessential girl from next door, which he found impossibly arousing, and endearing. "A lovely one?" he growled, even as his pulse thrummed, his shaft throbbing. "A lovely what? Big toe? Clavicle?"

"Don't make me say it." Her hand squeezed tighter, her grip firm as it went up and over the head of the shaft, then down again, and he groaned. He had no words, couldn't talk, didn't want to talk as she scooted away from him and then, still stroking him, moved down to take him into her mouth. Her mouth was so hot and tight around him that he gave himself over to the pressure and friction, as she touched and licked and sucked until he was going to come. But he didn't want to come that way, not in her mouth, and he rolled away. "Any position you want to try?" he asked, his voice deep, rough even to his own ears.

She moved onto her hands and knees, giving him her beautiful backside to touch. Margot on her knees was a sight to see. He put his hands on her butt, sliding his palms to her waist, and up her back before drawing them down again.

She shuddered, and he had visions of himself pulling her down on him, taking her this way with his mouth, but he was also impatient to bury himself in her, get lost in her, and coming up on his knees, he stroked her folds before pushing deep into her.

Her soft sigh made him ache. He had to hold back, not take her hard, not wanting to hurt her. But she bucked back against him, impatient.

Her impatience burned him, making him harder.

He listened to her breathing, letting her pleasure set the pace and his rhythm. It felt natural with her, everything right.

He couldn't explain the rightness, only that she fit . . . she belonged. With him. And he left that thought alone, not wanting to overthink, not when he could just relax and let go and feel.

SUNDAY MORNING MAX MADE HER BREAKFAST. IT WAS A late breakfast. They'd slept in and then had coffee sitting outside on the deck. She was wearing one of his T-shirts, topped with a long-sleeve flannel, and it was almost like wearing a dress, the hem hitting her midthigh.

They drank their coffee and hung out. Conversation was sporadic but they were both happy. Relaxed.

Finally Max excused himself and headed to the kitchen to make eggs and French toast. He topped the French toast with ripe berries and whipped cream since he didn't have any syrup.

Margot ate her breakfast on her lap, the sun warming her, the breeze riffling her hair. "I wish I'd met you earlier in my life. We have so much in common. I think it would have been fun."

"And it's not fun now?"

She laughed at his indignant tone. "You know what I mean." She was silent, thinking, her gaze fixed out on the water. "But maybe we wouldn't have suited. Maybe me traveling so much, and you always on location would have been too challenging. It's a hard life," she said. "I admire you for still being an actor. I got to the point I couldn't sustain it."

"Everyone gets burnt out. That's why so many of us take breaks, do different things, and then come back to it. You've come back to it."

"I'm doing a community theater production. It's not Broadway." She frowned. "And I'd never do Broadway again, or the traveling shows. I came back to California to do something else."

"Be close to your dad," he said.

"And maybe, possibly, hopefully, get married and have a family." She sat very still, lost in thought, before looking at him. "It's a dream. Dreams aren't always practical, and they don't always work out."

"But they're important. They keep us going."

"True." Margot rose to take both their plates into the kitchen. She returned and leaned against the railing and looked at him. "You've been married. What's it like?"

"Like all relationships there are good days and bad days."

"So you don't recommend it?" she asked.

"I wouldn't say that," he answered. "For someone like you—"

"Someone like me?" she interrupted, tucking a strand of hair behind her ear. "What does that mean?"

"Someone who grew up in a healthy, happy family. Your parents were loving and committed to each other. You've had good role models, which would help you know how to make it work, navigate pitfalls."

"But relationships take two."

He felt a prickle of pain, a flash of memory. So few of his memories were comfortable. "Very true."

"In that case, maybe you didn't fail both times. Maybe you didn't choose the right partners, women who were emotionally secure."

"That would still be my mistake."

Margot didn't immediately say anything. Instead he watched emotions flicker across her face: guilt, frustration, and something else he couldn't define. "Is something on your mind?" he asked.

"I finally looked you up, checked out your Wikipedia page."

"Why? What did you want to know?"

Her cheeks flushed. She shrugged as if embarrassed. "More about your childhood. And then there were a few questions about your personal life."

"Learn anything?"

"Annaliese is beautiful."

"She is," he agreed, choosing his words carefully. "But you are far more beautiful—"

"No. Not even close."

He rose, and went to the railing, and kissed her. She tasted sweet, like berries and cream, and as they kissed, he hardened with desire and need. She made him feel hungry. She made him want to strip her naked and carry her to his room and kiss every inch of her, make every inch of her his. It was a very primitive, caveman response, but she had stirred something in him that was fierce and alive. He couldn't explain the need, only that he wanted her here. He liked her here and he wasn't ready for her to leave. "You make me laugh. You're smart. And incredibly good in bed."

"Stop."

"But seriously," he added, voice husky. "I love acting with you. I loved last night with you. I loved waking up with you. I realized early on that being with you, Margot Hughes, was always the best part of my day."

"You make me happy, too." Her gaze searched his, emotion darkening her eyes. "I haven't felt this way in a long time."

"You deserve to be happy. You deserve to feel good."

"And I do. Thanks to you."

He clasped her face between his hands, thumbs stroking her cheekbones, tracing the delicate pink in her cheeks. "Sam's a fool. How he let you go is beyond me."

She blinked, and there were tears glistening in her eyes. "You're good for my ego."

"You have no ego."

"Maybe that was the problem," she admitted. "If I had more pride, I would have called Sam, forced him to admit he wasn't invested anymore. Instead I pretended everything was fine, afraid to be forty and single."

"It doesn't matter what age you go through a breakup, it's always hard. It always hurts."

"And now I'm getting attached to you," she said. "I didn't want this to happen."

"Why? Because I'll leave?" he asked.

She nodded.

"But you'll come see me," he said quietly, "and I'll come back and see you. Airplanes make those visits easy. Besides, goodbyes aren't for weeks. We have until late July."

She nodded again, blinking hard.

"So don't be sad," Max said, gently wiping a tear from beneath her eye. "We're at the beginning, not the end. Let's just enjoy this."

Chapter 13

MONDAY, BEING MEMORIAL DAY, THERE WAS NO WORK, and Margot canceled rehearsal so everyone could be with their family. Happily, Margot was spending the day with Max. They'd gone for a drive, stopping for lunch in Atascadero, and then returned late afternoon so he could grill something for them on his deck for dinner.

While Max prepared the shrimp kebabs, Margot read him the email she'd gotten from Heather. There were no available tickets left the first two weeks of the show. Sally had authorized them to add the extra row of folding chairs to add ten more seats to every performance.

"Ten seats," Margot said, looking up from her phone. "It's such a small number, but for Sally, this is huge."

"It is huge. She's very happy. She's been asking me about attending one of the dress rehearsals next week. I told her we wanted her to wait until opening night so she can be surprised."

"What did she say?"

"She complained but she's alright. It's good to see her excited."

"Now we need to get the rest of the kinks worked out and we'll be okay."

"We're getting there," he said.

Margot carried their drinks outside as Max put the shrimp on the grill. He had a big salad already prepared, as well as some fragrant pilaf on the stove. "Have you heard anything back from the audition, or is it too soon?"

Max shrugged. "I think I have the role."

"You do?"

He nodded.

"How do you know?" she asked.

"Lee told me."

"When?"

"Friday, after I read."

Margot fell back in her chair, baffled. "Why didn't you tell me? This is wonderful!"

He shrugged again. "It is good. I'm happy. I'm lucky to be working."

He didn't sound that happy. She could feel his tension across the deck, heard the resistance in his voice. Margot got up and went to him, arms wrapping around him, hugging him from behind. "This is a big role," she said, cheek against his back. "And it's Lee Sheridan."

"I know."

"So . . . ?"

His hands covered her hands. "I will be on set somewhere for the next year. I might have a couple weeks off, but it's going to be a lot."

"You're used to hard work."

"Yeah, but sometimes I want—" He broke off.

She waited for him to finish. He didn't.

She let go of him and stepped around to face him, fingers hooking into the waistband of his jeans. "Just tell me I can come see you sometimes and I'll be happy."

"Yes." He clasped her face, kissed her deeply, hungrily, kissing her so long that the shrimp began to smoke.

He reluctantly let go of her to tend the shrimp skewers. "I can't think around you," he said, but he was smiling and she knew he wasn't complaining. Neither was she.

During rehearsals that week, the sparks and chemistry were so strong that Margot knew others had noticed. None of the cast or crew commented, but Sally, having returned to work, called Margot in to her office and asked her to close the door.

Margot raised an eyebrow as she sat down opposite Sally's desk. "This only happens when something has gone wrong."

"I'm hoping that's not the case." Sally hesitated, studying Margot intently. "I'm concerned."

And Margot knew. She knew this was about Max and her. But maybe she was wrong. Maybe this was about the business. She hoped it was that. "What's worrying you?"

"There is a lot of talk right now about you and Max. Not sure if you're aware of the scrutiny and speculation."

Margot shrugged. "People have to talk about something."

"Yes, but it's never comfortable when people become unkind."

"Are people being unkind?"

"He's only recently divorced. There is considerable on-line criticism about that, and you two being so hot and heavy together."

"I didn't realize there was a proper time frame for dating again after a divorce."

"I'm not worried about Max. He has a pretty thick skin. I want you to be careful. I don't want to see you hurt."

"I don't have social media accounts. I don't pay attention to online comments."

"What about what people say here? In Cambria? In Paso Robles, or San Luis Obispo? These are small towns. You don't want everyone knowing your business." Sally opened a drawer in her desk and pulled out magazines and dropped them on her desk, one after the other. *In Touch. Us Weekly. OK! Star. People.* "You guys can't keep your hands off of each other. Which is great for *Barefoot in the Park* ticket sales—I think we've sold out the entire summer season—but this play will end, and then what? Do you even know?"

"No."

"Margot, you know how much I care for you, which is why I'm speaking to you from my heart. I love Max. He's the son I never had. I've watched him go from a troubled young boy to a successful, ambitious man—but he isn't perfect." Sally's gaze was somber as she studied Margot. "Be careful. I know you're an adult. I know you're smart. I know you've a good head on your shoulders, but Max has never had a lot of security, and while he has good intentions, he tends to put his career first, and relationships second. He will be back on set in August, and I don't want you hurt."

Margot looked down at her hands, which were clenched in her lap. She didn't know if she was more embarrassed or angry, but she did know she was disappointed that Sally would think she needed this talk. Margot knew what performers were like. She knew how this industry worked. Actors routinely fell in love and lust with their costars. On tour, actors were always hooking up with each other, regardless of the relationships back home.

Margot never had, but it wasn't something she'd boast about. She'd loved Sam. It was that simple, that difficult. She was faithful to him, and if Max were hers, she'd be faithful to him, but the odds of their ending up together?

A long shot.

Maybe impossibly long, but why couldn't she hope? Dream?

Margot rose and silently stacked the tabloid magazines into a tidy pile and handed them back to Sally. "He's already told me he'll never get married again. He's said he doesn't do commitments. You're not telling me anything I don't know."

Sally looked tired, and old. "I care about you."

"I know, but, Sally, I'm already buckled in. Can't get off now. I have to go for it and try to enjoy the ride."

Margot exited Sally's office and, stopping by her desk, she grabbed her phone and purse and kept walking out the front door.

Margot walked without a direction in mind. She walked because she needed to move, walked because her emotions were bubbling up and she wasn't going to cry. She didn't want to cry. Nothing had happened. Sally had been concerned for her. So what? Her dad was probably concerned, too, but Margot wasn't in danger. She was dating.

She was having fun.

She was falling in love.

Margot heard the word in her head, felt it echo in her heart. She didn't know how it had happened. She'd resisted it—him—until she couldn't, until resistance was futile. From the beginning the sparks had been so intense. Even now she didn't know how Max felt about her. Was she important to him? Was she different? So hard to say. But it didn't seem to matter, because she was in over her head. It was too late. She cared for him so much.

Margot's walk took her past the Cambria Playhouse with the oversized posters for the play out front, displayed in wood-and-glass frames.

Capri had drawn them—a vivid illustrated poster featuring Margot and Max in the costumes she was creating for the play. The typography on the posters was even more gorgeous. Margot wanted to be sure she had one at the end of the play. She'd save it, maybe even hang it in her little cottage. She hadn't been at her cottage very much lately.

She spent most nights with Max. Some nights she slept well. Other nights she was overwhelmed by it all. She'd lost control. She had no idea how this—she and Max—would play out, but she'd see it through, and try to embrace all the emotions and fizzy sensations.

Of course Max was going to leave. That was a given. He'd be filming season 5 coming up in August. And then he had several films lined up. Another commercial in Italy to shoot. He was addicted to work, but so were most successful actors. It was part of the business. You were either fighting to become someone, fighting to remain someone, or fighting the fact you were on your way out.

Margot itched to call Max, craving reassurance. But what could she say? And what could he possibly promise her in return?

Nothing.

Sally was right. Margot was on her own with this one.

THE FINAL REHEARSALS PASSED QUICKLY. THEY WERE now in the middle of dress rehearsals, with two more complete run-throughs before opening night, on Friday.

The crew got better every night, too, moving set pieces, providing the right props, getting the lighting right, working in the proper sound. Margot and Max were also getting comfortable with their costumes and making the quick changes as needed.

"Do Sally and your dad know each other?" Max asked.

Margot hesitated and then shook her head. "No, I don't think they've ever met."

"What if we have a little dinner at my place one of these weeks? Have them both over so they could get to know each other."

She arched a brow. "You're not matchmaking, are you?" she asked, thinking of how in the play Paul tries to set his mother up with their neighbor Victor.

He grimaced. "No. No. Sally doesn't need my help in that area, either. I guess she has her eye on someone. A radiologist at the hospital."

Margot laughed. "She's busy."

"She's quite the romantic. She's been this way ever since I met her."

Margot tipped her head back and looked up at the sky. It was clear tonight, stars bright overhead. The last few days had been warm and clear, the nights were cool but still beautiful. "You don't have to cook if we have Dad and Sally over. We could go out—"

"I like to cook, and it helps avoid the cameras, too."

"Good point. They pretty much stalk you."

"You're getting a lot of attention, too. Are you okay with it?" he asked, reaching out to take her hand.

She liked the way it felt, her hand in his. She liked his touch, his warmth, his energy. With him she was almost always happy. Things felt better when they were together. "Sally mentioned it to me last week, so I avoid going online or listening to what people have to say."

"I never read the comments. My manager runs my social media so I never have to deal with it."

"That's smart."

"Speaking of my manager, she rang me earlier to let me know that there will be some theater critics in the audience opening weekend. Not sure what nights, but I imagine Friday or Saturday. Looks like our play will be getting some coverage in the bigger papers. I shared with Sally already. She was ecstatic."

"Oh, Sally and her thespian ambitions." Margot smiled at Max and he smiled back, before lifting her hand to his mouth and kissing it.

"She is happy," he said. "The first two weeks of the play have completely sold out."

"The whole season is sold out completely. We knew it would happen when you joined the cast."

"I'm glad I could help."

"Be careful not to help too much. Sally and Jen were talking, and they wondered if we'd want to add some matinee performances. I told Sally we weren't being paid enough to do two shows a day. You better back me up on that."

He grinned. "Ah, good old community theater. Howard is still appalled I'm doing all this for free."

"Hopefully we're laying the groundwork for a successful future. May it never be this challenging again."

"You know, Sally is thinking of hiring a full-time theater director. Someone who wouldn't be in a volunteer role, someone who would choose the plays, be in charge of the season, build up the theater's reputation." Max looked at her. "Would you be at all interested in such a role?"

"*No.*" Margot was adamant. "I can't imagine doing that."

"Why? Why would you not be interested in something that is so clearly in your wheelhouse?"

Margot didn't know how to answer. She didn't even know if she had a logical answer. It had been a gut response, but truly she didn't know how or why to justify her answer other than when she left New York she'd been ready to do something else. Ready to be someone else. And she'd been someone else for a couple of years now.

Was she in love with her job at Cambria Coast Development? No. But at the same time, she could lock the door, walk away from the office, and leave the problems until the next day. Ultimately, the success and failure of the business belonged to someone else. Whereas, when she was an actor, the success or failure weighed heavily on her. Because theater was an ensemble, no one could make a play successful alone. It was the entire production.

"If you could be paid what you are earning now, or earn considerably more, would you consider it? Is there any part of you that might be a little interested?" Max persisted.

"I can't answer that, not right now. My stomach is doing flip-flops. I think I'd never want to take advantage of Sally's generosity, I wouldn't want for her to go in the hole financially if plays weren't successful or my decisions weren't the right ones."

"Just keep your mind open. You don't have to make any decisions now. Who knows how you'll feel when the play ends?"

Chapter 14

OPENING NIGHT HAD FINALLY ARRIVED, AND AS WIDELY discussed, it was a sold-out show, with every extra folding chair added to accommodate Sally, the office staff, plus a few other VIPs like Margot's dad, who'd bought a ticket for himself but waited a little too long, so he was in a back corner by himself. Heather did some rearranging of seats when they added that extra row, placing him near herself so she could make sure Margot's dad had someone to visit with before the show and again at intermission.

The play went off without a hitch, and after the week of rough dress rehearsals, Margot had expected at least a few problems, but there had been none, and the energy of the play had been perfect. No missed entrances, no forgotten lines, no props in the wrong spots, and they got laughs in all the right places. If anything, there were far more laughs than Margot had anticipated, and Max had known exactly how to play to the audience, holding the exaggerated expression, holding the pose.

Despite her initial worries, the audience loved the

switched roles, and the early murmurs of surprise gave way to bursts of laughter and frequent applause. From the corner of her eye, Margot could see her dad's face, and he was enjoying himself. Sally laughed hard. The standing ovation at the end went on and on, it was hard to say how long it actually was. One minute? Two? Max, of course, got the biggest thunder of applause. For a tiny theater, it was almost deafening with the whistles and cheers when he stepped forward to bow.

Max bowed, and again, and then he turned to Margot, and brought her forward, wanting her there with him. He took her hand, smiled at her, and facing the audience, he gestured to her. The applause thundered. Margot did a half curtsy, flattered, embarrassed, relieved, exhilarated.

The curtains closed and yet the applause continued.

The stage manager had the curtains open again. Jen shooed Margot and Max out. "They want you," she said. "Go."

Max and Margot walked out, hand in hand.

As they stood on the stage, bowing again, Margot could see Sally right there in the front row where she had been all performance. She was also on her feet. She had tears in her eyes. Margot had never ever seen Sally cry, and it made her own eyes water.

Jen suddenly joined them onstage. She was carrying a huge bouquet of roses and lilies in a glorious arrangement of reds and pinks. She motioned for Max and Margot to stay put, and then asked that the house lights come on.

"We wanted to take a moment and recognize our intrepid leader, and founder, Sally Collins. Sally, could you please join us?"

A spotlight hit Sally as she made her way to the small staircase on the side of the stage. Max was there to assist her up the steps. Onstage, Jen handed the roses to Margot, and Margot in turn gave them to Sally.

A stagehand set up a mic stand in front of Sally, positioning the microphone for her.

Sally looked at Margot and then Max. She hesitated, apparently speechless, but then she found her words as she looked out at the audience. "This is not my moment. This is Max and Margot's, and the cast and crew's. Didn't they do an incredible job tonight?"

The audience clapped. Someone in the back whistled.

Sally glanced from Max and Margot to the crew and cast standing in the wings, and then she looked back at the audience. "This is also your moment," she said to the audience. "I'm so happy to see theater returned to Cambria. Live theater. Cambria has a long tradition of excellent community theater, and I'm pleased I could do my part to help bring it back."

The audience began applauding hard, and more whistles, and then the curtains closed.

Margot exhaled, tired and yet thrilled. Tonight had gone so much better than she'd hoped, and now she could relax. Savor the good feelings. She couldn't call the performance a triumph—that was awfully grandiose—but she really couldn't find anything to criticize tonight. Maybe something would come to her later, but for now, she was happy, and she hugged Sally, Max, and then Jen, and the others circling them onstage.

Sally turned to the crew and cast. "Tonight we're celebrating," she said. "We have a party for all of you."

Margot glanced at Max, wondering if he knew about it. Max met her gaze, shrugged, in the dark as much as she was.

"This is my thanks to all of you," Sally said. "You deserve to be celebrated. You've earned it. Do what you have to do to get out of here, and I'll see you at Marion's. They are waiting for us. We are taking it over, ours for the night. I'll see you there!"

Sally turned to Margot. "I've invited your dad to join us," she said. "He's going to follow Heather to the restaurant in his car, so don't worry about him."

"Thank you for including him."

Marion's was on Moonstone Drive, directly across from the water. As the cast and crew arrived at the restaurant, glasses of champagne were passed around. Waiters circled with trays of appetizers, and as the room filled, the noise increased with all the different conversations and bursts of laughter. Margot introduced her dad to members of the crew, and as it turned out, one of the grandfathers of the Cal Poly theater students had worked with her dad in Paso Robles. Margot was glad her dad was having a good time, and then when it was time to be seated, Sally indicated that she wanted Margot and her father to sit at her table. Sally wanted Max at her table, too, but he was only just walking in and going to the bar directly, as Margot imagined he wanted something other than champagne.

Seated, Sally looked happy and regal, the Sally of old, holding court at the head table. With the cast and the crew, and Sally's team from the office, there should have been twenty-seven of them in all, but there were quite a few people Margot didn't recognize. "Who are they?" Margot asked, gesturing to a group talking in the corner.

"Don is from the *Paso Robles Press*. Meredith is with the San Luis Obispo *Tribune*. Chase is with the Monterey *Herald*." Sally's gaze scanned the room. "The others might be their guests, or they could also be from other media. I had Jen invite quite a few from the area. They're not critics—that would be unethical to wine and dine anyone who reviews—but there's nothing wrong with including some press at dinner. They might want to do some interviews later, some feature stories on the theater. It's historic and has cultural merit."

"You forget nothing," Margot said, so glad to be off her feet, and sitting down. Her father was enjoying the beer Heather got for him from the bar and content to relax. The last week had been hectic, and Margot had been worried. Theater was live. Anything could happen, and yet tonight had been almost perfect. Her relief was profound.

Max walked across the room toward them, a wineglass in one hand, and his whiskey in the other. He handed the glass of red wine to Margot before sitting down on the other side of Sally.

"Vina Robles 2018 from the Arborist Estate," Max said. "According to the bartender, it's a favored vintage. He said it's forty-one percent Syrah, thirty-five percent Petite Sirah, twelve percent Grenache, and twelve percent something else that I've never heard of." Max glanced at Sally. "And you, my dear Sally, get that one glass of champagne and nothing more. We're going to keep you healthy so you'll be here for a good thirty more years."

"I think wine is supposed to be good for the heart," Sally said.

"Yes, but you don't drink wine, do you?" Max retorted.

Everyone was starting to fill in at the various tables. Their table of six had two spots still open at their table, but no one joined them. Margot was fine with that. She liked the smaller group. Conversation would be easier.

Jen, like the star she was, hadn't yet sat down. She was circling the perimeter of the dining room, making sure everyone had a place to sit. Margot watched her, impressed as always by Jen's ability to take charge, make decisions, facilitate change.

Margot leaned toward Sally. "Sally, Jen is wasted as the office receptionist. She's brilliant. She's so good at so many things. You need to promote her, give her more responsibility, increase her pay. You don't want to lose her."

Sally glanced toward Jen, who was encouraging a few of the stage crew to get seated. "Is she thinking about leaving?"

"Not that I know of, but she's not going to want to be a front office receptionist forever. That girl can do it all, and she's wasted answering phones and handling mail and emails. You like smart people, and she's one of the smartest people I've met in a long time."

"Good to know," Sally said, still watching Jen.

Margot could tell from Sally's expression that she was taking Margot's words to heart, and it gratified her. Jen had kind of saved the summer, at least in Margot's mind. There was no way Margot could have handled everything, and she found it hard to trust others with important details, but Jen was such an outstanding communicator, and so thorough, as well as quick to respond, that Margot had been able to hand off tons of details, and problems.

A waiter appeared with salad plates, and placed one in front of Sally and then Margot and Max. During the salad course Jen dragged Capri over to meet Sally.

"You'd said you wanted to meet the designer," Jen said to Sally. "Well, here she is. This is Capri, and everything you saw tonight was her idea."

Sally's took Capri's hand and shook it. "Thank you for that gorgeous set, and the costumes. And thank you for finding experienced people who could help. Both Margot and Jen have been raving about you, but because everyone was so secretive about the play, I had no idea what to expect. But it was incredible, and worth the wait. You captured the nineties perfectly—just as I remembered them. I think I even owned a suit like the one Margot wore in the opening act."

"I haunted thrift shops," Capri said. "And then made what I couldn't find. It was a challenge only in that we had so much to do in a short period of time, but I also think that's what made it so fun. This last week we were at the theater until almost midnight every day, and then back early. It was intense but it brought us together, made it feel like summer camp."

"And now you have something else to add to your résumé," Sally said. Something caught her attention in the distance. "Oh dear," she murmured, half rising.

They all turned to look. A man had entered the restaurant and was standing in the doorway. He had gray hair, thick, a little shaggy, a scruffy gray beard, dark eyes. He was lean, dressed in a black T-shirt and jeans. He could have been a hippie or a biker, but whoever he was, Sally knew him, and she wasn't happy to see him.

Sally glanced at Max. "Did you know he was coming?"

"No." Max stood, expression grim. "I'll get rid of him."

"Don't make a scene," Sally warned.

Capri and Jen disappeared. Margot watched Max cross the dining room "Who is that guy?" Margot whispered.

"An old boyfriend." Sally's lips flattened. "And Max's dad."

Margot's lips parted. "That's Johnny?"

Sally nodded, and Margot watched, riveted, as Max approached his father. Side by side she saw similarities she hadn't noticed before. They were nearly the same height, although Max was a little taller. They had the same build. Johnny was thinner but he had the broad shoulders, long torso, lean hips. This is what Max would look like in thirty years. Rugged. Tough. Because Johnny had a vibe about him, an attitude, as if he were the someone. The actor. The star. Not his son.

Max stood at an angle from his dad. There was no hug, or smile. It looked tense even from their table. Johnny said something and then Max was speaking. Johnny shook his head. Max shrugged. Johnny glanced across the room to where Margot and Sally were sitting. Johnny looked straight at Sally, a long, hard look. Sally stared right back.

Max walked out of the dining room. Johnny stood there a moment before following.

Margot glanced at Sally. "Do you think he was at the show tonight?" she asked.

"No," Sally answered flatly.

"Why did he come, then?"

Sally glanced at Margot, unsmiling. "Money?"

Max never returned after walking his dad out. Margot had knots in her stomach. She couldn't help worrying and wondering. Sally didn't say a word about his disappearance, but Margot saw her look at the door a couple of times as if waiting, wanting, him to return.

After the dessert course, Margot walked her dad to his car, hugged him good night, and then headed home as well. Driving back to her house, she called Max but he didn't pick up. Margot left a brief message and then hung up, heart heavy. Tonight had started so well, but now Margot felt sad.

At home, she was able to shower and wash off the rest of her stage makeup. In cozy pajamas, she lay down on her bed and finally was able to read through all the texts and messages that had come in tonight.

There were best wishes from some of the office staff, a break-a-leg call from her dad. There were congrats from people she'd worked with in Cambria who'd come to the opening night performance, and then there was a group text from Paige, Elizabeth, and Andi, who were excited to share that they would be coming from Orange County to see the play the second weekend of July. They'd be making a girls' weekend of it, arriving Saturday by noon, and leaving Sunday, staying in Paso Robles, though, so Elizabeth and Paige could see their moms.

Margot knew it was late but couldn't wait until morning to respond. Can't wait to see you all. This is the best news! she texted, and it was. She needed her friends.

Elizabeth answered. Heard tonight was sensational. (But of course it would be, my mom taught you everything you know!)

Margot replied with a laughing emoji and then added, How did you hear about tonight's show?

Some friends from Paso were there, Elizabeth responded. They raved about it. Seriously, they couldn't stop gushing.

Margot grinned. Gushing is good. Love hearing positives. It's been intense.

Heard Max Russo is very gorgeous, Elizabeth added.

Margot paused, smiled to herself. He is.

You should know, Elizabeth replied immediately. I've seen some of the pics. Pretty hot.

Don't believe everything you read, Margot answered.

I SAW it. You two were kissing.

Margot bit into her lip, fighting her grin. Just practicing our scenes.

Elizabeth added an exclamation to Margot's text, replying, Um, sure. But we will discuss when there.

Margot sent a smiley face.

Now get some sleep, Elizabeth answered. You've earned it.

xox

Ending the text conversation, Margot plugged her phone in next to the bed, and headed to the kitchen for some water. She was tired but also still amped up. Tonight had been good. Everything felt good. The standing ovation at the end had felt fabulous. She'd had a lot of standing ovations in her life, but this one was special. The entire cast had performed well, and to stand there and take a bow with Max . . . that was so special.

He was special.

She was past falling for him. She'd fallen, and there was nothing she could do about it, not now. She'd tried hard not to care, or feel, but he was everything. Smart, interesting, kind, witty, fun. He was warm, too, and that warmth was what she'd missed all these years. The hugs, the affection, the laughter, the lightness. He made her feel beautiful. Valuable.

But . . . where was he? What happened when he left the party with his dad? Was he still with his dad, talking things out? Or was he somewhere having a drink, trying to drown his frustration?

She hoped he was okay. She wished he would have

called her or sent a message. She'd left him plenty. There was nothing else she could do—

Tires crunched gravel outside, a car approaching her cottage. Margot went to the living room window and peeked out. Max was parking his car. She unlocked the front door and waited for him on her little porch.

He was still wearing what he'd worn to the restaurant, but he looked rough. Exhausted. Her heart went out to him. "Come in," she said, opening the door wider. She'd never seen him like this.

With Max in the house, she closed the door and locked it again. Her eyes searched his. "You okay?"

He dragged a hand through his thick hair, messing it further. "Can I stay with you tonight?"

He wasn't slurring. He didn't smell like alcohol. But his features were hard and his expression hollow.

Margot took his hand, leading him to her dark bedroom. He sat down on the edge of the bed and, stepping between his knees, she began to unbutton his shirt. She was trying to peel his shirt off his broad shoulders when he lay back and pulled her down with him, bringing her close, her cheek on his bare chest.

"I missed the party," he said after a long minute.

"There were some toasts. Dinner, drinks. Obviously, people missed you, but you didn't miss that much."

"What did you eat?"

"Crab cakes." She kissed his chest, right above his beating heart. "They were good."

"What about your dad? What did he have?"

"The steak."

"Lucky bastard."

Margot pushed up on her elbow to look down at him. "Have you not had anything to eat tonight?"

He shook his head.

"You and your dad didn't get dinner?"

"No."

"What . . . what have you been doing this whole time?"

"Walking."

"Where?"

"Streets, beach, park, anywhere my feet would take me."

"And your dad?" she asked.

"Told him to go home. Don't know if he did."

She heard his stomach growl and she climbed off the bed. "I'm going to make you something to eat. It won't be fancy but it'll be food."

"Thank you." He rose. "Could I shower? Would you mind?"

"Of course not. You do you, and find me when you're ready. It's a tiny cottage, you won't get lost. Oh, and the towels on the upper rack in the bathroom are all clean."

Ten minutes later he emerged from the bathroom in nothing but a towel wrapped around his hips, his tan muscular chest with those hard carved biceps on full display. "I have nothing to change into," he said. "Sorry."

"I'm not," she teased, removing the grilled cheese sandwich from the hot skillet. "Those workout sessions have a nice payoff."

He smiled, but the smile didn't quite reach his eyes. However, he caught her, held her, and the hug was firm, tight. His body was so warm from the shower, and he smelled delicious, very much like her favorite vanilla-scented body wash. After a moment he kissed her, lightly, and let her go. "Thank you."

She wasn't sure if the thank-you was for the compliment, the shower, or the hug, but it didn't matter. He was thankful and she was, too. She was worried about him, and while she wanted to ask questions, wanted to understand what had happened tonight, curious about the conversation with his father, Max's reserve wouldn't let her pry. He didn't seem to want to talk, and it was enough that he was here with her.

Max sat down on the lone stool at the tiny counter and watched her dish up his dinner. Her dad had built the counter for her when she first moved in. She'd found the tiny kitchen limiting, and the extra counter space was used every day.

She glanced at him as she ladled the soup. "I should have asked you if you liked tomato soup. Hope grilled cheese and soup is okay. I didn't have a lot of choices."

"It's great."

She smiled as she placed the soup and plate in front of him. "What would you like to drink? I've some white wine, iced tea, water."

"Just a glass of water. Thank you."

She poured him water from the filtered jug in the refrigerator and then tidied the already tidy kitchen, giving Max time to eat, and he did. He concentrated on the sandwich and then the soup, and when he was done, he carried his dishes to the sink to wash them. She shooed him away, topped off his glass of water, and turned off the lights. "Let's go to bed. It's been a long day."

Margot woke up early to use the bathroom, and when she slipped back into bed, Max reached for her, pulling her close. She smiled as his arms wrapped around her. He was far more of a cuddler than Sam had ever been. Sam wasn't cold, but when it was time to sleep, it was time to sleep, each of them on their own sides of the bed. This being-held stuff was new to her, but she liked it. She felt safe.

The next time she woke, the sun was higher and Max wasn't in bed. She listened for him but the cottage was silent. Margot hoped he hadn't left.

Leaving bed, she went to look for his car, and it was still there. Max was outside as well, pacing and talking on his phone. She watched him for a moment, trying to read his mood, as he wasn't smiling.

She had a feeling that when he came inside, he wouldn't share about his call. He kept certain things close to the vest.

She exhaled a little, trying not to worry, reminding herself that none of this was personal. He was a mature adult who'd had forty-five years of living before he'd met her. He'd had relationships and marriages and his own way of communicating. He also had a big career with lots of demands, and he might just be talking to his agent, sorting through business stuff.

Margot busied herself in the kitchen, making coffee and then washing the dishes from the night before. She was drying the skillet when Max stepped through the front door.

"I didn't wake you, did I?" he asked, closing the door behind him.

"No. Not at all." She put the skillet away and reached for two cups from the cupboard for their coffee. "An *I Heart Paso* cup for you," she said, "and a *Daddy's Girl* cup for me."

He smiled and pulled out the stool and sat. "Last night went well," he said. "The audience loved it."

"They did," she agreed, realizing they were going to stick with safe topics, and that was fine with her. Yesterday was gone, today was a new day, and she was ready to move forward.

"That was Howard," he said. "We got good reviews. He's hoping to be here next week to see the play."

"That's great."

"I'd like to introduce you."

"Would love that," she answered, pouring coffee. Margot handed him his purple mug with the red glazed heart. "I have three friends coming in a couple weeks to see the show, too. Two are friends who were raised in Paso—"

"There's more of you?" he teased.

She grinned. "Does the prospect terrify you?"

"If they're anything like you, a little bit."

"Oh, they're a lot like me, but I'm sure they'll be on their best behavior. Paige and Elizabeth teach together at Orange University. Andi works there as well. She used to be in the math department, but I think she might be in administration now. Don't tell her I don't remember." Margot hesitated.

"Would you like to meet them? I don't want you to be un-comfortable."

His brow creased. "Why would I be uncomfortable?"

"I don't want to be pressuring you—"

"Margot, I met your dad. I went to your house to intro-duce myself."

She sipped her coffee. "Why did you do that?"

"I wanted to meet him."

Margot wasn't quite sure how to proceed, but since they were talking, there were things she wanted to know. Or say. Maybe ask. "He thinks we're together, as in a couple."

Max set his cup down. "Aren't we?"

She faced him across the counter. "To be honest, I wasn't sure."

"You sleep with me almost every night."

"Yes, but that doesn't necessarily mean anything for a lot of people."

"We're not a lot of people."

She didn't know if she was amused or exasperated. "And you don't make commitments."

"I'm not getting married again, but that doesn't mean I'm not committed to you." He frowned. "Have I misread the situation?"

The situation. Her. Them. The edge of her mouth tugged. She was glad he liked her, that was good, but it was a little painful having him tell her he wasn't going to marry her. He'd said he'd never marry again before, several times, but it had never been in the context of their relationship. At least he was being honest.

"It doesn't mean I'm not into you," he added. "Because I am."

"That's good."

He reached out, covered her hand resting on the counter. "But?"

She didn't want to do this, be vulnerable now, not when he

kept so much to himself. He had a whole world he didn't share. Margot tried to be respectful, but it was hard to feel like only part of him was available, accessible. "I know we're not even serious enough to talk about marriage—we've only started dating—but it's tough to know that there aren't a lot of options in the future. Unlike you, I haven't been married. It's not something I'm over. It's something I still hoped to do."

"Like kids," he added.

She shrugged and eased her hand from beneath his. She retreated to the sink, straightened the soap dispenser and the scrub brush. "I think about it." She glanced at him over her shoulder. "I think about the future and getting older and not having family left after Dad is gone." She hesitated. "That doesn't ever worry you?"

"My family isn't my family. My friends are my family."

Margot nodded, but there was a lump in her throat. This conversation depressed her. She had friends and she loved her friends, but she wanted all the things he didn't.

So what was she doing with him? Why had she let herself get emotionally involved? Sally's warning came back to haunt her. But Margot dismissed it, realizing she didn't have to go to the worst-case scenario. She didn't know the future. She couldn't anticipate how either of them would feel at the end of July. Why create trouble right now? Who knew how things would be when the play ended?

Max rose and came to her in the kitchen. "We're good," he said, drawing her into his arms. "I'm into you. In a big way." Then his head dropped and he kissed her. His mouth was firm, the pressure delicious. Her mouth opened to his, and he kissed her deeply, making her lips and body tingle. His kisses melted her, stealing her resolve.

She drew back a fraction, looked up into his dark eyes. "Are you in a hurry to get out of here?"

He shook his head. "You're the only thing on my agenda. I just want you."

* * *

THEY RETURNED TO BED, MADE LOVE, TAKING THEIR time, making the pleasure last, and then later, after, Max held Margot, their bodies still warm and tangled together.

He lightly caressed her back, fingertips tracing the lovely line of her spine, grazing the hollow in the low of her back. She meant so much to him. He wasn't good at putting his feelings into words, and the conversation about the future hadn't been comfortable, but he was glad they'd had it, glad they'd started talking about it.

Max didn't gush. He never said anything he didn't mean, and maybe she didn't know that about him yet, but he meant every word he'd said to her this morning. He was into her.

He had strong feelings for her. And no, he didn't make lots of promises and commitments—how could he now? He was only months from his divorce—but at the same time, he was committed to building what they had, committed to seeing them grow, and where they could go together.

Every day their relationship got stronger, not just physically, but emotionally, intellectually. He couldn't remember any relationship being so satisfying in so many areas. Margot was smart, and strong, and she held her own with him. More than held her own. He liked her. He respected her. He trusted her.

But it was when he held her that he felt the most peace. She felt perfect in his arms. She felt right. From that first night, she fit. There was a click between them, a meshing that made him want to open up more, as hard as it was. He wasn't good at talking about his past, but his past had shaped him, for the good and the bad, and at some point she should know the things he hadn't yet told her. She'd have questions, and maybe doubts, but once he explained, and he was certain she'd give him a chance to explain, she'd understand how hard it had been to leave Annaliese, despite everything she put him—and them—through.

There was a point he'd compared her to Johnny, but in the end he realized the reason he'd stayed with her, and protected her as long as he had, was that she was fragile like his mom.

Max never wanted to find Annaliese the way he'd discovered his mom. He couldn't ignore her cries for help and attention. He wouldn't be the reason she broke.

It had been so hard to untangle himself from her, though, but he was free, and he'd remain free. Margot would need the details, not just about Annaliese, but his mom as well, and that he wasn't ready to share.

Talking about his mom was the most painful thing he could do.

Margot tipped her head back, looked into his eyes, her hand gentle on his cheek. "A penny for your thoughts."

He kissed her lips, the kiss slow, hot, as hot as the shimmering energy between them. She was breathless when he lifted his head and pressed a kiss to her neck, and then she shivered. She always shivered when he kissed her neck. He liked that.

Liked her.

Maybe loved her.

Probably loved her.

How could he not?

She was the easiest person to love he'd ever met. She was so . . . her. Kind, smart, genuine. She was also beautiful, but it was her heart he loved most. When she smiled at him, she glowed, stars in her eyes, little bright bits of hope and happiness.

To feel such happiness again, to share such happiness.

Max smoothed her silky hair back from her forehead. "Not to scare you, or move too fast, but you feel like mine. Like we're meant to be."

She turned in his arms so that she lay on his chest.

"Well, I'm crazy about you. I fell for you fast, and hard. It wasn't the plan."

"There was no plan, was there?" he asked.

She smiled at him, smiled with such warmth that his chest tightened.

"Maybe no plans are the best plans," she said. "Maybe that's the secret. Not to look too far down the road, but rather, be grateful for today."

Chapter 15

IT HAD BEEN THE MOST BLISSFUL WEEKEND, A PROPER
weekend with the Fourth of July on a Tuesday, giving the
cast and crew two full days off. Last night they'd watched
fireworks in the park and had homemade strawberry ice
cream courtesy of one of the crew members, who'd dropped
off several pints at Max's house.

Now Max showered with Margot, enjoying soaping her
up, and down, feeling lucky that he got to start the day with
her in his home. In his bed. Every day they got closer, communication became easier, his heart more open. He trusted
her, too—significant, considering his past.

They'd made love earlier, after waking, but she felt so
good now, her body warm, wet, slick with the scented bath
gel. Cupping her breasts, he kissed her deeply as the water
streamed down, soaking them. She sighed into his mouth
as he kneaded her taut nipple and he grew hard in response.
It didn't seem to matter how many times they came together, he always wanted more. More of her. His desire was
quite specific. She was the one he wanted. She was the one

he needed. She reached down to capture his erection, her touch sure, confident, stroking him firmly.

His hips thrust into her grip, and he growled deep in his throat, hungry. He thrust a second time before reluctantly drawing away, aware she had an early-morning staff meeting at work, and he had a call with a producer that he needed to prepare for. Neither of them could afford to get distracted, not this morning. But they'd have later. They had tonight, tomorrow, the future.

Max turned the faucet off, and kissed Margot one last time. "Crazy about you," he said, slipping a hand through her wet hair, pushing it back from her face. His gaze roved over her flushed cheeks, her gaze dark with passion. They were like teenagers together. He smiled into her eyes and then kissed her neck right where she was so sensitive.

She gasped, leaned against him. "You are ruthless," she whispered, but she was smiling.

Out of the shower, he shaved while she dressed, and then while he dressed, she blew dry her hair, making the tiny bathroom work for the two of them.

There was time for just one more kiss, and then Margot picked up her bag and headed for the door. She paused as she opened it. "Have a good day," she said, shooting him a smile.

"See you at the theater tonight."

She blew a kiss and stepped outside, closing the door behind her.

IT WAS A BUSY DAY, BUT SATISFYING, AND AS MAX parked in the lot across from the theater, he felt good. He'd spent hours today on the phone, first with the producer in New York, then with Howard discussing the call, and then there had been a call with one of his costars on *Stardust Ranch* who was curious if Max would be interested in participating in an event she was involved with. The event raised funds for an arts program for underprivileged kids in Los Angeles. Max was definitely interested, deeply committed to community outreach, aware of how the arts and creativity allowed children necessary self-expression and building self-worth.

Pocketing his key, he crossed the street and entered the theater's brick courtyard, the illustrated *Barefoot in the Park* poster prominently displayed out front. Another framed poster hung on the wall next to the tiny theater box office.

A woman was studying the bright poster, and he drew up short, recognizing the slender shoulders, the artfully tousled blond hair, the long legs in white fitted trousers.

He went cold, the cold wrapped in nauseating dread.

Annaliese.

She turned and looked at him, sunglasses hiding her eyes but the corner of her full mouth lifted. "Hello, lover."

"What brings you to Cambria?" he asked.

She walked toward him, lips in that hard, fixed smile. "Why, you, of course." She stopped several feet from him, but close enough he could smell her perfume and the distinctive fragrance of her hair spray, the perfect long, loose waves framing her face. "It's been impossible to reach you. I was forced to go to Howard. He didn't return my calls, either. Have you blocked me on your phone?"

She was as beautiful as ever, and every bit as unpredictable, too. "Yes," he answered calmly.

"Why?"

Voices sounded on the street, and some of the theater crew entered the courtyard. He kept his back to them, his attention fixed on Annaliese. "You know why."

"And my emails? Not getting those, either, darling?"

"I haven't read them, no."

She looked away, arms tightly folded across her chest. "I can't believe you hate me that much."

Footsteps rang on the bricks. More of the theater crew arriving. He could feel the curious gazes. "I don't hate you," he answered. "But we have nothing to say to each other—"

"That's where you're wrong. I have something to say. Something important." She removed her sunglasses, revealing her blue eyes, the shade intensified by her colored contact lenses. "I'm pregnant."

He held his breath, irritation growing. Just one more game. She was queen of games, a master of manipulation. "So?"

"It's yours." She stepped closer, voice dropping, a spark in her eyes. "And don't insult me by saying how. You slept with me four and a half months ago. Remember?"

She never quit, did she? Endless games, endless BS. She loved to mess with his head, but he wasn't going to let it happen this time. "We never slept together, Liese."

"But we did."

"No, you told the media we did, but we know the truth. I know the truth."

"The media doesn't know it."

His irritation transformed into revulsion, and it was all he could do to speak civilly. "What do you want?"

"Money to support our child."

"We don't have a child, and if you're pregnant, it's not mine."

Her narrowed gaze swept over him, from head to foot and back again. "Should we share the big news with your costar?"

And just like that, there was Margot, entering the courtyard. She was on the phone, talking. She hadn't seen him yet. She looked animated, one hand gesturing as she talked. He watched her, chest aching with bottled air. He didn't want to have to introduce her to Annaliese. He didn't want to see worry in her eyes. Margot had been so happy these past few weeks. They'd both been so happy.

Margot suddenly lifted her head and spotted him. She smiled. Her wide, beautiful smile that made her lovely face come alive.

Annaliese followed his gaze. "Speaking of the devil," she said, lips pursing as much as they could, considering the overzealous use of fillers and plumping.

He said nothing.

"The reviews say you have incredible chemistry," Annaliese added.

He stared at Annaliese, even as Margot passed, heading into the theater. Then, and only then, he added coolly, "The play's reviews have been good. It's been a fun production."

Annaliese continued to watch the doors of the theater, even after they'd closed behind Margot. Max was glad he hadn't had to introduce them. He needed to talk to Margot first, warn her to keep her distance. Annaliese was as toxic as they came.

"Seems as if your publicity team is working overtime. Your relationship is in all the magazines," Annaliese said. "Not sure of your objective, but hey, everyone deserves a good time."

His watch vibrated with an incoming text, but he didn't look at his wrist. He knew he needed to go inside, warm up, get ready for the performance. "I'm not playing your games. You're wasting your time."

"Five million and I'll go away. You'll never hear from me again."

"I'm not going to be blackmailed."

"You have plenty of money."

"You might want to get a job. It's what people do when they need money. Or cut back on your expenses. But your problem isn't my problem. Goodbye."

Her head tipped, expression shuttered, hard to decipher. "The doctor said I conceived April twenty-third or so. Baby arrives January fourteenth—"

"We didn't have sex. We never touched. The baby, if there is a baby, is not mine."

"Until you prove otherwise, people will think what

they're told." She stared up at him, triumphant. "People love scandal, and your fans . . . they'll be so disappointed in you."

The theater door opened, and Jen stood there looking at him.

They were waiting for him inside. Margot would be waiting, too.

Max held his breath, counted to five, and then again. "I have to go."

"Dinner later?" she called as he walked away. "We have so much to discuss."

He kept walking, but he wasn't okay, not with her here.

MARGOT HAD DELIBERATELY LEFT HER DRESSING ROOM door open a few inches to keep an eye out for Max, wanting to know when he'd entered the theater.

She heard his voice in the hall. He was talking to Jen, and her stomach did a crazy flip-flop, nerves making her anxious. Max and Jen were talking about a lighting change for the final scene, and Margot exhaled slowly, telling herself not to get carried away. So what if Annaliese, the ex-wife, had appeared in town? Ex-wives did things like that. But Max wasn't married to her, and Max loved Margot, she felt it in the way he held her and kissed her. She felt his love every time he looked at her, and he wasn't going away.

Nothing was going to change.

And yet hot tears prickled the backs of her eyes and her pulse raced, her heart beating so fast she couldn't get her eyeliner on without smudging one side. Impatiently she took a Q-tip, dipped it in makeup remover, and wiped away the smeared blob.

Max knocked on her door before pushing it open and stepping inside.

She capped the eyeliner and turned to face him. "Everything okay?"

"Annaliese is here," he said, closing the door partway behind him.

"I saw," Margot answered, trying to keep her voice steady, needing to control the anxiety. She loved Max so much she was terrified something would happen. These past few weeks had been magical, and she'd wondered more than once if she would wake up one day and find out all of this had been a dream. "What brings her to Cambria?"

"She has some problems, said she wanted to talk to me."

"Is she okay?"

His jaw tightened. "I don't know."

"Are you going to meet her after the show?" Margot asked.

"No."

"But if she needs help . . . ?"

"She's a big girl. Trust me, Annaliese can take care of herself."

Margot searched his eyes. He wasn't happy. She had a feeling there was something else going on, but she wasn't going to push if he wasn't ready to share. "Just know I'm here for you, and if there's anything I can do, or any way I can help—"

"I know." He leaned over and kissed her. He deepened the kiss, and she felt an urgency that was different from passion.

She reached up, touched his cheek, and then he lifted his head, smiled at her. "Are we still having dinner after the show?" he asked.

"If you can," she said.

"I most definitely can. You're my number one." He kissed her lightly and then walked out, heading to his dressing room.

Margot watched him disappear, heart still racing, anxiety still bubbling, but then impatient with herself, she shook her head. Nothing bad had happened. Nothing bad would happen.

So what if his ex was here? The world was full of exes. She couldn't let her imagination run wild.

IT WAS A REALLY GOOD PERFORMANCE. THE ATMOS-phere was electric, and the cast was on. The audience was fully engaged as well, and their laughter and energy made a great show better. Margot loved being an actor on nights like this. She loved performing live, loved being able to see and feel the audience's appreciation. It might be a commu-nity theater production, but tonight it felt as professional as anything she'd ever been in.

After the show Max asked her to come to his place for dinner. He had some salmon he was going to grill, and with the clear sky it'd be beautiful to eat on his deck.

Margot was glad they'd be eating at Max's and not at a restaurant. Now that she had some time to process that Max's ex-wife was here, she had questions, not just about Annaliese, but about different aspects of his marriage and divorce, and it would be easier to have a real discussion without servers interrupting, or other guests seated close by.

She stopped by her house before going to Max's to shower and change. By the time she arrived at his place, the grill was hot, a bottle of wine was open, and the vegetable sides were ready to go.

Cozy in her sweater, she sat in a chair on the deck, sip-ping her wine and watching him put the salmon on. "It was a good show tonight," she said.

"One of our best," he agreed, glancing at her. "Do you like the wine?" he asked. "It's a Chardonnay that is sup-posed to pair well with salmon."

"It's delicious." She hesitated. "Can we talk about An-naliese?"

"Yes." He closed the lid on the grill and faced her. "What do you want to know?"

"Why has she come to see you now? You said she has

problems and needed to talk to you, but you weren't planning on talking to her. Why?"

"She wants money," he said bluntly. "But she receives a very generous alimony, and I'm not going to give her more. We had a prenup, and she's been taken care of—"

"What if it's not money? What if she's sad or lonely?"

"You have a big heart, Margot, but you don't know her. She's manipulative, extraordinarily manipulative, and I want no part of it."

Margot looked past him to the ocean, watching the waves take shape and the foam bubble as they crashed. "So if this is about money, is the alimony . . . enough? Or is it hard for her to live on that amount after being married to you?"

He looked somewhat exasperated. "What do you make a year working for Sally? What is your salary?"

Margot was taken aback by the question, but answered truthfully, telling him she made under six figures annually, but there were opportunities for bonuses.

"Annaliese's monthly alimony is more than your annual salary. She also got the Malibu house in the divorce, and the three cars I'd bought for her. She could sell any of those if she needed cash. She shouldn't be hurting for money."

Margot's eyes widened. She'd been thrifty her entire career, and often as the primary breadwinner, she'd gone without so Sam could remain at home, writing. "Does she not know how to manage money?"

"She's a very intelligent woman. She has an accountant and a financial adviser. She has a personal banker. She has a personal assistant. There are a lot of people who could help her, if she'd be willing to accept help."

"So why come to you now?" Margot asked, trying to understand Max and Annaliese's relationship. "Does she really need money, or is this about attention?"

"I don't know." Max leaned against the railing. "I've been ignoring her emails for the past six weeks, and, frustrated, she reached out to Howard. Howard said I should see what she wants, but I didn't. I don't want her in my life. I don't want to be dragged back into her games. I don't want anything to do with her, and she knows it, but she can't accept it, which is why she's here, threatening to create drama."

"But why? Does she think you still have feelings for her?"

Max laughed hollowly. "If someone blocked my number, and refused to answer my emails, I'd think I wasn't wanted. Only, Annaliese's mind doesn't work that way. The more you shut her down, the more determined she is to win."

Margot said nothing, brows pulled, concern growing. What kind of woman had Max married?

"Annaliese is insecure," Max said coolly. "She needs to be important, as well as the center of everything. We had some ups and downs in our marriage, but it wasn't until I was cast in *Stardust Ranch* that everything began to unravel. She hated that my career was taking off, and she couldn't get hers going."

"I didn't realize she was an actress," Margot said.

He made a rough sound and walked to the grill to turn the salmon steaks over. "She's not," he said flatly. "Not like you. She tries, and she's beautiful, and she can get cast in small parts, but she wants more, and the fact that she isn't a star drives her crazy. She thinks everyone is against her, when, to be honest, she hasn't put in the time, or the effort." He looked at Margot. "If I was a director, I wouldn't cast her. Not unless I needed a beautiful woman in a bikini in the background."

Margot wasn't sure if Max was bitter following a difficult divorce, or if he was telling the truth. Perhaps it was a little of both. "What was the attraction?"

He shrugged. "She was beautiful. She was fun. We had a good time together. Initially."

Margot waited for him to say more, but he didn't. She sipped her Chardonnay and then again. "That seems so shallow," she said after a lengthy silence. "It doesn't seem like you."

"I'd already been through a divorce, and I wasn't interested in getting married again. I just wanted to work, and put the past behind me." He hesitated. "She was also really into me, and after the divorce, it felt good to be wanted. She was interested in my career, and wanted my advice, and I introduced her to people, wanting to be supportive of her. Things felt new and exhilarating, and we were happy. It was a very physical relationship, and everything was good, until it wasn't."

Margot didn't particularly want to think about Max in a "very physical relationship" with anyone, but she understood how relationships changed. She'd seen it firsthand. Sam had changed. He'd outgrown her. She'd been so busy traveling and performing she hadn't even realized he'd moved on and emotionally left her behind.

"Do you want to eat out here?" Max asked. "Or would you prefer to be inside?"

The wind was cool, almost cold, and Margot felt chilled from the conversation. "Let's eat inside." She rose, needing a moment to sift through her own feelings. "I'll go set the table."

"Great. I'll be pulling the salmon off in another few minutes."

They didn't discuss Annaliese during dinner, nor while they washed the dishes together. Margot saw the time, it was almost midnight, and she had work tomorrow. She was tired, too, and needed sleep. After hanging up the dish towel, she faced Max. "I think I should go home," she said.

He drew her into his arms. "Why?"

"It's already late and I'll be getting up early. There's no point in waking you up, too."

"You know I go back to sleep," he said.

She did know, but she was worried, and afraid she'd toss and turn. "How long do you think Annaliese will be in town?"

He kissed her on the forehead. "That I don't know."

"I'm nervous," she whispered.

"Don't be."

She rose up to kiss him. "I think I'm going to go home. That way I won't have to worry about keeping you awake."

"You're sure?"

She nodded and he walked her out to the car. He kissed her goodbye and swept hair back from her cheek. "Everything's fine," he said. "Don't let Annaliese get to you. Okay?"

Margot nodded and climbed into her car. She waved goodbye as she drove away, but tears filled her eyes as she reached the end of the street. Things were changing, and as she knew all too well, not all change was good.

MAX DIDN'T SLEEP WELL. HE'D SPENT MUCH OF THE night debating whether he should have told Margot about Annaliese's threat, that if he didn't come up with more money, she'd go to the tabloids and reveal that she was pregnant.

He was hoping she was bluffing, which is why he hadn't said anything to Margot, but another part of him knew better. Annaliese had a temper. She craved control. Taking action, even punitive action, at least made her feel as if she'd taken control.

He now regretted not sharing the whole story with Margot, but he hoped to protect her from pain. Annaliese was far too good at creating pain. Maybe he should pay Annaliese off. Maybe not the millions she wanted, but a quarter of a million? Would that suffice? But that would also be setting up a never-ending cycle where she'd sweep in and make demands. He couldn't set a precedent. He couldn't encourage her in any way.

Just as thinking of Annaliese made him feel physically ill, thinking of Margot calmed him. He'd missed having Margot next to him last night, missed her warmth and her sweet smile when she woke. She woke up happy, eager to begin a new day, and her serenity and optimism steadied him. He hadn't even realized until Annaliese's appearance how much Margot affected his outlook. Margot made things better, she made his day brighter, her laugh made his heart lighter. Around her, with her, he felt optimistic. Hopeful. Excited about the future.

But he wasn't excited now. His gut was in knots. Dread filled him, dread that Annaliese was here, and Margot—open, honest, kind Margot—could get caught in the middle of Annaliese's drama.

LEAVING BED, MAX TOOK A HOT SHOWER, TRYING TO wash away his anxiety. The shower did no good, the worry remaining as he toweled off and dressed. He made coffee and yet he couldn't sit down and enjoy it. Instead, Max paced the small living room, the marine layer thick and pressing up against the glass. He felt claustrophobic. He hated the anger within him, and the panic. Panic that he was losing control, panic that he'd be trapped in someone else's bullshit again.

His dad's.

His mom's.

Now Annaliese's.

Grabbing his car keys, he left the house and drove down Moonstone Beach Drive, ending up at Sally's. There was a car in the driveway he didn't recognize. It was a black Audi, small and clean. Max parked behind Sally's car, leaving the Audi room to back out.

It took Sally a minute to come to the door. She smiled at him, but she half closed the door behind her, instead of inviting him in. "I have a guest," she said.

Max could tell from the sparkle in her eyes that it was a male guest. Sally the romantic, he thought, almost smiling, and then he remembered why he was there and his smile faded, the nausea returning. "Do you have time to talk?"

"Annaliese is in town," Sally said.

He nodded, not entirely surprised Sally knew. It was her town, and she seemed to know everything that happened in it, and knowing Annaliese, she was probably already talking. Telling stories. "I can come back later—"

"It's fine. Come in." She opened the door wider. "We'll go to the kitchen."

He closed the door behind him and followed her to the kitchen, which was distant from the main bedroom wing. Once in the kitchen, Sally turned on the coffee maker. "What does she want?" Sally asked, turning to face him.

"She wants money. She says she's pregnant."

Sally's brow creased. "Is it yours?"

"No."

"You're sure?"

"We haven't been together—slept together—since I was in London eighteen months ago."

"Then what is this about?"

"She's asking for a lot of money."

"Sit," Sally said, gesturing to one of the stools. "And how much?"

"Five million."

"Wow." Sally faced him, hands on her hips. "Do you have that much?"

"Not liquid, no. I have my New York condo, my place in Laurel Canyon, and investments. But even if I did, I wouldn't pay her off. I don't owe her anything more than what she's getting."

"Was the settlement fair?"

"More than fair. We should have divided the things purchased while married, but I handed over the Malibu house—she loves that place—and I'm paying for her cars, as well as the insurance. She's still on my insurance, at least until the end of the year."

"And the alimony?"

"Over six figures, monthly."

"So this can't be about money."

"No." He frowned at the marble island. "Maybe she really is pregnant, but that's not my problem. I'm not going to get involved, and I refuse to be dragged into her drama."

Sally poured a cup of coffee and then returned the carafe to continue brewing. "Still drink it black?" Sally asked him.

He nodded and she handed him the cup.

"So what are you most worried about?" Sally asked, drawing a stool out and sitting across from him.

"Margot." He looked at Sally, his stomach knotting, making even the smell of coffee unappealing. "And you. Annaliese can make things really unpleasant."

"Don't worry about me. Annaliese doesn't trouble me in the least. Now, Margot . . . I can see why you're worried. She's a sweetheart. She won't like having Annaliese around, so you're going to have to prepare Margot as best you can. Let her know there will be drama, and do your best to protect her from it until Annaliese is gone." Sally hesitated. "But you don't know when that will be, do you?"

He shook his head. Annaliese was unpredictable, and while she hadn't been able to carve out a career on the big or small screen, she excelled at getting attention from the tabloids. They loved her stories and her manufactured vulnerability. She created photo opportunities for them, and they showed up. Max was used to the gossip and cameras, but he didn't want this ugliness playing out in Cambria. It was a great little town, full of good people, and the last thing he wanted was to see the people he cared about dragged into the spotlight only to be trolled by people with nothing better to do than hate.

"Do you know where she's staying?" Sally asked.

He shook his head. "She was waiting for me outside the theater when I arrived last night. I don't know where she went after." He started to lift his mug but set it down. "Sally, don't get involved. Don't try to see her, or give her money. Stay away from her. Please? Promise me?"

"I promise." Sally studied him intently, her narrowed gaze searching his. "Does she think that you want a baby?"

"No. She knows where I stand on children. We discussed it a great deal, and we were in agreement on that. No kids. I'm not going to be a father. I don't want to risk it. I'm too much Johnny's son—"

"You're nothing like him," Sally interrupted. "He cared for no one, and you, dear Max, care for everyone."

He didn't reply to this. He sat silent for a long minute. "Annaliese is going to make things ugly. She's going to play the victim, create stories for the tabloids. She'll do her best to drag Margot into her circus." He took a deep breath, insides sharp, painful. "Look, my career is fine. The people I work with, they know who Annaliese is. My fans know who I am. But Margot . . ." He shook his head. "She's not going to know what hit her. It's going to be uncomfortable. The drama with Annaliese is going to get a lot worse before it gets better."

"Have you told Margot this? Have you prepared her?"

"That's next."

"Why haven't you said anything yet?"

He met Sally's gaze. "Because it's a lot. I wanted her to feel secure about us before I revealed how messed up everything has been in my past."

"Max, you have a past. Your childhood was challenging, but you rose above the circumstances. You're not Johnny, and you're not your mom. You can't control Annaliese, you can only do what you can to prepare Margot for what's to come. Don't let her be caught off guard. No one likes to be blindsided—especially not Margot."

Chapter 16

MARGOT ARRIVED AT THE PLAYHOUSE AT THE USUAL time, right round six. She checked in with the crew arriving, asked Jen about box office sales, making sure there were no issues, and then went around greeting the cast. Max hadn't arrived yet, but then he often came a little later, showing up an hour before the performance instead of ninety minutes early like she did.

They'd talked earlier. He'd gone to the gym, had a workout, and then was going to try to do some writing. She'd headed to Paso Robles for lunch with her father. She casually mentioned to her dad that Max's ex-wife, Annaliese, was in town, and that Max wasn't happy about it.

"Are you worried?" her dad asked, getting right to the heart of the matter.

"I don't like it," she confessed. "Max seems unsettled, too. He keeps telling me everything is okay, but—" She broke off, and shook her head. "The more he tells me not to worry, the more concerned I become."

"I think Max truly cares about you, so try not to get involved, and let him handle his ex, and with any luck, she'll soon be gone."

Margot nodded, agreeing. Her father's advice made sense, and it's what she intended to do.

She'd begun putting on her makeup for the show when there was a knock on the door. Margot called out, "Come in."

The door opened and Margot saw a stunning floral arrangement appear, and then the woman who was carrying the flowers. It was the tall, stunning blonde talking to Max before the show yesterday. His ex-wife, Annaliese.

Margot's heart jumped. She wasn't sure how Annaliese had managed to get back here, to the dressing rooms.

Annaliese entered the room briskly, her enviable curves wrapped in a formfitting red dress. "I wanted to drop these off and tell you to break a leg." She set the flowers on the counter littered with Margot's stage makeup. "I haven't seen the show yet, but I managed to get a ticket for tonight. I'm so excited. The reviews have been so good. You must be very proud, starring in the play, and directing."

Margot wished Max or Jen would arrive, or any of the other cast or crew. She didn't know what Annaliese wanted, but she didn't trust her, not at all. "Thank you," Margot said, managing a smile. "It's been fun."

Annaliese leaned against the counter. "The critics like you. They've been raving about your performance."

"I've spent most of my life on the stage. It's nice to know I'm good at what I do." Margot then forced herself to focus on her reflection, taking the lip pencil to her mouth and outlining the shape before coloring it in. "You're an actress, too, aren't you?"

"I prefer film over the stage." Annaliese adjusted a couple of the flowers, rearranging the long stems. "The money is better, too."

"That's probably true, but I've never done film or TV, so

I have nothing to compare it to." Margot reached for her lipstick, and slicked it over the pencil. She studied her reflection, seeing what she still needed to do. There was quite a bit, but she couldn't focus, not with Annaliese in her dressing room, sitting so close to her. Margot rose, adjusted her robe. "I appreciate the flowers, it's a lovely thought, but I need to change."

"Oh, of course." Annaliese straightened. "Well, have a great show. Fingers crossed we can all have dinner tonight. I've so much news I'm dying to share." And then, with a smile and a wiggle of her fingers, she walked out.

Margot locked the door behind Annaliese, and pressed a hand to her middle, queasy.

For a moment she stood there, trying to calm herself, when a knock sounded on her door.

"Who's there?" she called.

"Max."

Margot unlocked the door and stepped back. He entered the room. "You okay?"

She nodded.

He spotted the flowers. "Those are beautiful."

"From Annaliese." Margot smiled because she didn't know what else to do. "She was just here. She brought them to me herself."

"What?"

Margot nodded and sat back down, her gaze meeting Max's in the mirror. "She's going to be in the audience tonight. She managed to get a ticket."

"But the show's sold out."

"She's hoping the three of us will have dinner tonight." Margot's gaze met his again and held. "She says she has news." Margot's pulse raced. "What news could it be?"

"We're not having dinner with her," Max said firmly. "There is no chance of that."

Margot nodded, glad. Annaliese was not someone Margot

wanted to be around. "Can you maybe find a home for these flowers, too? They're gorgeous, truly extravagant, but I don't feel comfortable—"

"Got it," he said, crossing the floor to take the flowers. He leaned down and kissed her lightly, gently. "I'm sorry you had to deal with her. I'll make sure that Jen and the crew know not to let her backstage again." Max left, and he closed the door behind him.

Margot picked up her black eyeliner, wanting to extend the eyeliner further, but she couldn't focus on her eyes when her thoughts were so jumbled. What was Annaliese's news? Margot only realized now that Max hadn't answered the question. Did he know? Or was he avoiding answering? Either way, Annaliese was going to be a problem.

It took her a moment to pull herself together and finish her face, and then Margot stood and changed into the lavender-gray suit she wore in act 1, scene 1. Dressed, she scraped her hair back, drawing it into a relatively severe chignon, before adding the pearls to her ears, and the single strand of pearls at her neck. She could do this. She was a performer. Last night had been exhilarating. Everybody had been so cohesive and strong. During the curtain call, Margot had smiled at Max as he'd taken her hand for their final bow. She'd felt joyful. Strong.

She might not feel as confident now, but she was going to go out there tonight and give another outstanding performance. So what if Annaliese was in the audience? There were one hundred others there tonight, too. It would be a great show. Acting wasn't just her passion, she was damn good at it, too.

IT WAS A GOOD, SOLID SHOW, BUT MARGOT WAS GRATE-ful it was over as the curtains closed for the last time. She'd done her best tonight, and even though she'd spotted Annaliese in the first act, sitting on the aisle in one of the middle rows, she'd managed to block her out. It was Max who seemed to struggle tonight, his lines not quite as sharp, his laughter a little forced. No one else would notice, but Margot did because she'd come to know him so well. And then when he first kissed her onstage, she'd felt him hesitate, and later during the big kiss, he was holding back as well.

Margot didn't blame him. She didn't think she'd be her best if Sam suddenly showed up. Having an ex in the audience could be distracting, especially in such a small theater.

But it was over now, and after giving her a faint smile, Max headed to his dressing room. Margot could tell he wasn't happy, and she would have gone after him, but Jen was approaching her and Jen didn't look happy, either.

"What's wrong?" Margot asked, closing the distance between them.

"That woman that got backstage earlier—"

"Max's ex-wife," Margot said, wanting to be clear.

Jen nodded. "She's in the lobby, and she asked one of the ushers to bring her back to see you and Max, but the usher said she needed to get permission. She's making a bit of a scene. Apparently you three are having dinner tonight, and she wants to wait back here."

"No, and no," Margot answered.

"Well, she's not happy. Should I let Max know?"

"I'll let him know," Margot said. "And thank you." She started for the dressing rooms but slowed as she approached Max's door. She suddenly knew what she wanted to do, what she needed to do, and she wasn't sure how he'd react, but Margot didn't want to be drawn into anything, not with Annaliese, not with anyone.

She knocked on his door, and he opened after a moment. He'd already changed and had washed his face, removing the makeup. "Hey," he said. "It went okay tonight, despite everything. What do you think?"

"We got the laughs and the standing ovations. Everyone

enjoyed themselves," she agreed. She hesitated, gathering her courage, finding her words. "Max, Annaliese is in the lobby and she's making a scene, nothing particularly awful, but enough that Jen's uncomfortable. Annaliese wants dinner, and I think you should meet her, and have a conversation with her, and see if you can convince her to leave. Cambria really isn't big enough for all three of us." She tried to laugh, as if it were a joke, but her laugh fell flat and Max wasn't smiling.

"She doesn't operate like that," he said. "Knowing that we want her to go makes her even more determined to stay. We're going to have to suck it up for a while, pretend she isn't here, pretend she doesn't bother us—"

"But she bothered you tonight," Margot interrupted. "You weren't yourself onstage. You were tense and you weren't completely focused."

"You said it was a good show."

"Because I didn't want you to feel bad. But we can't continue like this, not indefinitely."

"Margot, she's been here one day. Give her time. Let her get bored. She'll leave eventually."

"And until then she hangs around and makes everyone miserable?"

"If you let her make you miserable."

"Please, have dinner with her. Let her talk. Be kind. Listen. Be supportive of whatever she needs so that she feels safe, and secure, and maybe once she feels safe and secure, she'll go."

Max made a rough sound. "You don't know her."

"No, but I know you, and you're a good person. You don't like those around you to suffer." Margot swallowed and forced herself to continue. "I'm having a hard time with her here. I'm not afraid of her, Max, but she makes me uneasy. I don't want to be bumping into her, or having conversations with her. I don't want her outside the theater, or bringing flowers to my dressing room. I don't want to be on her radar in any way."

He said nothing for a moment, brow furrowed.

"What?" Margot asked, searching his expression.

"Okay. I'll have dinner with her, but, Margot, I think this is a bad idea."

MARGOT WOKE UP TO HER PHONE VIBRATING WITH ONE text after another. She grabbed her phone and rolled over onto her back to look at the screen. Messages from the girls at work. Message from Jen. Messages from friends in Orange County. A missed call from her dad. She went to Jen's text first. WTF it read. She'd shared a screenshot of the headline, *Max and Annaliese Russo Expecting!* There were other headlines, too, from the rest. *Back Together Again. Baby Russo on the Way?* The headlines were accompanied by photos. Pictures of Max and Annaliese at dinner, sitting close, practically shoulder to shoulder.

Margot went to the TMZ website, which Jen had also mentioned, and watched a brief video where someone was asking Annaliese questions about the pregnancy news, and she smiled, incredibly coy. "I can't talk about it," she said, and then the next moment put a protective hand to her belly. The reporter persisted and she dipped her head as if shy. "We're happy, that's all I can say. Very happy to have a son on the way."

A son? What? Margot rewatched the video three times, unable to believe what she was hearing and seeing. It wasn't just the TMZ website, though. There were so many different headlines, from British tabloids to American morning entertainment shows. She knew this was manufactured drama, but it was still nauseating. Heartsick, she picked up the phone and called Max. He didn't answer. She left a message, asking him to call her.

Margot made coffee but it tasted bitter. She sat down on the couch, numb. It was Friday and she needed to dress for work, but she couldn't make herself move from the couch. She was still sitting frozen when she saw Max's car pull up, and watched him leave his car and walk to her front door.

She let him in and returned to the couch. He looked exhausted, lines etched around his eyes and mouth. "You've seen some of the tabloid headlines?" he asked gruffly.

She nodded. "Apparently, they're on the regular news, too. I've received a half dozen messages, including a call from my dad. Everyone is kind of freaking out. I wanted you to have dinner with her, but Max, wow. You're having a baby together now?"

He didn't laugh. "Haven't been intimate with her in eighteen months. So if she's pregnant, it's not mine."

"All those stories—"

"The stories look bad, but not one of them is true. I warned you she'd pull something. I didn't want to meet her for this very reason. I knew she'd use it as a photo opportunity, and she did."

"But a baby, Max?"

"There's no baby, Margot. Not with me."

Margot jumped up and paced the floor. "Why would she lie about something like this? Why wouldn't you tell me?"

"I did tell you."

"No. You *never* mentioned a baby."

"I'm pretty sure I said—"

"Not about a baby," she interrupted, voice rising. "You said other things, but I'd remember about a baby."

His voice sharpened. "Why is the fake baby such a big deal to you? There's no truth in it, Margot. I swear to you."

Margot returned to the couch and sat down heavily. She buried her face in her hands and tried to breathe, which wasn't easy when her chest squeezed and the air bottled inside her lungs. "Did you ever want children with her?" she said at last, looking up at him.

"No." His expression hardened. "I don't want kids. I've no desire to be a dad. It's not going to happen."

A lump filled her throat. She felt as if she'd run off a cliff and was free-falling. "Ever?" she whispered, looking at him.

He shook his head. "Ever, what?"

"You seriously don't want kids ever?"

"No. And it's a good thing. I'd make a lousy dad."

Margot wished she'd never woken up. She wished she were back in bed and this was a bad dream. "If you were with a different partner—"

"No. Margot, I love you, and I love being with you, but that's not in the cards. I thought you knew how I felt."

Clearly, she didn't. They'd never actually had a conversation about *their* future. She'd just hoped . . .

"Does it matter?" he asked, his voice rough. "Do kids matter that much to you?"

She looked down at her hands, which were tightly clenched in her lap. She forced herself to relax, ease her locked fingers apart. "I've shared with you before that I want to be a mom. Getting married, and having a family, is right there at the top of my bucket list. It's one of the main reasons I left New York."

"Along with being closer to your dad."

"Yes. Closer to Dad, and living somewhere more affordable so that I could have options that I didn't have in New York. Like buying a house. Having a family, whether through IVF or adoption. Maybe even becoming a foster mom, if that was the right next step."

"I didn't realize you were that serious about . . . kids."

"It's that dream of mine," she said softly. "Not sure I can let it go."

"Then don't. But you're wasting your time with me, sweetheart, because I'm not going to be the one that gives you babies or creates a family. I'm not a family man. But you know that."

He'd said it, yes, but she hadn't believed him. She hadn't

wanted to believe him. He'd been so perfect in every other way. Margot smiled grimly, if only to keep the tears from welling up. "I guess I should thank Annaliese for popping into Cambria and creating a little drama. Without her fake pregnancy news, we might never have had this conversation. It's good we did. Helps us both save time. Who needs to make another mistake?"

Max looked at her. "What are you saying?"

She was not going to cry. She was not going to lose control. She had goals. She knew what she wanted. "I need to fall in love with someone else, I guess."

"That's harsh."

"Max, you don't want to be a dad. I want to be a mom. I'm not going to change my mind—"

"And I'm never going to change mine," he interrupted tightly.

"So." She looked at him and then glanced away. "That's that, then."

He growled in frustration. "I swear to God I feel like I'm talking to Annaliese—"

"But you're not," Margot cried, jumping to her feet. "You're talking to me, and maybe, Max, maybe Annaliese isn't the problem. Maybe you are—"

"I'm sorry." He caught her, took her hands, held them in his. "That was uncalled-for. I shouldn't have said that. I haven't slept. I'm so tired I can't see straight. All I've wanted to do was protect you."

"I appreciate that." And yet her heart was filled with the worst kind of pain. She'd felt this before, years before. "Max," she said, holding tightly on to him. "I pictured a different future for us. I saw us staying together after the play, I saw us playing house, getting married, becoming parents, the whole thing."

His jaw tensed. "Even though I said I didn't want to get married?"

She laughed, feeling slightly hysterical. "Maybe I

thought I could change your mind. Maybe I thought you hadn't met the right person yet. But no need to make that face. You're still single. You're okay." She leaned forward, kissed him lightly, and then stepped away. "You're free," she said, going to the door and opening it for him, smiling despite the tears stinging her eyes. "No pressure from me."

MAX DIDN'T KNOW WHAT THE HELL HAD HAPPENED.

What was going on?

Everything had been going so well. The past seven weeks had been really good weeks. The play was a success, Margot was, well, Margot, and he couldn't remember ever being so happy. Margot made him happy. He felt good with her, right with her, he felt the way he'd always wanted to feel—and then Annaliese shows up and now he and Margot are done? Come on. How did that work?

While he'd like to blame Annaliese for this morning's implosion, he couldn't put all the blame at her feet. This . . . this was bigger than that. This had to do with his values and beliefs clashing with Margot's.

He didn't want kids. He couldn't.

It's not that he hadn't ever tried. He'd tried his best to be a dad, a stepdad, to Cynthia's daughter, but when their marriage ended, she yanked Gigi away and it had been devastating. The little girl had cried as he'd said goodbye, and for months he'd thought of her, missing her, missing his wife, but there was no second chance, no forgiveness. Cynthia was gone and so was Gigi, who'd become his daughter, too.

It was his fault, too. He'd been careless, he hadn't been thinking, and that lack of sensitivity and loyalty had destroyed the family he and Cynthia had been building together.

If he'd ever doubted his ability to be a responsible dad, it was cemented then. Parents shouldn't cause children pain. Parents shouldn't inflict hurt or heartbreak, and yet here he was, every bit as disloyal as Johnny.

Max never dated a single mom again, and when he did go out, he was careful to establish boundaries, be cautious, make certain that the women he pursued weren't women who wanted to get married or have a family, because he'd never do either.

So what had happened with Margot? How had he not heard her say how important children were to her? Or how had he heard and not paid attention?

Was he so taken with her that he didn't focus on the words, but on the feeling she evoked in him?

Or had he thought the issue of babies unimportant, and didn't matter? Because she was almost fifty, and therefore fertility wasn't an issue, not for him?

Max returned to his house and went to bed, blinds down, room shrouded in darkness. His head hurt and he felt flattened. Exhausted.

She'd shown him the door. Literally opened it and said goodbye. She'd wanted him gone. Margot had kicked him out.

Not because the attraction was gone, not because the love was gone, but because they wanted different things. She wanted a family. He didn't. And that was that.

So simple, and so complicated.

He put an arm over his eyes, pressing against the gritty burning sensation. His chest ached. His stomach was rolling. He felt terrible. He really did.

MARGOT DRAGGED HERSELF INTO WORK, ARRIVING MID-morning. It had taken her almost two hours to pull herself together, and lots of cool compresses to reduce the swelling under her eyes from all her crying, but at last she was dressed, and parking in the small lot behind the building, after finding a spot open—rare for this time of day.

The moment she entered the office, Jen and the rest of the team clustered around her, wanting to see how she was and if she'd talked to Max. Was there any truth in Annaliese's claim?

Sally emerged from her office, having ended the call she was on, and steered Margot back, pointing her to a chair facing Sally's desk, before closing the door to ensure privacy.

"I'm a mess, I know," Margot said. "I'm sorry—"

"Don't apologize. I could kill him. This whole thing with Annaliese—"

"But this isn't about Annaliese," Margot said, knocking away tears that she'd been determined not to cry. "It's something else. Something that can't be fixed." She drew an unsteady breath. "We've broken up. I was the one to end things. I'm crazy about him, but we want different things, and I can't continue with him, not if there's no future."

Sally plucked tissues from the box behind her and passed them to Margot. "What can I do? I feel responsible."

"You're not. You warned me. This—the pain—it's all on me."

Sally folded her hands on her desk. "Something triggered this. You two were doing so well until a few days ago."

"It's not what he did, but what he doesn't want. Max doesn't want kids. He feels very strongly about it, but I'm still wanting to be a mom. It's one of the reasons I returned to the area. It's something I hoped could still happen." She mopped her eyes and dabbed her nose. "The thing is, I'm upset because I'd started picturing all that with him. He's so good with me, I figured he'd be just as wonderful as a dad."

"There was a lot of stuff that happened when Max was a kid. Max blames his dad, and thinks that he'll end up being the same kind of dad."

"But how is he anything like Johnny?"

"He's not. But you can't tell him that. Max has scars, and those scars blind him to the truth." Sally's expression softened. "It's not something you can change, either. I've tried. He's stubborn. It's what initially helped lift him from his circumstances, but it's also what continues to hold him back."

Margot exhaled slowly, picturing Max even as she remembered their terrible conversation this morning. "I really love him."

Sally said nothing.

"Part of me wants to pretend he'll change his mind," Margot said after a long silence. "I want to think we can work through this. But the realist in me, the one that's lived through hard things, knows that hoping and wishing won't end up making me happy. For nearly two years after our breakup, I waited for Sam to miss me. I waited for him to realize he'd made a mistake. I don't know if it was pride or desperation, but I needed him to want me again. But he didn't change his mind. He hadn't made a mistake. I was the one that made the mistake by waiting, and hoping. I made the mistake putting my life on hold in case he wanted me back. It was so damaging to my self-respect, and it kept me from moving forward. I can't do that again. I won't."

"These next few weeks will be hard for you." Sally studied Margot. "Can you get through the rest of the month?"

"There's a little over two weeks left. I'll survive. We're professionals. We can make it work."

MAX HAD FINALLY SLEPT AFTER GOING TO BED THAT morning, and it was almost noon when he woke. Groggy, he made himself go for a run and returned to his cottage for a shower and late lunch. The afternoon was spent writing and then it was time to head into town. He'd been successful so far not thinking about Margot. Obviously he'd have to interact with her tonight, but everything was scripted. They'd perform and then it'd be over. At least until tomorrow, when they'd do it all again.

He arrived exactly an hour before the play, parking in his usual spot in the lot across from the theater. He didn't see Margot's car, which was unusual, but there was no time to dwell on it as he saw Annaliese leaning against the hood of her red Porsche, watching him. She waved as he parked, and then joined him as he walked across the street to the playhouse complex.

"What do you want, Liese?" he asked, keeping his gaze ahead.

"Just wondered how your day was. Thought I would hear from you but didn't."

He could smell alcohol on her. It wasn't the first time, nor would it be the last. "You've been drinking."

"I had some drinks at the bar over there. Had to pass the time one way or another."

"You shouldn't be drinking if you're pregnant."

"Maybe you should mind your own business since you don't care about me," she answered.

"Maybe you should return to L.A."

"Why? When this is vastly more entertaining?"

From the corner of his eye Max saw Margot cross the street, heading for the theater. She'd parked in a different lot today, as if making certain she wouldn't be parking near him.

Annaliese seemed very aware of who and what had distracted him. "Why do you like her?" she asked. "She's not that pretty—"

"Stop," he said quietly. "She's not part of this equation."

"That's true. You and me plus baby makes three."

He clamped his jaw, fought back the rage. Annaliese was deliberately provoking him. It's how she won. Fight hard, fight dirty, and soon enough he'd lose his temper and say things he'd regret. He didn't want to do that anymore. He didn't want to be the bad guy anymore.

He stopped walking and faced her. "Listen, stay here. Enjoy Cambria. Visit Paso or Hearst Castle. I don't care if you're here, I don't care if you go. Because either way the play wraps on the twenty-third, and I return to New York the next day."

* * *

MARGOT COULD HEAR MAX AND ANNALIESE TALKING AS they followed her into the theater complex. She walked into the theater quickly, wanting to put distance between them and her. After checking in with Jen and the box office, she headed to her dressing room but didn't close her door all the way, wanting to know when Max arrived, wanting to speak to him if he wanted to speak to her.

Since the start of rehearsals they'd never gone this long without communicating. Usually there were a dozen texts exchanged every day, plus phone calls and sometimes FaceTime calls, and quite often they'd have an early bite, too. Instead, today he'd left her place and there had been only silence, and now they'd have to go onstage and pretend.

As she sat down to do her face, she heard his voice in the hall. He was talking to someone, and laughing. Her insides fell, her emotions raw. She heard his footsteps pass her room, continuing to his. His door opened and closed. There was only silence in the hall now.

Margot's eyes burned as she clipped her bangs back to apply her foundation. Her eyes were pink. Her skin appeared sallow. She looked as sad as she felt. This wasn't fair. She loved Max. She wanted nothing more than to be in his arms, but she couldn't go there anymore. They weren't her arms. He wasn't her person.

She didn't doubt his feelings for her. That was the problem. She knew he cared. She felt the love. He was everything she wanted in a partner, except for the no-family stuff, and that was a deal breaker for her.

Why hadn't they discussed this more early on? Why hadn't she been more vocal, more clear? But it wasn't all her fault. He could have been more forthcoming as well.

Margot used the makeup sponge to smooth the foundation and then applied loose powder to help it set before picking up the tapered blush brush to shade beneath the hollows of her cheeks. Once the contouring was complete, she dotted the tops of her cheekbones with a hint of high-lighter. Margot hated thinking about Annaliese, but if she was pregnant, Margot envied her. Margot would be over the moon to have a baby. She should have used her early forties to pursue her options instead of waiting around for Sam.

She could have bought sperm. She could have tried ART or IVF. She was still fertile then. It would have been pos-sible if she'd been focused and making good decisions.

But she wasn't making good decisions, and here she was, jealous that Max's ex might be pregnant—even though it wasn't with his baby.

Applying eye shadow, Margot fought the envy, envy that Annaliese was pregnant when Margot couldn't get preg-nant. Envy that so many women could make a baby, and she was too old for that.

This is what she'd secretly dreamed—that she and Max could have a family. Of course she hadn't told him that at night, when she was falling asleep in his arms, she had a favorite image, a picture of them together, having a life together, and filling their home with one or more children. How could she tell him that she'd imagined this incredible life for him and her, when they'd known each other for what? Sixty days?

But until Annaliese arrived, it was her secret, her dream. Max could work, travel, act, and she'd be in Paso with their little human being and she'd stay busy. Not necessarily sure what she'd do—continue working for Sally? Create a little theater school? Margot didn't know, but she wouldn't be bored. She'd be a mom and she'd have a purpose and it would be exciting. Fulfilling. Wouldn't her dad love it, too? Being a grandad. Having someone else to love.

But that dream wasn't going to happen, not now.

* * *

THAT NIGHT THEY GOT THROUGH THE SHOW WITHOUT
any difficulty. Max knew he'd be able to rely on Margot,
and he was right. She was a consummate professional and
wasn't about to let any tension affect the evening performance. Just as they did every night, they came together at the
end, holding hands as they took their bow. Just as they did
every night, she looked at him, and smiled into his eyes,
before they turned back to the audience, who were on their
feet, giving a standing ovation.

After the curtain closed, she dropped his hand and he
walked away. During intermission Sally had sent a message
to him that she'd like to take him to dinner after the show,
if he was up for it. Max responded that he'd like that.

He changed and removed his makeup, washed his face,
and then met Sally in the foyer. She mentioned she'd made
a reservation at her favorite sushi place, and Max was glad.
He hadn't had sushi in a long time. It wasn't a long walk but
they drove together in Sally's car, with Max coming around
to open her door. "You were marvelous tonight," Sally said
to Max as they entered the restaurant. "Even funnier than
usual. I don't know how you do it."

"That's why I'm paid the big bucks," he teased, smiling
at her because he could tell Sally was a little troubled. "I
didn't know you were in the audience tonight," he added,
after they were seated.

"I heard there would be an empty seat due to a last-
minute cancellation and took it. The play gets better and
better. Who knew you were such a wonderful comedic
actor?"

"I'm glad you think so. I'd love to do more comedy in
the future."

The waitress appeared to take drink orders. Sally wanted
a small sake and Max chose Sapporo. Max had been determined not to bring up Margot, but the moment the waitress

walked away, he asked Sally about her. "Did Margot come to work today?"

Sally nodded. "For half the day. She came in right around noon."

He looked away, jaw tightening. "This is all so crazy. It doesn't make sense."

"Which part?" Sally asked quietly.

"All of it. We were good. We were happy. And then overnight she changes her mind and ends everything." He hesitated, remembering how she'd turned white this morning, her eyes huge in her face. "I can't help but wonder if Annaliese hadn't come to town, would any of this have happened? Would Margot and I still be together?"

"Maybe. But I can't blame Margot, and I'm not blaming you, either. I hate that this is happening to you, and her. I love you both. I think of you as mine, and always will, but Margot is really special to me, which is why from the beginning I was concerned, afraid you two were rushing things, afraid she'd end up hurt."

Margot wasn't the only one hurt. He was hurt, too, and maybe it wasn't something they could talk about, but the ache in his chest reminded him of that painful kickback he got when first learning to fire a rifle. "Sally, I wanted her in my life. I wasn't planning on breaking things off, not even when I left for New York and then on to Wyoming. I'd thought I could convince her to visit me, maybe even live with me while I was on location, and see if we could figure it out."

"Max, she works for me. She has a job here, and a life here. Margot's not the type to follow a man around."

"It doesn't really matter now, does it?" he retorted sharply, frustrated by the direction the conversation had turned. He needed Sally's support, not this . . . whatever this was.

The cocktail waitress delivered their drinks. Max took a quick sip of his beer while Sally filled her sake cup. "I'm not angry with you," he said after a moment. "I'm sorry for being an ass. I haven't felt this . . . confused . . . in a long time."

"It's because there is no winner and loser. No one did anything wrong. You're adults being true to yourselves, and you realized that while you have strong feelings for each other, your goals don't align. Max, it's okay to take a step back. Honestly, it's smart to do it now. It would only hurt more later."

"You say there is no winner or loser, but I feel like I lost my best friend. Margot meant that much to me. She was my future. I wanted that future."

"Can you two compromise somehow?"

"You mean, have just half a baby?"

Sally gave him a hard look.

"Or I live in New York while she raises the kid in California?" he said, lifting his beer. "Because that's the only way I can see not damaging a little human being. Admit it, Sally, I'm not cut out to be a dad. I wouldn't know the first thing about being selfless. That's not in my blood."

"Then why did you stand by Annaliese all those years? She wasn't easy. She resented your success and did her best to sabotage your career. But you stayed with her."

"I'm not a quitter. I made a commitment to her, and I intended to keep it. Unfortunately, she wasn't on the same page."

"Because of her affairs, not yours."

He sighed. "Sally, I know what you're doing, and I appreciate it, I do. You love me, and you love Margot, and what could be better than having us end up together? It'd make a perfectly wonderful happy-ever-after to our story, but in this case, it's not going to happen."

Chapter 17

SATURDAY MORNING MARGOT SLEPT IN, WORN OUT from the past twenty-four hours and needing decent sleep since her friends were arriving today. But her first thought on waking was Max, and she grabbed her phone to check and see if he'd possibly texted. If there had been anything on his end. But there were no messages, other than Elizabeth saying they were on the road at six, and then later, right before noon, Paige texted that they'd made good progress and were a half hour out of Paso Robles.

Margot had already showered and dressed and done her hair, and so once that text from Paige came in, she jumped in her car to meet them at the hotel where they were staying. Although both Paige and Elizabeth still had mothers living in Paso, they were making it a girls' weekend, and a hotel suite seemed a lot more fun than sleeping in one's childhood bedroom complete with the obligatory twin bed. When Paige and Elizabeth would see their moms, Margot and Andi planned to slip away and have some catch-up time of their own.

Margot always loved the drive to Paso. She loved the hills covered by grapes. Cambria wasn't home. Paso was. She was going to enjoy her day in Paso Robles with her friends, too. She was not going to be emotional, discuss Max, or share anything personal that was painful. She'd focus on the fun things she and the girls would be doing this afternoon, like the lunch followed by wine tasting. Obviously she wasn't going to do more than sip the different wines, as she couldn't afford to be buzzed tonight. She was not an actor that improved with alcohol. To be fair, she didn't know a single actor who was actually better drunk.

She reached the hotel minutes after Elizabeth had pulled in. She was in reception, checking them in while Andi and Paige hung out by the car.

Margot pulled up and honked. They spun around and then, seeing it was her, rushed to the car, leaning in to hug her.

Elizabeth stepped from reception then with keys and directions to their unit, which took up the wing of the second floor. There were more hugs and lots of talking all at the same time, and then Paige reminded them of their one o'clock lunch reservation, and the restaurant was a fifteen-minute drive from their hotel.

Margot followed Elizabeth to the parking spots assigned to the room, helped her friends carry their overnight bags into the suite, and then after quickly freshening up in front of the two bathroom mirrors, they trooped back down to the cars. Elizabeth knew the area well and said she'd drive. Margot knew the area well, too, but she was happy just being a passenger in the back seat next to Andi.

Andi leaned close to Margot as Elizabeth drove. "I heard about Max," she said under her breath. "I'm sorry."

"How did you know?" Margot asked.

Andi handed Margot her phone, showing her a headline and photo of Max and Annaliese at dinner from a national entertainment magazine's website. From the angle, they looked quite intimate. Margot knew it was the effect of a telephoto lens, but still it made her swallow hard. The headline, *Max and Annaliese Together Again*, was sensational as well.

"They're not back together," Margot said carefully. "But Max and I aren't together anymore, either."

Andi gave her an incredulous look. "I saw the photos of you two. You couldn't keep your hands off of each other."

"It's a theater thing. Actors always fall for each other. I knew this would happen, and I knew it would end, and I'm fine."

"Really?"

Margot nodded. "He's not sticking around here. He'll be in Wyoming for four months starting in August, and then he'll be overseas to film a movie, and then there's a pilot for a show that he's auditioned for and his agent thinks he'll get." Just reciting all the work he'd be doing, and all the traveling, put an ache in her chest. When he left, it really would be goodbye. But that was still a little more than two weeks away, and despite how hard it would be to see him again tonight, it would be even worse when he was gone for good.

The topic of Max and Margot came up again at lunch, and Margot repeated herself, saying virtually the same things. She hadn't expected the romance to last. It had been a summer fling, fun, but not something permanent, and she was good. In fact, as soon as the play was over, she was thinking of doing a little traveling. Did any of them have time? She was hoping to escape for at least the first week of August.

No one could get away, they all had families and commitments, especially with the university starting fall semester in a few weeks, but they discussed all the places Margot could go. Paige suggested Yellowstone. Elizabeth was a huge fan of Puerto Vallarta, although it would be too hot in August. Maybe Margot should try in March. Andi suggested a drive down to Orange County, a few days in Laguna, a few days in San Clemente, and maybe a few days in the mountains. They talked about which they liked better, mountains or ocean, reading by the fire or reading on the beach, as they did their wine tasting. As they tried the different wines, Margot warmed to the idea of escaping. She didn't even care where she'd go, she wanted to be somewhere else, and feel something new.

As they returned to the hotel so Margot could get her car and head back to Cambria, Margot mentioned that she'd made a dinner reservation for them all after the play, asking if Elizabeth thought her mom, Mrs. Ortiz, would enjoy dinner after as well.

Margot blew kisses to her friends and drove back to Cambria, remembering how she'd invited Max to join them back when they were together, back when he made her feel like the most beautiful woman alive.

Her chin quivered, and she struggled to hold back the tears. She had a show to do tonight, She had to be strong and keep her feelings in check.

She wouldn't tell anyone, but she was glad she'd see him soon. It felt awful not talking with him, not hearing his voice or seeing his face throughout the day. She still felt the connection between them, felt all those little nerves and bits of energy and desire that made him feel like hers. Her Max. Her love. Her heart.

It would take time to wean herself off him. It was probably good they did a show together six nights a week. It was better having that hour and a half at the playhouse than losing him cold turkey. And tonight would be fun. Her friends would be in the audience, and they were such wonderful friends. Margot was looking forward to performing for them, and eager for Mrs. Ortiz, her high school drama teacher, to see how far she'd come.

AT THE THEATER, MARGOT WENT BEHIND THE STAGE TO the tiny dressing rooms in the back. She unrolled her yoga mat in the corner and did some stretching, and a few of her favorite yoga poses, trying to relax and get focused for to-night. She was keyed up, and excited, but also emotional. Working with Max made her feel, and now that they weren't together, those feelings were hard to manage.

She was still sitting on her yoga mat when a knock sounded on the closed door. "Come in," she called, getting to her feet.

Max opened the door.

Her heart rose and fell. She met his gaze and for a second couldn't look away. He was still everything. "Hi."

"Looks like Sharon's understudy is going to go on for her tonight," he said. "Sharon's running a fever and has chills now. She can't risk exposing everyone."

Margot picked up her mat and began rolling it up. "Did she call you?"

"No, she phoned Jen but I just saw Jen—who was on her way to get the understudy here pronto—and she asked me to tell you."

Margot tucked the mat back into the corner. "My friends will be here tonight, and my high school drama teacher."

"Mrs. Ortiz," he said.

She couldn't hide her surprise. "You remembered."

"You said she was important to you."

For a second she couldn't speak. Part of her longed to throw her arms around him and beg him to forget the past day and a half and let them go back to the way things were, but the rational part of her brain reminded her that she was the one who'd initiated the break. She was the one who'd decided she couldn't do this. "How are you?"

"Doing okay." He hesitated. "Annaliese is gone. She re-turned to L.A. this morning."

"That's good."

He opened his mouth to say something but then shut it, saying nothing. She wished she knew what he'd intended to say.

Silence stretched, the kind of silence that wasn't easy,

the silence that made you ache. Margot ached. How she missed the comfort she'd once found in him.

"I should get ready," he said.

She nodded.

Max turned at the door. "I don't suppose I'm joining you all for dinner tonight."

Her gaze focused on his mouth because she couldn't look into his eyes, nor could she let him see how raw she was, how much pain she was feeling. "Probably not a good idea," she agreed huskily. "It'd be a little awkward with the way things stand."

She didn't add that her friends were upset for her, and circling around her, because even though she didn't blame him, they knew something was wrong. They knew she hurt.

"Perhaps I could still say hello to your teacher, Mrs. Ortiz? You'd said she'd like to meet me. I'd love to introduce myself, if that is okay with you."

Margot swallowed around the lump in her throat. "I'm sure Mrs. Ortiz would enjoy it. I'll bring them onto the stage after the show. Would that work for you?"

"Sounds great."

The performance was almost like the first one, opening night, charged with an electric energy. The understudy for the mother role missed a line, but quickly covered the mistake, and everything else went incredibly smoothly. More than smoothly. Margot felt filled with honey and heat, her body tingling, her heart pounding. This was what she'd loved. Being onstage, being alive. And when Max kissed her neck she sighed, missing him, missing everything between them, which only made the rest of the play more intense, and the final scene so very bittersweet.

My God, she loved him. She had a sneaking suspicion she'd always love him. But wasn't that a good thing? At least she was feeling again.

After the standing ovation, Margot sent Jen to get her

friends and bring them up on the stage, behind the closed curtain.

Margot was conscious of Max waiting beside her, and then her friends were there, with Mrs. Ortiz leaning heavily on Elizabeth's arm.

Andi's eyes widened and she took in Max at Margot's side. Margot focused on her drama teacher. "Mrs. Ortiz, Max wanted to meet you. He's heard me rave about you, and how you taught me everything I know."

Mrs. Ortiz was tiny, a hair over five feet tall, and she moved forward, hands outstretched.

Max stepped in to take her hands, giving her a steadying arm. "Hello, Mrs. Ortiz. It's a pleasure to meet you."

"I have followed your career since you started performing at Yale, Mr. Russo." Mrs. Ortiz's voice quavered but her eyes were bright. "You have accomplished so much. It's not easy doing what you've done."

"You must call me Max," he answered, "and thank you for all your years of teaching. You have inspired many."

"I hope so." She hesitated. "Can I hug you?"

"Absolutely." Max gently hugged Mrs. Ortiz, the top of her gray head barely reaching the middle of his chest. When she stepped away, she was beaming.

Margot felt a wash of emotion, and gratitude. Max might not be hers anymore, but he was still lovely, and he'd made her teacher feel special. She used the moment to quickly introduce her friends. "Max, this is Mrs. Ortiz's daughter, Elizabeth. This is Paige, who is also from Paso Robles. Elizabeth and Paige grew up together and are still best friends. And then this is Andi, who works with Elizabeth and Paige at the university. Andi has become a close friend of mine."

Max shook hands with each, and there was a minute of stilted small talk. Then he excused himself, and they headed outside to go to dinner. Margot wished, how she wished, things had been different, and Max could have gone to dinner with them.

SUNDAY, MARGOT MET THE GIRLS IN PASO ROBLES FOR brunch, and they lingered over their meal until almost one, when they had to get back on the road for the drive home. Margot had been feeling good with them, and safe, but when they all said goodbye and began climbing into their car, Margot started to cry.

Mortified, she wiped the tears away, and everyone came back out of the car and hugged her all over again. She laughed at herself, trying to explain that she'd been so happy seeing everyone again, and being together again, that it was hard to watch them go.

Again Elizabeth and Paige got into the car, Elizabeth in the driver's seat, Paige in the passenger side, but Andi lingered for a moment, wanting to speak with Margot.

"You should come see me," Andi said, voice low. "We could go up to the cabin. It's gorgeous in the summer. When the play ends, come for a visit. Or maybe if you can take a few extra days, join me in Blue Jay for Labor Day? Wolf is working a lot and I'd love your company."

"I'd like that," Margot said, holding on to her smile. "We need to spend more time together."

"Let's plan on Labor Day weekend, okay? Put it in on your calendar," Andi said firmly, giving her one last hug.

"I will," Margot answered, hugging her back, grateful, so grateful for friends that truly cared.

WITH HER FRIENDS GONE, MARGOT SETTLED INTO THE new week, working hard during the day, and then off to the theater each night. She wasn't crying this week. She was no longer in shock. Instead she felt numb, and a little bit dead.

Even though she wasn't drawing attention to herself at

the office, Margot could feel Sally's gaze rest on her. She'd often look up from her computer to see Sally watching her, and every time Margot would smile or wave, not wanting Sally to worry or feel guilty. This wasn't Sally's problem. She wasn't responsible for the breakup. That was Margot's decision, and while she might regret making it so hastily, she knew that, ultimately, it was the right thing.

On Wednesday, exactly a week after Annaliese had put in her appearance, Sally asked Margot to take a walk with her during their lunch. Sally drove them to Moonstone Beach, where they strolled along the boardwalk. The sun had burned off the clouds, and the sky was a light delicate blue, while the water shone sapphire. Margot lifted her face to the sun, savoring the warmth and light. She could smell the fragrant wildflowers growing along the boardwalk and hear the squawk of seagulls overhead, and the delicate sandpipers running on the beach eased some of the ache within her.

"I hate seeing you so unhappy," Sally said after several minutes. "Thank heavens Max is leaving soon."

But thinking of Max gone didn't make Margot feel better. If anything it created more pain. "But then you won't see him," she said huskily.

"He was going to leave anyway. You, you're supposed to stay." Sally glanced at her. "But when the play is over, I do think you deserve a break. You need some time off. Maybe even get away."

"I'll be fine—"

"I've been thinking about it a lot," Sally said, overriding Margot's objection. "You need a holiday. You've earned a holiday. I'd like you to go somewhere warm, somewhere new. I owe you. I promised you the moon if you took on the play, and I haven't delivered."

Margot wrinkled her nose. "You owe me nothing. Despite this . . . with Max . . . it's been a good summer. It's been a great summer. The play's been fun. You've got me acting again. Imagine that!"

"Have you been to Greece?" Sally asked abruptly. "I have friends with a villa. On Santorini, I think. Or is it Mykonos? It's fully staffed, and it's empty this summer. They invited me to use it, and before my heart attack I was thinking about going in August. How about I send you instead?" She gave Margot a naughty look. "You might like a gorgeous Greek. Greek men are lovely. Excellent in bed, but the very traditional ones don't make American wives good husbands."

Margot shook her head and laughed despite the lump filling her throat, making her eyes burn. "Oh, Sally. You and men!"

"Why not? They're fun." And then she took in Margot's watery eyes and quivering smile, and her smile disappeared. "Well, not when they go stomping on your heart. That's not fun, but, Margot, my dear, you're young, you've got so many adventures ahead of you. Just go for it. Live."

"I'm not that young anymore." Her voice cracked. "Next birthday it's the big five-oh."

"So? I'm seventy-six—"

"Sally! You said you were sixty-six."

Sally shrugged. "And Max thinks I'm sixty-three. The age doesn't matter, Margot. It's the attitude. I want to enjoy this life, squeeze every little drop from it. I think you should, too." She pulled out her phone, typed something, and then turned the screen so Margot could see it.

"The view from my friends' home," Sally said.

It was turquoise water, a rocky hill with whitewashed buildings with tiled roofs, cobalt-blue doors, and pink, red, and purple flowers everywhere.

"Gorgeous," Margot said.

"It is. So consider it done. I'm getting you a ticket to Greece. I've got the miles, too. How would you like to go first class? Champagne on the airplane, a seat that folds flat. Let's spoil you a little, shall we?"

Margot's eyes prickled but she was smiling as she hugged Sally. "Okay."

"Okay, yes?"

"Yes. Why not? Greece sounds great."

MARGOT WENT TO THE THEATER THAT EVENING THINK-ing how much everything had changed in a week. She was glad, too, for her acting career, and that again tonight she could pour all of herself into the play.

Performing with Max kept her close to him, even if it was for ninety minutes every night onstage. Being touched by Max, held by him, kissed by him made her feel so much. Tonight, it was almost too painful, but she'd take the pain over feeling nothing.

If only the play were real life. She didn't want to just be his wife in a play, onstage. But what she wanted didn't matter. Just like with Sam, what she wanted wasn't part of the equation, and that's where Max and she were now. Which is why, during those last scenes of the play tonight, where she as Corie felt such desperation, Margot was there, in Corie, living all of the emotions.

It was a relief to be fully alive, to feel free to be at the end of her tether, in need of saving.

In the play, Corie needed Paul to help her.

In real life, she needed Max, and wanted Max, but she couldn't see how to bridge the gap between what was, and what they each needed. He didn't want a family but she did. He didn't want to marry again, and she'd never been married. Could she love him enough to let the other dreams go? Could he love her enough to fill those empty places within her heart?

She didn't know, and wasn't even sure how to talk about it with him. So at least they had this, these acts, these scenes. These moments that were increasingly fleeting.

Soon the play would be over.

After tonight there were only eleven performances remaining, and then this terrible, wonderful, life-changing time would end.

THURSDAY NIGHT MAX WOKE UP IN A COLD SWEAT. HE pushed the covers down to his hips, cooling himself, while trying to calm his racing pulse. What a terrible dream. It wasn't even real and yet the words Annaliese had said to him in the dream were the very words Cynthia had said as she left him all those years ago. *It's always about you, Max Russo. There's only room for you.*

Cynthia might have been right. Annaliese wasn't. He'd learned from his first marriage, and he'd tried hard to be a better husband for Annaliese. He tried hard to give her everything he could. But it wasn't enough. She had needs he couldn't meet. She had struggles he couldn't fix. He gave and gave but like in tonight's dream, he still wasn't enough.

Max left his bed, pulled on his boxers, and walked to the living room. The landscape spotlights were off, but the moon was nearly full and illuminated the foamy surf crashing on the rocks.

He hated the feeling of inadequacy. Hated being someone who constantly disappointed others. This isn't the man he'd wanted to be. He'd achieved the career but not the personal success. If he were truly successful, he wouldn't let fear drive him. If he were truly mature, he wouldn't let the past haunt him.

Maybe Cynthia was still right. Maybe there would never be room for anyone else in his life. It was a depressing thought. But at least he was being real.

FRIDAY MORNING, MAX HIT THE CAMBRIA GYM AND worked out with a vengeance, putting every bit of his anger and self-loathing into the weights, lifting heavier, doing more reps, pushing himself until he hit the wall on every exercise. By the time he was done, he could barely walk out of the gym, but he was calmer. Quieter. He'd managed to silence some of his demons.

Outside on the sidewalk, he looked up at the sky. The sun was starting to break through the marine layer, bits of blue and rays of light through the billowy gray.

It crossed his mind that he needed to let all the demons go—the guilt over his mom, his dad, Max's wives, and the mistakes. There were so many mistakes. But how could you get anywhere if you're constantly dragging all the bad feelings with you?

It was time to let the past go. It was time to stop hating himself so much. He was a man, not a demigod or hero. Mistakes happened. People failed. People screwed up. It was a part of life. Part of being human.

For the rest of the day, he was just going to be human. No more, no less. He would feel and he would be, and if he made a mistake, he'd forgive himself because he honestly was doing his best.

That evening during the performance, Max held Margot onstage as if it were the first time. He kissed her neck, feeling her shudder, her skin so sensitive, her skin so familiar, her soft sigh as his lips trailed her neck a bittersweet pain. He loved this woman. He adored her.

He'd missed being with her this past week, and it had been only a week, but it felt like forever.

He'd missed holding her and kissing her, talking and listening. Laughing. Missed the walks, the visits to Sally, the lunches at her dad's. He missed talking with her and listening to her. Missed sitting with a drink and rehashing the evening's performance. He missed the little navy and gold flecks in her eyes you could only see when close.

In short, he missed everything about her.

After tonight there were only ten performances left. Ten

more nights to look into Margot's eyes. Ten more nights to hold her close. Ten more nights to hear her laugh. It wasn't enough. He had to find courage, and the words, to let her know that he didn't want to lose her. That maybe, as Sally had said, there was some kind of compromise, something that would work for them, so they could have a future.

He wanted a future with her. That's what he had to tell her. He didn't have all the answers, but the one thing he knew, the one thing he believed, was that they were meant to be together.

After changing, he stopped by her dressing room. He rapped on the door, and when there was only silence, he opened it and discovered the room was dark. She'd already gone. Disappointment surged through him. He'd worked himself up, gathered his thoughts, and was ready to express himself, and so, feeling like a kid in high school, he drove to her place. The shades were down but he could see a shadow moving inside. Max parked, turned the engine off, incredibly nervous.

Not sure what to do, he called her.

She didn't answer.

But from the shadow moving inside, he knew she was there. He drew a rough breath. He hesitated, uncertain, but then he called her again.

She didn't answer still.

He texted her. I'm outside.

He waited, and waited, and just when he thought he'd have to leave, the front door opened, and she stood on her little porch, silhouetted by light.

She wasn't beckoning him in. But she also wasn't sending him away.

He got out of his car, and walked halfway to the front door. She was in her pajamas, her hair in a ponytail high on her head. She looked sixteen. He felt fifteen. "It's late, I know," he said.

"I can't invite you in," she said.

"Alright. But could we talk out here? I need to talk. *We* need to talk."

"Will it change the outcome?" she asked, coming down the stairs, approaching him in the driveway. "Are you ready to be a dad? I doubt it. Am I ready to give up my dreams to be an actor's wife? No."

"You sound so cold putting it like that."

"Max, I'd be thrilled if I could figure out how to make this work so we're both happy and have the futures we want. I mean that. My feelings for you haven't died. I don't keep you out here because I hate you. I keep you out here because if I invited you in, I'd make you stay with me all night. I miss you. I miss everything about us. But I gave everything to make Sam happy, and it was never enough. I don't want to do that again, give and give and feel empty at the end."

"Maybe there wouldn't be an end. Maybe we'd find a way—"

"How?" Her voice broke. "Are you going to stay here? No. Am I going to move and leave my dad again? No. Do I want to do another long-distance relationship? Because that's what I had with Sam. And that's another big no. You need to find that wonderful woman who will love you and support you, and only you, because that's what you need. Someone who will make you the center of her universe, and sadly, despite how much I love you, that won't be me."

He nodded. Her words hurt. It all hurt. He'd driven here tonight with high hopes. He'd imagined that tonight would be the start of something new, something better. He was wrong. "I hear you, and I don't agree, but I respect you too much to argue." He looked at her, taking in her silhouette, her face shadowed, but even with the distance between them, he remembered how she'd felt in his arms, in his bed. "Good night, Margot."

Her voice was nearly inaudible. "Good night, Max."

* * *

INSIDE THE HOUSE, MARGOT PRESSED HER FOREHEAD TO the door.

She'd come so very, very close to going to him, reaching for him. But if he touched her, kissed her, she'd melt. She'd need him even more than she already did.

Love this big was consuming. Love like this made her crazy. Margot climbed into her bed fully clothed and cried.

Margot was still feeling emotional and raw Saturday night as she waited in the wings to go on the stage. Max was already out there now. With the role reversal, the character Paul opened the play, and Margot watched him, breathless, anxious, her heart in her throat.

All day she'd waited for this performance tonight. All day she wrestled with herself—call him, don't call him, talk to him, don't talk to him—and soon she'd be onstage, soon she'd be with him, and touched by him. The kisses were almost too painful, the sensation overwhelming. Close to him, she wanted to stay there. Alone at home, she couldn't imagine him leaving and never seeing him again.

Margot took a quick sip of water from her water bottle, squared her shoulders, thinking of her first line, creating the energy necessary for the stage. In a moment she'd walk onstage and be Corie Bratter, Paul's wife.

Energy pulsed through her. The nerves had turned to excitement. Acting with Max, she came alive. And even when the play ended, she was determined to stay alive. Love might hurt, but this time around, she was older, wiser, stronger.

This time love wasn't going to break her. She had friends, she had work, she had her dad—she'd be okay.

SUNDAY MORNING MARGOT HAD A BRUNCH DATE WITH Sally. They were going to Sally's favorite, the Madonna Inn's Copper Cafe, the inn loved as much for its pink exterior as the comfort food in the—also pink and gloriously whimsical—restaurants.

Margot looked forward to getting out of Cambria and heading toward San Luis Obispo. She picked up Sally at eleven, and Sally was in a great mood, wearing a new blouse with crisp white trousers, and from her never-ending smile, Margot suspected Sally had something good happening in her personal life.

"So, are you going to tell me about it?" Margot said, glancing at Sally as she drove. "What, when, who, all the juicy stuff?"

Sally shrugged delicately. "It's very new still."

"But he's making you happy."

"Russ is terribly sweet. He's a doctor at the hospital."

"Oh, Sally!"

"And he's not a youngster. He's reasonably close to my age."

"What?" Margot cried. "Your age? What's happened to you, Sally? Where have all the pups gone?"

Sally adjusted her chunky gold necklace. "You can tease me, but age doesn't matter, not when you meet someone wonderful."

"Was he your doctor?"

"No. He is a cardiologist, and Russ was making rounds while I was taking a walk around my floor. I thought he was quite attractive, and quite elegant, so I commented on his tie, and we struck up a conversation."

"Now you're dating?"

"As much as we can. Fortunately, it's about quality of time, not quantity."

Margot loved how Sally couldn't stop smiling. "As a cardiologist, does he worry about your heart?"

Sally put a hand to her chest, indignant. "I have a wonderful heart."

Margot laughed. "Yes, you do."

Reaching the inn, Margot parked, and she and Sally

walked around the hotel's public rooms and grounds, enjoying the fairy-tale elements, until it was time for them to be seated in the café. They talked about a little of everything, skirting the subject of Max.

"One week left," Sally said as they each enjoyed a chocolate mousse for dessert. "How is it possible?"

Margot exhaled slowly. She wasn't ready for it to end. Performing, she could pretend he was still in her life, not just at the theater, but in real life. At least there was that stage kiss. The stage hug. The contact that kept her going.

"I don't know," Margot said, remembering the challenging start. "It was hard in the beginning, but it all came together."

"If Max didn't need to go to Wyoming, you could continue for another month."

Margot didn't know how to respond to that, so she didn't. "I'd dreaded doing any theater here, and yet, I've enjoyed it. It's been good for me. I feel like me, the old me, the one who could do anything."

Sally smiled smugly. "I knew you'd be sensational."

"To be fair, Max made a huge difference. He's a tremendous actor with a huge fan base."

Sally arched an eyebrow. "You've developed your own. I've seen the cards sent to the theater. People love you."

Margot hesitated. "I'm not opposed to possibly doing something at the playhouse again. Depends on what it is, of course."

Sally feigned shock, and patted the table and then her purse. "Wait, let me get my phone out. I want to record you saying that."

Margot laughed. "Make sure you record the part where I say, 'It depends on what the play is.'" She smiled at Sally, grateful at how well Sally was doing, grateful Sally had a new man in her life, a man who happened to be a doctor. "I wish you were coming with me to Greece. We'd have so much fun together."

"As soon as I'm cleared for international travel."

"If something came up," Margot said carefully, "would you be able to get the miles for my ticket back? Or would they be lost for good?"

"Why? Are you having second thoughts about Greece?"

Margot shrugged. "I think it'd be more fun to go with a travel buddy. Going on my own seems rather lonely."

"But you'll be able to meet more men this way. Who knows? You might come back engaged—or even married."

"That's not going to happen." A lump filled Margot's throat. She blinked. "You know I love Max."

"Then invite him to Greece with you."

"Sally, be serious."

"I am. Maybe a getaway is just what you two need. Maybe you'll be able to have a real conversation and figure this out."

Margot rubbed at a bead of moisture on her water glass. "He came by last night. He wanted to talk."

"That's good. How did it go?"

"Not well. I'm struggling. I love him but I don't see how we can make things work, and I don't want to be the one who sacrifices my dreams because he doesn't like kids."

Sally gave her a look. "Max loves kids. If you knew him, you wouldn't say that."

"Then why is he so opposed to children?"

Sally looked across the bustling restaurant, every table filled, then back at Margot. "He blames himself for things he couldn't control, and it was awful, it really was. But he was a little boy. What could he do? What can any seven-year-old do?"

"What happened?" Margot asked, pain rushing through her.

"Maybe you should ask him. Maybe once you understand some of those scars and secrets, you two can find a way around them."

Chapter 18

MAX WAS THE ONE WHO TOLD HER. HIS CALL WOKE HER up and, sleepy, Margot made him repeat the news twice. The playhouse was on fire. It had been burning for the past two hours. The firefighters almost had it out now.

Margot dressed quickly, numb. She drove straight downtown. She could smell the fire from the highway, and as she approached Main Street, the smoke still trailed up.

The street had been blocked in front of the theater. Margot's chest squeezed tight as she parked on the street and then walked to the theater. Sally was there, with a handsome bearded man, his arm around her.

Margot approached Sally, tears in her eyes as she struggled to take in what was left of the theater. The roof was gone, the huge beams sticking out of the hollowed theater, burnt edges poking into the sky.

As Margot joined her, Sally repeated what the fire chief had told her. The fire seemed to have started backstage, and had swept across the stage, into the auditorium, destroying the lobby, too, which meant virtually everything.

Tape was up, keeping everyone but the fire department back. The theater was still smoking, and even though it wasn't yet six in the morning, there were dozens of people on the street, watching.

The smell was terrible. Margot put her fist to her nose, trying to block the acrid smell. It broke her heart to see the playhouse like this. It had become such a big part of her life this summer, and she might have resisted its charms earlier in the year, but she had come to love it. And now all that was left was this blackened shell.

Margot didn't even know she was crying until Sally wrapped an arm around her shoulders. "It's okay," Sally said quietly, firmly. "I'm thankful no one was inside. Things can be replaced. People cannot."

Sally's calm and strength made Margot swallow hard, the lump in her throat making it hard to speak. "We were having such a great summer season. We were on fire—" She broke off, sniffed weakly. "No pun intended."

"It was a great summer season. I'm so proud of you, and Max. So proud of everyone. You all pulled together. You became a family. It's what I always envisioned for the playhouse. And you and Max brought it star power. How extraordinary is that?"

"You're being so positive." Margot reached up to dry her eyes. "Why aren't you more upset? You poured yourself into this theater. You have worked so hard to make this dream come true."

Sally squeezed her shoulders. "Because the dream came true. We had the summer season I always dreamed of. People were happy. The community came together. We sold out. Folks came back again and again, bringing family and friends. Others drove here to see the play. Isn't that amazing?"

"But we weren't done yet. We had our final week left."

"Don't focus on what didn't happen, but on what did. Every night, a full house. Ovation after ovation. Reviews in all the big papers. This theater sat empty for ten years before

I bought it, and it has been a struggle, bringing it to life, but we did it. That was the goal. That was the challenge. And we met it. More than met it. We succeeded beyond my wildest dreams."

"What about the fall production? We're just about to cast the show."

"There's not going to be a fall season. I was talking to Russ before you arrived, and maybe it is time for someone else to take this property over. I'm not sure it can be rebuilt. I don't know the extent of the damage, but the city might not want to protect it. They might want to develop this square. In that case—"

"Sally, no. You've shown everyone that Cambria loves its theater. You've shown everyone what we can do here with the arts. I can't bear to think that it's all over." She looked at Sally, held her gaze. "I don't want it to be over. We have to finish the season. I don't want to refund a single ticket. Let's honor those tickets, and end strong. I'm sure there has to be an auditorium we can use. I'll have Jen start making calls—"

"Now I need to remind you to be practical. It would be far easier to refund the tickets, and go out on top, with a win. The reviews for *Barefoot in the Park* have been incredible. Let's savor that. There's no need to keep pushing so hard, not anymore."

"I disagree." Margot felt so strongly she couldn't let it go. She was passionate about the play, committed to what they'd been doing this summer. "Let me talk to Max—wait, where is he? He called me."

"He was here earlier. He had an errand to run, said he'd be back later. I think he'll be back soon."

"I'm going to call him. I want to get his thoughts. If he thinks we should close, then we will, because I can't force him to continue. However, if he wants to finish the season, I'll get Jen researching our options. I know we have options. I know this isn't over. Not like this."

Margot returned to her car, and sat down heavily in the driver's seat, her legs shaking. Her entire body trembling. She'd imagined a lot of things happening this summer, but not this. Never this.

She was about to call Max, when her phone rang. He was calling her.

"I'm parked down a block from the theater," she said. "I can't believe it. It's totaled. It's gone."

"They think it might be an electrical fire. Something with the lights."

Margot sighed. "That's what Sally said."

"Is Sally still there?"

"Yes. She's with her new guy, Dr. Russ."

"That's good. She doesn't need to be alone right now."

Margot felt like crying. The poor theater. Such a beautiful historic playhouse. Gone. "Where are you? Can we talk?"

"Want to come here?"

She hesitated, and then didn't even know why she was hesitating. Being with Max now was all she wanted. "I'll grab a coffee and head over."

"Or I could make you coffee here," he suggested.

"Even better. See you soon."

It still felt strange to be back at Max's house. The 1960s cottage was exactly the same. The garden was the same. The interior and deck all the same, but she wasn't the same, and from the looks of it, Max wasn't, either.

The coffee finished brewing as she entered the small kitchen. It felt weird keeping her distance from him, weird and empty with all this distance between them. She'd found security and comfort in his arms. But he wasn't hers anymore . . . or was he?

They carried their cups out onto the deck, and they both stood at the railing and looked out. Margot knocked away a tear. She didn't know why she was crying. She felt beaten. Broken. And she didn't like it.

It was breezy, and Margot's hair kept blowing in her

eyes. She tucked a tendril behind her ear. "Sally thinks we need to end the season now. Wrap it up. Refund the tickets for the remaining shows."

"She told me the same thing earlier."

Margot glanced at him. "What do you think?"

"That I shouldn't always listen to Sally."

Margot pressed her lips together. Her eyes felt scratchy, and a lump filled her throat. She wanted to put a hand on his arm. A hand to his chest. She missed his warmth. Missed his skin. Missed the way he kissed her when they were alone.

But she couldn't go there now, couldn't think those things. "We're lucky it's Monday, I suppose. The theater is dark today. It gives us time to strategize. We could reschedule performances for Tuesday and Wednesday, maybe even Thursday, and hopefully by Friday we could be live again. Somewhere. If we can tap a lot of volunteers, we can organize sets and costumes in three days. Just need a place we could perform." She glanced at his profile. She couldn't read him at the moment. "If that's what you wanted to do."

"It's a lot of work for our crew. The burden of making the adjustment falls mainly to them."

"I know there are so many others who'd love to help."

He sipped his coffee but said nothing.

"In the beginning we didn't have a lot of volunteers," she continued. "But that's changed. We have fans—and friends—here in the community, people who'd love to step up. Our set isn't that complicated—"

"It took them two full weeks to build it the first time," he interrupted.

"That included painting. We know what we're doing this time." She looked at him hopefully, not wanting to force him, but hoping, hoping he'd want to finish the season. She'd been counting on finishing the season.

She'd wanted this last week with him.

It was selfish, but there it was.

"Thoughts?" she asked quietly.

"There's a ranch in Paso Robles that does concerts and events. They have nothing scheduled the next couple of weeks. EV Ranch has no built-in seats. Everyone would need to take folding chairs or blankets, but they have a decent stage with lights and sound. It's a permitted venue. We could take our play outdoors, theater in the park." Max looked at Margot, expression revealing nothing.

"How do you know all this?"

"I started making calls as soon as I left Sally, and it's so early that no one was up, but then I got a call from Jason, the manager of EV Ranch. He'd heard about the fire on the morning news. I guess it's everywhere, and people are upset—"

"How did he even have your number?" she interrupted, confused.

"Jen had given him my number a couple weeks ago. Remember we'd discussed doing a benefit there, but things got crazy and we let it go."

She nodded, holding her breath, eager to hear the rest.

"Jason straight up offered their venue. I was on the phone with him just before I called you. He's promised to do whatever he can to help us." Max's expression eased, a faint smile curving his lips. "I wanted to have a plan before we talked. I didn't want you to feel the burden of making this work . . . *if* you wanted it to work."

"I want it to work." She paused, and frowned, still not totally clear. "Why would Jason offer his venue to us? Does he want a percentage of the tickets?"

Max's gaze rested on her mouth and then lifted, locking with her eyes. "He saw the play when it first opened. He'd brought his wife and mom, and they had a great time. It was his mom's idea for him to call me. The ranch used to be hers." He hesitated. "Apparently, she went to school with your drama teacher, Mrs. Ortiz. They were good friends in school, and she followed your career. She's always been very proud of you."

Margot's eyes smarted and she blinked hard. "When we started rehearsing in May, I didn't think anyone remembered me."

"You were wrong."

"About a lot of things," she said.

His expression tightened and Margot shook her head. "Not about you. Oh, not at all about you. I meant about myself. About my confidence, and my self-worth. I'd stopped believing in me. I'd stopped imagining a future for me. But it's changed. I've changed, and that's a good thing."

He looked as if he wanted to say something, but instead Max's jaw firmed. There was silence for a moment, an uncomfortable silence that Margot needed to fill.

"Should we check out the venue? Make sure it works?" she asked.

"I've looked at it online. It has a stage, parking, restrooms, concessions. It's not the Greek Theatre or the Hollywood Bowl, it's pretty rustic, but if they can put up chairs for us, and then have open seating in the back, on the lawn, allowing us to sell a few more tickets, it could work."

"I love the idea of performing under the stars. Let's lock this in and then we can tell Sally, before she tells anyone else that the summer season is done."

He gestured to the house. "Do you want to see EV Ranch's website?"

"Later I will. Right now I need to start making calls. See if we can get a new set and props, and I've got to have the office staff reach the ticket holders for the next couple of nights, see if we can get them rescheduled. Or refunded. Whatever they prefer."

She smiled at Max, glad they were in this together. "I hate what's happened to the theater, but I'm excited. Performing outside, on a summer night? What could be better?"

He smiled back at her. "Nothing, as long as I'm performing with you."

* * *

MARGOT WENT HOME, SHOWERED, AND DRESSED FOR work. Sally hadn't come in yet this morning, but once at the office, Margot met with Heather, Kelly, and Ali. Jen was off talking to the local radio station, doing an interview about the fire, and how the play was going to find a new home at EV Ranch in Paso for the final week.

"I'll update the website," Heather assured Margot.

"I can help reach out to the ticket holders," Ali offered. "When would they be able to use their tickets, if they can't this week?"

"We'll add a couple more shows at the end," Margot said. "We were supposed to wrap on Saturday, July twenty-second. Let's continue into the next week, with Sunday, and then Tuesday, Wednesday, and Thursday. That should take care of those who'd bought tickets and don't want to miss out."

"What about the lawn area? How do you want to handle that?" Heather looked worried. "It could be a bit of a nightmare. You'd need more security, more concessions, more everything."

"What if we make a total of one hundred lawn tickets available for each night at the ranch? They can be discounted. So instead of forty-five a ticket, they'd be, say, fifteen?"

"Twenty," Ali said promptly. "It's you and Max Russo. This isn't community theater anymore."

"But it's supposed to be," Margot said.

"And yet it's not." Ali glanced at Heather. "If you can send me the spreadsheet with the tickets purchased, I'll work on emailing everyone. I think the best thing is to make it a straight exchange, Tuesday tickets for Tuesday, Wednesday for Wednesday, etc."

"Good plan," Margot agreed.

"Have you seen the venue?" Heather asked.

"No." Margot glanced back at Sally's dark office. "I'm

thinking of scooping up Sally and dragging her out there with me. It's her production after all."

"No," Ali corrected. "It's yours."

Heather nodded. "And that's what Sally always wanted. She wanted you to own this. She wanted this to be your success."

Margot thought about it for a moment. "Then maybe I don't bother Sally at all. Maybe we go for it. Make it happen."

Heather nodded. "That's what I'm talking about. Let's go, Queen Margot."

BUT SALLY DID NEED AN UPDATE, MARGOT REALIZED, AS she was wrapping up her office work late that afternoon. Sally would need to know what was going on, since lots of things were happening. Like an additional week of performances being added to accommodate the canceled performances this week. And more tickets being sold for the lawn areas so more people could see the play before it closed.

Margot would have loved Max to be with her, explaining the plans to Sally, but he was tackling big things like set, sound, and lights, so Margot called Sally and asked if she'd like some company. Russ was working tonight, and Sally would love company, so Margot picked up dinner and she and Sally ate outside on her antique wrought iron table. It was warm but there was a breeze to keep things pleasant, and as they ate, Margot told Sally about the changes being made, and how they were moving forward, finishing the summer season as planned.

Margot had been pushing around her salad greens with the prongs of her fork but put her fork down. "We're going to miss a couple performances this week, but they'll be rescheduled at the end. We'll be back onstage Friday night."

"You found a theater?"

"Not a theater, but a venue. The EV Ranch in Paso Robles

reached out to us. They offered us their outdoor space. It's not an amphitheater, but they have all the essentials and they've offered to bring in folding chairs for the one hundred paid seats, which means we don't have to close, and we don't have to refund tickets. We can finish the season, and we'll have time to figure out what you'd like to do for the fall season."

Sally put her fork down and looked at Margot. "No."

Margot frowned. "No what?"

"No fall season. No more. I don't have it in me to rebuild the theater. It took two years to get it open, and we'd only been open six months and now it's gone. I'm not a quitter, but I don't have the heart for it. I don't have the energy. I'm sorry."

"You don't need to apologize to me. It's your theater."

"But you've invested so much of yourself this summer. I don't want you to think—"

"I understand," Margot said. "This has been a hard summer for you as well. I doubt insurance will cover all the improvements you made. I'm sure you're taking quite a financial hit."

"I am, but that's not why I'm walking away. I'm walking away so I can focus on new things, happier things. This theater has been a struggle. Once I was invested, I was determined to see it through, but it's been hard, and exhausting. Maybe the fire is a blessing in disguise. Maybe it's going to free both of us. I'll be able to focus more on doing things with Russ, and you can look at your future in a new light."

Margot frowned. "How so?"

"You knocked it out of the park with *Barefoot in the Park*." Sally winked. "Pun intended. You and Max have been sensational. Everyone's talking about it. It's been the thing to do this summer, and not just here, locally, but all over California. But you shouldn't be tied to that theater. You shouldn't feel any obligation to future seasons, and knowing you, you would. But as you've repeatedly told me since you first started working for me, there's more to you than being an actor. There's more than performing. You have hopes, dreams. Maybe this is fate's way of saying, 'Go for it. Take those risks. Have that life you always wanted.'"

Margot looked at Sally steadily. "I don't think I have to choose one thing or another. I could still act, I could be a mom, I could teach theater."

"Whatever you wanted."

"You don't mind if I don't take over your empire?"

"I realize now it's not the right path for you. You have too much in you that's creative, too much that needs expression, to make real estate your future."

"So what is your succession plan?"

Sally shrugged. "I don't know yet. Maybe Jen might want to learn the ropes, or maybe I'll sell. There are those who have expressed interest. But let's be honest, I'm not ready to lose control of my company, or ready to stop working. Retirement is light-years away."

Margot smiled. "And Dr. Russ agrees?"

"Dr. Russ supports me in whatever I want to do." Sally smiled back, but gradually her smile faded. "What are we going to do about Max?"

"Nothing," Margot said firmly. "I trust Max to do what's best for him, because that's what I want. I want him happy, and if he's happy, I'll be happy, too."

IT WAS A HECTIC FEW DAYS, AND HECTIC WASN'T EVEN capturing the frenzy of shifting the production to a venue thirty minutes away, a venue in the middle of the hills with rather limited infrastructure.

But everyone pulled together to make it work. Max adjusted his flights, pushing back his return to New York, and the cast and crew brought their energy and excitement to adapting the production to the ranch, because although it was the same play, it was now quite different. An outdoor production had unique requirements, with lighting and sound just one aspect. Making the set work without significant changes was another challenge, as there were no curtains, or stage wings to store things. The set became more of a circle that could be turned for different acts and scenes.

They pared down the furniture required. Limited props.

Thursday night was the final dress rehearsal at the ranch, and it wasn't smooth. The crew was struggling with the changes, and the cast wasn't comfortable with the new set.

Margot was feeling the stress. The perfectionist in her didn't like that the final rehearsal was so rough. The comedic timing was off. But hopefully all those problems meant things would be better tomorrow night. Fingers crossed.

Margot was going over notes with Jen when Max approached. "It's getting late. We should head home. Try to unplug for a little bit."

Jen eased away, waving good night, leaving Max and Margot alone.

"Don't stress," Max said. "It's going to be great."

"I'm not stressing." She saw his expression and made a face. "Okay, I am stressing, but this is harder than I thought it was going to be. I tend to forget not everyone is a professional with twenty years of stage experience."

Max looked at her, really looked at her, deep into her eyes, and she saw the old warmth there, the fire that had burned between them. "If anyone can pull this off, it's you," he said.

"What you meant to say is that it's you and me. Because we couldn't do this without each other."

He smiled a little bit, but enough that she felt heat rush all the way through her, the tingle and fizz, the electric chemistry, the affection, her desire and dreams.

Maybe they weren't going to end up together. Maybe he had those other commitments. But that didn't mean they couldn't work together, pull together, still be a team.

"Okay." She glanced at her watch, checking the time, exhausted out of her mind. No wonder. It was past ten. They'd been here working, rehearsing, and then doing it again since five this afternoon. But thanks to Sally's small but mighty staff, the remarkable Cal Poly theater crew, Max's wit and star power, and her grit and determination, they would open at the ranch tomorrow night. There would be a show, and even if there were problems, they'd survive.

"I'll walk you to your car," he said. "If that's okay with you."

The heat was back in his eyes, and there was a growl in his voice, a need that felt like the pulse in her veins. She had to be careful with him. She'd already given too much. But she didn't have it in her to argue with him, or to resist. Tonight she was too tired.

They exited the venue, crossed the trampled grass to the gravel-covered parking lot. They said nothing as they walked, and neither of them looked at each other, but he was close, his warmth reaching out to her, his energy tangible.

If she leaned toward him, she'd feel him.

If she lifted a hand, she could touch him.

She couldn't touch him.

At her car her gaze lifted. His eyes met hers and held. For the longest time they just stood there, inches apart, heat and need snapping, crackling, desire filling the night air.

Whatever existed between them wasn't dead, and it wasn't one-sided. The awareness was too strong for that.

But there were other feelings involved now, other emotions that made wanting him, and being with him, impossible.

She stepped back, reached for the door handle. "Good night, Max." Her voice cracked and she couldn't even look at him, afraid he'd see everything she wanted, afraid he'd know how much she still loved him, but the play was ending so soon now. Ten days until it was over. Nine performances to go.

"Good night, Margot."

She smiled at him, and it was an act, the smile. It was hard driving away from him. Hard keeping the distance between them. But if that's how she'd survive these next ten days, then that's exactly what she'd do.

Chapter 19

IT WAS OPENING NIGHT ALL OVER AGAIN. THE CURTAINS
would open in ten minutes. From backstage they could hear
the crowd. Earlier, Max and Margot had both peeked out.
The folding chairs were full. The lawn was full. The tem-
perature was perfect—seventy-eight degrees.

As the rest of the cast and stagehands started to fill the
wings, Max smiled at Margot. "How do you feel?"

"Good. Ready to go."

"Try to have fun."

"I love performing with you," she said, and it was true.
He was an incredible actor, and her favorite costar. Ever.

"Even when you're mad at me?" he teased.

She shook her head at him. "I think you're fishing for
compliments. You're not going to get them."

"That's okay. I'm crazy about you, girl. Never met anyone like you."

Her eyes burned, and Margot fought to hold back tears.
"It's been a fun summer. It really has. You got me out of my

comfort zone, you got me back onstage. You reminded me of who I am, and who I always wanted to be. I'll always be grateful to you for that."

Max stepped toward her, wrapped his arms around her, and held her in a long, solid hug. It wasn't passion, it wasn't sex; it was comfort, and love. She could feel his love. And honestly, wasn't that everything? It was so cliché, but it was so much better to have had this time with him, and to feel love, and to be loved, to have her heart broken open so she could feel again. She felt alive again. She felt hope, for her future, for whatever was to come.

"You'll always be my Max," she whispered. "No matter who else you might belong to, you'll still be mine, too."

He kissed her forehead. "I love you. Just remember that. Wherever you go, whatever you do, you'll have me cheering you on. I'm your biggest fan, and forever your friend."

Margot slipped out of his arms. She wiped away tears, because it was impossible not to cry. In his arms she always felt safe and strong. But she could also be safe and strong on her own. She'd learned things about herself this summer, and those lessons would not be forgotten.

She smiled through the tears. "Let's make this work. The show must go on."

THE SHOW WAS EXCITING, EVEN BETTER OUTSIDE, UNDER the stars. It was a different show, with a different energy, but Max relished the bigger stage and the bigger audience. The outcast kid in him, who'd never belonged, belonged here. These were his people, and this was his home. It had taken the summer to realize he could love this part of the world, and feel good here. The past wasn't here. The past didn't exist. He could let it go. He could be free. Tonight, onstage, he felt free. Light. Engaged.

Margot had been on fire tonight, too. She was beautiful.

She was talented. She understood story, she understood people, she understood how to bring out the emotion and humor.

He glanced at her as she was taking her bow. The audience was on their feet, applauding, whistling, shouting.

His chest grew tight, his heart filled with love and pride. Margot deserved the applause. She deserved only good things.

She turned to him, and as they did every night, she took his hand and they stepped forward together, for one last bow, together.

Her hand felt good in his. He gave it a squeeze. She looked at him, smiling, radiant.

With her he felt good. Not high, not drunk, not puffed up. Just real. Grounded. Happy.

The last couple of weeks hadn't been happy, and not just for him. He didn't think Margot had been happy, either. She cared for him, he knew she did. He decided he wasn't going to let her go, not without the fight of his life. And thanks to Johnny, he knew how to fight.

Max walked Margot to her car after they'd changed and hung up their costumes so they'd be ready for tomorrow night.

"How do you think it went?" Margot asked him as they approached her car.

"Are you kidding? It felt like opening night all over again."

"I agree." She smiled up into his eyes. "I never thought I'd want to act again, but this has been amazing. I am going to miss it when the play closes."

"And me? Will you miss me?" he asked, tone light, playful.

"A little bit," she said, holding up her fingers, showing an inch.

"More than that." He pushed her fingers apart, creating two inches. "There. That's better."

Margot laughed, swatted his arm. "You know I'll miss you. You and this play have been my summer, and as we already established, it's been a great summer."

He stopped her. "Margot, I'm sorry—"

"No. Don't apologize anymore, Max. I'm okay. Things are okay. We're okay. We're friends, right?"

"Right." Yet his chest felt tight and his gut cramped. It hurt losing her. It hurt being close to her but not with her. Hurt looking at her and not touching her—the sweet curve of her cheek, the fullness of her mouth, the firmness of her chin. He didn't want anyone else to have her, not when she felt like his.

Not when he wanted to be better for her. For them. For a life they could have together.

That's what he had to focus on. Not the past, but that which was still ahead.

"If you won't let me apologize anymore, would you at least take a drive with me? Tomorrow, before the show?"

He could see her reserve return, the wariness back in her eyes.

"I want to show you where I grew up," he said. "It's not that far from the EV Ranch. We don't have to do it tomorrow. We could do it Sunday, or Tuesday. Whenever."

She hesitated. He could feel her weighing the invitation, trying to figure out what was behind the suggestion.

"Margot, no pressure—"

"Yes," she said decisively. "I'd like that. Very much. I don't even know when I was last there."

"Hasn't changed much," he said. "It's still a tiny downtown."

"But you still have the grain elevator?"

He smiled and brushed a wispy strand of her blond hair from her cheek. "Still there, still our landmark."

"Then let's try for tomorrow."

"I'll pick you up at three. We could grab an early bite somewhere if we're hungry."

"Sounds good." She smiled at him, and it was a real smile, and for a moment he stood transfixed, remembering that smile while they rehearsed, remembering that smile as they ran around the theater "warming up," remembering her smiling up at him in bed and in that moment he thought he'd give everything to have her smile at him like that every day of his life.

But he couldn't go there. He couldn't—wouldn't—rush things.

She needed time. And he needed to respect the damage done by not sending Annaliese away immediately, and not sharing Annaliese's threat with Margot. Because that would have been the better decision, the right decision.

He watched as she started her car and pulled forward. Her hand lifted. He lifted his hand in response.

She'd smiled at him. The old smile. The smile gave him hope.

SATURDAY DRAGGED BY. MAX WORKED OUT, SHOWERED, tried to write, but gave it up. He had another coffee, a yogurt, he probably should stop with the coffee. His stomach hurt. He dreaded returning to Templeton, but he needed to show Margot more of who he was. He needed her to see where he came from—not the charming downtown with the pretty historic park, but the street he'd lived on. The house he'd been raised in.

These were the things he never shared. These were the things he had to share. He had to talk. He had to trust. He had to open up or Margot wouldn't understand how hard he was trying to learn and change—not just for her. For him. For them.

How he wanted a *them*.

She was already his best friend—or had been. Before Annaliese arrived and he'd messed everything up by not setting those boundaries with her.

Finally, it was almost three, and Margot was outside waiting for him when he pulled up to her house, wearing a lemon-yellow sundress with slender straps that set off her golden tan and gorgeous collarbones. She had such sensitive collarbones. He wanted to kiss her there, and on her neck below her ear.

"You look beautiful," he said, opening the car door for her.

She flashed a shy smile. "Thanks."

"Is that a new dress?"

"Yes." She settled into the car and tucked strands of sleek blond hair behind her ear. "I bought a few things for my trip to Greece. It's going to be hot, and dresses are so much cooler."

Greece? She was going to Greece? His chest tightened again, air bottling in his lungs. Max climbed behind the steering wheel and focused on buckling up, giving himself time to gather his thoughts. "When do you head to Greece?" he asked, starting the car.

"The first of August. Sally thought I needed a getaway. She got me a ticket to Greece." Margot's eyes widened. "First class."

"Is she going?"

"No. Just me. I've always wanted to go, and I'm staying at the villa of friends of hers. Sally's travel agent has planned the itinerary."

He'd been to Greece, and he knew the men would go nuts for her. And she'd be alone. He smashed his jealousy, along with the overly protective voice inside of him wanting to tell her that she should at least go with a friend. Or him. But no, he wouldn't do that. It was her trip. She deserved to feel good. Have fun. Be admired. Desired.

He swallowed the bitter taste in his mouth. He couldn't be possessive. She wasn't his. And yet he felt sick, almost physically sick, because he'd had her and lost her, and there was no one to blame but himself.

He'd respect her plans, even if it killed him.

"Sally loves Greece," he said, forcing himself to fill the silence. "She's been a number of times, hasn't she?"

"Four. She came close to buying a place there, but then

the pandemic came and she realized she was better off investing in real estate closer to home."

"As if she didn't have enough real estate already."

Margot laughed. "Sally prefers land over stocks."

"But she has invested in tech."

"Yes. She's incredibly savvy." Margot glanced out the window, and was quiet for a moment before adding, "I still find it hard to believe that Sally and your dad were—together. For years."

"A couple of years. But yeah." His lips twisted and he didn't know what he was feeling. "She likes a pretty face. Years ago Dad was a good-looking man—"

"He still is." She met his astonished gaze, shrugged. "He's rugged. Masculine. A bad boy. Women love those."

"You, too?"

"You were my bad boy. Think I've learned my lesson."

He looked at her, emotions even more unsettled. "And what was that?"

"Stay back. Keep your distance. It hurts to get burned."

He wanted to take her hand and hold it. Kiss it. Kiss her. He wanted to kiss her until she melted into his arms, melted against him. Kiss her senseless. Kiss her until she forgave him. Kiss her until she was his again.

But that wasn't fair to her.

He'd always used the physical to be close, to connect and communicate. The physical kept him from having to use words. But sex couldn't fix anything. Sex masked the truth.

Today he was going to share things with Margot he hadn't shared with her—or anyone. Sally knew some things, but not everything, and even though it was hard for him to be open, he had to try, for Margot's sake.

For their sake.

The drive to Templeton was similar to the drive to Paso Robles, but instead of going north on Highway 101, he turned south. The highway bordered his hometown, so he took the proper exit and drove Margot down Main Street.

This wasn't a tour of Templeton, but a visit to the place where he grew up, so they continued to the outskirts of town to where he'd once lived.

As a child, his house had been surrounded by pastures, open land. Much of the land had been turned into new developments, but his home was still there, with less land, but it still had the same gravel driveway, the same weathered barn, and the house looked every bit as ramshackle as when he'd lived there.

"This was home," he said, pulling up to the curb. There hadn't been a curb thirty years ago. "I lived here from the time I was born until I went off to college. I wasn't sure how it would look after all these years, but it hasn't changed. It's the same color as then. It was supposed to be robin's-egg blue, not sure what shade that is. My dad painted it himself for my mother when they got married." He looked from the house to Margot. "Blue was her favorite color."

"You don't talk about her a lot."

"Deliberately." He glanced back at the house, the windows to the right of the front door were his bedroom windows. The windows to the left were the living room. It wasn't a big house. The kitchen and the bigger bedroom were in the back. "That was my room," he said, gesturing to the two narrow windows on the far right. "My parents' bedroom was behind that. We shared the bathroom. Just a two-bedroom, one-bathroom house. Maybe eight hundred square feet?"

"Small," she agreed.

"There was no proper dining room. Sound traveled. The walls were thin. You couldn't block out their fighting, even if you wanted to."

"Did they fight a lot?" she asked.

He nodded. His parents had wild fights. They'd argue all night. They'd break things. They'd throw things. And then they'd eventually make up, with wild, almost violent sex he could hear in his room.

He'd been terrified as a kid. Bewildered by the chaos.

He hadn't even known how much damage had been done until he was an adult and couldn't figure out what a normal relationship should look like, or feel like. "I didn't know how to deal with it, so I'd try to be somewhere else, which wasn't easy when you're only four or five."

"You remember the fights that young?"

He didn't want her pity. He wanted her to understand why he'd made so many mistakes in relationships, but also why he wasn't going to keep making the same ones. "My parents weren't happy. Johnny wasn't faithful. My mom's parents, they wouldn't let my mom come home. They said she was married, she needed to live with her husband."

Margot shook her head. "That's wrong."

"My mom couldn't sleep when my dad wasn't there, so she'd take something to help her sleep. But then in the morning, she'd need something to wake up. On the days he didn't come home, or they'd have a fight, she'd take something to numb herself. Mom ended up taking lots of things, and the pills turned to harder stuff. She'd shoot something into her arm—"

"You saw her do this?"

"She'd go to the bedroom. She didn't want me to see, but it was just her and me a lot, and I'd hear her crying. I'd try to tell her Dad would be home soon, and that I'd take care of her until he did."

Margot reached for his hand.

"I did try to take care of her, too," he added after a moment. "I loved her. I was going to be the man. I was going to get rid of Johnny and be the man and make everything okay. And then one morning I went to wake her up because she hadn't come out yet and she was . . . cold. I think I knew she was dead, but I didn't want her to be dead. I wanted a miracle. I wanted to fix things, save her. That was my job, you know."

"Max, it wasn't your job. You were a child, a little boy."

"Not that little anymore. Not that innocent. I used to

pray Johnny would die so my mom and I could live together here without him. I had this silly idea that if it were just the two of us, she'd be happy. Instead *she* died." He made a rough sound in the back of his throat. "God had a funny way of answering prayers."

"That wasn't God."

"It felt like it, and I was being punished because I hadn't done enough. I hadn't gone into her room earlier. I hadn't thought to check on her." Max was ready to leave, but he needed to tell Margot the rest. He needed her to understand . . . him. If she could. "I should have checked on her hours before. I didn't. I thought she needed sleep."

He looked out the window at the old barn, now leaning to the left. Boards had fallen off. A hole gaped in the roof. "So I stayed outside, playing. Riding my bike, jumping over things. I found out later that if I'd just gone into her room earlier, if I'd tried to wake her up earlier, I might have been able to save her. But by not going to her, by playing outside, she died."

"That's not fair! How could you know?" Margot unbuckled her seat belt and turned in her seat to face him. "How could you, as a little boy, save her?"

"I could have called for help."

"You were a *child*."

He shrugged uneasily. "But I'd promised her—"

"Children shouldn't have to save their parents. Parents should be protecting their children. Not the other way around."

He glanced at her, and then back at the house.

"Max." She placed her hand on his chest. "You have to let the guilt go. It's time. Stop punishing yourself for something that happened a lifetime ago."

"But the guilt is there," he said. "And I haven't dealt with it, not until this year, when I realized I was making bad decisions, decisions based on the past."

"Like what?"

Now was the time to explain the rest, but it was ugly and embarrassing. "I didn't realize until recently—and I mean, the last year of my marriage—how much Annaliese was like my mom, and why I couldn't walk away from her. There were red flags, right from the beginning, but we had a very intense physical connection and I let that override my better judgment. I did try to slow things down, put some distance between us, but Annaliese freaked out. I'd already failed my mom. I couldn't fail Annaliese, too."

"You're breaking my heart, Max," she whispered.

"That's not why I'm telling you. I don't want sympathy, or pity. I needed you to know who I am. Who I really am. I'm not this awesome guy, or sexy Max Russo, heartthrob from TV. I'm a man who has made some really shitty decisions and am only now, at forty-five, realizing how I need to come to terms with my childhood, and the guilt, and that I spent my marriage to Annaliese being a fixer. I'm not proud of any of it."

"We all make mistakes."

"My marriage was terrible, but I kept trying to save it. I didn't want to abandon her, but at the same time I didn't want to be with her. I failed my mom and my first wife. I wasn't going to fail Annaliese—"

"And does no one owe you anything? Does no one reciprocate? Who takes care of Max?"

"I do," he bit out.

"Well, I'd like to, too."

He looked away, his jaw working.

"Do you know what I see when I look at you?" she asked, voice low. "I see my favorite person. My best friend. The one I want to share everything with. The one that makes waking up every day fun and exciting."

"But does this change the future?" His voice was pitched low. "Does this change what you want, and what I want? I don't know."

Her hand slipped into his, and she held it tight. "Maybe we don't have to have all the answers right now. Maybe that's asking too much." She smiled at him, gave his fingers a squeeze. "Baby steps, okay?"

"I don't want you disappointed again. I don't want you to end up with nothing—"

"That won't happen if I've got you. I've been thinking a lot about things, and what I want and need. Wants and needs are two different things. I want kids, but I need you. I need a family, but why can't we be a family, you and I?"

"I don't know how to make a family," he said flatly, feeling raw.

"I do. It's about love, respect, communication. Nothing you don't already know how to do. But again, baby steps. Let's take this slow. No pressure. No expectations." Margot leaned into him and kissed his cheek, and then when he turned toward her, she kissed his mouth, her hand cupping his nape, her mouth cool, her hands warm.

He felt hunger rush through him, a wave of need so intense he wanted to pull her onto his lap and devour her. But time was needed. For both of them.

At the same time, he wasn't going to end the kiss, not until she'd had enough.

She lifted her head a few inches, looked into his eyes. "I have one question for you."

"What is that?" he asked.

"You have to be honest."

"Always," he swore.

"Am I really a good actress?"

Max had expected something entirely different, and when he saw the laughter in her eyes and the curve of her lips, he couldn't resist those lips. He kissed her again. "Very good," he said, his mouth brushing hers. "One of the best I've ever worked with."

"Good answer."

THAT NIGHT WAS MAYBE THE BEST PERFORMANCE YET.

It was one of those nights where the stage couldn't contain him. Max felt impossibly alive. Sharing with Margot, going back to that place where memories were dark, dragging all the pain into the light, made him see that he was a different person now. He wasn't stuck, wasn't broken. Margot's heart had healed something inside of him, and tonight, taking the stage, he could see the world in 3D. His body hummed. His pulse pounded. He didn't think life had ever been better, bigger, or brighter.

As he performed opposite Margot, he felt the same shimmering energy. She was as alive as he was—filled with something that couldn't be articulated, only lived. Felt.

They were part of a cast, but there was no one else. It was just them and hope.

When the show ended, Margot came to his dressing room still in her costume from the final act. She had a wipe in her hand and was starting to remove her makeup. "So, what are you doing after?" she asked.

The energy still hummed between them. Bright, hot, electric. They felt connected. One.

"I'd say you," he drawled, leaning against the counter, "but I don't think we're there yet."

She braced herself against the doorframe, hands behind her back. "You have to admire a man with confidence."

He smiled, a slow, warm smile, enjoying every single thing about her. The fact that she was here, giving him a chance, blew him away. His Margot was everything. Brave. Strong. "It's an act," he said. "I'm quaking on the inside."

Her gaze swept over him, from head to toe, lingering briefly on his hips before looking up into his eyes. "I see no quaking."

"That's because I'm a good actor."

She laughed, shook her head. "Tonight was fun, wasn't it?"

"I think it was my favorite show yet."

"It was good. I felt you in every scene."

He'd felt her, too. It had been pure love. There was no other way to describe it than that. Max hesitated. "I'm glad we're talking."

"We should never stop talking. You've become my best friend. You mean everything to me."

"Do we still have a chance?"

"Max, I love you." She reached for the door and closed it behind her. "It's that simple, and that complicated." She crossed the small room, walking to him until she was toe to toe with him, her fingers hooking on the waistband of his jeans. "You've changed me. You've made me feel again, and have reminded me that I'm a big girl, and can take big risks. Not that you're a risk." She rose up on tiptoe to kiss him. "Just tell me there's no more wives lurking about," she whispered. "Or at least warn me so I can be prepared."

He cradled her face, kissed her deeply. "I haven't heard from Cynthia in years."

She laughed, wrapped her arms around his waist, pressed herself to him. "So you know, if she shows up, I'm going to show her the door."

"Good idea." He kissed her again. And then again. The door to his dressing room opened, and neither of them paid it the least bit of attention, and the door gently closed again.

"So my place or yours?" she asked breathlessly, when they'd finally come up for air.

"Whatever you want. As long as you're there."

"Oh, I'll be there."

AT MAX'S COTTAGE, HE COOKED A QUICK STIR-FRY AND they sat down on opposite ends of the couch, eating, talking, reliving the highlights from the play, and discussing how much they both enjoyed performing under the stars. Margot couldn't stop smiling. An enormous weight had been lifted off her chest. She'd been struggling these past few weeks, struggling to see a way forward without Max, and she didn't want to. That was the bottom line. She didn't want the future if he wasn't in it. It sounded dramatic, but she felt this truth all the way through her, to the very heart of her.

She wasn't meant to go through life alone. She needed a person, a partner, someone to love her, encourage her, and push her, someone who needed her, someone who needed her conviction and her enormous capacity to love.

She didn't realize she'd stopped eating and was staring off into space until Max cleared his throat.

"You okay over there?" he asked, a hint of laughter in his voice.

She blinked and, looking at him, nodded.

"You were very deep in thought," he added.

"I was thinking how we're good together. We have so much in common. And it's not just Sally, or the fact that we were raised in towns next to each other, but we're both so ambitious, we've spent our lives putting ourselves out there. You get me in a way no one else ever has, and I'm grateful. So grateful." She put her bowl down on her lap. "Romance and sex . . . that's all great . . . but having someone who really understands you, and has your back, that's even more important. That's what I get with you—"

"Hopefully with romance and sex," he interrupted, eyebrow arched.

"Max, we don't have to have kids—"

"No. No." His smile disappeared. He rose from the couch. "You're not going to do that again. You're not going to give up what you want to make others happy. That's not okay. I'm not okay with you putting yourself last."

"But it's not last. There's you, and me, the two of us, and what I want is what will make us strong. United. We can be a family without kids—"

"You said that before but, Margot, come on. Don't do this. We've been through this before, and it almost tore us apart. You've got to be honest—"

"I've thought about this a lot, and I don't want anyone else. I don't want to have kids with someone else, or even have kids on my own. I'm not going to get younger. Life's going to get harder. There will be challenges ahead, health challenges, financial challenges, and I don't think I could, should, be a single mom, not at this stage in my life." She placed her bowl on the coffee table and rose. "But you, I could be happy growing old with you. I could be happy sharing a life with you."

"It doesn't have to be one or the other," he said roughly. "I'm not giving you an ultimatum."

Her brow creased. She didn't understand. "I'm not . . . wait. What are you saying?"

"That we can figure this out, together. We can make this work together. It's not about compromising, but finding what we want together. We do those baby steps you mentioned. We continue making a life together, perhaps buy a home here, and figure out how to be together more, despite our careers. We spend time growing secure with each other, and continue discussing what's right for us, and what we want those next steps to be."

"You're leaving the door open," she said carefully, "for whatever could be."

"If we're solid, and happy, I'd be open to discussing . . . children." His voice deepened. "I've never held a baby. I don't know anything about babies, but I loved Cynthia's daughter. I was proud to be Gigi's dad."

Margot crossed the floor and wrapped her arms around his waist. "Just knowing we can talk about this is everything. I'm also simply happy to focus on the next few months. How do we make us work when you're based in New York, and I'm here? Could I come see you when you're in Wyoming—"

"Yes." He clasped her face, kissed the tip of her nose and then her lips. "I want you there. I need you there. Can't do four months without you."

"What about Sally?"

"Can't you do some work remotely? Or take a break— you've earned a break—and spend a couple weeks with me?"

"Well, I do have that Greece trip."

His expression fell. "That's right."

Margot almost laughed at how miserable he looked. "I'm considering postponing Greece, at least until you could go with me. What do you think about that?"

"Or maybe I can shift my travel plans, and we could do Greece together?"

Margot's eyes widened. "That would be so fun. Could you? Could we?"

"I'd love to get away, and have time alone with you."

"In *Greece*."

He drew her even closer so they were standing hip to hip, chest to breast, heat and energy streaking between them. "What about *after* Greece? What if we found a place here that we both liked? What if we made this area our home base?"

Her heart raced, and she looked up into his gorgeous face, so wildly, madly in love with him. "That's an excellent idea."

"I'm never at my New York place. I'm thinking of selling it, and investing in some decent property here. We could build. You could have your dream home—"

"Any home is a dream home if I'm with you."

"Such a sweet talker." He gathered her hair back from her face, drawing it into a ponytail. "But there's no reason for us to go anywhere else. Your life is here. Your dad is here. Sally's here. We've been happy here. Why not keep a good thing going?"

"Couldn't agree more."

He kissed her, and the kiss deepened, the heat and the longing growing stronger, the desire overwhelming. Kissing her, he walked her backward into his bedroom, where he swiftly disposed of her clothes and then carried her to the bed, where the lovemaking was fierce and consuming. The intensity of her orgasm shattered her, and Margot cried in Max's arms, feeling as if she'd finally come home.

* * *

THEY BEGAN DRIVING TOGETHER TO THE EV RANCH FOR the nightly performance. It was so easy to be together, night and day. They talked about everything, from the Greece trip, as Max had bought a ticket, to the scripts still arriving for Max to consider. After the Greece trip, Max would be working a lot. His schedule was going to be hard, and Margot would miss him. There would be visits, but they both knew it wouldn't be the same.

Max worried about her being alone, left behind. Yes, she had a job. She had friends and her dad. She'd lived alone for years, so it's not that she couldn't do it, but he wanted more for her. He wanted to give her more, and he could.

More security. More love. More family.

One day Max told Margot they needed to leave earlier than usual for EV Ranch, as he had an errand to do on the way. They took their normal route from Cambria to Paso Robles, and then got off the highway, heading to the EV Ranch, but partway, Max turned south, as if they were going to Templeton, but then he made a couple more turns and they were traveling down a quiet road. Margot noticed the real estate sign at the front of the narrow dirt lane, but said nothing, although she was curious, and darted a quick glance at Max. His expression revealed nothing.

He drove another quarter mile, slowing to pass through open wrought iron gates, and then she saw the house in the distance. It was an old farmhouse, two stories, white with tall windows. Max kept driving toward the house with the black shutters, glossy black door, the large covered front porch marked by square columns. Behind the farmhouse rose a big barn, and there was a detached garage, too, with the same white paint. She could see a lavender and rose garden on one side of the farmhouse, blue hydrangeas against the front of the house, and lush pink roses along the picket fence. It was charming, picture-perfect.

"What do you think?" he asked, parking in the driveway.

"I think it's gorgeous."

He shifted into park and turned the engine off. "Would you want to go check it out?"

She shot him a look of disbelief. "Now?"

The front door opened, and a woman in a suit stood there. She lifted a hand, waved to them. Max nodded at her and turned to Margot. "It's the original farmhouse for the Decatur family, built in 1902. They owned extensive land around here in the early part of the century, and created a thriving farm. Most of the land has been sold off, but the house and five acres remain." He smiled at her. "And it's for sale."

She looked at the stately farmhouse, framed by a cluster of huge coastal oaks, and then past to the gardens and barn. "Five acres is still quite big."

He stepped from the car and came around to her side, opened the door for her. "There's an old orchard behind the barn. A chicken coop, room for goats or whatever you want."

She accepted his hand. "Vegetable garden?"

"Yes."

She glanced at the realtor waiting for them, then back at Max. "This isn't a test, is it?"

"No. I saw this property online, and then drove here a few days ago, thought it could be a perfect place for us, but wanted to see what you think."

She held his hand tightly as they climbed the front steps. The interior of the farmhouse was even better than she'd imagined, with high ceilings, spacious rooms, beadboard, elegant woodwork, clean lines, crisp paint. The walls between the living room, dining room, and kitchen had been taken down to create one big open room with windows on three of the four sides. Light streamed into the room, and the handsome kitchen featured beautiful stone counters and the original hardwood floors, which had been skillfully patched, sanded, and stained.

Margot's heart was in her throat as she stood in the

middle of that beautiful sunshine-filled room. She could see herself here with Max, and children. Should there be children. She still hoped, but maybe if they got a dog . . . or two. A cat perhaps.

And yet as she toured the house a second time, she could see everything she'd ever wanted here. She pictured herself making dinner with Max, and spooning mashed oatmeal and bananas into the mouth of her baby. She could see the dogs at her feet, trailing after her, following a toddler around.

It was picture-perfect, but in the end it wasn't the house that would fulfill her. The dogs and kids were options. It was Max she needed. It was the one thing, the only thing, she was sure of.

Leaving the house, Max glanced at Margot. "You'd have a commute for work," he said. "It'd be almost a half hour each way, and maybe Sally could let you work remotely a couple times a week."

"Maybe," Margot said, thinking she was happy, happy just like this. The two of them. It was good. They were good.

His fingers laced with hers. "Should we make an offer?"

Her gaze traveled over his face. How she loved that face. How she loved this man. "Can I be honest?"

"Always."

"It's a big house for two of us, and with you gone, I worry I'd feel isolated."

Max opened the car door for her. "Fifteen minutes from your dad's house."

"True," she said, sliding into the passenger seat.

He walked around to the driver's side and climbed in. "There's room for your dad. It's a big house, four bedrooms." He started the car and didn't speak until he'd shifted into drive. "That detached garage could be converted into a house for him."

For a second she couldn't speak. "Have Dad live with us?"

"He's a family man. He should be with his family."

Margot's eyes burned, and she looked out the window, overcome. "It's a lot of money."

"It'd be a good investment. Land holds its value."

She nodded, knowing it was true. "Can I think about it?"

"Whatever you want." He took her hand, kissed it. "I want you to feel secure when I head to Wyoming."

"I'll be fine, knowing you're coming back."

"Always coming back," he said. "You're my person. My forever person. Believe that."

She leaned across the console and kissed his cheek. "I do. It's going to be good. We'll make it work, because you're what I want. Not property, not a house, not an engagement ring. Just you."

"Well, you've got me. You don't ever need to worry about that."

MARGOT DREAMED ABOUT THE FARMHOUSE THAT NIGHT. She dreamed of making love to Max in the big bedroom on the second floor, and the dream was so real that when she woke up and discovered she was in Max's empty bed in his rental house, she felt a stab of loss.

She pulled on one of his T-shirts and went to the kitchen, where he was on the phone. He wasn't talking, but listening, and he crossed to her, covered the phone, and kissed her.

He was still on the phone when she had to leave for work, and she kissed him goodbye and headed for the office on Main Street.

Three more days until the play was over. Three more performances. Tonight, Saturday, and then it all ended after Sunday's show.

A couple of days later, she and Max would be flying to Athens, and they'd have their romantic escape, and then . . . then everything would change.

After they returned from Greece, he would still need to

go to New York, this time to prepare the condo for sale, and then it was straight to Wyoming for table reads and rehearsal.

It would be hard once he'd be gone. She knew she wasn't being left behind, but he wouldn't be here, and they wouldn't sleep together and wake up together. They wouldn't have those late-night dinners together. They wouldn't be sharing the same experience. They'd be back to separate lives. His work. Her work. His life. Her life. How little it would intersect until one of them got on a plane and went to see the other.

They did need a home here. They needed a place that was theirs, a place where they both felt comfortable and looked forward to being, whether alone or together.

If they bought the Decatur farmhouse, her dad could join her. They could get a dog, and Max had been talking about a dog. He'd always wanted one as a boy, but Johnny wouldn't permit it. Buy a house, get a dog, have a kid . . . .

She closed her eyes at her desk, held her breath. The idea of being a mom still teased her. The idea of holding a little person who'd be her person made her ache. She could be happy without children, but she could be even happier with them.

Should she bring it up to Max? Was it rushing things? Because the farmhouse made sense if there were to be little people. The farmhouse was made for kids and dogs and active families.

"Hey," Jen said, leaving her desk to go to Margot's. "You okay? Does your head ache?"

Margot swallowed around the lump filling her throat. "No, feeling a little emotional, that's all. Can't believe it's ending this weekend."

"But you're going to Greece. And Max loves you. I heard him talking to Sally about this beautiful old farmhouse and how he thought it would be a perfect place for you guys to raise a family."

Margot straightened. "He said that?"

"To Sally."

"And those were his words? To raise a family?"

Jen looked baffled. "Yes, why? Is that a bad thing?"

"No. But . . . he didn't want kids. That's why we had that huge breakup earlier this month. It was all about kids. I want them, he doesn't."

"It didn't sound that way from what I heard. But you know him better. Whatever you two have discussed—" She broke off, and put a hand on Margot's arm. "Don't cry. Margot, everything's going to be fine."

Margot nodded and tried to smile. "I know. Don't mind me."

"It's been an intense summer."

"Yes, it has." Margot agreed, drawing a breath, pulling herself together. "Do you want to go get coffee? I could use a coffee and some fresh air."

"I'd love to," Jen answered, before asking the rest of the team if anyone wanted anything, but everyone was good, so Jen transferred the phones to Heather, grabbed her wallet, and stepped outside with Margot.

They walked in silence down to the coffeehouse, stood in the long line, most of the people waiting looking like summer tourists. Finally, it was their turn, and they placed their order and stepped to the back to wait for their drinks. Margot looked out the window where the marine layer was slowly burning off, happy to see the sun. Cambria was so picturesque but frequently gray, whereas Paso was almost always sunny. She thought of the 120-year-old farmhouse and how bright it had been, filled with light. She wouldn't be lonely at the farmhouse if her dad were there. But would he want to move? He took such good care of her childhood home.

She glanced at Jen, who'd become a good friend this summer. She'd worked her butt off, putting in long hours without complaining or asking for recognition. "You have to be ready for the play to end. It's been so much work for you."

"It has, but I've enjoyed it. It's been a challenge, but also a thrill. Come on, I've been able to work with Max Russo every day."

"Now that you know the real him, has your opinion changed?"

Jen shook her head. "No. If anything I'm a bigger fan than before. He is so nice, and so considerate. The crew loves him. I love him. You always worry that I've worked so hard, but this summer has changed me. It's given me experience and skills I didn't have before. It's made me confident. You've taught me confidence. I owe you."

Margot hugged her. "We've made a good team, haven't we?"

"We have. The best." Jen's smile faded. "I want to share something that no one else knows yet. Not even Sally."

Margot's heart fell. "You're leaving."

Jen nodded. "It's an outstanding opportunity. In San Francisco. I'd be closer to Bryan. I'd be a fool not to take it."

"Oh, Jen." Margot was thrilled for Jen but, selfishly, sad for herself. She'd miss seeing Jen every day, miss working with someone so smart and confident, someone who was always positive and fun. "I'm happy for you." She blinked hard, not wanting to tear up. "I really am."

Jen's name was called, and they stepped forward for their coffees, and as they were about to leave, a little girl approached Margot with a notebook. "Can I have your autograph, Miss Hughes?" the girl asked shyly.

"I'd be happy to," Margot said. Jen took Margot's latte so Margot could accept the notebook and pen. "What's your name?"

"Charlotte."

Margot sucked in a breath, holding it as she scribbled a

quick message in the notebook and then signed it. As she handed the notebook back she said, "I love that name. That's my sister's name."

Charlotte smiled. "Is your sister an actress, too?"

Margot only hesitated a moment. "No. But she loved seeing me in shows."

"I've seen *Barefoot in the Park* twice. On Wednesday we went and sat on the grass. I liked it even better the second time." She hesitated before adding, "I want to be an actress like you."

"Are you taking acting classes or in a children's theater?"

"There isn't anything like that here right now. They used to have a children's theater, but it closed last year."

"Does your school put on plays?" Margot asked. When Charlotte nodded, Margot encouraged her to audition for those. "Do anything you can, even if it's working behind the scenes. It's good to learn everything you can about the theater."

The little girl thanked her and scampered back to her mother, and Margot watched her, seeing herself in young Charlotte. Little Charlotte had touched her heart. It was so important to have dreams. "Adorable," Margot said as she and Jen exited the coffeehouse.

"A cutie-pie," Jen agreed.

Margot glanced back at the little girl. "I always wanted kids. Never would have thought I'd be almost fifty and childless."

"It's not too late—"

"Maybe not to adopt, but having a baby? Carrying a baby? That's not going to happen now. My eggs are done. I should have frozen my eggs when I was younger. I waited too long. It's funny how you can put all the creams and serums on your face and keep that youthful, but you can't do anything about the ticking clock."

They walked a block, and then Jen gestured to a bench and they sat down, stretched their legs out, and soaked up the sun. For several minutes they sipped their coffee and watched the world go by, and then Jen cleared her throat. "You don't have to use your eggs," she said carefully. "You're in really good shape. I don't know why you couldn't try to get pregnant through IVF using a donor egg."

"I don't know very much about the process."

"I was approached by a fertility clinic when I was at Santa Clara. The clinic wondered if I would be interested in being an egg donor, saying there could be some good money for me. I read the literature they gave me and, later, did more research. On one hand it was flattering, but it was also uncomfortable. It made me feel uncomfortable. I'm not attached to my eggs. They get wasted every month, but at the same time, I didn't want to put my DNA out there without knowing what would happen to it." She smiled at Margot. "With you, I know what would happen to it. My DNA would hit the jackpot. You'd be an amazing mom."

Margot couldn't speak, stunned by the rapid shifts in conversation. "I couldn't—"

"You could." Jen reached for Margot's hand and held it in both of hers. "If this is your dream, I want to make it come true. I'd like to help it happen. If I could."

"But I couldn't take your—" Margot broke off, unable to even say *egg*. It sounded like a chicken farm, and beautiful, brilliant Jen wasn't a hen.

"Eggs?" But Jen was smiling. "Why not? It's an egg that will be taken to a sterile lab where they will add the sperm, trying to make a zygote, which the doctor would turn around and transfer to you, or a surrogate, if that's what you thought best."

Margot was speechless.

Jen was still holding Margot's hand, and she gave it a squeeze. "You might not need a surrogate. I don't see why you couldn't carry. But that's something you'd have to discuss with your doctor."

Margot's head was spinning. This was wild . . . incredible. "I didn't even think it was possible at my age."

"Women can be surrogates in their forties and fifties. There are plenty of women who have carried babies even older. I'm simply saying, you should look into your options, and a fertility clinic would have a list of egg donors, and you could definitely do that. But rather than go with a stranger, I'd love to help you if I could. No obligation. No money. I don't want anything other than the knowledge that I was able to help you have your family."

Margot's eyes burned, and she blinked. "Why?"

"You're really important to me. You inspire me. This summer you've come to feel like family, and if I can help you, why not?"

"What if someday you change your mind and want the baby?"

"Why would I want *your* child? I'm not giving you a baby, I'm giving you DNA. Cells that you and Max would create an embryo from. But there's no baby until egg and sperm come together, and the cells start doubling, growing from a zygote into an embryo. You're the one who'd carry the embryo, not me. And I don't want anything other than to support you. You might want to pursue a different path, and I'm fine with that. I won't be hurt. But I wanted you to know you've got me, and you've got options."

"But you're moving to San Francisco."

"It's not very far away, and the egg retrieval is scheduled, so it's not like a surprise to anyone." Jen leaned forward, hugged Margot, whispering, "It would be a very cute baby, too. You know it would be!"

HOW DID YOU GET THROUGH THE REST OF THE WORK-day after that? How did you sleep? How did you think about anything else?

Magot couldn't.

After the performance, after making love, she slipped from Max's bed and went to the living room, where she used his laptop to begin researching what it meant to be an egg donor, and how it worked. She read how it was done, reading everything she could find online, and there was a lot online, pros and cons, stories by donor women, and stories by women who were beyond grateful to have had someone help them make a family.

Make a family. Oh, it sounded so good. It sounded like something she'd given up on, but now, now the possibility hovered just beyond her reach. And yet . . . she could see it. She could dream it. Maybe it wasn't too late.

Maybe there was hope for her yet. She closed his laptop and returned to bed, slipping close to Max, craving his warmth. He turned, facing her, his arm wrapping around her. "Can't sleep?" he asked, voice raspy.

She pressed her face to his chest. He smelled so good. He felt so good. "Just have a lot on my mind."

"Anything you want to talk about?"

"Maybe tomorrow. Go back to sleep."

Max didn't forget their conversation, and the next morning after he returned from the gym, showered, and sat down to the scrambled eggs and toast she'd made for them, he asked her what had been troubling her last night.

Margot took a bite of her eggs, and then another.

Max lifted a brow. "That bad, huh?"

"Maybe we should finish breakfast first."

His brow creased. "You don't have bad news for me, do you?"

"No. But it's a . . . conversation."

"Is this about the farmhouse?"

"Yes and no."

"About my work?"

"No," she said, feeling nervous. "Let's finish breakfast and we'll talk."

They ate in silence, and then Max cleared their plates,

put them in the sink, and after topping off their coffees, led the way into the small living room. He sat at the end of the couch, and she sat down next to him.

For a minute she didn't know how to start the discussion. Finally, Margot decided to jump in. "Max, would you consider becoming a parent with me?" she asked him, facing him on the couch, hands clasping the coffee cup. "I know this has been a sticking point for you, and it's been an issue for me, and I don't want this to become an issue. I wondered, after looking at the farmhouse, and talking about us, and possibly moving my dad in, if . . . if you could imagine having a baby with me."

"I've thought about it, too. Even discussed it with Sally. She thinks I'd be a good dad. A devoted dad."

The lump in her throat grew. "I think so, too," she said softly. "But I would hate for you to resent me later—"

"That wouldn't happen."

"Or the baby?"

"Never. That's not me. I don't abandon those I love, and I would love you, both of you. How could I not?" He hesitated. "I'm afraid more than anything."

"Afraid of what?"

"Losing. Losing my family." His voice deepened. "When Cynthia divorced me, I never saw Gigi again, and I'd come to love her as if she was mine. But then the marriage was over and she was gone. No goodbyes. No explanations. Nothing. It was awful. It hurt like hell."

Margot's heart ached. His life had been a revolving door of people and goodbyes. Except for Sally. Sally had been a constant.

Margot wasn't going anywhere, either. "I don't have to have children to be happy with you."

"And yet you've always wanted to be a mom," he said. "It's the one thing you've never been, it's the thing you've never done." For a minute there was only silence, before he gruffly added, "And it's something I want for you. For us. But I thought you couldn't. Your age, and everything."

"There are options." Margot shifted, trying to keep her voice calm, steady. "I'd work with a fertility clinic, use a donated egg, fertilize the egg with your sexy, smart sperm, and hopefully if the embryo takes, I'd become a mom."

His expression was guarded. "Sounds like a long shot."

"I've been reading about this, and if you're interested, I'll reach out to different clinics, make an appointment for next spring, or whenever you have a break from work—"

"Don't wait that long for information. See if you can get us in sooner. How can we make a decision without knowing the steps?"

She nodded, trying hard not to get too excited, aware, too, that not everyone was successful doing IVF.

As if reading her mind, he asked, "What are the odds of it working?"

"Hard to say, but, Max, what were the odds of me, little Margot Hughes from Paso Robles, making it on Broadway?"

"Good answer." He smiled at her, warmth in his dark eyes. "I like that answer. So you're serious?"

"If this was something you supported, I'd be very motivated." She hesitated. "I know there are different ways to be a mom. I know it's not necessarily about being pregnant, but I always wanted to be pregnant. If you were on board, I'd embrace the whole experience. I want the worries. I want the hopes. I want things that I never had, and this is what I've never had . . . being a mommy."

"What if your body can't do it? What would you do then? Would you be devastated?"

"I'd probably be a little devastated, but I've been devastated before and I recovered. I would recover again, and explore other options." She chose her words carefully. "Like surrogacy. I could try to find someone willing to carry for me. It's a significant financial investment, and it's a lot of legal paperwork, but I won't want to do that until I try first. I want to try. It's important to me." Margot swallowed. "But I would only want to do this if you want to go down this path with me."

Max was silent, and Margot searched his dark eyes. "It's a lot to throw at you, I know. Only a week ago I was saying no babies, no pressure, and now here I am, talking about egg donors and surrogacy. I'd like to blame the farmhouse. I'd like to blame that beautiful, wonderful property where dogs could run and kids could play, but it's not the farmhouse, it's me, that quiet little voice within me that is still hoping." She lifted her shoulders, and then let them fall. "I'm sorry—"

"Don't be sorry." He kissed her. "I want you to always talk to me, share with me. That's what best friends are for, right?"

She nodded.

"Here's the thing," he said after a moment. "The timing is tough. Greece, New York, Wyoming, and then after Wyoming it's Europe and then New Zealand." He hesitated. "Something would have to give."

Margot held her breath, thoughts all over the place, emotions barely controlled. He hadn't said no. He hadn't laughed. He'd asked questions. He sounded . . . open to it. "What do you suggest?" she asked in a small voice.

"Maybe instead of Greece we try to see a specialist. Use the next few weeks to figure out how this would work. But even then, you'd have to be the one to coordinate everything."

"I can do that. I don't mind doing the heavy lifting. And I don't need Greece. I'd much rather use this time to figure out . . . things." Her eyes felt hot and her throat ached. "Max, I've never had anything just handed to me. I'm used to working hard, making sacrifices. But making a baby means we're tied to each other, committed—"

"I'm committed."

"It would break my heart to start down this path and have you walk away."

"I'd never walk away." He set her coffee on the table, and lifted her onto his lap, as he did every night in the play. Max smoothed her wispy bangs back from her face. "Not from you, not from the child we made. Not now, not ever."

She looked deep into his eyes. His expression was so serious, his brown eyes intense.

"We had some hard times," he said, "but we've also had truly wonderful times. I love you, Margot. I really do love you, and I want to spend the rest of my life with you. I want to do everything with you—marriage and babies, Easter and Christmas. Fourth of July. Halloween, Thanksgiving. I want it all with you."

She blinked back tears and kissed him, and then again. "That's the nicest thing anyone has ever said to me."

He smiled, cupped her cheek. "Wait. Let me see if I can do better."

"How?"

"Margot Hughes, will you marry me?"

Her eyes widened. Her heart raced. "Are you serious?"

"If we're going to try for a baby, we should get married. We should do this properly."

She kissed him, and the kiss went on for quite some time. When the kiss finally ended, they were both a little breathless.

"So, was that a yes?" Max asked.

She grinned. "Of course it's a yes. A one hundred per-cent yes."

Then Max was kissing her, and any phone calls to share the good news would have to wait until much, much later.

Chapter 20

SHE WAS FIFTY AND ATTENDING HER FIRST BABY shower. *For her.*

Her shower. Her baby. A baby arriving very soon. Two weeks now, if the baby appeared on time.

Margot put a hand to her enormous belly, feeling the little guy kick. It was a boy, a little Russo boy, and with any luck, he'd look like his gorgeous dad. Dark, wavy hair, warm brown eyes, beautiful smile.

He kicked again, as if saying hello.

Her heart felt so full—so much joy. Max was gone, working, but she had him on speed dial, and he'd vowed to jump on a plane the second she went into labor. He had a private jet at his disposal, too, so there would be no problem flying directly into Paso Robles airport.

Jen had come down from San Francisco for the shower and would be arriving soon to the farmhouse to pick Margot up. The office staff had planned a celebration for Margot, hosting the baby shower at Sally's home. The lunch was being catered, not because it was too much work hosting a lunch for six, but because Sally didn't cook. She did her best to even avoid boiling water. Her new husband, Dr. Russ, cooked, but he hadn't been tasked with a baby shower.

Sally had been itching to throw the shower for months, but Margot was adamant they wait until she was in her final month. Just in case. She couldn't help being a little superstitious. Theater people were. First-time mothers were, especially when they weren't young moms.

Happily, the "just in case" didn't happen, and baby Russo was doing great. At Margot's appointment yesterday, the doctor said the baby looked great, and he was already seven pounds, and during the next two weeks he'd be getting plumper.

Standing at the family room window, Margot saw Jen's car approaching. Margot grabbed her purse and a light wrap, should the fog move back in. She was outside on the big, covered porch ready to greet Jen when she parked.

Jen climbed out of the car and gave her a hug. "Look at you! You're going to be a mommy."

"Very soon now," Margot answered. "Thanks to you."

"I'm so happy for you and Max. Speaking of Max, how is he?"

"Great. On location in Wyoming, filming season six, but ready to jump on a plane as soon as he's needed."

Jen reached out, patted Margot's belly. "You're huge."

Margot laughed. "Crazy what a body can do." She'd been working remotely the last two weeks, finding the desk chair at the office too uncomfortable for long periods of time. At home Margot could shift from a chair to the couch, to her bed, back to a chair. Sally and some of the others had stopped by, but it had been months since she'd last seen Jen. "How's life in San Francisco?"

Jen grinned and flashed an engagement ring. "I can't complain."

"No way! Jen! Were you expecting this?"

Jen laughed. "No, but I'm so happy. We've been together for a long time, and he's my one."

"Have you set a date?"

"We're going to hold off on the wedding for a little bit. It's fun to be engaged, but we're both young and I don't think we need to rush into the rest, you know?"

Margot's eyes stung. She blinked, and smiled. "I'm so happy for you. You deserve all kinds of wonderful things. You have the biggest heart—"

Jen hugged her hard. "You, too," she whispered. "Love you, Margot." She stepped back, tears in her eyes, too. "We should get going. Sally doesn't like to be kept waiting."

"No, she doesn't."

It was a half-hour drive from the farm to Sally's in Cambria, and when they pulled up, there were a few cars already in the driveway, and yet there was still plenty of room for them to park. It was also growing misty, the marine layer rolling in.

As they stepped into Sally's, the foyer was empty, but voices could be heard toward the back. She and Jen walked through the house to the big backyard with its rose-covered arbor. A long table filled the lawn, the table covered with a blue batik fabric, the centerpieces a line of blue mason jars filled with white roses, lavender snapdragons and blue sweet peas. White folding chairs flanked the table, and in the corner of the garden stood a cart filled with sweets—a blue frosted cake, platters of miniature cupcakes and cookies, jars of blue, purple, and green candies.

It was gorgeous. So gorgeous. But why was the table so big, and where was everyone?

Margot did a slow circle, and then everyone emerged all at once—Sally and the office staff, Capri from the play, and oh, her friends . . . Elizabeth, Paige, Andi, and Mrs. Ortiz. Margot, already so emotional with all the pregnancy hormones, couldn't hold back the tears. She'd expected her work friends but not her friends from Orange County. What a long drive for a baby shower.

"What are you all doing here?" she cried, facing them.

"Celebrating you," Andi answered, rushing forward to hug Margot. "And oh, look at you."

Margot was soon hugged by Paige and Elizabeth. "You're glowing," Elizabeth said.

"You are," Paige agreed. "You look wonderful."

Mrs. Ortiz held Margot's hands and smiled into her eyes. "My magical Margot," she said. "So full of miracles and life. I think this baby of yours is going to be a star, too."

"I hope not. I want him to have a normal life." But Margot was crying, happy tears, hormonal tears, every nerve and fiber within her, overflowing with joy.

It was a gorgeous baby shower, with lots of photos and wonderful food, delicious cake, a fizzy nonalcoholic drink, and gifts, so many gifts. Sally, who'd already given her a travel playpen, had a high chair with a bow on it, as well as a swing.

After the shower, Elizabeth and the Paso Robles crowd drove Margot back to her 1902 farmhouse with the detached garage being remodeled to become a home for her dad, who was thrilled to become a grandfather. Margot thought he'd resist the idea of coming to live with her, but he was truly pleased by the invitation, confessing he didn't like Margot being alone so much, and as soon as his house sold, moved in with her.

Elizabeth couldn't linger, needing to take her mother home, but assured them she'd return as soon as she could. Paige and Andi stayed, wanting to help Margot carry in all the gifts, the flowers, and the extra cake, which had been boxed up.

In the kitchen Margot found a note from her dad. He'd gone to his friend's to watch the baseball game and would be back later.

After putting the leftovers and gifts away, Paige, Andi, and Margot sat in the family room off the farmhouse kitchen, relaxing and sipping glasses of peach herbal iced tea.

"What a wonderful day," Margot said, sighing and stretching. "That was better than a wedding."

"How do you know?" Andi teased. "You eloped instead of having a wedding."

Margot glanced down at the ring on the fourth finger of her left hand. It was a beautiful diamond, a rather large stone, and it was both engagement ring and wedding ring in one. They'd eloped to make things easy, but one day there would be a reception, a big party, and they'd invite everyone, but there were priorities, and a quick ceremony at the San Luis Obispo courthouse, followed by fertility treatments, had taken precedence. "We'll have our reception someday. I promised my dad, and it will happen. But we're both so happy being together, making a life together, and that was more important to either of us than a party. I didn't really miss the whole wedding thing, either, not when I'm so committed to Max, and this guy," she said, running a hand over her belly.

Andi teared up. "I'm happy for you."

"Love you guys." Margot's voice thickened. "Who would have thought any of this was possible when we first met? That first Thanksgiving, Elizabeth was the only married one. Now we all have someone. Love really is better the second time—" She broke off, eyes widening.

Margot awkwardly stood up, and glanced at the chair, and then at her friends. "Um, I either peed myself, or . . . my water broke."

Andi and Paige both jumped up. Andi looked at Paige. "How do you know?" she whispered.

"You know." Paige's smile was huge. "We need to call Max. And Elizabeth, because she has the car."

"You can drive me in mine," Margot said. She was in shock. Was this really happening? "Let me change, and get my overnight bag."

"It's packed, isn't it?" Andi asked.

Margot nodded. "Once we're at the hospital, will someone please call Sally? She needs to know, too. Oh, and I need to tell Dad!"

THAT WAS THE LONGEST THREE-AND-A-HALF-HOUR flight of his life. Max kept checking his phone for updates, getting regular progress reports from Margot's birthing partners—Elizabeth, Paige, and Andi—that everything was going well. She'd only dilated to a two. Then a four. Then a five.

Max wanted to be there. He just wanted to be with Margot.

Glancing out the window of the private jet, he took in the terrain below. They were no longer over the Sierras. The big mountains had turned to a valley. Ahead were lower hills, the coastal foothills, and then Paso Robles.

Sally was waiting for him. She'd guaranteed she could get him to the hospital faster than any professional driver. He wasn't going to argue with her.

She was there at the executive airport, too, as he stepped off the jet. She had a new car, a black luxury car that wasn't gas dependent, and a new hairstyle, too. A little shorter. A little sassier. He gave her a fast, hard hug before they jumped into the car and raced to the hospital, the same one where Sally had been a year ago recovering from her heart attack. So much had happened in a year. Even with the ups and downs, it had been the best year of his life.

"Go in," Sally said, pulling up front. "I'll park and wait with the others."

He leaned over and kissed her. "Thanks, Sally, for everything."

IT WAS A LONG NIGHT FOR MARGOT, THE BABY TAKING his time making an appearance, but before dawn he arrived, shrieking furiously at all the indignities he was subjected to.

Margot was exhausted when her son entered the world, but she was also relieved. At peace. He was perfect, according to Max. Every finger, every toe, his reflexes perfect, too. Margot couldn't wait to hold him, but she loved watching Max watch his boy. His expression was reverent, and the love and wonder in his eyes brought her to tears.

So many people made this miracle happen. Jen—wonderful Jen. The fertility clinic, what an incredible team of doctors and nurses, and front desk, too. And then there was Max, the love of her life, who wanted babies and more.

Gorgeous, sexy, wonderful Max. She looked at him and smiled tremulously. None of this would have happened without him.

And Sally.

But that went without saying.

An hour later, Margot was in her private room, the baby in her arms, while Max fed her bites of mango and pineapple from the fruit bowl he'd bought for her from the hospital cafeteria, since that's what Margot craved.

Sally entered the room with blue and purple balloons tied to a huge stuffed elephant. Her gaze immediately went to the baby.

Max rose, took the balloons and stuffed elephant from her, and steered her closer to the bed. "Sally, we want you to meet our son."

She stood transfixed, hands clasped in front of her. "He's beautiful," she whispered. "Just beautiful."

"He is," Max said. "And healthy."

"Of course he is," Sally said stoutly. "I never doubted it."

Margot exchanged glances with Max. She smiled at him, a smile she knew he'd understand. But then he seemed to understand everything when it came to her. They didn't need words. They were already on the same wavelength. "Did Max tell you his name yet?" Margot asked.

"I have not," Max answered. "It's a traditional Italian name."

"Because you're a traditional Italian?" Sally teased.

"No. It just fit him. It was really the perfect name," he said.

"The only name," Margot added, feeling ridiculously emotional.

"Well, are you going to tell me?" Sally asked.

"It's Salvatore." Max wrapped his arm around Sally. "Salvatore Russo. In Latin it means 'savior.'"

"We plan on calling him Sal for short." Margot glanced at Max and then at Sally. "He's named after you. Our very own Sal."

Emotion darkened Sally's eyes. "No."

"Yes." Max hugged Sally. "You brought Margot and me together. If it weren't for you—well, and Neil Simon—we wouldn't be here now. With our Sal."

"He's right," Margot said. "Meeting Max changed everything, and doing the play together changed me. I found myself—" She broke off, drew an unsteady breath, tears filling her eyes. "I remembered what I loved, and remembered who I am, and found someone who loved me, really loved me." The tears were spilling and she couldn't stop them. "I felt like I'd lost everything, and yet now I have so much." She used her free hand to wipe away the tears. "Fifty and a first-time mom."

Sally plucked some tissues from the table next to the bed and used them to dry Margot's cheek. "This is why we can't ever give up," she said, blotting the other cheek. "Love is always just around the corner."

Margot smiled at Sally, always the optimist. "Do you want to hold him? You're going to have to be his godmother, you know."

"I was thinking she was more of a grandmother," Max said.

"Oh, stop it," Sally said. "I'll be both. And I'd love to hold him at some point, but right now he's so happy with you, Margot, let's leave him there in his mother's arms."

Sally's voice thickened. "I'm simply overjoyed. So happy for both of you. He's absolutely beautiful."

Margot looked down at her sweet baby boy, and he was beautiful, wisps of silky black hair, a tiny nose, and perfect rosebud lips. Her heart swelled, aching, the love overwhelming. She took a quick breath, trying to hold back the emotion.

Max leaned over, kissed her. "You're beautiful," he murmured.

She smiled up at him, a watery smile. "Love you."

He placed his hand on hers, where she held their son. She linked her fingers through his, keeping him close, savoring the warmth of his hand. There was so much she was grateful for.

She drew an unsteady breath, thinking of all the advice different people had given her, but her favorite advice was from Paige, who'd told her, "Just love him. Hold him. You can't possibly spoil him. Babies need love to flourish and grow." And Margot was going to hold him, and love him, and make sure he had everything he needed. She'd waited forever to be a mom. She was going to enjoy this.

Her second act.

It would be the best act of all.

ACKNOWLEDGMENTS

I grew up dancing and acting, and wanted desperately to be a ballerina, and then later, an actress. I loved musical theater (such a shame I couldn't sing!) and auditioned for every local high school, college, and community theater production I could. I lived to be onstage and dreamed of a career in theater. I was fortunate to be involved with the short-lived but much-loved California Shakespearean Festival in Visalia in the late seventies and early eighties, and was accepted into UCLA as a theater arts major, but changed my sophomore year to creative writing and then again to American studies. I haven't performed since my early twenties, but I still love plays and musicals. *Flirting with Fire* is an ode to all the community theaters across the country that create beauty and magic on a shoestring.

As always, thank you to my fantastic agent and publishing team at Berkley, thank you to my family and friends, and thank you wonderful readers for buying my books. I'm here because you're here!